"INTRUDER!"

Yelling out a warning to his GuildMaster, Healer Bantu dropped the scroll he was holding.

Jeryl fled from the Healers' wrath, visualizing the sanctuary of his room at the inn as he popped out of, and into, existence. The cold walls of the Healers' library were still around him. He tried again, this time seeing the street outside the Healers' wall. Still the library enclosed him. Someone was holding him there, preventing his flight in a way he did not understand. He channeled all his energy into breaking that hold. For an instant he was free but then something imprisoned him again.

This time he saw the GuildMaster's right hand reaching toward him, all six fingers cupped around the palm. Jeryl felt those fingers grasping him, holding him in the library.

Bantu rushed to join his GuildMaster, extending his own cupped hand to reinforce Jeryl's prison. "It is the one who came with Hanra-bae. Jeryl, of Clan Alu."

The GuildMaster twisted his arm, and Jeryl felt his prison shrink. Panic quickened the pulsing of his energy net. He pushed against the barrier, seeking a way out. These Healers were skilled. Their powers were almost a match for his own. If they severed the filament that connected him to his body, they would kill him. He spun in their grasp, seeking, seeking. . . .

DAW Science Fiction Presents

KRIS JENSEN'S

magnificent novels of the world of Ardel:

KRIS JENSEN
MENTOR

DAW BOOKS, INC.

DONALD A. WOLLHEIM, FOUNDER

375 Hudson Street, New York, NY 10014

ELIZABETH R. WOLLHEIM
SHEILA E. GILBERT
PUBLISHERS

First Printing, February 1991

1 2 3 4 5 6 7 8 9

DAW TRADEMARK REGISTERED
U.S. PAT. OFF. AND FOREIGN COUNTRIES
—MARCA REGISTRADA.
HECHO EN U.S.A.

PRINTED IN THE U.S.A.

For Jim Frenkel,
who helped make it possible.

Titan Station

"It's all right, honey," said Elissa Durant, hugging her three-year-old daughter Miranda. "Wake up, baby. Kitty didn't die. It's only a bad dream."

Miranda shuddered and opened her eyes. "Kitty's gone!" she wailed.

"Kitty's in Arizona with Gram and Gramps. They'll take good care of her. Cats aren't allowed to come to our new home." Elissa held Miranda close and rocked her. She hated uprooting her children, forcing them to leave friends and familiar places to move to a world they had never seen. When she and her husband, Sinykin, had been offered new posts a few months ago, they had thought it would be a wonderful opportunity for the entire family. Now she feared that their decision to accept these jobs was selfish and ill-considered.

Miranda's wails subsided into soft crying, then hiccups, and finally sleep. Elissa wiped the tears from her daughter's face and shifted her weight to a more comfortable position. She yawned. Miranda's nightmares had kept her up most of the past three nights. She was exhausted, and her nerves were frayed.

The space station's intercom announced the docking of another interstellar transport. Elissa turned to watch through the viewport.

The class III jump-ship slowly approached the docking arm, its attitude jets releasing puffs of gas into the vacuum as the pilot adjusted the ship's position and locked the grapnel in place. *Blue Heron*, a class IV jump-ship, nestled nose-in on the next docking arm. Two maintenance bugs scoured its surface, repairing minor hull damage. Elissa watched them, remembering her own days in similar bugs, when she and Sinykin Inda were newly married and living on Titan Station. They had transferred to ground assignments when she became pregnant, so that they could raise their children in a stable environment away from the uncertainties of station life.

Now they were dragging Miranda and Jaime off to live at an unfinished spaceport on a planet where they would not be allowed to travel beyond the Terran compound. *What sense did it make?* she wondered. They had discussed all the advantages of the move to Ardel: leaving the pollution, crime, and overcrowding on Terra for clean air and water, and a chance to spend more time together as a family. Yet when she held her crying daughter, none of that seemed to matter. She feared that Ardel would change her family in ways she could not begin to imagine.

The stateroom's door slid open. "Mom! Dad took me to see our ship," cried her son, Jaime, as he ran to the viewport. Miranda stirred in Elissa's lap, but did not wake.

"Please be quiet," she said slowly, trying to suppress the irritation she felt. "Your sister is finally sleeping."

"Our ship's bigger than that new one," said Jaime in an exaggerated whisper. "We can board this afternoon!" He was two years older than Miranda, old enough to be excited about his first trip into space.

"Too soon," muttered Elissa. She looked at the scattered toys and discarded clothing that littered their stateroom. It was no more than the usual debris generated by two children living in a confined space, but it all had to be cleaned up and repacked before they could transfer to the jump-ship. "Pick up your toys and put them in your duffle bag so you'll be ready to go," she said to Jaime.

Sinykin stopped beside her chair. "Let him be, Lissie. He wants to watch the ships."

The reprimand was more than Elissa could bear. She would not let her family see her fear; instead she lashed out in anger. "And who will pack all this? Me? Will you stay and comfort Miranda while I clean up this place? Will you be there for us when we get to Ardel?"

Miranda pushed away from her mother and opened her eyes. "Mom?" She sounded frightened.

Elissa stared at her daughter. *Our children trust us to be strong, and to make the right choices for them. But what if we've made the wrong choice this time?* she wondered. She pulled Miranda close, kissed her cheek and hugged her. "I'm sorry, honey. Everything is fine. You can go back to sleep."

Sinykin knelt beside them and brushed a stray hair from Miranda's forehead. He slipped his right arm around Elissa's shoulders. "It'll be all right, Lissie. Whatever happens, we'll all be together."

Chapter 1

Alu Keep, Ardel

Wind whispered at the shutters. Tendrils of smoke vanished into darkness. Jeryl leaned forward, drew a breath, held it until he could feel the drug working.

He squatted on the floor beside the brazier, watching armata leaves shrivel on the coals. Their ruby glow was the room's only light. He wedged his shoulder into the corner so that he would not fall, and spread a six-fingered hand against the wall. The stone was rough and cold, but his awareness of it was already fading. He closed his eyes and saw the elliptical sunburst of his fingers as a network of pulsing blood vessels, quiescent tendons, and muscles. That vision dimmed as he inhaled more smoke, until he saw only the nerves that spread like fine silver wires throughout his hand. He was ready.

It took a moment to disentangle the filaments of mind from the static net of body. Then he was free, fleeing room and keep to soar the thermal gradients within the storm clouds above.

His language had only one word for cloud, but fourteen names for storms. This was *alkaia*, ''thunder-snow,'' a fitting prelude to winter solstice.

The world turned toward dawn. Warming air currents stirred, clashing with cold along the front, fueling the storm. Lightning flashed, and the ionic discharge swept through Jeryl's mind-net. Light and darkness meant nothing. In the atmosphere of Ardel all was energy—reflected, conducted, transmitted.

Jeryl became the storm. He was buffeted by the powers that drove it, by the sun rising above clouds heavy with moisture, heat radiating from the warm soil below, strong winds pushing cold air down from the mountains. He climbed above the clouds to dance with the ice crystals, floated down a rising shaft of warm air, rose again through falling snowflakes. Riding the cold wind, he felt the momentary touch of another mind. He queried, "Who?" and received no answer. The other fled from him, vanishing into the clouds.

The last of the yellow leaves had shriveled to ash on the brazier, and the smoke was dissipating, slipping out through the shutters and the cracks around the door where daylight crept in. Jeryl's body, too long unmoving, was cold and stiff. He opened one eye, then the other, tried to move his right arm and could not. A deep, shuddering breath pulled his shoulders back and raised his head. Across the room, on his sleeping platform, he saw a blurred form move in the dimness.

"I smelled the smoke," said a cold, dry voice—Viela, the clan's Healer.

Jeryl blinked. His eyes burned. "What . . ." he rasped, cleared his throat and tried again, "what do you want?"

"Has your common sense fled with your manners, Mentor?" asked Viela. "You are the spiritual leader of my clan. Your health is my responsibility."

"Do not lecture me about trance drugs, Healer." Jeryl coughed and pushed himself away from the wall. "You use them."

Viela rose, swept a fur from the bed, and crossed the room to Jeryl's side. He pushed the brazier aside with one foot as he dropped the fur onto Jeryl's shoulders. "I only use the drugs when my work makes them necessary, and then under carefully controlled conditions. You use them irresponsibly."

"That is a matter of opinion." Jeryl struggled to his feet, one hand clutching the fur, the other pressed against the wall for support. He closed his eyes, and light flared in the wooden wall sconce. "As long as I fulfill my obligation to Clan Alu, what else I do is not your concern."

Viela opened the clothes cupboard and rummaged inside. "If you make yourself ill, and cannot fulfill your obligations this season, or the next, it becomes my concern." His voice was muffled, but ruby flares of anger in his aura were clearly visible to Jeryl.

Jeryl and Viela, Mentor and Healer respectively, often

disagreed. Yet they had worked together for many seasons. Four winters had passed since Jeryl took the band of office from the last Mentor's wrist and assumed the guardianship of Clan Alu, fighting and winning a battle that had determined the clan's future and his own. The gray cloak and copper wristband were a part of him now.

A few deep breaths cleared the smoke from Jeryl's lungs. Trance often left him feeling irritable. Clean air and a cup of tea usually restored his good nature and his strength.

"Dress," said Viela. Blue woolen tunic and leggings sailed through the air toward Jeryl. He dropped the fur, caught the clothes. In one graceful move he slipped out of his nightshirt and into the tunic. Then he sat on the sleeping platform and pulled on the leggings. Viela brought his boots from their place next to the cupboard. Jeryl settled the soft leather over the three round pads of his foot, buttoned the slender ankle strap, then wrapped the criss-crossing thongs up to the knee. While he put on the second boot, Viela laid the heavy winter cloak beside him. "You will need this today."

Jeryl looked up, saw the damp traces of snow on Viela's shoulders and hood. "I know," he said quietly. "I was riding the storm."

Viela's anger flared again. "Fool!"

Jeryl lifted his fine gray hair with one hand and let it fall to his shoulders. His aura was still clouded by the drug, but ruby sparks flickered in the murk. There were risks in leaving his body for long periods, risks that he weighed against the knowledge and experience he gained each time he entered trance. Viela did not believe he was capable of judging those risks. Jeryl wondered what Viela would think if he knew there was another mind riding that storm. He said nothing.

"Your recklessness will kill you. One day you will stray too far, or be gone too long from your body, and it will die!" Viela stalked out the door.

Jeryl rose, pulling the cloak about his shoulders. He blinked, extinguishing the light in the sconce.

"There are other things that should concern you, Healer," he said. "How many Mothers lie ill in your infirmary? Why are you harassing me when you have plague victims to care for?" The door slammed behind him as he followed the now silent Viela down the back stairs to the kitchen.

Warm air and the delicious smell of hot bread ascended around them. Jeryl expected to find the huge kitchen filled with workers so soon after dawn, as the kitchenmaster Ortia and his crew of tentacled younglings prepared the day's meals. Ortia baked bread for the entire clan in his huge wall ovens, and fed Jeryl and the guests who stayed at the clan-hall. He was usually too busy to talk, but his good nature suffused the kitchen and its occupants with a bright, cheery warmth. Younglings bustled about on their stubby legs, washing platters, cutting meat and vegetables for stew, and kneading dough. The long wooden table was laden with crocks of preserved fruit and bowls of nuts. A lone Master sat at one end, cupping a mug of tea in one hand. Jeryl greeted him.

"May the great sun shine upon you and yours, Hatar. How do you fare this morning?" Fear and frustration colored Hatar's aura a sickly green. His mate, the Mother Alain, had contracted the plague a hand of days earlier, and there was no real hope for her survival.

"I am well," he said, his words belied by the tremor in his hand. "I cannot bear the emptiness of my House now that the younglings are fostered out. With Alain in the infirmary there was no one to care for them. I came here for some warmth and breakfast, but I have lost my appetite."

"And the work? How goes the tapestry?" Hatar was a Master weaver, the best in Clan Alu, and Jeryl had often watched him at his loom, weaving fantastic landscapes with the warm, earthy colors from Alu's dye pots. He worked surrounded by apprentices, his hands moving too swiftly for the uninitiated to follow, as a constant stream of instructions and humorous comments issued from his mouth. Younglings vied for a place at his shop.

Hatar's aura darkened. "My loom has been idle since Alain fell ill. I cannot concentrate on the work."

"That tapestry was promised for winter's end Festival," said Viela. "If it is not ready, the Healers Guild will be offended."

Jeryl glared at him. If the guild's elders suffered offense, it was their problem. Hatar's peace of mind was much more important. Viela, never having had a mate to lose, would not, could not understand that. Then Jeryl remembered Viela's kindness to another young Master who had lost a mate years ago, and wondered. Perhaps the old Healer was practicing his art when he suggested the weaver return to his loom; the distraction of work might be good for Hatar.

Viela ignored Jeryl's look and sat beside Hatar. A youngling trundled over with a fresh pot of tea and a pair of cups. Viela filled them both, and added more of the strong, fragrant brew to Hatar's proffered mug.

"A meat pie for the Mentor," Viela called to Ortia, "and some warm bread."

Jeryl opened his mouth to protest, then closed it again. Further bickering with Viela would not be productive. He sat, accepting the plate Ortia brought him. Ignoring the meat-filled pastry, he spread preserves on a slab of bread. He offered a second slab to Hatar, but the other waved it away.

"You must dine with me this evening, Hatar," said Viela, cracking nuts with the pommel of his knife. "I would like to commission a new tapestry for the infirmary. We could discuss patterns and colors."

"I think not. I am in no mood to take on new projects."

The back door thumped. A youngling ran to open it, and another youngling tumbled in, its poncho spattered with snow. "Healer," it cried as it trundled across the room, "come quickly. You are needed. The Mother Alain is worse. . . ."

"Worse!" Hatar jumped to his feet, bumping the table and overturning his mug. Tea pooled on the table and dripped to the floor before the mug stopped rolling. Hatar backed his chair toward the hearth, snatched up the cloak that was drying there.

"Calm," said Viela, rising. "What has happened?"

The youngling caught its breath. "Convulsions."

Viela looked at Jeryl, shrugged in Hatar's direction. The weaver was still struggling with his cloak. "Stay. There is nothing you can do." He followed the youngling out.

Jeryl ignored Viela's instructions. The pain Hatar broadcast touched his memories of the day his own mate died. Hatar's place was at Alain's side, to comfort her in her last moments, and bring himself some peace. Jeryl helped the weaver with his cloak, followed him out into the dissipating storm.

They were barely outside the clanhall when Alain's death cry reached them. It swept through Jeryl's mind, stirred his heart, and quickened his breathing. He fought the physical response, tried to concentrate on helping Hatar. Hatar sank to his knees in the snow, his aura darkening. Jeryl pulled him to his feet, dragged him back to the kitchen door. He spared a thought to open the latch, tugged Hatar over the stoop as he began to struggle.

"Let me go!" Hatar shouted, twisting away from Jeryl. He ran outside, stumbled, and fell headlong into the snow.

Jeryl was at his side in an instant, and Ortia dashed from the kitchen to help. Between them they hauled the weaver back to the warmth. He struggled, but weakly. They had no trouble settling him on a bench before the hearth.

Ortia brought hot, sweet tea and pressed the mug into Hatar's hands, but Hatar ignored it. He looked at Jeryl with darkened eyes. His murky aura was shrinking, retreating to the limits of his physical body.

"Let me go," he whispered.

"Alain is dead. There is nothing you can do."

"Let me join her," said Hatar, turning his face to the fire.

Jeryl's room still smelled sickly-sweet from the armata smoke. Jeryl threw open the inner and outer shutters, letting chill air and tiny snowflakes rush in. He breathed a deep, cleansing breath, blew it out through his mouth, then breathed another. His stomach churned a little; stale armata smoke always made him ill. Holding his breath, he picked up the brazier and tipped it out the window. The few remaining coals tumbled down the lower roof to the gravel walk below. Ashes danced among the snowflakes on the wind. He slammed the shutters before the ashes could blow back in.

He pulled his leather travel pouches from the cupboard and began packing. Usually he enjoyed riding into the mountains to the FreeMasters' guildhall, but there was too much tragedy about this mission. He was escorting three of Alu's mateless Masters and two hands of scarred and handicapped younglings. All victims of the plague, they went to the FreeMasters for rest and training. And Hatar waited in the kitchen below, to join them after Alain's funeral rite.

There had been too many funerals since midsummer. Nearly half the Houses in the keep stood empty, their family lines lost to plague or accident. There must be a way to change that, to create new families and strengthen the clan.

The ancient scrolls talked of rituals and potions, but they were not specific. Someone, somewhere, must know the answer. Jeryl was determined to find it.

The ache of his own loss, five winters past, was still fresh. His mate Hladi, Mother of his House, had been murdered by a member of a rival clan. In that instant he had lost his House, his younglings, and his future. He would never undergo metamorphosis, never become a Mother, raise younglings, be the living center of an active and growing House. Yet he did have a legacy from Hladi—her death unleashed his psychic powers, and made him a FreeMaster. That was power he could use. He would find a way to repopulate Clan Alu, in the name of every Mother whose urn graced the mourning wall.

Jeryl tossed a pair of tunics and spare leggings onto the bed. It would be a short trip, only overnight, but in cold stormy weather he always packed two changes of clothing. Wet clothes were uncomfortable, as were cold temperatures, and the two together could be fatal. He slipped his favorite dagger into his wrist sheath and strapped it to his arm. No tent this time; he would spend the night with the FreeMasters at their mountain hall.

His thoughts were interrupted by a knock at the door. A quick psychic probe told him that Secko, his apprentice, waited outside with another member of the clan. Jeryl worked the latch with a thought, and the door swung inward.

"May the great sun smile on you this morning," said Secko quietly.

Jeryl shrugged. "My greetings to you both, but I think the sun smiles on none of us this season. You felt Alain's death cry?"

"Yes. I was at the stables, checking on the mounts and carts for your trip." Secko brushed a piece of straw from his legging, then tugged at the hem of his short gray tunic. "Will Hatar be accompanying you to the FreeMasters' hall?"

"He will. You should send some younglings to his House to pack his clothing and take it down to the stables. Then the bier needs to be readied for Alain's funeral, and her body must be brought down from the infirmary. We will leave as soon as the ceremony is completed." He glanced at Secko's companion. It was Ertis, Clan Alu's esteemed

Historian and storyteller. Jeryl wanted to discuss some
things with Ertis, things he would rather not speak of in
front of Secko, who lacked discretion and had an unfortu-
nate tendency to repeat everything he heard. Secko's training was nearly completed. Soon Jeryl would send him to a
post at one of the northern keeps and take a more suitable
apprentice.

"When will you return to Alu?" asked Secko.

"Tomorrow." Jeryl added an extra tunic to his pack.
"Please check on Hatar before you leave the clanhall. He
was in the kitchen a short time ago."

Secko looked from Jeryl to Ertis and back again. "I will
see to it, Mentor." He backed away from the door.

"Ertis, come in and sit down," said Jeryl. He closed the
door behind the Historian with a thought, leaving Secko to
walk down the hallway alone.

Ertis smoothed the sleeping furs before perching on the
edge of the platform. "Will you stop at the Terran spaceport
tomorrow, Mentor?"

"Yes. I have much to discuss with Sinykin Inda." Jeryl
enjoyed his rare visits to the spaceport. The Assistant Administrator always welcomed him warmly, and showed a
great deal of interest in matters affecting the Ardellans. "I
want to talk with him about the plague, and about this un-
seasonably bad weather."

"The weather is what brings me here. I received another
message from my GuildMaster."

Jeryl looked at the little Historian. The edges of Ertis'
clean white aura glowed topaz with concern. He wore the
traditional copper-colored tunic of his guild, with the twelve
gold ribbons he had won in competitions pinned to the
shoulder. His hair was almost white, and tiny lines surrounded his warm brown eyes. He had been respected and
honored as his clan's Historian since Jeryl was a youngling.
Next year Alu would need to select a new Historian, for
Ertis' metamorphosis from Master to Mother would occur
soon after that.

"What concerns your esteemed GuildMaster?"

Ertis ran his fingers through the golden ribbons. "He
sends a warning about the weather. Reports have come from
some Historians in the mountains that the storms are not
natural. Someone may be working the weather."

Jeryl recalled the other mind riding the storm, the Master

who had fled rather than identify himself. Was he a weather-
worker?

"Does your GuildMaster know that the storms have kept
Terran ships from landing at the spaceport?" This was the
other matter Jeryl intended to discuss with Sinykin Inda.
Only two ships had been able to deliver their cargoes since
the spaceport was completed last season. Many guilds and
clans were anxiously waiting for Alu to bring them the Terran metals they had been promised.

"He knows, and that is why he is concerned. He fears
that the problems at the spaceport are connected to the
weather-working." Ertis shrugged. "I would like to go with
you to speak with the Terran. It is time for the Historians
to establish communications with a Terran representative."

Jeryl made a negating gesture with his hand. "The situation at the spaceport is too unstable. Some of the Terrans
are not comfortable with Ardellans. Let me meet with Sinykin Inda alone. Perhaps he can send one of his people out
to talk with you. The Masters of Alu have become more
accepting of the Terrans. I think soon we will again be able
to let a few of them move among us. If they feel secure in
our keeps, perhaps they will allow more of us to visit their
spaceport."

Ertis shrugged his narrow shoulders. "Each time you go
to the spaceport, I will ask permission to go with you." He
watched Jeryl fasten the buckles on his pouches, then picked
up a pouch and followed the Mentor from the room.

Hatar still sat in the kitchen, staring numbly into the fire.
Jeryl helped him up and led him through the clanhall to the
circular court where Alain's body lay. It rested on a cold
stone bier that had seen too much use of late. A saffron
cloth covered her form, and the few snowflakes that fell
upon it were melted by the dwindling warmth of her body.

At her head sat the funeral urn, three hands high and two
hands wide, carved from a single piece of rose quartz. Its
base was circular, its top a square, and it bellied out in the
center to almost twice the base's diameter.

Secko stood beside the bier, holding Clan Alu's runestaff.
Jeryl left Hatar and Ertis on the clanhall's steps, and walked
down to take the staff from his apprentice. The intricately
carved wood fit comfortably in his hand, as if it was made
for him, but the staff was older than memory. He received
impressions from it, fleeting thoughts and feelings of pre-

vious Mentors. These he pushed aside, and set his mind to the unpleasant task at hand. He knew the ritual by rote. In the span of five winters, he had performed it more often than most Mentors did in a lifetime.

He stood at the foot of the bier, slid one hand toward the top of the staff and the other toward its foot. Drawing power from the earth, feeling energy climb from the soles of his feet up through his legs and torso, he lifted the runestaff high above his head. He sent the energy into it, charging it for the task ahead. When the staff was ready, he began to walk clockwise around the bier.

His hands tingled where they touched the staff. He felt its power, lost himself in its mystery. When he reached the center of the bier, he extended the top of the staff toward the center, almost touching Alain's body. The briefest spark of energy jumped from staff to corpse. Drawing more power upward to the staff, he continued his walk. At each corner he stopped, extended the staff, watched the energy transfer. Then he was back at the foot of the bier, breathing hard, his whole body trembling from the exertion.

He leaned the staff against the bier, took three deep, slow breaths, and went to fetch the urn. It was cold and hard in his hands, and the top stuck when he tried to remove it. He pulled harder, and it came away with a sudden pop. He set the lid on the ground, and put the urn beside Alain's body.

One more deep breath.

He picked up the runestaff, lifted it above his head. With a single, fluid motion he extended it to touch the center of Alain's body. Flames erupted from the shroud, engulfing corpse and staff and Jeryl's arms. Heat beat at him, but he felt no pain. He did not move.

It was over. The flames died, leaving the bier clean and cool, the runestaff untouched. Of Alain's body there was no sign, but the urn glowed with light and warmth. He picked up the lid, settled it tightly on the urn, and returned the runestaff to Secko's hands.

Jeryl rode his favorite mount, the big gray dappled alep that had belonged to the previous Mentor. It was old now, nearly ready to retire to the breeding pens, but Jeryl would ride it for another season or two. Its slender legs and broad flat feet carried it at an easy pace on the steep, icy trail. The central pair of legs, set farther apart than the front and back pairs, gave the animal extra stability on uneven ground. With those two legs folded up and tucked under its torso, an alep could run with the wind, but it lost much of its stability. Only a fool rode four-legged into the mountains in winter.

Beside him one of the new FreeMasters rode in morose silence. Hatar and the other two who had lost their mates to the plague followed, with the cart full of younglings behind them. Depression settled like gray mist around the group, clouding even the rudimentary auras of the younglings. The FreeMasters mourned their lost mates inside forbidding whirlpools of mud brown and vile green auras. The younglings had their own griefs. Plague-caused deformities would prevent them from undergoing metamorphosis and reaching adulthood.

There was nothing Jeryl could do for any of his companions. That was the source of his depression. The snow had stopped and the midday sun was melting the flakes from his shoulders, but he found no joy in the warmth and light. He led the funereal procession up the twisting mountain road, between tall conifers and the bare trunks and branches of deciduous trees. Snow clumped in some of the low spots, but most of the forest floor was bare. Dead leaves in all shades from blood to russet were caught in piles against scarletberry thickets. The berries were gone, eaten by birds that had flown on to warmer regions. The red lizards were hibernating, the small mammals hiding from the plodding aleps. Jeryl saw a gloomy landscape, stark and barren.

Yet it would bloom again. This was winter solstice, the shortest day of the year. Tomorrow the sun would begin its slow return, bringing with it warmth and life. First would come the season of storms, but when it ended the days would be noticeably longer and warmer. The cycle of growth would begin anew.

The road took them across a wooden bridge over a narrow stream. It was too early in the season for ice to form on the swiftly moving water, but on the shaded side of the bridge icicles were growing. The bridge had no side rails, so they crossed in single file. Jeryl was almost on the other side when he heard a splash and a shout behind him. He turned, and saw one of the FreeMasters and an alep in the rushing water.

"Hatar!" he yelled, jumping from his mount as he struggled out of his cloak. Hatar was out of his saddle and spinning free in the stream; his alep climbed the bank. Jeryl dove from the edge of the bridge into the rushing torrent, felt cold slide up his arms and hit his face with a shock. He held his breath, touched bottom sooner than he expected, and surfaced in the swift current. Hatar's cloak caught on a rock, keeping him from being swept down the mountainside.

Jeryl's feet scraped against the stony bottom. The water was only waist-deep. He struggled to stand, bending the flexible pads of his feet around rocks and gripping the boulder that had caught Hatar. He wrapped his free hand in Hatar's cloak and pulled him upstream. A loop of rope settled over Jeryl's shoulders. He braced Hatar against the boulder and pulled his head free of the water, then knotted the rope beneath Hatar's arms. The FreeMaster swallowed water, sputtered and choked. Jeryl looked at the others on the bank, saw that the rope was tied to an alep's saddle, and signaled them to pull Hatar ashore. He turned to follow, but the current pulled his feet out from under him. He clutched at Hatar's cloak, tangled his hand in the hem, and was dragged the few feet to the bank. Strong arms pulled him out of the water.

The others had already expelled the water from Hatar's lungs. He was coughing and gasping for breath. Jeryl shivered. His right thigh burned. Looking down, he saw his torn legging, and a long abrasion welling red-gold drops of blood. He stripped off the wet tunic, calling to the others, ''Get Hatar out of those wet clothes.''

Jeryl pulled a pouch from his alep's back, rummaged for a pad of soft cloth, and tied it over his wound. The bleeding had already stopped. He pulled off boots and leggings, rubbed his body dry with one spare tunic, then put on the other. Hatar was naked and shivering violently, but except for bruises he appeared unharmed. One of the FreeMasters helped him struggle into dry clothing. Jeryl tossed his spare tunic to the other. ''Rub that alep down before its coat gets icy,'' he ordered.

His boots, soaked through, were probably a total loss. He unfolded his extra pair and slipped them on, but his chilled fingers could not close the fasteners. He walked over to the FreeMaster currying the wet mount, and addressed him quietly. ''You rode behind Hatar. What happened?''

The FreeMaster refused to look at Jeryl. "He forced his mount over the side of the bridge into the water," he said.

Jeryl understood an attempt to kill himself, to join his lost mate in death. After Hladi's death, he had considered throwing himself from the keep's high wall. A strong Mentor had prevented it, keeping him alive to serve Clan Alu in other ways. Now he had performed the same service for Hatar.

Was it a service? Would Hatar thank him for saving his life? Not today, certainly, and perhaps never. Jeryl looked at the bleak, winter-dead forest. The clans were like this forest, barren, stark and cold, approaching death. Unless he could find a way to increase the clans, to create new Houses and new family lines, they were doomed to a long, slow death. He stared at the sun glowing huge and amber overhead, and made a silent vow. If he could find that key, the secret that had been lost or hidden for so many years, he would return to this mountain on midsummer day and make a blood sacrifice, as the ancients had done. He would pour his own blood upon the soil in thanksgiving.

The sun had already dipped behind the mountain peak when they arrived at the FreeMasters' guildhall. It was mid-afternoon, and the sky was bright and clear above them, but they moved through shadow. The sprawling stone hall was shuttered against the cold, its ancient gray walls solid and reassuring. Inside, a huge fire warmed the main room. The enormous hearth filled most of one wall. Jeryl sat on the bench before it and accepted a mug of hot spiced cider. His companions had shed their cloaks and were huddled close to the fire. Across the hall younglings were setting out platters of roast fowl and loaves of bread on a long table. Two of the servants trundled over and took Alu's younglings off toward the kitchens.

Logs snapped and crackled on the hearth as the flames consumed them. The fire's warmth brought feeling back to Jeryl's numbed feet and hands. He closed his eyes, and held the cup of fragrant cider close to his face. The scent was a heady reminder of fall harvests and summer spice-gathers.

"Jeryl, it is good to see you," called someone from across the room. The Mentor reached out with his mind, and touched the welcome presence of Arien, leader of the

FreeMasters. Jeryl was too weary to rise. He opened his eyes and raised his cup to salute his old friend.

Arien slipped out of his cloak and shook the water droplets off its shoulders. "I was out all day, checking for storm damage in our orchards. A mug of that cider would suit me well right now."

A youngling appeared at Arien's side to take his heavy cloak; another handed him a steaming mug. The leader joined Jeryl on the bench, his back to the flames.

"Did your trip go well?" he asked between sips.

"Well enough," replied Jeryl. "We had a minor mishap. Hatar fell into the stream."

Arien looked at the newcomers. "Which is Hatar?"

"The tall one. His mate died this morning. I pray she was the last."

"The deaths must end soon," said Arien quietly. "The 'mishap' was deliberate?" It was not quite a question.

"Yes," said Jeryl, gazing into his mug. He shivered despite the warmth of the fire. "Can you blame him?"

"When my mate died, I spent ten days wandering alone through the mountains, hoping something would kill me," said Arien, watching Hatar. "I did not have the courage for suicide."

Jeryl touched Arien's arm. "I rejoice in your continued existence," he said.

Arien returned the touch, clasping Jeryl's hand palm-to-palm, fingers intertwining. "And I rejoice in yours," he said, so quietly that no one but Jeryl could hear.

They sat together for a long time, sharing cider and warmth. They were still there when the younglings announced the evening meal and the FreeMasters gathered at the long table to eat. Jeryl was not hungry. He felt safe and warm by the hearth, and for the moment his problems seemed far away. Arien stayed with him, talking softly.

"I am concerned about the storms, Jeryl. They have started much earlier than usual this year, and they are more intense. The storm season is just beginning, and we have already seen damage in the orchards."

Jeryl shared his friend's concern. "We lost our last crop of hay because the younglings could not cut it before the first snow. We sent the herds to winter pasture early, and with them as many younglings as we could spare.

"The weather is also causing problems for the Terrans.

Their ships cannot land during the storms. Most of the captains have taken their goods elsewhere rather than wait for the weather to clear. The trade agreement promised us a hand of shipments before winter, more iron and copper than the metalworkers could use in two seasons. Instead we have received only a few cartloads." Jeryl swallowed the last of his cider. "This is becoming a serious problem. The Terrans say that if the storms continue, they will close the spaceport until spring."

Arien shrugged. "Perhaps the Metalworkers Guild will have to buy its metals from the mining clans until more shipments arrive."

"I think not. The miners are refusing to sell any of their metal. They say they will not trade with us until the Terrans are forced to leave Ardel."

"The mining clans are not self-sufficient. They always trade for grain."

"The miners controlled our supply of iron and copper until the Terrans came. They were the most powerful, the wealthiest of the clans until we began to trade with the Terrans. If they can use a metal shortage to force the Terrans to leave Ardel, they will not give up their advantage for a few carts of grain."

"I suppose not," said Arien. "By trading with the Terrans, we have broken the miners' monopoly. Yet if the miners refuse to trade with us, we only exchange one monopoly for another."

Jeryl set his empty mug on the bench. "You are correct. That is one of the things I hope to discuss with Sinykin Inda when I go to the spaceport tomorrow."

Arien's aura brightened. "I am traveling in that direction myself. I intend to visit our new guildhall near the spaceport. My assistant manages the hall adequately, but he is young and inexperienced in some matters. He has requested that I come to inspect the stable, and advise him on a problem he is having with the aleps. We can ride together, if you like."

"I always welcome your company, Arien." Jeryl rose, gesturing toward the table. Most of the FreeMasters had finished eating, but the platters were not yet cleared away. "Shall we eat?" he asked.

Arien piled a plate high with meat and starchy tubers, but

Jeryl took only fruit and cheese, and a fresh mug of cider. The thought of heavy food unsettled his stomach.

"You have been using trance drugs again," said Arien, his aura flickering with disapproval. "You always lose your appetite afterward."

Jeryl's annoyance flashed in his aura, then died away. He spoke softly. "I have had one lecture today, Arien. I do not need another. You know why I use the drugs."

"I know," Arien said. "But have they done any good? Do you feel any less lost and alone?"

Jeryl did not answer. He walked back to the bench beside the hearth and sat, balancing his plate on his lap. Arien joined him a moment later.

"My apologies, Mentor," said Arien. "I know that trance is more than an escape from your problems."

"You speak out of concern for my well-being. My anger is not justified." Jeryl blinked, and a tiny flame of cool white light appeared before him, dancing and flickering in the air currents. "I am the one who should apologize."

Arien set his plate aside and touched Jeryl's hand. "Take care, my friend. I could not bear to lose you as I lost my mates," he whispered. Arien produced his own shimmer-light, slightly larger and more yellow than Jeryl's. As they watched, the flames moved slowly toward each other until they touched and flared, becoming one. "What have you learned since our last discussion?"

"The storms are not entirely natural." Jeryl stared at the shimmer-light. "I touched another mind riding the storm this morning. He was unfamiliar, and unwilling to identify himself. The Historians are also suspicious; they sent warnings of weather-workers practicing their ancient art in the mountains."

Arien shuddered. "I thought that all the weather-working rituals were lost long ago."

"That may be so. Perhaps I touched only a trancer like myself, and frightened him."

They ate in silence, Jeryl fastidiously peeling and slicing fruit and cutting cheese into chunks, Arien attacking his food with fingers and fork.

"Your appetite has not changed," Jeryl said, watching his friend with affection. He set his empty plate aside. "If you continue to eat like that, you will get fat like an old wool-deer."

Amusement flitted through Arien's aura. He shrugged, pulling meat from the bone with his fingers. "I work, Jeryl. Outdoors. In the cold." He popped a piece of meat into his mouth. "Hard work."

Jeryl knew how hard Arien worked, guiding the growing guild of FreeMasters, helping new members adjust to the loss of their mates and to their new lives in the guild. The FreeMasters grew most of their own food, and kept a herd of wool-deer and maintained a weaving house, and traded services for the rest of the goods they needed. They worked as mountain guides, and animal handlers, and guards for caravans making the long trek to the towns of the fisherfolk. Arien organized it all, sometimes with great difficulty, for by nature FreeMasters were an independent lot.

"I know you work hard, Arien," said Jeryl quietly. "I have come to ask you to work even harder. I need your help."

Arien set aside his plate, and wiped his fingers on a scrap of cloth. He laid his right hand over Jeryl's. "We are closer than littermates, Jeryl. You know I will help you."

Jeryl's troubled aura cleared to luminescent white. "I have vowed to find the secret of creating new Houses, of restoring the clans' populations by beginning new family lines. It was done long ago, but the knowledge has been obscured by time and politics. I think the Healers and the guilds may hold the key, and I intend to wrest it from them. Will you help me?"

Arien did not hesitate. "I will. Where do you intend to begin your search?"

"In Berrut, at the Healers' guildhall," said Jeryl.

Chapter 2

Sinykin Inda sat in full lotus on a reed mat, meditating in the manner of his Hindu ancestors. He connected with the power of the earth below him, pulled that energy up his spine from his tailbone to the top of his head, and let it flow up and out and cascade back to the ground like a fountain. In his mind he saw the power cleansing and activating the chakra energy centers of his body. He began to chant a single syllable, holding the note until his breath was almost depleted.

Sadness welled in him. He let it grow, experienced the hollowness that comes with the loss of someone very dear. The warm, vibrant energy of his heart chakra spread to touch the emptiness, to flow into it and fill it. With it came happy memories—his daughter's bright smile, the warmth of her tiny hand in his. The way a strand of her fine, soft hair strayed across her cheek. For an instant she was there again, whole and healthy.

The moment faded. He did not clutch at it but let it drift away. Miranda was with him, would always be with him whenever he chose to look inward. She would always be six years old, beautiful and happy and full of life. He could not lose her again.

Sinykin sighed. He thanked the planet for its energy, and slowly opened his eyes. He arched his back, stretched his arms and legs, then stood and rolled the meditation mat. He tied the roll with a white ribbon and stowed it in a closet before going to the kitchen. Miranda's funeral urn was on the window sill, the opalescent stone shimmering in the sunlight. Jeryl of Clan Alu had given him the urn when he heard of Miranda's death. Sinykin stroked it with a finger as he passed.

In the kitchen he heated water and measured camomile petals, harvested from carefully nurtured Terran plants, into a cup. He found fresh scarletberries and ground-plums in the cooler, rinsed a handful of each under the tap, and set them to drain on a napkin. While the tea steeped, he slipped into underwear and a yellow coverall that had physician and xenobiologist emblems side by side on the left shoulder.

He ate quickly, thinking about the day ahead. Two years of intense study and careful preparation might come to fruition today, when he asked Jeryl for permission to travel to Clan Alu. Not since the death of the first envoy, Trade Attache Sarah Anders, had any Terran moved freely among Ardellans.

He had studied Anders' journal, read her reports of the psychic phenomena she had witnessed. She claimed that the natives could ''think'' balls of light into existence and carry them in the palms of their hands, could send thoughts over great distances, and heal by the laying on of hands. She even hinted that they had mastered telekinesis. After her death her journal had been returned to her superiors at the Terran Union's Interstellar Trade Commission. Most of them discounted her descriptions as a product of the overactive imagination of a mentally ill operative. The official reports said that she had caused her own death. Secretary Sandsmark of the Terran Trade Commission, the man who had given her the Ardellan assignment, seemed to be the only bureaucrat who did not believe that.

Sandsmark had called Sinykin into his office, given him the journal and Anders' personnel record. Inda smiled. Like Sandsmark, he believed the things Sarah Anders described. He was not an adept, but he could see auras, and sometimes diagnose and help heal his patients by the touch of his mind and hands. At Sandsmark's request, he had come to Ardel to learn the truth about Anders' death and the abilities of the Ardellans. He had not yet solved the mystery, but he and his wife had learned to love Ardel.

He struggled into his insulated parka as he stepped outdoors. Two inches of fresh snow had transformed the landscape from dirty brown to sparkling white. Sinykin picked his way along the narrow path Maintenance had cleared with the blower. He stopped at the weather station where Jeff Grund, the spaceport's meteorologist and computer special-

ist, had climbed to the top of the stationary ladder and was
inspecting the equipment on the roof.

"Morning, Jeff," called Sinykin. He saw a new tower
extending more than thirty meters above the devices that
measured wind speed, humidity, and precipitation. "Is that
part of another experiment?"

Grund waved and nodded. He pointed out the thick cable
that ran from the tower to a large black box perched near
the edge of the roof. "Maintenance installed it yesterday.
I'm trying to get some accurate measurements of the electromagnetic disturbances that have been occurring during
the storms."

"Good." Sinykin watched Grund climb down the ice-
covered steel rungs. The meteorologist wore heavy boots,
and a thick red sweater over his coverall, but no parka or
gloves. He seemed to be inured to the cold. "How can you
go out in just a sweater?" Inda asked, shivering at the
thought.

"I grew up in northern Minnesota," said Grund. He
laughed. "This weather is mild compared to the winters
there."

"Six days of freezing temperatures and three days of snow
doesn't feel mild to me. What's the forecast?"

"It looks promising. No snow for the next few days, lots
of sun, clear nights, and midday temperatures that may creep
above freezing. Some of this snow should melt."

Sinykin shrugged and pointed to the clouds that hovered
over the distant mountains. "The forecasts have been wrong
more often than right this season."

Jeff grinned at him. "Care to make a wager on the date
and time of the next lunar conjunction?"

Inda looked up at the big redhead. "I'm not ready to
compete with your computer," he said. He kept detailed
records of the complex celestial movements around Ardel,
and was just beginning to see a pattern in the lunar phases
and conjunctions. His prediction of the last lunar conjunction had been off by less than three days, but Grund's computer program had pinpointed it within a few minutes.

Grund shrugged. "Why don't you just let the computer
keep the records and make the predictions? You'll never be
as accurate as it is."

"I don't need to be as accurate as your computer," said
Inda, smiling. "I do this to counteract my Terran condi-

tioning, to become one with the cycles and seasons of this world.''

"You intend to stay, then? Permanent resident, not temporary posting?''

Inda nodded. "Yes, Elissa and I have decided to stay here. Jaime may leave when he's of age, but this is our home now.''

"Well, you're welcome to it. If we can't learn more about those electromagnetic disturbances, and find out why they disrupt the navigation systems on the ships, there won't be much of a future for this spaceport.''

"We didn't have this problem last winter, or the year before. The supply ships always landed without difficulty.''

"I know,'' said Grund. "I've checked the records. Before this year's winter storms started, no ship had reported navigational problems or electromagnetic disturbances when landing on Ardel. Now at least half of them file reports, and some are refusing to land during bad weather. The difficulties always occur during the storms, and they never affect the spaceport itself.''

Sinykin nodded. This was becoming a serious problem, for both the Terrans and the Ardellans.

"Sinykin, the Old Lady sent down a memo yesterday. Said I'm to be prepared to take over your duties as Assistant Administrator on a day's notice. Are you planning a trip?'' asked Grund.

Inda shrugged. "I may be unavailable for a while. The details aren't worked out yet.''

"Well, I really don't want to be ass-ad,'' Grund grumbled. "I have enough to do keeping the weather station and computer running, and investigating the electromagnetic disturbances. We can't let another ship land during bad weather until we find a way to shield the navigational systems.'' He looked at the bank of clouds in the east. "I hope the forecast is correct and the snow stays away a few more days so we can get another supply ship in here. My wife is juggling inventories. She says we're running short of vitamins and diet supplements for the chickens.''

Inda grinned. "I think they'll survive for a while without their diet supplements. And if they don't, you omnivores can eat them for dinner.'' He looked out over the landing field. The big power blowers were clearing snow from the landing surface and loading docks behind administration.

Elissa was probably driving one of them; she had driven power vehicles for sport on Terra, but here there were no sport vehicles, just farm equipment and maintenance rigs. He had never understood the attraction she felt for heavy equipment, but he accepted it, and she accepted his work with psychic powers. He smiled, remembering his wife scrambling over the hull of a disabled ship, a thin safety line snapped to her tool belt to keep her from sliding off, holding a magnetic wrench in one hand and a diagnostic tool in the other, a satisfied grin on her face. She found the same joy in mastering machines that he found in mastering his mind.

The administration building was a two-story prefab, shipped in sections and assembled on Ardel. A wooden box with vinyl siding, polarized plexiglass windows, and a nearly flat roof, it had had no personality until a few of the spaceport workers turned its walls into a huge mural. Now a twentieth century big-city skyline reminded them of their heritage. Inside there were other scenes—the Kremlin, Tokyo Interstellar Spaceport, the Albuquerque Amusement Arcade. Inda and Grund entered through the Empire State Building and separated, Sinykin taking the stairs to the second floor. He stopped at the central processing station to get his appointment schedule from Lindy Zapata.

"Good morning, Dr. Inda," she said. "Administrator Griswold wants to see you before the alien gets here."

Sinykin sighed. No matter how often he told her that Jeryl was a native, Lindy persisted in calling him "the alien." "We are the aliens here, Ms. Zapata," he said sarcastically. "Tell Griswold I'll be in in five minutes."

Inda's office was large, with a huge window facing sunrise and the landing field. When the mural painters had asked him what he wanted on the walls, he requested an Ardellan forest. Now scarlet conifers marched around the room, accented by berry bushes and a few leafy green deciduous trees. No one else liked it, except Elissa.

Pulling off his parka, he looked out across the landing field. The great wind generators were shut down again. The methane generators must be running. His ancestors had burned dried cow dung; he burned methane made from human waste. As he changed his boots for thin black slippers, he wondered if the human race had made any real progress.

The Administrator's office was down the hall to the right. Inda knocked once and entered when he heard Griswold's acknowledgement.

"Morning, Anna. You wanted to see me?"

She waved him to a chair. Her office was one of the few without a mural. Instead, her walls were covered with photographs of the spaceport during construction. "I have considered your request to travel among the Ardellans. I'm sorry, Sinykin, but I have to deny it. Our agreement with Clan Alu limits contact to the spaceport compound."

"There is a provision for individuals to visit Alu Keep, if the Mentor of Clan Alu gives his permission." Inda was determined to win an invitation from Jeryl.

"You still need my permission, and I will not give it. The situation here is too delicate to allow anyone to leave the compound. The last envoy to visit Clan Alu killed herself, and three other Terrans were killed by the Ardellans."

Inda sighed. This argument was getting him nowhere. Griswold knew that the Ardellans had killed Terran criminals in self-defense. "I am administrator of the science division, and the scientific charter allows me to make decisions about research and investigations. You cannot interfere in a scientific mission if Alu gives permission for the investigation."

Griswold's face flushed. "If you want to turn this into a power struggle, Dr. Inda, I'll be happy to oblige you."

"I do not wish to challenge you," said Inda, rising. He was wary of Griswold's quick temper, and of her distrust of scientists. "I only want to be allowed to do my job."

The Administrator slapped her hand against the desktop. "Dr. Grund is prepared to take over as scientific administrator. If you propose this trip again, I will have you replaced. Now get out!"

Inda stalked from the room, slammed the door behind him. Lindy Zapata stared as he passed her desk. He ignored her. He closed his office door quietly, took a deep breath. The window showed him clouds rolling down the distant mountains. He sighed, picked up Sarah Anders' journal, opened it at random and began to read.

"I am beginning to piece together the life cycle of these strange and complex beings. I still do not fully understand it; it is so different from anything documented in the literature. Most species have two sexes, some only one, but here there are three.

"The younglings, the young of the species, are neuter, like the workers of some Terran ant species. Most of them remain so all of their lives, but a few are chosen to be cocooned. The youngling joins a House made up of a Mother (adult female) and a Master (adult male). It is cocooned, and after a period of time emerges from the cocoon as a Master.

"Mrann tells me that the two Masters mate with the Mother. She is the womb in which their seed merges. From that time until her death, she does not leave the mating chamber. After the mating, the new Master cocoons the old Master.

"The young grow within the Mother, consuming her body until they are mature enough to survive outside. She dies as they burst forth into the world, and her death cry awakens her cocooned mate, who emerges as a Mother. She nurtures the younglings and lives with her new mate for many years. When at last she becomes fertile, the Master cocoons a new youngling and the cycle begins again."

Inda heard a sharp tap on the door. He closed the journal and returned it to its place on his desk.

"Come."

The door opened, and Inda saw Lindy Zapata step aside. Jeryl, Mentor of Clan Alu, walked past her into the office. The door closed.

Jeryl raised a hand in greeting, holding it circular palm outward, all six fingers spread in a sunburst. Inda raised his hand in answer, approximating the gesture as best he could with a rectangular palm, four fingers, and an opposable thumb. "May the great sun smile upon you, Mentor," he said. He willed his psychic shields down, his mind open and receptive.

"And on you, Healer Sinykin Inda," answered Jeryl.

They both sat. Jeryl looked awkward in the Terran chair. The Ardellan was not tall, though he seemed so to Inda, who had the short stature of his Indian ancestors. Jeryl was gaunt, his legs slender and his knees bulbous in tight-fitting leggings. His steely gray eyes were bright, not cold, and his fine gray-white hair was a nimbus about his head.

"I am pleased you could come," said Inda. He enjoyed speaking Ardellan, with its formal structure and lilting accents. It was a language of few intimacies, designed for keeping distance between people who were otherwise too close.

"Your message said you wish to discuss the weather and the plague," replied Jeryl. "I have control of neither. How can I help you?"

Inda chose. He would ask Jeryl to let him travel to Alu Keep. "In the case of the plague, I would like to help you, Mentor. When the first cases appeared, I thought it might be a disease we Terrans had brought to Ardel. We work hard to guard against such things, but contaminations have occurred before, with disastrous results. It is rare for an illness to affect both the native population and our people, so when our people became ill, I assumed it was a Terran disease. We have isolated the virus, the tiny cells that cause the sickness, in our laboratory. To my surprise we found it is native to Ardel, and is carried by an insect, a small red flier. Do you know the insect I mean?"

"Yes," said Jeryl. "The fliers are usually rare, but this year there were many of them."

"They spread the virus through the clans and cities, and to our compound. It did not kill any of our people, but it did make some of the children very sick." Inda did not like the word youngling, which connoted servitude and inferiority. Since Jeryl spoke Terran standard, he chose to substitute the word "children" and hoped Jeryl would understand the difference. "We are developing a vaccine, a liquid containing the dead virus. We inject it into the bodies of our people, and it teaches their bodies to fight off the illness."

"I knew that the illness was not brought here by your people," said Jeryl. "There have been plagues as long as we have been keeping records. The oldest scrolls are moldy and moth-eaten, and four hands plus three plagues have swept through Clan Alu since they were written."

Four hands plus three, thought Sinykin. Twenty-seven times the plague had swept across the face of Ardel in recorded history, and still they could do nothing but treat it with bark tea and herbal remedies. But to tell the truth, he and his physicians had been almost as helpless. Megadoses of vitamin C and lots of liquids, and something to stop the diarrhea if necessary, were their standard treatments. The vaccine would prevent further outbreaks among the Terrans, but would it work for the Ardellans? He gazed across the desk at Jeryl. "Since the disease affected my people as well as yours, though in different ways, perhaps our method of prevention would work for your people. I would like to return with you to Clan Alu to get some blood and tissue samples. If I could visit some of the other clans, that would be even better. I will bring the samples back here and analyze them in our laboratory to discover whether the vaccine will work for your people."

Jeryl was quiet for a long moment. Sinykin closed his eyes and concentrated, focusing his mind's eye on Jeryl. The area just beyond the physical limit of the Ardellan's body was filled with softly glowing white light, flickering with distinct streaks of emerald and topaz; different from a human's aura, which usually showed large, fuzzy patches of color that changed very slowly.

"I am not certain I can accept your offer," said Jeryl suddenly. A streak of ruby light flashed across his aura. "It falls in the realm of the Healers. We could not use your vaccine without their approval."

"I understand," replied Sinykin, suddenly afraid that Jeryl would not let him go to Alu. He opened his eyes and his mind, projecting security and self-assurance. "If we find that the vaccine is safe for your people, we would present our idea to the Healers. Ideally, we would like to train them to make and administer the vaccine themselves."

Jeryl brought his hands together, touching palm to palm. "That is not so easily done," he said. "Most of the Healers who have power in the Guild are old, and resistant to change. It might be more effective to teach some of the younger Healers, and let them present the proposal to the Guild."

Inda nodded. "I thank you for your guidance in this matter."

"My guidance is perhaps not all it should be," said Jeryl, angry sparks flashing in his aura. "Knowledge and willingness to act are not the same as wisdom. I chose to trade with you for iron and copper and steel, and now you are unable to supply them, and the mining clans in the

mountains choose not to trade. Our supplies of metal are
small, and the metalworkers and the trade guilds are complaining.''

Inda swiveled his chair to look out across the landing
field, where Maintenance was clearing away the last of the
snow. ''We are also running short of some things. A cargo
ship is expected in two days, bearing supplies for us and a
load of copper for you. If there is no storm, it will land.''
He turned back to Jeryl. ''The weather has made it very
difficult for our ships to touch down safely. The equipment
that guides them is very important, and something in the
storms damaged that equipment on two ships that landed.
We cannot allow a ship to land during a storm until we can
protect that equipment. The ships have other places to go,
and often cannot wait for the weather to clear.''

''I understand that your ships are having problems,''
said Jeryl. ''I have tried to explain this to the guilds. Their
representatives point out that there were storms last year,
and the year before, and they did not keep the ships from
landing.''

''That puzzles us also. We expected stormy weather during the winter season, and built this facility to withstand
cold temperatures, high winds, heavy snows, and ice.'' Inda
shrugged. He did not know how to explain to Jeryl that
electromagnetic interference was disrupting the ships' navigation equipment. ''Something else is happening, something that may have nothing to do with the violence of the
storms.''

Jeryl clasped his hands in his lap, weaving his fingers
together. ''This is not at all normal weather for this area
and season. Storms like this are seen in the mountains, but
not on the plain until late in the season. The reports I have
had say the weather in the mountains is mild this year, the
big clouds passing over quickly to spill their burdens of
snow and cold here.''

Inda nodded. ''Our weather sensors tell us the same
thing.''

''I fear there is more at work here than the impersonal
violence of nature.'' Ruby streaks flashed in Jeryl's aura
like red lightning bolts. Inda watched this manifestation
of the Ardellan's anger, wondering what other powers it
connoted. These people were far beyond the class four
''pre-industrial'' rating the Terran bureaucracy had as-

signed them. Would he ever be able to convince anyone else of that?

Jeryl's gray eyes met his. "I would like you to come to Alu," he said, "but the decision is not mine alone. I wish to consult with Arien of the FreeMasters Guild. We will send word to you tomorrow morning, yes or no."

Chapter 3

Jeryl rode away from the busy spaceport into the silence of the rocky, barren plain. The mid-afternoon sun warmed his shoulders, and melted the dusting of snow on the trail. The water disappeared quickly into the sandy ground. The heavy snows of winter would bring the plain alive with slender grasses in the spring, but the grass would soon burn and die in the hot summer, leaving only fat succulents to brighten the landscape. To Jeryl the plain was a dormant thing, a place of potential that might or might not be realized.

This relationship with the Terrans was also a thing of potential. After four summers of building, four winters of sharing food, after riding lessons and instructions on how to keep predators away from their silly flightless food-birds, the Terrans were finally able to offer something of value to Ardel. Iron for blades and tools; and steel, stronger than iron and never rusting; and copper, precious copper, the metal that conducted psychic currents and helped store energy. And in exchange they would take sand from the plain, to extract something they called titanium.

The Terrans bought other things from Ardel—fabric and pottery, crystalline sphene, and soft, pliable, iridescent leathers. Trade was channeled through Clan Alu, since the Terrans had first landed in territory owned by the clan. By tradition a clan governed all activity that occurred on its land. Alu made a small profit on the transactions, which rankled the trade guilds but not the Terrans.

Now the Terrans offered something else, something unexpected. An end to the plague. Would Ardel accept the gift?

Jeryl hoped so. It would do more than save the lives of Mothers and prevent deformities among younglings. It would prove that the Terrans had something other than metals to offer Ardel. Jeryl wanted desperately for that to be true. He needed to believe that Sarah Anders' death meant something beyond a few rolls of copper wire and some shiny bars of steel.

Sinykin Inda seemed to possess the same honesty and openness that Jeryl had found so attractive in Sarah. That was both reassuring and frightening. Jeryl had dealt with enough Terrans to know that honesty was not a universal trait among humans. Some Terrans tried to lie to Ardellans, tried to conceal their feelings and disguise their motives. It was a futile exercise, but no Ardellan would tell them so. Only those who gained a Mentor's trust, as Sarah Anders had, would be allowed to travel freely among the Ardellans. Ardel had repaid Sarah with death. Jeryl hoped that Inda would not suffer the same fate.

Jeryl's alep tugged at the rein. After a morning of slow plodding down mountain paths, and a long wait at the spaceport, the animal was impatient. The trail ahead was bare and level, perfect for a four-legged run. Jeryl leaned forward and gave the alep a gentle nudge with his heels, just above its central pair of legs. It pulled them up and tucked them tight against its belly, then broke into a smooth, four-legged gait, the broad pads of its feet slapping the damp sand. The wind tugged Jeryl's hood back, blew his fine hair off his shoulders. He hunched over the alep's withers, right hand gripping the rein, left arm laid along the animal's slender neck, shivering. His right thigh ached. The long abrasion rubbed against his legging with each of his mount's strides. He concentrated, flushing the awareness of pain from his mind.

The ride was invigorating. The trail skirted a rocky outcrop, and Jeryl eyed it warily, then shrugged and gave his mount its head. It was rare this late in the season for predators to be hiding, waiting to ambush unwary coneys and basking lizards. Wild dog packs followed their prey to warmer regions before the snows came, and solitary tols sought shelter in mountain caves. Only highly adaptive, intelligent species like Ardellans and Terrans were foolish enough to stay in the path of winter storms, building walls and taming fires to protect themselves.

Yet walls and fire were not enough to keep a clan safe. If its population continued to decrease, in a few generations

Alu might be forced to return to nomadic life, following the herds instead of sending a few Masters and a gaggle of younglings to tend them in the winter. Jeryl feared there would not be enough Masters and Mothers to dye the wool and work the looms, to oversee the gardens and maintain the keep. His life span had been quadrupled by the death of his mate. He might live to see Alu Keep abandoned.

Gloomy thought. If Sinykin Inda's vaccine worked, it would halt the massive losses caused by the plague. The clans would die more slowly, losing Houses to accidents and occasional severe illnesses. Jeryl still needed to find a permanent solution to the problem. Long ago there had been a way to create new Houses. Healers and Mentors had done it together, until the Healers decreed that there were more Houses than the land could support. They had stopped gathering the necessary herbs and preparing the secret potions, had instead taken the mystery back to their guildhall and hidden it away. Now even Healers like Viela had no knowledge of it.

Jeryl rounded another enormous rock pile and saw the new FreeMasters' guildhall in the distance. It sprawled beside the road—stables, corrals, gardens and halls, and a Terran windmill and deep well. Small trees, imported from the seaward forests, shaded the well pool. Younglings bustled about the yard, tending to aleps and stacking wood brought from the mountains in carts.

This guildhall was an extension of the FreeMasters' hall in the mountains. It housed the guild members who had helped the Terrans build their installation, those who carried messages between the spaceport and Alu Keep, and those who transported goods to and from the Terran compound. Anyone who wished to travel to the spaceport was required to stop at the guildhall and present evidence that Clan Alu had granted permission for the visit. Few carried such evidence; the FreeMasters turned away most would-be visitors.

In addition to the road from the spaceport, three other roads led away from the guildhall. One continued across the wasteland toward Alu Keep and another cut through the plain to Berrut, city of the trade guilds. The last climbed the foothills and the mountains to the ancient FreeMasters' hall, and beyond to the mining clans' keep. Jeryl followed that route with his eyes, his mind dwelling on the historians' reports of weather-workers in the mountains, and the mining clans' refusal to trade unless the Terrans left Ardel.

As Jeryl reined his alep to a stop next to the corral, he saw a rider racing down the mountain road, cloak flapping behind him. Suddenly the stranger's beast went down, flipping its rider feet over head onto the sand.

"Call the Healer," Jeryl shouted to a passing youngling. He turned his mount and spurred it toward the downed rider, who was already struggling to his feet. "That is no way to treat an alep," Jeryl admonished the limping FreeMaster, his own exhilarating ride from the spaceport forgotten.

"I have an urgent message for GuildMaster Arien," said the FreeMaster. He knelt beside the injured alep, and began to examine its legs. The animal lay without kicking, breathing in huge windy puffs. Its torso jerked when the FreeMaster touched its left foreleg.

"Torn ligaments," he said, looking up at Jeryl.

"Foolish thing to do to a good mount," said Jeryl. Serious damage to a delicate foreleg meant the animal must be destroyed. Jeryl deplored the waste of a healthy alep. No animal should be ridden hard on uneven ground unless lives were at stake. He wanted to reprimand the rider but would not usurp Arien's authority to do so. Instead, he unsheathed his dagger and tossed it to the FreeMaster.

"Put that blade away!" A Healer was sprinting up the trail, sleeves billowing, right arm waving, left hand clutching a medicine bag. He skidded to a stop and dropped to his knees beside the injured alep, pushing the FreeMaster aside. He stroked the animal's legs gently.

"Tell the stablemaster to send up a cart and a winch," he said, pulling wrappings and a jar of salve from his pouch. "This animal has torn ligaments and cannot walk."

"Destroy it now, then. Why let it suffer?" asked Jeryl. He stared at the Healer's tattooed face. Blue lines snaked around his features, highlighting eyes and mouth before trailing down his neck to disappear beneath his tunic. Fisherfolk! Did this Healer know secrets that could make the alep's leg sound again?

"This animal can be saved," said the Healer as he spread salve on the alep's injured leg. "I need to concentrate. I must rejoin the ligaments before we move the alep."

"What of me?" asked the FreeMaster. "I wrenched my leg in the fall. Will you examine me?"

"Can you walk?" queried the Healer.

"Yes. It is not too painful." He limped to Jeryl's side and returned the dagger.

"Then walk to the hall, or sit here and rest until I am finished. I will examine you after the alep is settled."

Jeryl was astonished. "You treat an injured animal and let a Master wait? What kind of Healer are you?"

"A sensible one. You feed your mount before feeding yourself, do you not? I care first for the patient who cannot care for itself." He looked up at Jeryl. "If you are so concerned about the FreeMaster, you can dismount and let him ride your beast to the guildhall. I need your help to immobilize this leg."

"What is your name, Healer?" demanded Jeryl as he dismounted. The fisher's self-assurance bordered on arrogance. That irritated Jeryl. He searched the fisher's aura, expecting to find evidence that he was angry with the rider or disapproved of the way he had treated the alep. Instead he found the soft blue haze unmarred.

"My name is Hanra-bae," said the Healer. He pointed to one of the gathering crowd of younglings. "Fetch the stablemaster with that cart and winch."

Jeryl handed his rein to the FreeMaster, and knelt beside the injured mount. He wanted to help save the animal, even though his experience told him the effort was useless.

"Place your hands here, and here," said Hanra-bae, showing Jeryl how to hold the leg above and below the injury. Jeryl grasped the leg gently, but the Healer squeezed his hands, made him hold tighter. He sensed the animal's pain, a sharp, pulsing agony that beat at his shields. The alep kicked, and Jeryl struggled to hold the leg steady.

"No, no!" shouted the Healer. "You must keep it immobile." When he touched the injury, the alep tried to nip him, but he turned and struck it a sharp blow on the nose.

Hanra-bae placed his hands between Jeryl's, directly over the torn ligaments. Jeryl had never seen a Healer work on an animal. Closing his eyes, he watched with a Mentor's psychic vision as Hanra-bae unleashed his Healing powers. The blue haze of his aura extended downward to engulf the injured leg. With intense concentration, the Healer probed the injury and traced the torn ligaments. When he brought the jagged ends together the alep struggled, but Jeryl managed to hold its leg steady. Pouring energy into the leg, Hanra-bae knitted the torn filaments together. Then he withdrew, and bound the leg with strips of linen.

When Hanra-bae was finished, Jeryl released the alep's leg. Certainly the Healer's confidence was justified. He was good, better than Alu's Healer. "I have never seen such fine control without the conscious aid of the subject. You are very skilled. How will you keep the alep from reinjuring itself?"

"The animal must not be allowed to use this leg for at least a hand of days. We will hang it in a sling in one of the stalls, and immobilize the leg in a splint."

The stablemaster arrived with the cart. Jeryl left them to discuss moving the animal, and returned to his own mount. How had one of the fishers come to be Healer for Arien's FreeMasters? The fisherfolk were rarely seen more than a day's ride from the sea. Only the FreeMasters who guided the yearly trading caravans to their ports knew them well. Jeryl considered that as he helped the injured FreeMaster mount and led his alep toward the compound.

Arien ran from the guildhall as they entered the stableyard. "Jeryl! Ramis! What happened?" Younglings left their tasks and crowded close, frightening Jeryl's alep. It did a fast sidestep, bowling over half a hand of the rotund younglings.

Younglings could be a nuisance, especially here, where there were no Mothers to teach them proper behavior. Half a hundred black eyes peered, their supporting stalks quivering with excitement. Arien waded through the crowd, grabbing tool straps and tentacles to pull the ovoid bodies aside. He cleared a space beside the alep, and helped the injured FreeMaster dismount.

"Are you all right, Ramis?" he queried. "What are you doing here?"

"GuildMaster, I bring bad news. One of the new FreeMasters from Clan Alu took an alep and rode into the mountains this morning, after you left the guildhall," said Ramis. "We did not learn of this until midday. A search party was sent out immediately."

"Who was it?" asked Arien.

Jeryl did not wait for Ramis' reply. "Hatar!" he said. "By the great sun, I should have had him bound until he came to his senses. He knows nothing of survival in the wilds. Did he take anything with him?"

"No, Mentor," said Ramis. "Only the clothing on his back and a saddle for the alep."

"I must go and find him," said Jeryl, feeling the weight of another death settle on his shoulders. "Can you spare me an extra mount and some supplies, Arien?"

"No. Let my FreeMasters search for him. They may have found him already."

"He is my responsibility!" And if I had been more careful, he would be safe at the guildhall or at Alu Keep.

Arien stepped close to Jeryl and touched his shoulder. "Hatar is no longer your responsibility," he said quietly. Jeryl stared at him. "He is a FreeMaster now. He belongs to the guild. Let us take care of our own."

Jeryl sighed and placed his hand on Arien's. The GuildMaster was right. Hatar's future was out of his hands. His time and energy belonged to Clan Alu. He had a far more important quest—to find a way to start new family lines and increase the clan's population.

"The searchers will find Hatar," said Arien as he showed Jeryl and Ramis into the main hall. The room was long and narrow, with a hooded firepit in the center dividing the work area from that used for eating and socializing. Arien helped Ramis to a bench near the firepit and propped his injured leg on a stool.

"I hope that they do," said Jeryl, shrugging off his cloak, "but I do not expect it." A youngling with a single eyestalk took the garment from him and offered him a steaming mug. The youngling carried the cloak away, then it brought another mug for Arien and a third for Ramis. The youngling had five well-formed, active tentacles. The sixth was withered, like its second eyestalk. Another victim of the plague, thought Jeryl, come to haunt me. Each dead Mother, each maimed youngling, was a reminder of his powerlessness.

Arien shrugged, and pulled a stool close to the fire. "There is nothing we can do for him. He chose his fate, as ultimately we all do. Let it go, Jeryl. There are other matters needing your attention."

Jeryl spurned a proffered stool, and sat on the thick rug beside the fire. Arien was right, there was nothing he could do for Hatar. Many others depended on him now.

"Who is this fisher who practices his Healer's arts on your aleps?" he asked. "Has he been with you long?"

"Hanra-bae? He came from Port Freewind with the last caravan. He claims to be traveling to Berrut." Arien paused to sip his tea. "He offered to stay with us for a few days and show our Healer, Lirra, some new techniques."

"He is very skilled for one so young."

"Perhaps, but how does one tell the age of a fisher? Those tattoos can hide many wrinkles."

Jeryl almost choked on a swallow of tea. "Arien, your sense of humor becomes stranger with each passing season." He set down his mug and looked at his friend. "You visit the fishers each year; certainly you know more about them than do I. How does this one come by such skill?"

"He has told us little about himself. He received some training at the Healers Guild in Berrut, then studied with the fishers' senior Healer at Port Freewind. I know nothing beyond that. Lirra has spent much time with Hanra-bae during the past six-day, and seems to be impressed with his skill."

"I should like to invite Hanra-bae to visit Alu Keep. Perhaps he would be willing to share his techniques with Viela."

Arien snorted. "But would Viela be willing to learn them?"

"He is a good Healer, even though he is set in his ways. He will not spurn a chance to improve his skills." Jeryl gazed into the fire. He heard the crackle of the flames and the clicking of the loom in the far corner, but his mind saw Sinykin Inda's tissue samples and vials of blood. Would Viela be willing to cooperate with the Terran Healer?

"I had another message from Berrut today," said Arien, "from GuildMaster Reass of the Metalsmiths and Guild-Master Mikal of the Merchants. They wish to meet with me, to talk of having FreeMasters permanently assigned to their guilds."

"What?" asked Jeryl. He pulled his eyes away from the flames, dismissing the vision of Inda's cure.

Arien sighed. "Those trance drugs you use are interfering with your connection to the real world, Jeryl." Topaz flickers of annoyance danced in his aura, and were quickly extinguished.

"No, no. I was thinking of something Sinykin Inda told me. What did you say?"

"The trade guilds sent me a message. They want FreeMasters assigned to their guildhalls to act as permanent guides and translators. . . ."

"They want to subvert the loyalty and power of Free-Masters to increase their own fortunes," said Jeryl quietly. A ruby stain of anger spread through his aura. He took a deep breath and blew it out slowly. The red stain receded. "The trade guilds want to establish direct contact with the Terrans. A FreeMaster in each guild gives them reason to send members here, to infiltrate your hall and mingle with the spaceport caravans."

"I know that. They use any strategy that brings them closer to the spaceport and the Terrans. Every six-day we turn away delegations of merchants that attempt to visit the spaceport without Alu's permission." Arien waved for a youngling to bring fresh tea. "I will deny the guilds' request, and they will protest, and it will lead to another argument before the Assembly."

Jeryl stretched out a hand to clasp Arien's leg. "And we will prevail again. Tradition rules, my friend. Alu fought the Assembly once before. This time they will not dare challenge clan-right."

"Do not be too sure of that. The metal shortage is causing unrest among the clans as well as the guilds. My informants say many of the elders think allowing Alu to trade with the Terrans was a mistake."

Ruby streaks flashed in Jeryl's aura. He pulled his hand away from Arien, not wanting to transmit his anger through the contact. "What Alu does on Alu land is no one's concern but Alu's. It has always been so. The Assembly cannot change that now."

"Perhaps. But there is contradiction in what you say, Jeryl." Arien touched the Mentor's shoulder. "Trade with the Terrans itself breaks tradition. Their presence has brought new ways to our people. Many things are changing."

Jeryl gulped the last of his cooling tea, then watched a youngling refill the mug. "More things than you know are changing," he said, looking up at Arien. "Sinykin Inda wishes to travel to Alu. He claims he has found a way to stop the plague!"

"A way to stop the plague?" Hanra-bae was striding across the room from the far door. "Which Healer has discovered this boon?"

"The Terran Healer," said Jeryl. He heard the edge of anger in his voice, and tried to eliminate it. After all, the fisherfolk had different ways. Hanra-bae might not realize he was intruding on a private conversation. "He has made a preparation that keeps his people from catching the plague. He believes it might work for us, too."

Hanra-bae knelt beside the bench and began to examine Ramis' injured leg. "Does he claim to know which poison causes the plague, and how it is spread?"

"Yes, he does. The red fliers carry the poison." Perhaps this chance meeting with the fisher could benefit them all. Hanra-bae might be more willing than Viela to aid the Terran Healer. Jeryl decided to approach the subject carefully, after learning more about the fisher. "Will the alep recover?"

"Yes." Hanra-bae did not look up. "It must stay in the sling in the stable for a few days, while the ligaments begin to mend. Then we will tether it in a stall so that it cannot walk. It will be sturdy enough for riding on the plain, though I do not think it will take the mountain trails again."

Ramis spoke for the first time since entering the hall. "It is an old alep. We were talking of retiring it to the breeding paddocks soon."

"That is no reason to mistreat the animal," said the Healer. He handed Ramis his boot. "I find no damage to your leg, only a slight sprain. Avoid long walks and try not to fall off your mount for the next six-day." He rose and turned to leave.

Arien stopped him. "I do not believe that you and my friend have been properly introduced. The great sun smiles on you both today. Jeryl, Mentor of Clan Alu, this is Hanra-bae, Master Healer of Port Freewind."

Surprise flared in Jeryl's aura, though he tried to damp it. Arien should have told him that the young fisher had already attained senior rank in his guild. "You are young to have reached the rank of Master Healer."

"Sometimes natural ability can achieve more than experience can." Hanra-bae sat and signaled for a youngling to bring him tea.

"But you spurn the symbols of your rank. Where are your sash and medallion?"

Anger flashed in the Healer's aura. He seemed to be easily provoked, a failing common among Healers. "I do not care to advertise my position in the guild. My skill is all that should matter."

Jeryl chose to answer the fisher's arrogance with praise. "I have witnessed your skill. You have earned your rank."

Arien agreed. "We are very pleased to have you with us. I know you plan to continue your journey soon, but you are welcome to stay as long as you wish."

Hanra-bae shrugged. "Lirra has learned most of what I can teach him. I do need to leave for Berrut in the next few days. Meanwhile, I would like to know more about this preparation the Terran Healer has made. What is it? How does it work?"

"I know little about it, except that it teaches the body to no longer be susceptible to the plague. Inda claims it works for the Terrans, and he wants to come to Alu to gather blood and tissue samples for testing. If he can make a preparation that will work for us, he will teach the Healers to make and administer it."

"Induced immunity," said Hanra-bae. "I have read about this, in some translations of the ancient scrolls. We have lost the skill to make preparations like that. Many of the ancient skills are now mysteries to us."

Jeryl tilted his head and stared at the fisher. "The Terran Healer is called Sinykin Inda. I would like to allow him to travel to Alu Keep. He speaks our language, but he will need a guide and companion, preferably a Healer. I fear that Alu's Healer, Viela, will not approve of Inda's presence at the keep. Viela does not like Terrans." He sighed. "It would be a shame to lose this chance at halting the plague because Viela will not cooperate with the Terran."

"It would indeed be a shame," said Hanra-bae. "Surely there is a Healer at the guildhall in Berrut who would work with Inda. Have you made inquiries there?"

"Not yet. I just learned of Inda's plans today."

Hanra-bae nodded. "I will be visiting the Healers' compounds in Berrut. I could interview some of the young Healers for you, and if one of them is suitable, send him to Alu Keep."

Arien snorted. "No youngster will be able to stand up to

Viela. That stubborn old Healer has decided that Terrans do not belong on Ardel. He makes life miserable for anyone who tries to work with them.''

"Yes," said Jeryl. "What we really need is someone with the stature and skill of a Master Healer, someone who will command Viela's respect."

Hanra-bae stared at Jeryl. "I am not a guide or companion, Mentor. I am interested in the Terran's preparation, and would learn to make it, if it works. But I have a mission of my own that I must complete."

"Think of all you could learn from Inda. Would it not be worth a hand of days. . . ."

"No!" The Healer rose, then sighed and sat again. He looked at Arien. "I do not mean to be impolite. Your guild has been hospitable, and I thank you. I must leave soon, and go on to Berrut. The future of my people depends on it."

"I accept your thanks. You are free to come and go as you please. You will always be welcomed here," said Arien, giving Jeryl a reproachful look. "Jeryl and I are also traveling to Berrut. May I ask the nature of your business there?"

"The plague has decimated my people. It is over for this season, and they are safe until the warm weather comes again. There are so few of them left! Each time the plague comes, or there is an accident with one of the fishing boats, we lose more families." Hanra-bae's aura swirled with anguished emerald and topaz mist. He paused, looking at Jeryl. "You must have some understanding of this. The plague has not been kind to your clans. The FreeMasters' Guild grows larger as Houses stand empty in the keeps."

Jeryl stared at him. Did they seek the same key? "Alu has lost many people. Over half the Houses in the keep are empty, most sacrificed to the last three plagues. I have read the ancient scrolls. The plague has come before, and killed in even larger numbers, but always the clan recovered and thrived afterward."

"It is the same among the fishers. Once we knew how to create new lines, make new families. Now we die, and only in the guilds does the population grow."

"Hah!" There was new bitterness in Arien's voice. "Our ancestors made a grave error when they allowed the best of their craftsmen and traders to leave the keeps and build the

trade city. They believed that Berrut and its guilds would
remain allied with the keeps, that the guildmembers would
continue their family lines, that younglings would be fostered between city and keeps. That did not last long. Now
the city guilds have crèches where all the Mothers and
younglings live, and the Masters live in a guildhall as if
they were FreeMasters. Younglings grow up knowing only
their Mothers. Some guildmembers remain Masters well beyond the age when they should have metamorphosed into
Mothers. Who knows what perversions are perpetrated
there? Do not emulate them.''

"I will not copy their ways, but I would know their
secrets.''

"So would I," said Jeryl. "If the Terran's preparation
works, it will halt the plague deaths. Is that not worth your
time?''

"It will only resolve one aspect of the problem. We must
repopulate the empty Houses, replace the family lines that
have died out,'' explained Hanra-bae. "I am the most skilled
Healer my people have. I am the only one who has studied
in Berrut. They selected me to return there, to search the
old records for information that may help us. I am expected
at the Healers' compound in three days.''

Jeryl looked at Arien. They were going to Berrut; it would
be to their advantage to ally with this Healer. Arien made a
brief gesture of assent. "We are returning to Alu Keep tomorrow, then leaving for Berrut the following morning. We
would be honored to have you travel with us.''

"I thank you. I do not care to travel alone," said Hanra-
bae. "Now let me examine your leg.''

"My leg?" Jeryl resisted an impulse to touch his throbbing thigh.

"Your right thigh. You have an abrasion. I can feel the
irritation from here.''

The sun was rising as they saddled their aleps. Arien was
still giving orders to his apprentice.

"Send a messenger to Sinykin Inda at the spaceport.
Ramis will do, if he can avoid trouble. Tell Inda that a guide
will be there tomorrow at dawn to escort him to Alu Keep.
Send along one pack animal in case he has extra gear.''

"I will see to it, GuildMaster," replied the apprentice.

"I will be at Alu today, and tomorrow night I will be in

Berrut, at the Inn of the Blue Door. I trust that you can handle anything that comes up,'' said Arien as he swung into the saddle.

"Certainly, GuildMaster. May the great sun light your way.''

The day was clear and cold. Prodding his old mount with his feet, Jeryl leaned forward, one hand holding the rein and the other resting on the alep's withers. He rocked with the smooth, even gait, supporting his body on muscular thighs, his buttocks just brushing the saddle. Arien and Hanra-bae followed him on younger animals. The ride was swift. By late afternoon they could see the tall gates of Alu Keep.

Hanra-bae stopped his mount on the road before the keep and stared at the high stone wall. "Does it extend all the way around the keep?''

"Yes,'' said Jeryl. "Have you never seen a keep before?''

"No.'' The fisher dismounted and led his alep to the open gate. He hesitated there, looking up at the arch of stone overhead.

"Come.'' Jeryl led the way into the keep. Hanra-bae slowly followed.

They left the aleps at the stable just inside the gate, and Jeryl sent one of the grooms to find Ertis. Then they walked, carrying their packs, down the long gravel road to the clan-hall. Arien, to whom Alu Keep had once been home, pointed out things of interest to Hanra-bae, but all Jeryl could see were the darkened windows of abandoned Houses. House Rastee, which he had shared with his mate, stood just inside the gate. A tangle of dormant vines, their leaves lost to winter winds, covered the walls like crisscrossing scars. Across the road was Hatar's House, its walls still clean. And somewhere in the mountains Hatar rode alone, as desolate as his House.

Jeryl counted two hands of empty Houses along the main road. The clanhall was a welcome sight, but Arien led them around it to the mourning wall. The sun was low, and the great wall cast a deep shadow. Jeryl hung back, his head and shoulders in sunlight. Arien went straight to the urns of his dead mates, but Hanra-bae approached an older part of the wall.

"What are these jars?" he asked, stroking a red granite urn. "The runes below them are in a dialect I cannot read."

Steeling himself against the coldness of the shadows, Jeryl approached. "These are burial urns. They hold the ashes of every adult member of Clan Alu who died since the founding of Alu Keep." He stared at the ancient runes, sifting through old memories to render them in words. The runes identified each of the deceased, and described his life and death. "This is Allie'a, twelfth Mentor of Clan Alu, who died in dispute with Clan Sau."

"You cremate your dead? I had heard that when I was in Berrut, but I never believed it. And 'dispute'—that is some kind of ritual challenge, is it not?"

"The Terrans have an ugly word for it. War." Jeryl followed Hanra-bae along the wall, watching as he stopped now and again to stroke an urn and decipher the runes below it. Here the history of Clan Alu was kept, in the memories the living wrote of the dead.

They passed Arien. Hanra-bae stopped before a moss green urn. He stroked it, and the marble glowed with soft, shifting light. "Who is this?"

Arien's hand clasped Jeryl's shoulder. His touch eased painful memories.

"That urn contains the ashes of a Terran," said Arien. "Her name was Sarah Anders."

"And she died here? Why was her body not returned to her people?"

Arien shrugged. "That is a long and complicated story that is best saved for another time."

Jeryl shivered. "The air grows cold," he said as he climbed the stoop to the clanhall's back door. The others followed.

The kitchen was warm, the air heavy with the smell of food and the dampness of wash-water. Secko was just finishing his meal at the long table. He started to rise when he saw the fisher; Jeryl gestured for him to remain seated.

"Enjoy your tea in peace," said Jeryl. "We will eat in the main hall. When you are finished, please have our packs taken upstairs. Arien and Hanra-bae will be spending the night with us."

Arien and the fisher took fresh bread and tea from the hearth. Jeryl led them through narrow passages to the meeting hall. The huge old room was dark and empty. He blinked and two wall sconces flared.

An ancient tapestry insulated one wall, but the hearth was cold, the firebox empty. A long stone table dominated the chilly room. Jeryl took the end chair, with Arien to his right and Hanra-bae to his left. They were barely settled when Ertis, Alu's Historian, appeared in the doorway.

"Come join us. Are you hungry?" Jeryl waved him to an empty chair. "You remember GuildMaster Arien, and this is Hanra-bae, Master Healer of Port Freewind."

"It is good to see you again, GuildMaster." Ertis sat, and raised his hand in greeting. "Welcome to Alu, Master Healer. It has been many years since I spoke with a fisher. Your people tell many interesting tales. May the great sun brighten your visit."

Hanra-bae shrugged acknowledgment; his mouth was full of bread.

"Our visit is necessarily short," said Arien between gulps of tea. "We leave for Berrut in the morning."

Jeryl waved them all to silence. He swallowed a last bite, and pushed aside the remains of his supper. "There is a matter we must settle, Ertis. One of the Terrans is coming to Alu. I cannot be here to host him. I need someone who is discreet and experienced to be his guide and companion."

Excitement erupted through the Historian's aura in a sudden swirling of topaz and aquamarine mist.

"If you are to host the Terran, you must be prepared to deal with some opposition among our people. You know that there are some Masters in Clan Alu who do not wish to have Terrans among us." Jeryl sighed. "This Terran is Sinykin Inda, one of the spaceport administrators. He is also a Healer. He will be taking blood and tissue samples from victims of the plague."

"He will do what?"

The voice boomed from the outer chamber. Anger impinged on Jeryl's awareness as he turned to chastise the interloper. Alu's Healer, Viela, stood outside the doorway, his body and part of his flashing ruby aura framed in the opening. Jeryl could see Secko standing behind the Healer.

Jeryl let his own anger show in his aura. "Apprentice, you should not have disturbed the Healer. We have no need of his skills this evening."

"I am here to protect my clan," said Viela as he stepped into the room. "By what right do you bring a Terran to Alu?"

"Mentor's right! By what right do you interfere?" Jeryl felt Ertis cringe. The Historian disliked arguments. Arien gazed at Viela, watchful but unperturbed. Hanra-bae did not turn to look at his fellow Healer.

"The health of this clan is my responsibility," declaimed Viela, approaching the table. "The last time a Terran came to Alu, it cost the lives of a Mentor, his apprentice, and your mate. Have you forgotten?"

Jeryl had not. Sarah Anders' time at Alu Keep had also cost the Terran her own life. He would never forget her death, nor his own part in it. Arien laid a steadying hand on his forearm, but Jeryl brushed it away as he stood. "You overstep the bounds of your office, Healer. It is in the best interests of the clan that this Terran come to Alu Keep. I require you to cooperate with him in every way."

"I will not stay at the keep if you bring a Terran here." Viela stopped an arm's length from Hanra-bae's chair, his right hand clutching his Healer's medallion, his left raised in a gesture of challenge. His fine white hair was an unruly cloud around his head.

"You are bound to Clan Alu by your oath," said Jeryl. His own aura flared with ruby lightning. "You will not leave the keep without my permission, as long as the Terran is here. To do so would break your Healer's oath, and bring the wrath of the guild upon you. You will cooperate with the Terran to the best of your ability because what he does will aid Alu."

"Do not threaten me!"

Hanra-bae's chair scraped the floor. He rose and turned to face Viela. Blue lines snaked across his face, taking on sudden, impossible life. "Do you deny your oath? I am Hanra-bae, Master Healer, and I represent the interests of your guild. Think well on what you do!"

Jeryl's anger flared anew, this time at Hanra-bae. This was a clan matter, and the fisher's interference was unwelcome and unnecessary.

The Master Healer did not seem to notice. "Come," he said to Viela, "I would inspect your infirmary." He grasped Viela's outstretched arm, turned him around, and walked him out of the room.

Arien touched Jeryl's hand. "He meant only to help," he said, looking after Hanra-bae.

Jeryl took a deep breath and calmed his aura. Arien was correct; as Master Healer, Hanra-bae did have authority over Viela. If the fisher could convince Viela to accept the Terran's presence at Alu Keep, Inda's visit would go more smoothly. Besides, as Mentor Jeryl had other responsibilities. Not the least of these would be disciplining his loose-mouthed apprentice.

Ertis coughed, reminding Jeryl of the purpose of this meeting. There were many details of the Terran's visit to settle. They had much to do before they could leave for Berrut.

He would deal with Secko later.

Chapter 4

Sinykin Inda pulled the white plastic plaque from his office door. In carved block letters it announced his name and title: ASSISTANT ADMINISTRATOR—SCIENCE DIVISION, CHIEF MEDICAL OFFICER, XENOBIOLOGIST. Jeff Grund's would be even longer. He tossed the plaque into the smaller of two boxes on his desk. If things went well, he would no longer need it. Three years of planning, studying, and working to establish trust between himself and Jeryl were finally coming to fruition. The next plaque Maintenance made for him would say: SINYKIN INDA, ENVOY.

"You've decided, then?"

Inda spun around. Anna Griswold stood in the doorway. Her blue dress tunic hung almost to her knees, making her appear shorter than her meter-and-a-half height. The Spaceport Administrator's insignia on the breast shone brightly, as if she had just finished polishing it. She leaned against the door frame, slender arms crossed under her tiny breasts, toes just outside the limits of Inda's office.

"It was not a difficult decision," replied Sinykin.

"The consequences may be more than you care to deal with."

"Do not threaten me, Anna. You have power over the science division only during declared emergencies. You cannot interfere with a legitimate scientific mission."

Griswold straightened up, dropped her hands to her sides. "You are making a mistake, Sinykin. Don't risk everything you've worked for."

He laughed. "This is what I've been working for. I'll be the new envoy, Anna."

She shook her head. "I hope you won't be dead," she said before walking away.

Inda shrugged. Griswold was stubborn. She might try to make life difficult for Elissa and Jaime while he was gone. That would be a mistake. Elissa was strong, and she had many friends among the spaceport personnel. She could take care of herself and their son. Sinykin picked up the holo-cube that contained her image and put it in the smaller box. Then he carried the larger box out and set it on Lindy Zapata's desk. "See that Jeff Grund gets this," he said. "He'll be Acting Assistant Administrator while I'm gone."

"I'll tell him to come pick it up. We'll miss you, Dr. Inda. Who's been assigned to your office?" she asked.

Inda stared at her. How could a human being be so lacking in tact? "My office will be empty until I return," he said as he turned away.

He took one last look at the painted conifer forest. Perhaps Jeryl would take him to the mountains, and he would see the scarlet trees. Jaime would like to have some of the spiral cones. Sinykin picked up his box of personal things, and nodded a curt good-bye to Lindy Zapata on his way out.

The afternoon was clear and cold now, as the sun dropped toward the horizon. Night came on so quickly this time of year. The short days left him little time for outdoor exercise. He and Elissa could work out in the gym, and next year, if the deep well brought in enough water, there would be a swimming pool. But Jaime liked to play outdoors, so every four-day when he and Elissa were both off, they all went hiking among the rock piles or rode the six-legged aleps. Today Elissa was working, but Jaime was waiting for him at the apartment, ready for one last rock-climbing expedition before the winter storms put a stop to climbing until spring.

Jaime was watching for him at the window. He had the door open before Sinykin reached it.

"Are you ready, Father? Can we go now?" he asked, taking the box from Inda and putting it on the table. "What's this stuff?"

"Some things from my office," said Inda. "Let me put on my hiking boots. Do you have your gloves?"

"Yeah." He pulled the nameplate from the box and held it up. "Why did you bring this home?"

"I won't be working at my office for a while, Jaime."
Sinykin placed a hand on his son's shoulder and steered him
to the folded futon under the window. They sat side by side,
their backs against the cool wall.

"I'm going away for a few days." He saw his son's eyes
dart to the kitchen window, where Miranda's funeral urn
shimmered in the sunlight. He felt the momentary panic that
swept through the boy. "Not like your sister. I am going to
Alu Keep, to spend some time with the natives, and I will
return."

"Is Mom going with you?" asked Jaime, knees drawn up
against his chest and right arm wrapped around them.

Sinykin put an arm around his son's shoulders and hugged
him close. "No, she's staying here with you. I should be
back in eight or ten days. You can wait that long, can't
you?"

Jaime looked up at him and smiled. "Yes. I'll mark each
day on my calendar until you come home."

"Good. Now put on your coat so we can go outside."
Inda watched his son's compact body uncoil and spring
across the room. Jaime scooped up gloves and jacket as he
dashed to the door. Sinykin followed, pondering the wonderful resiliency of young minds and bodies.

Elissa was waiting when they returned. Her hair was wet
from the shower, curled in little ringlets across her forehead. Tiny lines of tension showed at the corners of her
mouth, and her eyes lacked their usual sparkle. Her tur-
quoise kimono with the graceful swan embroidered on the
back was limp and wrinkled.

Jaime ran to hug her, leaving the apartment door open.
Sinykin closed it.

"Uhh," said Jaime, stepping back and looking from his
mother to his father. "Tommy Grund invited me for supper.
His mother's making chicken!" he said all in a rush.

Sinykin met his wife's eyes. In deference to him, she never
served animal flesh in their home, but sometimes she and
Jaime ate it elsewhere. Lately, chicken was his favorite meal.
Elissa nodded, and Sinykin said, "All right. You can stay
and study with Tommy, too, if you want."

"Great!" Jaime grabbed a stack of brightly-colored plastic computer disks from the desk and stuffed them in his

pocket. His only good-bye was the slamming of the door behind him.

Inda went to Elissa, wrapped her in his arms and held her close. Her distress concerned him. "Lissie," he said, "what's wrong?"

She broke away from him and walked to the window, touching Miranda's urn. It seemed to glow, but perhaps it just reflected the brightness of her robe.

"I don't want to lose you, too," she said, staring into the twilight. "We might have lost Miranda anyway, here or on Terra. But you. . . ."

"This is a medical mission," he said softly, trying to be reassuring. "I'll be in no danger."

"The first envoy died, Sinykin. No one knows how or why. . . ."

He followed her, turned her away from the window to face him. "The Ardellans know how she died. Jeryl has promised that it won't happen to any more of our people. Perhaps, when I visit him, he will tell me about it."

She shrugged. He knew she wanted to believe him, and that she was still afraid. In the past, her job had been the dangerous one. He remembered the years on Titan Station, before Jaime was born. Often he had stood at the maintenance viewport, and stared out at some disabled ship, searching among the clusters of workers for Elissa's suit with its distinctive purple stripe. He usually found her working in the most dangerous locations, clinging to the scarred hull near the engines, with a slender lifeline her only protection. He had feared for her safety then, as she feared for his now.

"Has Griswold contacted you?"

Elissa nodded.

"What did she say?"

"She's convinced you're going to die if you leave the compound." He saw tears gathering in her eyes. "She wants me to make you give up this idea."

He muttered an oath under his breath. "I'll be perfectly safe, Lissie. Don't let Griswold's paranoia make you fear dangers that don't exist."

Elissa smiled at him. "I love you. I'll always worry about your safety."

With the lightest touch of hands on shoulders he drew her toward him. She stepped into his embrace, slipping her arms around his chest and hugging him close, the flat of her palms against his back. She was strong; when she held him he often felt she could pull his smaller body into her own.

He put one hand behind her neck and pulled her head down. "Make love with me?" he whispered, and delighted in the response that swept through her body.

At dawn they walked with him to the corral at the edge of the compound. Elissa held his hand, but Jaime ran ahead to see the guide who waited for Inda.

"Jaime told me he wants to be a xenobiologist," said Elissa.

Inda squeezed her hand. "He'll have to go off-planet to one of the big universities, or even back to Terra to train at Stanford. And then he could choose an assignment with an exploratory mission, rather than coming back here."

"I know," whispered Elissa. "We left our families, and someday Jaime will leave us."

Inda slipped his arm around her waist, holding her close. He and Elissa had been together for a long time. Miranda was gone, and Jaime would leave them some day, but they would always have each other.

"I love you, Lissie. Don't worry about me. I'll be back soon."

She hugged him.

The sunrise was murky, the air crisp and cold. A cargo ship was due soon, had already contacted the ground crew judging by the lights and activity on the landing field. Elissa should be there. He was keeping her from her work.

"I'll go straight to the field from here," she said, giving him a kiss on the cheek. Her eyes roamed the landing field; she was analyzing the placement of people and equipment.

At the corral, Jaime's hot breath made puffs of fog as he stood looking at the guide. He asked no questions, but stared at the six-fingered hand that rested on the gate.

"May the great sun smile on you, Ramis," said Inda in Ardellan. "These are the members of my House, my mate and our child."

Ramis held up his right hand, fingers spread in a gesture of greeting. "The great sun smile upon you and your House," he replied in halting Standard.

Jaime extended his hand, trying to mirror Ramis' gesture

with fingers that were too few and too short. "May you have clear weather and a safe ride," he said.

"Perhaps we will not have either," said Ramis to Inda, lapsing into the low, bell-like tones and chopped syllables of Ardellan. He pointed toward the mountains. "There is a storm coming. Your gear has been loaded on the pack animal. We must leave now."

Sinykin kissed Elissa and hugged Jaime. Jaime's attention was on Ramis; he seemed to have forgotten that his father was going away.

The pack alep was tethered outside the corral. Ramis led two saddled mounts from the enclosure. The tall one was gray with black stripes across its shoulders. The other was short, broad in the chest, with stocky legs and a speckled coat. It shifted restlessly on its six round feet when Inda mounted. Ramis leapt easily onto his alep's back.

Elissa stood with Jaime, right hand on his shoulder and left in her pants pocket, watching Sinykin. His eyes sought hers, he smiled and nodded, and she smiled at him. Jaime waved. Then they both turned away, Jaime toward school and Elissa toward the landing field.

Inda tugged back on the rein and pressed with his right knee to make his mount turn. It plodded along behind Ramis and the pack animal, following them past the landing field to the main gate. Maintenance personnel opened the gate, then locked it behind them.

The huge amber sun had just cleared the eastern horizon, and the sandy plain was suffused with golden light. Here and there snow filled a hollow, or nestled in a shady spot on the north side of a boulder. They traveled toward the newly-built FreeMasters' guildhall, where Inda and some of his coworkers were infrequent visitors. None of the Terrans had been allowed to travel elsewhere. Alu Keep was nearly a day's ride farther north, out of the wasteland.

They passed the guildhall before mid-morning, and soon after left the wasteland behind. On either side of the trail fields were plowed in neat spiral patterns, the furrows white with snow and the ridges bristling with brown stubble. Their aleps walked six-legged on the rutted track, placing their flat, flexible feet with care.

At midday they stopped to water the animals. Ramis brought out cold tea and bread rich with nuts and fruit. While they ate, heavy gray clouds moved out of the moun-

tains and obscured the sun. The wind turned easterly and
icy. Before they remounted, Inda wrapped his scarf over his
mouth and nose. Soon snow began to fall, and the wind
drove the sharp crystals against his face, freezing them to
his scarf and his eyebrows. He wished for a pair of snow
goggles. His nose ran.

Ahead, Ramis shouted and pointed at the black sky to the
west. The blizzard was moving swiftly toward them. The
Ardellan pushed his mount to a jerky trot, and Inda did his
best to keep up. He had no time to watch the scenery now.
He was bumped and jostled from side to side as his mount
trotted over the ruts. He tried to keep his eyes on the trail
and to guide the alep to the smoothest parts. Once the animal stumbled and nearly threw him. He gripped tighter with
his knees, hunching low over the alep's neck. His thighs
cramped.

The trip seemed interminable. Cold penetrated his boots
and robbed him of sensation in his toes. Snow covered the
road so that he could not see the ruts. Ice crystals crept
down the back of his neck and into the tops of his gloves.
The front of his scarf became stiff where his breath melted
the snow and the wind turned it to ice.

Finally he lost sight of Ramis and the aleps. He gave his
mount its head, hoping that it could follow their trail through
the blowing snow. He was exhausted and frightened, lost in
a world obscured by whiteness. Nothing existed but Inda
and his mount.

Suddenly a dark wall loomed before him. One second it
was not there; the next it sheltered him from wind and snow.
He felt its presence unmistakably. It was high and wide,
and very old.

Inda's alep snorted. Another answered. Sinykin saw
Ramis waiting beside an open gate. He smiled beneath his
frozen scarf. His hands were shaking.

"Welcome to Alu Keep," said Ramis. He took the rein
from Inda's hands and led the alep inside. Others closed the
thick wooden doors behind them. Inside the high stone walls
there was no biting wind. The snow fell straight down, covering the ground and Ramis' shoulders.

Younglings were waiting to take Inda's mount. His gear
was already unpacked and stacked under a sheltering eave.
Inda stood in his left stirrup, lifted his right leg over the
alep's rump and tried to dismount. His left leg cramped. He

grabbed for the saddle, lost his footing and slid to the ground. It was firm and unmoving, a welcome change from the alep's back. He sat in the snow, breathing hard and massaging his leg, while his mount was led away.

Ramis helped him up. Inda leaned against a post and looked around. The keep was large, covering more ground than he could see through the snow. The outer walls snaked away to left and right, disappearing into the storm. The ground sloped away from the gate for a hundred meters, then climbed upward again. Huge dark shapes, some tall and narrow, others long and low, lined the road. Buildings, he thought, seeing oval, circular, and triangular patches of light that must be windows. Night was approaching. He checked his chronometer. They had spent more than eight hours in the saddle with only one break.

A ball of light floated up the road toward them. As it neared, Inda saw that it hung above the head of an Ardellan Master. Sinykin hobbled forward, one hand lifted to greet his host.

The Ardellan was wrapped in a voluminous cloak. Inda could not keep from staring at the shimmering ball of light that danced in the air over the alien's head. It was a trick, it must be a trick.

"Come," said the newcomer. He turned back down the road. Ramis followed him, carrying his pack, and three younglings toted Inda's gear. Sinykin trailed after them, watching the ball of light. This must be the shimmer-light Sarah Anders had described in her journal. It was real!

The air was colder; the storm was nearly over. Only a few flakes still drifted to the ground. The keep was silent, except for the crunching sound their feet made on the snow-covered gravel. Apparently Alu Keep was on the edge of the storm. Less than ten centimeters of snow covered the road. Inda thought of Elissa plowing the landing field, and smiled. Had the cargo ship landed, or had the storm come too soon?

Their guide led them down the slope and up another, then to the right past a walled complex and left down a narrow lane. The sky was dark, but light from the windows was reflected by the snow. They walked through a kind of inverted twilight, led by their guide's glowing globe.

The arched door of a sprawling stone building opened to them. Heat and light and noise flooded out, engulfing Inda.

He entered the building, stood shivering in the narrow anteroom. His wet cloak clung to his shoulders, and his thighs
and buttocks were damp and aching. While he watched, the
ball of light faded out of existence. Their host threw back
his hood and raised his hand in a gesture of friendship.

"Welcome to House Actaan," he said in near-perfect
Standard. "I am Ertis, Historian and storyteller of Clan
Alu. Please remove your cloaks. I will show you to rooms
where you can change to dry clothing."

"Thank you, Master, but I will not be staying," said
Ramis. "I am expected at the clanhall. I will take my supper there, and spend the night."

"We have room for you here," Ertis protested, but Ramis
had already opened the outer door.

Inda backed away at the sudden blast of cold air. "Your
help and guidance was much appreciated, Ramis. May the
great sun guide you on your return journey."

"And you also," said Ramis. The door swung closed
behind him.

Ertis shrugged out of his cloak, and hung it on a peg
beside the door. "Give me your outer garment, please," he
said. He took Inda's parka and hung it on a second peg.
Then he led Inda along a curving, windowless corridor.

Carved wooden sconces were pegged to the walls every
few meters, but they did not hold candles or torches. A ball
of light, smaller than the one that had hung above Ertis'
head, rested on each sconce. The ceiling of the corridor was
arched, and curved down to meet the walls; the whole was
made of stone, with not a crack or a seam. Inda felt as if
he was walking through a tunnel, or a cave.

The corridor widened to become a room with wooden
doors along one wall. Crystal panels in the doors showed a
lighted courtyard garden, with snow falling softly among
the trees. It appeared that nearly the whole wall could be
opened to the garden in good weather.

The next room held two looms, and baskets and skeins
of yarn and thread. There were no seams in the walls here
either. It was as if the building had been carved from solid
stone, or the rock had grown up around the rooms.

The corridor curved again, sharply, leading to a huge central room. Doors were spaced at intervals around the curving walls, and a long, low hearth dominated almost a fourth
of the wall space. Tapestries hung between the doors,

wooden benches and large stuffed cushions were scattered about the floor, and a big oval table filled one curving corner. There were no windows, but a skylight opened the room to the outdoors.

Ertis led Inda to one of the doors, which opened into a private chamber. The room contained a low, wide platform covered with sleek silver and black furs; a cupboard; and had a single window opposite the door. A bright tapestry hung on the wall. Like the other tapestries in the house it was of abstract design, this time swirls of blue and green on a gold background. His packs were already in the room, piled beside the sleeping platform.

"This will be your room, as long as you stay with us," said Ertis. "Unpack your belongings, and rest. I will come for you when food is ready." Ertis left, the door swinging shut behind him.

Sinykin was still shivering. The air was warm, but his clothing was wet and he was chilled from the ride. He stripped, found a rough towel in his gear, and enjoyed a brisk rubdown. Then he wrapped himself in one of the luxurious bed furs and began to unpack. His clothing and personal gear filled one shelf in the cupboard. He had brought Anders' journal; he slipped it between the shirts. The medical equipment he left alone, settling the packs on a lower shelf. He hung his wet clothing from pegs to dry and dressed in trousers, a shirt, and soft black slippers. Then he sat on the platform with his new journal and stylus. He was accustomed to using a portable disk recorder, but the Ardellans no longer permitted powered equipment outside the spaceport grounds and mining compound. He could not even carry a transceiver to keep in touch with the spaceport.

Inda began to write.

"2262:6/27, Alu Keep"

"The ride from the spaceport to Alu Keep was long and cold, but uneventful. The lands and fields were barren and snow-covered. I saw few animals and birds because of the season.

"The keep itself is impressive. Its walls are massive, obviously built for protection. Inside the architecture is curving and delicate, with few angular lines.

"I was not met by Jeryl, but by a Master named Ertis. He carried above his head a ball of light that must be the 'shimmer-light' that Sarah Anders described in her journal.

I have no idea how he generated it. I saw more of it in Ertis'
House.

"Ertis is older than any Master I have met. His hair is
white and thin, and floats about his head like wisps of silk.
He is small, only a few centimeters taller than I am, and
while I am slender, he seems emaciated. The map of lines
on his face obscures whatever beauty or symmetry he might
have possessed but hints at fascinating experiences and
wondrous stories to tell. I look forward—"

There was a single knock at the door. Sinykin set aside
his journal and rose. "Come," he said. For the first time
he noticed that the door had a latch but no handle.

It was Ertis. "I am told that you cannot work our latches.
Is that true?" he asked.

"I am not certain," replied Inda. "How are they operated?"

"One simply thinks them open, or closed."

Just as Anders reported! "Show me, please," asked Inda.
His heart beat faster as he watched Ertis manipulate the
locking mechanism without touching it. What would he give
for such an ability? "Please do it once more."

Ertis touched the latch. "Here, inside the door, is a small
iron bar. Simply tilt it, like this—" he moved his hand
clockwise, "and it will trip the latch. Then push the door
open with your mind."

Inda closed his eyes, and tried to see the latch with the
second sight that sometimes guided him in treating his patients. It was no help. He could not see the bar, much less
move it. "No, I cannot open that latch."

Ertis held out a lumpy metal knob obviously meant to be
fastened to a door. "We will install a latch of the type we
use in younglings' quarters. It will be ready before you sleep
tonight. Now the evening meal is served. Come."

Inda grabbed his cutlery kit and followed Ertis into the
main room. The oval table was laden with platters and bowls
of food. The scents of roasted flesh, hot grain cakes, and
alien spices enveloped Sinykin. He realized suddenly that
he was very hungry. He reached out, touched Ertis' shoulder. "Your pardon," he said, "but I do not eat animal
flesh." He was truly apologetic; the meal looked and
smelled wonderful.

Ertis turned to face him. "That is no problem. Many of
our Healers will eat nothing but grains and fruit. I will show

you which dishes you may choose from." He handed Inda a pottery plate. "Our kitchenmaster baked fresh nutbread today."

Inda came away from the table with a well-laden plate, heaped with bread and nuts and a green tuber that he had never seen before. Ertis assured him that Sarah Anders had eaten it often, with no ill effects. He settled on a bench next to Ertis, and watched the Ardellan use his knobby utensils. They were much different in shape from Terran knives and forks, built to fit a circular hand with six fingers that all behaved like thumbs, but they were no less efficient.

"I had expected Jeryl to meet me," said Inda between bites. "Will he be here this evening?"

"Jeryl was called away to Berrut. I do not know when he will return," replied Ertis. "He asked me to see to your needs."

"I thank you for your willingness to be my host. You speak excellent Standard. Did Jeryl teach you?"

"Yes, Jeryl and FreeMaster Arien." Ertis deftly picked apart a small roast fowl. "I have a special interest in different manners of speech. I have studied the dialects of the mountain clans and the fisherfolk, but Standard is far more difficult."

Five large younglings entered the room, helping a plump cloaked being to a pile of cushions. Ertis leaned close to him and whispered, "That is my mate, Poola. I will not introduce you; she rarely speaks, and never sees guests. She honors you by taking her meal in your presence."

"Thank her for me, and convey my respects to her," said Inda. He tried to keep from staring—even Anders had never seen a Mother. Poola was short and plump. A youngling removed Poola's cloak, exposing short, fat arms and dexterous tentacles. Her face showed none of the lines and creases that gave Ertis character, but her eyes were warm and friendly. An aura of bright blue light surrounded her and extended to each of the younglings. They brought her tidbits from the table, feeding her, and in return she groomed them with her tentacles. It was a very intimate ritual.

According to Anders' journal, Mothers were Masters who had undergone a second metamorphosis. Inda looked at Poola and tried to see her as a slender, gray-haired Master. Her body was as different from a Master's as was a Master's from a youngling's. A shiver ran up Sinykin's spine as he tried to imagine what it would be like to change sex in the middle of his life.

Ertis touched his arm. "Would you like more food?" he asked.

"No. Thank you very much, but I have had enough," he said. Ertis signaled, and a youngling came to take their empty plates. It scooped up Inda's cutlery, too.

"The utensils will be returned to you after they are cleaned," said Ertis. "Are you fatigued? Would you prefer to rest, or will you join us for music this evening?"

"I would very much like to hear your music." He thought again of the disk recorder he dared not bring with him. He would have liked to record some of the music.

A bell tinkled; a youngling led a Master in from the outer corridor. Ertis rose and went to greet him. He was tall and slender and much younger than his host.

"Welcome, Septi. Come and meet our Terran guest."

Septi? Anders had written frequently of a youngling, naSepti. Could this be the same being, in its adult phase? Inda rose and raised his hand in the Ardellan greeting, but Septi grasped it in a weird imitation of a handshake.

"I am very pleased to meet you," said Septi in excellent Standard. "I have not spoken your language in a long time; forgive me if I am awkward."

"Your command of our language is not at all awkward," said Inda. "Where did you learn to speak it so well?"

"I was personal servant to Sarah Anders while she lived at Alu Keep. I heard the language as a youngling; it is natural for me to speak it as a Master."

That pricked Sinykin's curiosity. "Were you with Anders when she died?" he asked.

"No. That is a story I cannot tell you." Septi released Inda's hand. "If you wish to view a memory of Sarah's death, you must ask it of Ertis. He is our Historian. He holds all important memories of Alu."

Sinykin was both excited and afraid. Anders' death was part of the mystery that had brought him to Ardel. He turned to Ertis. "Can you tell me of the death of Sarah Anders?"

"I can, but I will not do it now," Ertis replied. "It is a story of tragedy, and tonight is a time of happiness. We shall share music and joy. I will tell you the story of Master Anders another time."

"Thank you," said Inda. He did not force the issue. Anders had never mentioned the existence of Historians and storytellers, and Sinykin did not know the rules of courtesy for dealing with them. He could only hope that Ertis would tell the story when he was ready.

Septi had brought a circular wooden box with him. He opened it and lifted out a glistening opalescent object. "This is a shell-pipe," he said, holding it up for Inda to look at. "It is made from two kri shells, fastened together, with six holes in each one." The shells spiraled like huge snail shells, but they were narrower. One was slightly larger than the other. Septi turned the shell-pipe to show an opening between the shells. "I blow here, and control the sound by placing my fingers over the holes."

Ertis gestured to one of the younglings. "Bring my harp," he said. They brought an object that Inda recognized, though it was quite different from any Terran harp. Its base was circular, about thirty centimeters across. A carved wooden arm extended up and slightly out from the base, following the curve of the base's edge. Strings stretched from base to arm, the shortest ones almost vertical, the others acquiring more slant as they grew longer. The harp could not be played by human hands; only the broad reach of an Ardellan could encompass all the strings.

They played. Ertis' melodies flowed through the room, bringing images of summer wind, bubbling water, and warm moonlit nights. Septi piped and stars appeared, sparkling brightly after moonset. Inda sat, eyes closed, hands folded in his lap, with his back against the stone wall. His mind floated on the edge of trance. He concentrated on the music, trying to name the scale that was certainly neither diatonic nor pentatonic. But other thoughts appeared, strange thoughts, bits of information he could not know. "This house is all of one piece," the wall said to him, "and its stone is as ancient as this world." He accepted that; the rock would not lie.

He could see the room now, though his eyes were still closed: the walls and floor that were carved in living stone; the tapestries that glowed with the energy of their weavers; nebulous, unformed auras that had to be the younglings'; the well-defined auras of Poola, Septi, and Ertis. Every object in the room had its own aura, compact and simple for the most part, generated by handling and use. The harp and shell-pipe were surrounded by more complex clouds of energy. As Ertis and Septi played, the instruments' auras grew and changed in color and intensity. It was as if the instruments had lives and souls of their own.

The music was over, and the auras were fading. Sinykin tried to impress them in his memory, but the images were slipping away too quickly. The living rock became cold stone again. Had he experienced a new kind of reality, or was his imagination running wild? Inda took a deep breath and opened his eyes. Everything seemed perfectly normal. The younglings were escorting Poola from the room, and Septi was packing away his pipe.

"The music was wonderful," said Sinykin. "Thank you both very much for sharing it with me."

"It is our custom," replied Ertis, rising.

Inda rose also. "I am tired. I will go to my room now."

"Rest well," said Ertis.

The new latch was on the door to Inda's room, as Ertis had promised. Inda opened it and slipped inside. A candle burned beside the sleeping platform. He picked up the journal, then set it aside. He was too tired to complete the entry he had started earlier; he would record his observations in the morning. He stripped and slipped between the furs. As he drowsed, the music came back to him along with one clear thought. Before he returned to the spaceport, he would learn the exact nature of Sarah Anders' death.

Chapter 5

Jeryl dismounted in the stableyard. The hood of his fur-lined riding cloak was caked with ice. He used both hands to brush it clean, then peered through the swirling snow at Arien. Somewhere behind them Hanra-bae's alep snorted.

A youngling appeared out of the darkness and took Jeryl's mount. A second came for Arien's alep, and held the rein while he dismounted. Hanra-bae dismounted also, but seemed loath to let the youngling lead his mount away.

"They still do not allow aleps on the city streets? In Port Freewind we have a system of gutters and sewers to keep the roadways clean."

"Berrut is far larger than Port Freewind," said Jeryl, "and flushing gutters is difficult in the winter."

"I forgot how cold and snowy the winters are here. Along the coast we have cool weather and much rain at this time of year, but we rarely have snow." The fisher gave up his rein to the stablemaster, and picked up his pack. A tongue of shimmer-light flickered above his head. As the wind died, the tiny crystals of *ranaia*, ice-snow, were giving way to large, dry flakes. They drifted down to powder his shoulders. "Is it a long walk to the inn?"

"Not too long, if we stop wasting time and get on with it." Arien started down the road, his pack tossed over one shoulder and his cloak billowing behind him. Hanra-bae followed.

Jeryl trudged after them, following the shimmer-light that was their only illumination. Arien was familiar with the roads; Jeryl trusted him to find the inn. He let the silence and the snow close in around him as he thought about Hatar, alone, without shelter in this storm. The weaver must still be alive, because they had not yet felt his death cry. Perhaps that meant the searchers had been successful, and he was safe at the guildhall or at Alu Keep. If they did not find him, he would surely die of the cold.

They passed a lighted window. Jeryl looked in, saw a group of Masters gathered before a blazing fire. He shivered and shifted his pack to the other shoulder. They passed three more lighted windows before Arien turned off the road. The arched door of the inn opened as they reached it, welcoming them with light and warmth. Younglings took their cloaks and overboots, and the innkeeper greeted them with mugs of hot spiced cider. The common room was almost empty.

"How many rooms?"

Jeryl touched Arien's shoulder. "An adjoining pair for us."

"A room on the courtyard, second floor." Hanra-bae set down his mug without tasting the cider. He waved away the youngling that tried to take his pack. "Send up a pot of fresh boiling water and a clean mug. I am not to be disturbed until morning."

"Take the green room, top of the stairs on the right." The innkeeper turned to Arien and Jeryl. "For you, the pair of rooms across the hall. I hope you will find them satisfactory."

Hanra-bae looked at Jeryl and Arien. "Thank you for allowing me to ride with you. Please excuse me now. I must prepare for my visit to the Healers' guildhall tomorrow." He stalked up the stairs without a backward glance.

Jeryl sipped his cider and watched the fisher leave. "He is even more arrogant than the other Healers I have met," he commented to Arien.

"That may be so. Healers are often quite sure of themselves. I know some who would say Hanra-bae is much like you, prideful and overconfident."

Jeryl almost dropped his cup. He turned to stare at his friend.

Arien touched Jeryl's arm. "You are not like that, but sometimes you appear that way to Masters who do not know you. Perhaps it is the same with Hanra-bae. We should take time to know him before we pass judgment on him. You said he is very skilled; perhaps his pride is well-founded. Besides," Arien said with a humorous glint in his eyes, "he is a fisher. They have different ways."

Jeryl shrugged, then set his empty cup on a table. "Come, let us go to bed. We have much to do in the morning."

Arien took the first room, and Jeryl took the second. Someone had shuttered the windows and filled the braziers with hot coals. Both rooms were warm and smelled of smoke. There was a narrow doorway connecting the rooms. A heavy tapestry, its design muddied by seasons of accumulated smoke and dirt, hung in the doorway. Jeryl capped the brazier in his room and opened the shutter a crack to clear out some of the smoke. Then he pulled the tapestry to one side and tied it to a hook in the wall so that he could talk with Arien.

"Are the fishers really so different from us?" he asked. "I have traveled as far as Bentwater, and did not find those fishers to be too strange. It is true that Mothers sit on the village council, but that has happened occasionally in the keeps."

"Bentwater is a river village. The people there call themselves fishers, but they are still much like us. As you travel closer to the sea, the customs become stranger." Arien had already changed to his nightshift and was arranging the furs on his sleeping platform. "Did you not hear Hanra-bae ask about the urns, and how we cremate our dead?"

"Yes. He spoke as if the custom was strange to him."

"It is. Fishers throw their dead into the sea."

Jeryl coughed. "That's disgusting!"

"They think our custom of keeping our dead in urns is disgusting," said Arien. "Each spring I travel to Port Freewind to negotiate the caravan schedule with the council of Mothers there. Come with me this year. You will learn much about the fishers."

"I would enjoy traveling with you, but I fear my duties will keep me at Alu this spring. Perhaps I could join you next year." Jeryl yawned. The sleeping furs looked inviting. It had been a long and tiring day. He stripped off his clothing and left it in a pile next to his pack. Arien's room was already dark. Jeryl called out softly, "Sleep well." He slipped between the furs and extinguished his shimmer-light.

Jeryl lay on his back in the darkness. He closed his eyes, and let his thoughts slip into the twilight space between wakefulness and sleep that is almost trance. He was aware of Arien's even breathing in the room next door, and of the snow falling softly outside the window. His breathing slowed, and his mind drifted toward sleep.

The air was cold. Hatar shivered, and wished he had brought some extra clothing, or a tent. And food. Some bread; a flask of tea; some grain for the alep. He sighed, and nestled against the warm flank of his sleeping mount. They were huddled in a small hollow surrounded by a stand of conifers. The interlaced branches of the trees broke the wind and sheltered Hatar from the snow, but they could not keep out the cold nor satisfy his hunger.

In the morning, if he lived that long, he would go . . . where? He could not return to Alu, to an empty House and Alain's ashes in a jar on the mourning wall.

The FreeMasters were searching for him. Hatar could feel them moving across the countryside. They were coming closer to his hiding place. Soon they would sense his presence. They would find him, and wrap him in a warm cloak, and offer him a flask of steaming tea. They would take him back to the FreeMasters' guildhall, where every Master mourned a lost mate. He would never find peace there. Better to wander in the mountains until he died!

Hatar climbed to his feet. He awakened his alep with a sharp rap between its ears. It brayed at him, and angrily shook its head. He kicked its shoulder, and it struggled to rise. While it untangled its six legs, Hatar examined their trail. The snowfall had obliterated their tracks. The FreeMasters would have a difficult time following them. Hatar wrapped his cloak close about his body, firmly grasped the alep's rein, and began walking deeper into the forest.

Jeryl's eyes opened. He stared into the darkness, experiencing again the despair that had consumed him after his own mate's death. He wanted to wander the wilderness with Hatar, to punish himself for surviving by depriving his body of warmth and nourishment. His hands were trembling, and his mouth was open and dry. He tried to close his lips and swallow. A spot of warmth touched his right wrist. He flexed his arm, and felt the cuff of iron and copper and gold-green sphene against his skin. The wristband had been worn by every one of Alu's Mentors. Its power warmed his arm, then spread the warmth across his chest and into the rest of his body. It drove out his feelings of despair, and replaced them with a sense of duty to clan and to keep. He tried to swallow again, and succeeded. His breathing slowed, and his hands stopped trembling.

Sleep was a long time coming.

Hanra-bae was waiting beside the hearth when they came down for breakfast. He was bundled in a thick wool cloak and baggy leggings, and had a steaming mug clutched between his hands. Arien stopped to greet him while Jeryl walked on to get their food.

"May the great sun smile on you today, Master Healer. May we join you?"

"If you wish." There was no insolence in his tone, only fatigue. "I do not remember it being so cold here. I slept with three furs last night, and still I could not stay warm."

Jeryl returned from the sideboard with two mugs of tea and a plate of breakfast cakes. He handed a mug to Arien, set the other down, and pulled out a chair. "It is always cold in the winter." Hanra-bae had taken a chill, like a youngling on his first winter ride! What did these warm-water fishers know of cold weather? "You will become accustomed to it."

The fisher glared at him with eyes gone dark and cloudy. "I spent an entire winter in Berrut when I was a student, and I never became accustomed to the cold. I will quickly transact my business here, so that I may return to Port Free-wind and warmer weather."

"Ask the innkeeper to have some hot stones placed in your sleeping furs tonight," suggested Arien. "They will not stay warm for the entire night, but they will help."

"Eat more food, and drink hot tea or cider before you go to sleep," added Jeryl, pushing the tray of cakes to the fisher's side of the table. Hanra-bae was a skillful Healer, but he seemed to know little about practical matters. "And wear a pair of leggings under your nightshift."

"Thank you. I will try all of those things." Hanra-bae took a cake and passed the plate to Arien. "I have an appointment at the Healers' library today. Do you wish to come with me?"

Arien waved his dissent. "I must meet with several GuildMasters. They are expecting me before midday."

"Jeryl?"

The Mentor had never been inside the Healers' compound. Few outsiders were given access to their facilities. He could not pass up an opportunity to visit their library and read some of their most ancient and secret scrolls. Jeryl tried not to sound too eager when he answered. "I will accompany you."

They consumed all of the cakes and each drank two cups of tea before they bundled into fur-lined cloaks and boots. Jeryl opened the inn's door and sunlight streamed into the dim common room. The world outside sparkled. Ice had transformed the trees along the road into crystal sculptures dusted with white powder. In the still air, the crunch and squeak of their footsteps on the snow-covered roadway filled the space between the stone walls. Icicles decorated many eaves, dripping into puddles where sunlight struck them. Second-moon danced in the clear blue sky above the peaks of the eastern mountains.

Arien left Jeryl and Hanra-bae at the beginning of red street. "I will wait for you at the inn after midday," he called as he walked toward the Metalsmiths' guildhall.

Jeryl sighed. Nothing good ever came of his visits to Berrut. Only crises brought him to this misbegotten city. His mate had died while he was in Berrut. Sarah Anders had been killed here, in a park near the inn. Yet here he was again, hoping that this time he might find the key to saving his people.

The Healers' compound was vast and imposing, filling both sides of yellow street with three-storied stone buildings connected near their roofs by covered walkways. Yellow stone walls hid the buildings' lower windows, and wooden gates kept the curious outside. Everyone was welcome in the infirmary. Only Healers and apprentices were permitted beyond that area. The guild guarded its secrets well, for it claimed to have knowledge that could be dangerous to the uninitiated. It was more likely though, that it feared the usurpation of its power.

The Healers did have power, though it was less visible than that of the Messengers, or the Metalsmiths. With the Terrans' unwitting help, Clan Alu and the FreeMasters were undermining the power of those guilds. In a dozen seasons, if Clan Alu could survive that long, Jeryl might have the deciding vote in the Assembly.

When Jeryl and Hanra-bae arrived at the main gate next to the infirmary, the fisher lifted the wooden knocker and let it fall. Immediately a small panel slid open and a pair of eyes peered out at them.

Hanra-bae held up his Healer's token.

The panel closed.

Ice crackled, a bolt thumped, and the creaking gate swung inward. The gatekeeper, a young apprentice muffled in a threadbare cloak, confronted them. He looked at Jeryl with suspicion.

"Where is your token?"

Hanra-bae answered. "He has none. He is my guest."

The gatekeeper considered this for a moment. Then he began to close the gate.

"Come." The fisher grabbed Jeryl's arm, and stepped sideways through the portal. Jeryl shouldered the gate open another hand's breadth and followed. He tugged the tail of his cloak free as the gate slammed.

Sparks of anger and fear flashed in the gatekeeper's aura. "That one," he pointed at Jeryl, "is not permitted here."

"Do you deny a Master Healer the aid of his assistant? Fetch the GuildMaster, then, and we shall discuss this with him."

The gatekeeper scurried off, leaving them to stand in the cold. Jeryl stared at the grounds and the buildings. The walls hid more than Healing secrets. The buildings were old and sagging, mortar crumbling, doors weathered, windowpanes cracked. The court was little better, with trees in need of pruning, and straw poking through the snow. Ice had not been cleared from the paths, though someone had tossed a few handfuls of sand about."

"Was this place so run-down when you were a student here?" he asked Hanra-bae.

"I believe not. I was not too observant that year because I was so involved in my studies, but I think I would have noticed this."

"Hanra-bae! Healer, it is good to see you." A jovial Master trundled down the path toward them, slipping and sliding. "We have been expecting you since your message arrived a six-day ago. What brings you to visit us?"

"Research, Bantu, research. Greetings from Port Freewind and the Mothers' council. Where is the Guild-Master?"

"Instructing. The gatekeeper thought I might know you,

so he asked me to come out. Who is your companion? Your message did not say that you were bringing an assistant.''

"This is Jeryl, of Alu Keep. He is my translator. You know I never did master those ancient runes.'' Hanra-bae turned to Jeryl. "This is Bantu, one of my instructors, and assistant to the GuildMaster.''

Jeryl raised his hand in greeting. "May the great sun smile on you and your guild,'' he said, hoping his distrust did not show too plainly.

Bantu returned the greeting absently. "You are certainly welcome here, Hanra-bae. Unfortunately, in recent seasons we have had to restrict access to our facilities. I am afraid we cannot allow your associate to remain on the grounds.''

"How am I to complete my work without a translator?''

"I can assign a student to help you,'' offered Bantu.

Hanra-bae waved. "No, no, it would certainly not do to keep one of your fine young apprentices from his studies. If I cannot complete my work I will have to disappoint the Mothers' council in Port Freewind. I had believed the Healers Guild would be more cooperative, but I see we cannot sway you.''

Bantu hesitated. Jeryl watched, hoping against hope the bluff would work. Hanra-bae's tongue was as smooth as a Terran's, and that was no compliment as far as the Mentor of Clan Alu was concerned. Jeryl had learned about lies from a Terran.

"Our restrictions are not absolute. I could let you use the library, but your assistant must remain there until you leave the compound. Would that be sufficient?''

"Yes, I am sure it would be,'' replied Hanra-bae. "I am looking for some old texts on reproduction. I was told your library had copies of them.''

"That might be,'' said Bantu, leading them across the court. "We have preserved many ancient manuscripts here.''

Hanra-bae leaned close to Jeryl. "Keep your Mentor's wristband out of sight, and tell no one of your rank. Be silent when others are near, unless I address you.''

Jeryl shrugged his assent, pushing the copper band far up his arm and clamping it tight. He followed Hanra-bae and Bantu into a building that was better kept than the first one he had seen. Its windows were intact and its door painted. Inside, neat racks of scrolls filled all the walls and many of the tabletops. The order in this room contrasted favorably with the disorder of the rest of the compound. The Healers seemed to care more for their manuscripts than for their buildings.

They settled at an empty table. Bantu wished them well, then stopped to talk with an apprentice who was returning scrolls to the racks. The apprentice said little but shrugged frequently. Jeryl guessed Bantu was charging him to watch the visitors.

"They really don't want to let you use the library, do they?" he asked Hanra-bae.

"No, though I am not certain why. I requested some texts last season, and the GuildMaster refused to send copies." He pulled a small roll of writing-cloth from his cloak. "You!" he called, and when the apprentice with the scrolls turned, Hanra-bae held the roll out to him. "Please locate these scrolls and bring them to us. Are you the librarian?"

"I am his assistant. He is ill today. I can help you." The apprentice dropped his scrolls on a table as Bantu disappeared through a doorway in the far wall.

"Come, then. Let me show you what I need." Hanra-bae unrolled the writing-cloth and spread it on the table.

From bottom to top the sheet was covered with poorly sketched runes. The list included "Allal's Notes on Reproduction" and "The Diaries of Healer Rondi," along with many other works that were unfamiliar to Jeryl. If they had to read each of these scrolls, they would be here for days.

"How much of the list is important?" he whispered after the apprentices took it away.

"Only five of the titles interest me. The rest is camouflage. I do not want the guild to know which manuscripts are important to me."

The apprentice returned with three of the scrolls. Hanra-bae checked the titles, handed two to Jeryl. "Look for references to reproductive dysfunction," he said loudly.

Jeryl pretended to read. Sometimes a passage would catch his attention—"Black tongue can be eliminated by forcing the infected youngling to drink an infusion of two parts powdered wool-deer's foot, one part violet leaf-mold, and one-third part toxic ellberry. This mixture will cure the youngling, or kill it. Either way, the spread of the disease will be stopped." More scrolls appeared at the table, and

Hanra-bae sorted through them, dropping most in a pile before Jeryl.

"He has not brought the titles I need," whispered the Healer.

Jeryl looked at him. Perhaps the Healers had known all along which scrolls Hanra-bae really wanted.

"Master Healer?" called the apprentice from across the room. "There are several scrolls that I cannot bring to you. They are stored in a special room, and no one is allowed to enter it without the GuildMaster's permission."

"Then fetch him," said Hanra-bae.

Bantu burst in through the back door, with the apprentice in tow. "Hanra-bae, the GuildMaster sends his greetings. Of course you may view the old scrolls. He apologizes for the inconvenience this stupid apprentice caused you by making you wait."

"It is all right, Bantu. We used the time to good advantage with these other texts." Hanra-bae rose and stretched.

Jeryl knew something was wrong. A green haze drifted through Bantu's aura, contaminating its clean white openness. It had something to do with Jeryl, though the Mentor was not certain what that might be.

"Come," said Hanra-bae as Bantu opened a door in the far wall. "Let us see what information these other scrolls have for us."

Bantu stepped between Hanra-bae and the door. "I am sorry, but your assistant cannot be allowed to enter this room."

Hanra-bae's aura flared bright red. "What? I cannot work without his help. He must accompany me!"

The green haze around Bantu thickened, becoming opaque near the edges. Jeryl's heart lurched, and tension banded his forehead. Had Hanra-bae played the bluff too far?

"We cannot allow the Mentor to remain inside the compound. You must continue your researches alone, or leave with him."

Jeryl flexed his arm so that the band of office slid to his wrist. So much for deception. It was a Terran practice, and he needed no further proof that it should be left to Terrans. "I am indeed Mentor of Alu. Why would you bar me from your compound?"

"We need not explain ourselves," said Bantu. Ruby flames curled through his murky aura, driving out the ugly green haze.

"You and I are members of the same guild, Bantu," exclaimed Hanra-bae. His anger was a ruby cloud, his words cold and hard and threatening. "You owe me an explanation, even if you will not give one to the Mentor."

Jeryl knew threats would gain them nothing. Perhaps if he left now, peaceably, Bantu would still allow Hanra-bae to see the texts. Their visit would not be a total loss.

"I will go."

"No!" Hanra-bae was adamant. "There is no reason for you to leave."

Jeryl stared at him. How could this Healer be so foolish? Or had he another deception in mind? No matter; Jeryl was leaving. He closed the clasp at the neck of his cloak. "There are other matters to which I must attend. I will see you at the inn this evening." He turned and strode to the door.

Bantu accompanied Jeryl to the gate and barred it behind him. It was a symbolic gesture, for no lock would stop a Mentor. He toyed with the idea of lifting the bar, but dismissed it as a waste of energy. Instead he turned his thoughts to Arien. His meeting might be over; perhaps he was already at the inn. The wind tugged at Jeryl's cloak as he stepped away from the wall. He pulled his hood up, tucked his hands up his sleeves, and hurried through the snowy streets to look for his friend.

Blue paint was peeling from the inn's door. The latch had been worn smooth by hundreds of turnings. Jeryl visualized the iron bar inside it, twisted the bar with a thought, and the door creaked open. Warm air and cooking smells escaped. He entered, leaned against the door to shut it, then shrugged off his cloak.

"Jeryl!"

It was Arien's voice. Jeryl turned, saw his friend sitting with a Master who wore the copper tunic of the Historians Guild. Their table was in a dark corner far from the hearth, well away from the other patrons. Jeryl took a mug of hot spiced cider from the sideboard, and joined them.

Arien's aura was dull and faintly green. Jeryl took that as a warning and let his friend lead the conversation.

"Allya, this is Jeryl, Mentor of Clan Alu," said Arien.

Allya waved a tense greeting. "Jeryl, this is storyteller and songsmith Allya, a traveling Historian. He has visited my guildhall often, and cheered us on many cold winter nights."

Jeryl returned the wave, moving his hand in a casual arc. Allya's acknowledgment was short, though his aura glowed at Arien's praise. Jeryl could see that the Historian was troubled.

"Allya has just returned from a visit to the mining clans. When he heard that I was in Berrut, he sought me out. He has troubling news to share with us."

Jeryl shrugged. The world was full of troubling news these days. What was one more problem?

"It is my habit to stop at the Iron Keep at least once each season," said Allya. "The folk are glad to see me, for I bring the news of the plains and entertain them. But on this visit they were less than cordial. In fact, they were secretive. They kept me away from certain areas of the keep, especially the watchtowers.

"Being a gatherer of news, I was, of course, curious. One night I managed to elude my hosts, and climb one of the towers. What I saw in the upper room frightened me, and I returned to my quarters immediately."

Jeryl sipped his cider. There was no hurrying a storyteller. The tale would out, but in its own time.

"A group of Masters had gathered in the top room of the tower. They were standing in a circle, chanting about storms. I think they were trying to control the weather!"

Allya seemed to expect amazed gasps or sudden flashes of anger at his revelation. Jeryl disappointed him.

"You confirm what I have long suspected," he said, setting aside his mug. "Do they know you witnessed their rite?"

"I thought not, but when I left the keep the next morning, a storm chased me down the mountain. I nearly crippled my mount trying to keep ahead of it."

"That would be the storm that swept through Berrut last night," commented Arien.

"That is correct. I spent the night at your guildhall, and rode to Berrut after the storm passed. The FreeMasters were hospitable, as always."

Jeryl felt a surge of hope. "Have they found Hatar? Was he safe at the guildhall?"

"No. There was no word from him. The FreeMasters were still searching, and they had heard no cry of distress. They thought he might have found shelter at a keep."

Jeryl stared into his cup, saying nothing.

"Thank you for the information, Allya." Arien rose, offering his palms to the Historian in farewell. "Please speak to no one else about what you saw in the mountains. We will deal with the problem."

Allya accepted the dismissal. He rose, touched Arien's palms, and left the table. Two steps away he turned back and addressed Jeryl. "Hatar is not dead," he said.

"Thank you. May the sun light your travels."

"And yours, Mentor." Allya disappeared through the blue door.

Arien touched Jeryl's hand. "Where is Hanra-bae? Did he find the information he seeks?"

"I do not know. The Healers recognized me and forced me to leave before our search was finished. Hanra-bae is still at the library, looking through some ancient texts. He will join us later." Jeryl pulled his hand away, and wrapped his fingers around his mug. "How was your meeting with the GuildMasters?"

"Not much better. They have invited me to visit a crèche tomorrow, but they will not allow you to come with me. I cannot guess how they knew we came to Berrut together."

"It seems that I am not to be allowed any freedom in Berrut," complained Jeryl. Worry wrinkled his brow. Hatar was lost in the mountains, or hiding who-knew-where; the Healers were hostile and unwilling to share their knowledge; the mountain clans practiced long-forbidden weather magic; the guilds maneuvered to cut into Alu's trade; and at Alu Keep, a Terran moved freely for the first time in five winters. A vision of a sleek, many-clawed tol stalking a rutting buck wool-deer appeared to Jeryl. Who was the wool-deer, and who the tol? Would the tol's long fangs prevail, or would it be gutted by the buck's sharp antlers? And did he dare to step between them? "The guilds are hiding something from Alu."

"From more than Alu!" Hanra-bae appeared at their table, shrugged off his cloak and sat. "The texts they would not allow you to see hold the secrets we seek. I could decipher enough of the ancient runes to know that the information I need is there. They would not let me bring in an

interpreter, so I tried to copy some of the vital passages.''
He set a rolled scroll before Jeryl.

Jeryl unrolled the writing-cloth and stared at it. Blots of
ink and misdrawn strokes made the runes unreadable. He
crumpled the cloth, tossed it back to Hanra-bae. ''I can see
it is useless to have you copy the texts. We must find another
way to obtain the information in those scrolls.''

''Impossible!''

''Few things are impossible,'' said Arien. ''Let the problem rest for a day, and come with me to see a crèche. The
GuildMasters will not let Jeryl come, but you may accompany me tomorrow.''

''Do not discount me so quickly, friend.'' Jeryl slapped
his palms against the table. ''All three of us will see the
inside of that crèche, and before we sup tomorrow night, I
will tell you how we shall outwit the Healers Guild!''

Chapter 6

Elissa Durant slipped into her seat near the end of the long conference table. She was early; the other department heads had not yet arrived. Anna Griswold would arrive last, as she always did.

Three new photos had been added to the display on the wall opposite the windows. They clearly were Griswold's work. One showed the empty landing field at night, lit by the soft yellow glow of halogen lamps. The second was a study of bars and pipes that produced a series of geometric shapes. Elissa stared at it for a moment before she realized that it had been taken from below one of the control towers, looking up through the struts. The last one was a shot of the "conga line," the three big trucks, snowplows lowered, forming a diagonal line as they swept down the landing field. The snow curling up and away from the plows was one of the few natural things Anna had ever photographed. Her subjects were made things, not people or nature. Elissa had not noticed that until Sinykin pointed it out to her.

Marta Grund, director of Supply and Procurement, came in with her husband Jeff. Elissa smiled when she saw them.

"Have you heard from Sinykin yet?" asked Marta as she settled into the chair opposite Elissa's. Jeff took Inda's usual seat.

"No, but I didn't expect to hear anything this soon."

Jeff nodded. "You should get a message tomorrow, or the next day. It takes half a day for the messenger to ride here from Alu Keep."

"You and Jaime should join us for dinner tonight," said Marta. "It's Jeff's night to cook. He promised to make stuffed trout."

"Freeze-dried, or fresh?" asked Elissa. She grinned at

Jeff. His unsuccessful attempts to turn a shipment of freeze-dried fish into something edible had become well-known on the base.

Marta laughed. "Fresh, of course. The trout tank in the fish farm has just produced its first crop."

"Thank you, we'd love to come." She missed Sinykin most at mealtimes. Dinner with the Grunds would be a nice diversion, and Jaime would enjoy spending the evening with their son Tommy.

"When can we stop by and pick up some of that trout?" asked Alec Harwood, the Security Chief, as he sat down beside Elissa.

"It's being put on the availability list today. It's first come, first served, but there's plenty to go around."

"I'm glad to hear that," said Anna Griswold as she came in. She set down her mug and looked around the table. "Are we all here? Let's get started. Jeff, can you tell us why that supply ship refused to land yesterday? The storm wasn't severe. It should not have caused any problems."

"There was an electromagnetic disturbance in the atmosphere during the storm. It was the same sort of thing that other ships have reported this winter—disruption of navigational equipment and interference with their guidance systems. The captain elected not to land rather than risk being stuck here with damaged equipment, or being unable to lift off because of the interference." Grund tossed a sheaf of papers into the center of the table. "Our new monitoring equipment was operational during the storm, and we recorded a lot of data about the disturbance. We're running computer analyses now."

Griswold nodded. "Do you have any speculations?"

"Preliminary results suggest that the new shielding system that's being used on military craft would be adequate here."

"I'll need more than your best guess to support a request for state-of-the-art equipment," said Griswold. "You all know that we're a low-priority base. Until we start shipping titanium from the mining operation, we are a liability rather than an asset. Get me some hard facts to send to the trade commission.

"Now, when is the next supply ship scheduled to arrive?"

"*Manatee* is due in six days," said Marta. "We've already checked; the ship has no special shielding."

"What's our supply situation? Can we hold out if they pass us by?"

Marta shrugged. "We're starting to run out of a few items. Nothing critical yet, but if *Manatee* doesn't land we may have to break into some of the emergency supplies. We're not in danger of starving. Life will just be a little less comfortable."

A bitter smile touched Griswold's face and quickly fled. "Jeff, I think you should get together with Maintenance and Engineering and see if you can jury-rig some kind of shielding before that ship gets here. Give me a report on your progress tomorrow morning.

"Now, let's move on to departmental reports. Security?"

Sinykin Inda slipped the vial of Master Kalen's red-gold blood into his sample case. He swabbed the Master's arm with an alcohol wipe and bandaged the tiny wound.

"This sample of your blood will help us test the plague-stopper," he said. Trying to render technical explanations in his inadequate Ardellan embarrassed him—he sounded at once stupid and condescending. These people were not children or backward aborigines who needed simple explanations. He needed a more complete vocabulary so that he could tell them what he was doing and why he was doing it.

He had spoken to Ertis and Septi about the problem. The Historian's command of Standard was excellent, but his reply made little sense to Inda. "Be not concerned," he said. "We see all that is spoken, and our eyes understand intentions." It sounded like the mystical double-talk of some pseudo-occultist. Inda was pleased when Septi offered to accompany him. He hoped that the young translator would keep him from inadvertently offending any of the Masters who gave him blood and tissue samples and their histories.

Kalen had contracted the plague at the end of the harvest season. He was still very weak from his illness and could not leave his House. He sat beside the central hearth wrapped in furs, his feet propped on a stool, a bowl of herbs smoldering on burning charcoal at his side. "When I became ill, I was very much afraid my mate Nenii would also contract the disease. I would not let her see me. In Alu, every Mother who became sick eventually died. We lost fourteen Mothers.''

Inda closed his eyes and looked at Kalen with his psychic sight. The Master's aura was thin and muddy. Instead of forming a glowing halo around his body, it obscured him with its dirty haze. Inda sensed Kalen's weakness and general ill health, but nothing more specific than that.

The reasons for the differing reactions of Masters and Mothers to the illness seemed important. It might provide a key to preventing deaths in the future. ''Why did the Mothers die? Did the disease affect them differently, or are the Masters stronger than the Mothers?'' asked Sinykin. He managed to pose the question in adequate Ardellan, but could not understand all of Kalen's reply. Septi seemed to sense Inda's confusion, and translated for him.

''I do not know why the Mothers died. I only know what the disease did to me. I could not eat or drink, my body became hot, and my heart beat to a strange rhythm. The Healer burned leaves and made me breathe the smoke, and he rubbed my body with pungent oils. That brought my heartbeat back to normal, but still I could not drink or eat. It was a hand of days before my stomach would take the herbal teas he prescribed.''

''Did any younglings of your House become sick?''

Kalen called to a youngling working at the hearth. ''Send in your littermates,'' he said. The youngling disappeared, and a moment later two others came into the room.

Inda had seen many healthy younglings. They had round bodies, stubby legs, constantly-moving tentacles that girded their torsos, and waving eyestalks that sprouted from the tops of their bodies. They possessed mouths of a sort, and other, unidentifiable sense organs. Their coloring was pale, almost white, and they had not a single hair on their bodies.

These two younglings were horrendously deformed. One had lost more than half of its tentacles. They were shriveled to useless, wormy nubs. The other was blind. Its eyestalks were bent and withered, the organs at their tips milky white instead of healthy blue or gray. Inda had seen a dozen other deformities today, at least one at each House he visited.

Kalen dismissed the younglings with a wave. ''You see what the plague does to younglings,'' he said. ''Many younglings in Alu were deformed like this. None of them can metamorphose into Masters; we do not know how their deformities would manifest. They are condemned to be younglings until they die, whatever their intelligence or skills.''

''My House was not untouched,'' said Ertis. He crossed the room and stood beside Kalen, touching his shoulder briefly. ''Three of our most promising younglings suffered gross deformities, and one died. Poola and I nursed them ourselves. I do not understand how we escaped the illness.''

''Perhaps your bodies were strong enough to fight it off,'' said Inda. Inwardly he cringed—how could he explain natural immunity when he did not know the Ardellan words? He had drawn blood samples from Ertis and Poola first thing that morning. Only future analysis would give him the answers he sought. ''I have all the samples and information I need from you, Kalen. Thank you very much. I appreciate your help.''

Ertis touched Kalen again to keep him from rising. ''We will take our leave now. Rest, my friend. Septi and I will come again soon.''

They stepped through the oval door into the cold, clear afternoon. ''It is time we go to the Healers' complex,'' said Ertis, pointing to the sprawling buildings near the keep's center. He turned to Septi. ''We do not mean to keep you from your House. You need not come with us.''

Septi shook his head. ''Today there is nothing more important than spending time with you and Healer Inda.'' They set off down the road together.

The Healers' complex was surrounded by a low wall that joined the front of the main building. The only entrance Inda could see was an arched opening in the building's facade. This led into a sheltered antechamber with a broad door at the far end. They entered, and Ertis knocked once at the door. ''Since we are not here seeking aid, it is polite to wait for a response,'' Septi told Inda.

A youngling wearing a gold-colored sash opened the door to them. It stepped aside and ushered them into the bright lobby.

''We are here to see the Healer. Please fetch him for us,'' said Ertis.

''There is no need. I am here.'' The Healer stepped out of a dark corridor. He was the oldest Master Inda had ever seen. His hair was white and wispy, wrinkles traversed his forehead and spread from his eyes and mouth onto his cheeks, and his tunic hung like a sack on his stooped and emaciated body. He looked very fragile, but he moved with dynamic speed and precision as he crossed the room. "Go on about your business," he said to the youngling. "I will handle this matter."

Sinykin stepped forward, making a gesture of greeting. "My name is Inda, and I am also a Healer. I have come to ask your help in gathering information about the plague's victims."

"My help? What possible help could a simple Healer be to a great Terran physician?"

He said the last two words in Standard. Sinykin heard the Healer's anger, closed his eyes and focused on Viela's aura. He saw a ruby red haze close about the Healer's body. It darkened as Inda watched. He opened his eyes, looked at the Healer's impassive face. How would Viela react if he learned that Sinykin could read auras, even if only at a rudimentary level?

"I only wish to take samples of blood from the younglings and Masters still recovering from the plague. I will not interfere with your work, or your patients' recovery."

"You will not interfere, because you will have no opportunity to interfere," said Viela.

"Jeryl ordered you to cooperate with Healer Inda." Ertis was also angry. His red aura pulsed with the beating of his heart.

"Jeryl has no authority within the Healers' complex," said Viela, herding them toward the open door.

"I have no wish to be your enemy," said Inda. "What I am doing will help your people. It may prevent the next plague."

"You are already my enemy, Terran. You and your people have caused far more trouble for mine than the plague ever has." He forced them into the anteroom and slammed the door in Inda's face.

"Viela is not always that rude," said Septi as they trudged through the snow toward House Actaan.

Ertis touched Sinykin's arm. "The Healer is angry that Jeryl ordered him to cooperate with you. He does not like change, and your people have brought much change to Alu Keep."

"We have tried not to disrupt your way of life. Some

change is inevitable when different cultures meet and inter-act," said Sinykin. "Living on your planet has changed us also." He looked at the huge golden sun hanging over the western wall of the keep. The small moon had already set, and the larger moon would rise just after sunset. Inda's body and mind accepted the rhythms as if he had been born to them. He was adapting to the solar spectrum, the lessened gravity, the thinner air, the alien diet.

Once, in an effort to understand the link between the eyes and the brain, Terran scientists had rigged a man with a mirrored visor that inverted all the images he saw. In a few weeks, his brain compensated for the inversion and every-thing seemed normal to him. When the visor was removed, the man suffered severe psychological and physical prob-lems readjusting to normal vision. The human brain would accept a change in its perception of the world, but once it assimilated that change, returning to its original perception could be difficult and painful. The human body was even more fragile. Returning to Terran gravity after time spent in a low-gravity environment presented many problems. This made the choice between "temporary posting" and "permanent resident" an important one. The postees ate Terran food, used special lighting in their homes, worked out in gravity simulators, and did all they could to maintain the illusion of Terran normalcy.

Inda and Elissa had chosen permanent resident status. They had no intention of returning to Earth. Jaime was young enough to adapt easily if he chose to return to Terra, but for Sinykin and Elissa the process of becoming Ardel-lans had already begun.

"Does Viela speak for all the Healers?" asked Sinykin.

"He has rank," said Ertis, "but he cannot answer for the entire guild. I do not know how the others will feel about your offer of help. I am certain there will be much discussion."

Inda shrugged. They had reached the door of House Ac-taan. It opened for them, though no one waited in the hall.

Ertis took the sample bag from Inda and set it on a shelf. "Are you ready for some tea?"

"I was told that there are some traders at the weaving-house. We could invite them to the clanhall for tea," sug-gested Septi. He turned to Inda. "It would be a good opportunity for you to meet someone from another clan."

"And for me to hear the latest news," added Ertis.

"I would like that," said Sinykin. He followed Septi back into the cold.

The weaving-house was on a street of shops that ran from the clanhall to the main gate. The building was a little taller than those next to it, but not enough to house a second story. It was built of dry-mortared fieldstone, with one large, irregularly-shaped window in the front wall. They entered through the broad arched door.

The main room was large, and crowded with looms. Huge spools of thread were skewered on dowels stuck in the back wall, and hanks of yarn hung from pegs driven into the rafters. Rolls of finished cloth were stacked on a long table.

A half-dozen Masters were in the shop, most of them looking at rolls of cloth. A wooden scale sat at the end of the table, where two Masters studied it. On one end of its balance arm was a flat pan, on the other a vertical dowel. One of the Masters held a box of stone weights, the other a string of rusty iron rings.

"Your coin bears cleaning," said the Master who held the weights.

"I said as much to your stablemaster when he gave it to me," said the one holding the iron. "We delivered clean, new harnesses and saddles, and received rusted coin in exchange."

"The traders of Clan Sau have long been known for their honesty. We will adjust the knife-weight to make up for the rust," said the oldest Master. He took a roll of cloth and spread the fabric across the table. "This pattern is the work of our finest weaver. Six knives for the bolt."

"I offer four," said one of the traders.

Inda whispered to Septi, "They trade knives for the cloth?"

"No, a knife is a standard weight of iron. It is enough to forge a good blade." Septi pointed to the balance. "When a price is decided, they will weigh the iron rings."

The haggling on that bolt had already stopped, at five-and-a-quarter knives. The weaver put weights on the balance pan, and the trader slipped iron rings over the dowel until it balanced. Then he added one extra.

The bargaining went on for quite a while. Inda watched in fascination as bolt after bolt of bright cloth was unrolled and examined, a price set, iron exchanged for fabric. One of the traders wrapped the cloth carefully and stacked the rolls in a hand cart. A few bolts were rejected; they disappeared quickly into a storeroom.

The cart was full before the trading was finished. The last two rolls were laid across the top and tied down with a bit of yarn.

"You may leave the cart here until morning," offered the weaving-master.

"No, no," replied the trader. "We leave at dawn, and do not wish to disturb you so early. We will take it with us." He took his cloak from a peg near the door and put it on. The loop of iron rings disappeared into an inner pocket. One of his companions began wheeling the cart toward the door.

Ertis stepped forward. "I am Ertis, Historian of Clan Alu, and my companions are Master Septi and Sinykin Inda, a Terran Healer. Would you care to join us for tea at the clanhall?" he asked. "We would like to hear the news you carry."

Inda met the traders' eyes openly, wondering if they were as curious about him as he was about them. They had obviously never met a Terran.

The traders exchanged a quick glance. Then the one who carried the iron stepped forward. "My companions must take care of our goods, but I would like to share tea with you." He made a sweeping gesture of greeting. "My name is Jemma."

They walked up the road to the clanhall. Once they were inside the great double doors, Jemma excused himself for a moment and went up the broad staircase to the second floor. Inda removed his parka and hung it near the door, next to Ertis' cloak. Then he followed Ertis through the main hall to the kitchen.

The room smelled of warm bread, stewed fruit, and tea. The hearth filled most of one wall. Ertis and Inda sat at the long table. Septi spoke to a youngling, and then brought over mugs and a pot of tea. The youngling followed with a plate of bread and a bowl of preserves. Ertis was pouring the tea when Jemma joined them.

The trader looked like most of the Masters Inda had seen: tall and slender, with fine pale hair and gray eyes. He had discarded his outer cloak and tunic, and now wore a short blue quilted cape, one side thrown back over his shoulder to reveal a gray lining covered with buttoned patch pockets of all shapes and sizes. An enterprising peddler could carry most of his stock in that cape. Jemma's trousers were brown leather, his boots knee-high and soft. A quilted gold tunic extended almost to his knees, and was slit to the waist in front, revealing a plush blue lining. Around his neck, he wore six fine chains of copper, each one longer than the last.

Ertis handed Inda a steaming mug. The tea was fragrant, conjuring in Inda's mind memories of apricots and cinnamon. Sinykin tasted it, then imitated Septi by adding a dollop of sticky green sweetener and stirring the tea with his knife. Ertis and Jemma discussed mundane matters—where the traders were bound, with what goods, and what news they had of their previous stops. Inda drank his tea and spread preserves on a slice of bread.

The talk turned to weather, and Inda began to pay attention. "Aren't these storms abnormal for this area?" he asked, remembering Jeryl's comments.

"Not abnormal," replied Jemma, "but early, with more wind and ice than we would expect. The storms are not following their usual patterns. This year most of them have swept down from the mountains to strike in the wasteland, instead of on the northern plain. Already the barren lands have more snow than they get in a normal winter. If this keeps up, there will be flash floods in the spring, and the greatest blooming season the wasteland has seen in my lifetime."

Inda again wondered if yesterday's storm had kept the supply ship from landing. "The storms are causing great problems at the spaceport."

"And for us. We were four days late reaching Alu, and if another storm strikes we will miss our appointment at Eiku. We must be there by nightfall tomorrow."

"You should have no problem. The weather is clear and cold, and should stay that way tomorrow," said Septi. "It will be a good day to travel."

Ertis offered some bread. "Since you will only be with us for one night, I would like to offer a story this evening at the clanhall."

"Yes, a story-telling would be appropriate," said someone behind Inda.

"Ah, Secko, come and join us." Ertis signaled to a

youngling to bring another mug. "Sinykin, have you met Jeryl's apprentice? This is Sinykin Inda, and Jemma of Clan Sau."

"We would be honored to hear one of your stories," said Jemma. He nodded to Secko, then turned to Inda. "Are you visiting Alu to hear the stories of Ertis? He is one of our most renowned Historians."

Inda smiled. "No, Ertis' stories will be an added bonus. I am here to study the survivors of the plague."

"To what purpose do you do such a thing?"

"We have made a preparation that prevents our people from falling sick," replied Inda. "It may also work for you, but it must be tested. I am gathering samples and information to help us with our tests."

Jemma poured himself a second cup of tea. "Then you should visit Sau Keep," he exclaimed. "We have a Mother who survived a bout of the plague. She is hideously deformed, and our Healer says she will never be fertile, but she is the only Mother I have heard of who lived through the illness."

"If I journeyed to Sau, would I be allowed to see her?" asked Inda.

"I believe so."

Ertis touched Inda's arm. "Jeryl said nothing of traveling beyond Alu."

"Did he tell you I must stay at Alu?" Sinykin thought back to his last conversation with the Mentor. Jeryl had said nothing about going beyond Alu Keep. Griswold probably would be angry, and might accuse him of violating the trade agreement. Still, this was important research; the lives of many Ardellans might depend on it. Besides, the traders were inviting him to visit their keep. His sixth sense was telling him that he would learn much on this trip. "I would like to go to Sau. It could be very important to my study."

"If you go, I must accompany you," said Ertis.

Inda nodded. "Of course." He turned to the trader. "Could we ride with your party, Jemma?"

"We would be happy to have you, but we must go to Eiku before we return to Sau. We leave at dawn tomorrow."

"Could I go with you?" asked Septi.

"I think it would be best if you stay here." Ertis looked at Secko. "What do you think?"

"I cannot advise you. Jeryl did not give me any authority in this matter. You must use your best judgment."

Inda looked at Ertis, who made a small gesture of assent. "Inda and I will meet you at the stable at dawn," he said.

Secko knocked on the door of the Healers' compound. When it opened, he shouldered his way past the youngling who greeted him. "Take me to the Healer."

The youngling led him to the door of Viela's office, knocked and turned away, leaving Secko to face the Healer's wrath alone.

"I said I was not to be disturbed!"

"Healer, it is Secko. I bring you news of the Terran."

The door slowly opened. Secko stepped into the private chamber, and the door slammed shut behind him.

Viela was working with stylus and writing-cloth at a broad table on one side of the room. The shelves behind him were filled with pots and jars of many shapes and sizes. Bundles of drying herbs and net bags full of roots and bulbs hung from the beams overhead. Covered baskets were stacked in two of the corners.

A circular skylight opened the center of the room to sun and air. A pit had been carved through the stone of the floor below the skylight, then filled with sand and circled by a thin copper wire. A sunbeam touched the far edge of the sand and made a hand's span of the wire shine.

"So, what is this news?" Viela put aside his stylus and rolled the writing-cloth. "What does the Terran do now?"

"He is leaving Alu in the morning. He and Ertis are journeying to Eiku Keep, and then on to Sau Keep, in the company of some traders."

"And why did you think this would interest me?"

Secko swallowed. "I know you do not approve of the Terran's presence here. I thought you would be pleased that he is leaving."

Viela rose and went to stand at the edge of the sand pit. "I do not approve of the Terran presence on Ardel. It troubled me that the Terran came to Alu; it concerns me more that he is journeying beyond the keep.

"I had intended to send a message to my guildhall about the Terran physician's plans. If he is leaving Alu, Jeryl's orders no longer bind me; I need not remain here. I will deliver the message myself."

"You cannot leave Alu without a Healer!"

"By the rules of my guild I can leave the keep for three days. My apprentice will remain here and care for my patients. If I find that I will be gone for more than three days, I will send a replacement from the guildhall."

"And what will I tell Jeryl if he returns?"

"The truth," said Viela. "I have gone to Berrut to lodge a complaint with my guild, to keep the Terran from meddling in Healers' business."

News of the story-telling brought many Masters to the clanhall. The floor of the great hall was covered with cushions, a patchwork of varied shapes and colors, except for the cleared space in the center where Ertis would stand. The traders sat on the first row of pillows, where they had the best view. Inda almost joined them, then chose a red cushion near the outer wall, outside the main cluster of Ardellans. He wanted to observe them as well as listen to Ertis.

"May I join you?"

Inda looked up. Septi stood over him, pointing to the pillow next to Inda's. "Of course," said the Terran. "I would be glad of your company."

Septi sat with a smooth, graceful movement, settling the hem of his cloak around himself as if to delineate his territory. All through the room the Masters maintained distance one from another, sitting far enough apart so that they would not accidentally touch, would not brush against each other when changing position. Each sat quietly on his own cushion, staring at the place where Ertis would appear.

At some unseen signal the flames in all the wall sconces dimmed, throwing the corners of the room into shadow. Nearly every cushion was occupied. Inda counted quickly—well over two hundred Masters waited for Ertis. As he finished his count, a low murmur started at the front of the room, swept through the Masters like a rushing stream, then died. Ertis had appeared.

Inda had not seen the Historian enter the room. There was no path to walk from the door, no place but cushions for Ertis to put his feet, and Sinykin could swear he had not been in the hall a moment ago. Yet now he stood in the center of the gathering. A dozen yellow ribbons had been pinned to the shoulder of his tunic. They hung in a broad fan across his left breast, rippling as he moved.

The Historian turned slowly, taking stock of his audience. Sinykin no longer saw the quiet, self-effacing Ertis. This person was in control. Inda would not have been surprised to see him ordering people to move forward, to fill in the few gaps in the first circles. Ertis did not do so. Instead he seemed to examine each member of his audience. No one looked away from his gaze. His eyes met Sinykin's and rested there a moment. Inda felt himself pierced, studied, and approved before Ertis' gaze moved on. When the story-teller completed his circle, he turned once more, quickly, then raised his hands and began his story.

"Many seasons past, in a snow-covered field outside Sau Keep, challenge was issued. The Mentor of Clan Renu, whose name shall not be spoken because of the great shame he brought upon his clan, disputed with Attar, the Mentor of Clan Sau. The cause of their dispute is long forgotten; the bravery of Attar lives on.

"It was a day much like this one, falling soon after the beginning of storm season. The omens were great, for the moons were approaching conjunction. It was a sacred time. Attar asked to postpone the dispute for three days and nights, until the conjunction had passed, for he respected the old traditions. Renu's Mentor refused.

"Now it happened that Molti, Mentor of Clan Alu, was visiting Sau Keep at the time. He heard the words of Renu's Mentor and was angered, so he offered advice and aid to Attar of Clan Sau. Attar's apprentice, Helil, was young and inexperienced, and Molti believed he would be of little help in the dispute. Molti offered to take Helil's place in the circle, to stand beside Attar and ally Clan Alu with Clan Sau. Attar would not accept his offer. He feared that Molti might be hurt or killed and the autonomy of Clan Alu would be compromised. Instead he asked Molti to be an outrider during the dispute.

"In those days, the office of outrider was important. Each Mentor was allowed two outriders, whose task it was to keep others from interfering with the dispute. Molti accepted, and before dusk he followed Attar and Helil to the field of dispute and helped set up the tents. The Renu delegation was already there. In the first moment of darkness, Attar stood alone before the Renu Mentor and accepted his challenge with upraised arms."

Inda was listening, and looking at the rest of the audience. They all stared at Ertis with rapt attention.

"Do you see it?" whispered Septi, leaning close but never taking his eyes off Ertis.

"See what?"

Septi laid a hand on the Terran's arm, and Inda stared in astonishment as the room faded to a shadow and he gazed upon a vast outdoor scene that centered around the storyteller. Ertis moved among slightly wavering images, almost interacting with them as he told their story.

"Attar and Helil went alone to Attar's tent, to spend the night in meditation. Before dawn Molti called Attar, and dressed him, and took him to be fed. Attar and Helil did not eat, and drank only cold tea, because the moons' conjunction was imminent. Then Attar walked to the runestaff and lifted it from its resting place, and bore it to the circle of dispute himself. Helil followed him, and Molti and the other outrider mounted, and took their places outside the circle."

Inda watched as Attar walked through the darkness, his cloak billowed out behind him by a gust of wind, the runestaff carried upright at arm's length before him. He moved with the deliberate steps of an old man approaching a task that frightened him.

"Once again Attar met the Mentor of Renu, and they faced each other in the center of the circle. Words were spoken and sparks flashed in the darkness. Runestaffs touched, then were carried around the field of dispute as the Mentors cast a circle to contain their power. As the sun rose, they faced each other across the circle.

"Renu's Mentor stood with his apprentice. Two hands of younglings gathered behind them, Renu's sacrifice. Behind Attar and Helil, just outside the sacred circle, a group of Sau's younglings waited. Attar had selected one from each of the twelve founding Houses of Sau Keep. The younglings stood together, tentacles entwined, drawing strength from each other."

Renu's Mentor attacked first. Inda watched him cast a ball of orange flame across the circle at Attar. Behind him the bodies of two younglings shriveled and blackened as they fell to the ground. Helil took the runestaff from Attar's hands and used it to counter the attack. The flaming ball touched it and burst apart, showering Helil with sparks and ash. A tendril of smoke rose from the tip of the runestaff.

Attar countered with a flaming ball of his own. His blue fire was intercepted by Renu's apprentice, who struck and destroyed it with his runestaff. Renu's Mentor had already cast a second ball of flame across the circle. Helil reached for it with his runestaff. The power touched its tip, and flowed downward.

Helil screamed. The runestaff slipped from his scorched hands. His arms were burned and blackened. He fell to the ground, moaning.

Attar was angry. He sent a huge white ball of flame straight at the Renu apprentice. It struck his hands, ran down his arms to envelop his body. He burned with a bright flame, dropping the unscathed runestaff as he collapsed.

Now it was a battle of Mentors. Power surged from Attar's hands, leapt across the circle to meet the attack of his opponent. With each burst of power, more younglings died. Attar screamed as a ball of flame struck his left shoulder. His cloak burned and was quickly quenched, but his arm hung useless after that.

Renu sent a huge ball of fire at Attar. Inda gasped as he watched it fly across the circle; the wounded Mentor could not possibly survive this strike. Attar raised his right arm. Flames shot from his fingers, streaked like arrows across the circle toward the Renu Mentor. Sinykin lifted a warding hand just as the ball of fire struck Attar's leg. The Mentor fell to the ground, his leg aflame. Across the circle, one of Attar's fire arrows found a home in the Renu Mentor's chest. He screamed as the flames engulfed his body.

"Attar's right leg was scorched and smoking. Still he tried to rise, to see the fate of Renu's Mentor. When Attar fell back to the sand, Molti hurtled from his mount's back and ran into the circle. He knelt beside Attar and helped him to sit, so that the Mentor of Clan Sau could raise his arm high into the air and proclaim his victory. Sunlight glinted on his copper wristband.

"Attar died in the arms of his friend Molti, who carried his blackened body from the circle, wrapped it in fine cloth, and returned it to Sau Keep. Helil survived, but lost the use of his fingers. He wore the copper wristband and was Mentor of Clan Sau for a season. Molti conducted the funeral for Attar because Helil could not hold the runestaff. Attar's

black urn still rests in Sau's mourning wall, under the runes
that Molti carved there.

"All the wealth and power of Clan Renu passed to Sau,
for two generations. Because of the love of Molti and Attar,
Clan Alu and Clan Sau are allies to this day."

The circle was dissolving. Inda blinked several times as
the images of Attar and Molti faded. He sighed. The scene
had been so compelling that he had forgotten he was in the
clanhall, listening to Ertis. It was more convincing than any
hologram he had ever seen. He felt as if he had witnessed
the event, not a retelling of it.

Ertis turned about once again, gazing at the Masters who
stared at him in rapt attention. He blinked, and the Masters
began to move and stretch. Before Ertis completed his circle, Masters were rising to congratulate him.

Septi turned to Inda. "Did you enjoy the story?" he
asked.

Sinykin did not know how to reply. Enjoy? He had been
so immersed in the action that he had no sense of enjoyment, only a feeling of total involvement. "The story absorbed me completely," he said. "Is it intended to do that?
Am I supposed to feel as if I was there?"

"Of course," said Septi. "Why else tell a story?"

"Are all of Ertis' stories told this way?" asked Inda,
thinking of the tale of Sarah Anders' death.

"They are," said Ertis, joining them.

The Terran smiled. "Then I would like to hear more of
them in the future. Septi, thank you for sharing this experience with me."

"We must rise before dawn tomorrow to meet the traders.
I think it best if we return home now." Ertis exchanged a
farewell gesture with Septi, and led Inda from the clanhall.
The night sky was clear and the air cold, foretelling fair
weather for their trip.

Inda's room in House Actaan felt comfortable and familiar. He stripped and washed, then sat cross-legged on the
bed with his stylus and journal before him. As he relaxed
and grounded the excitement he felt about the day's events,
he realized how much he missed Elissa and Jaime. This
would be their quiet time together, to share dinner and talk
about the day. He wanted to tell them of all the things he
had seen and done at Alu Keep, and to hear about their day
at work and at school. And he must tell Elissa that he was

going on to Eiku Keep and then to Sau Keep. He tore a page from the back of his journal and began writing.

The letter was three pages long when it was finished. He had been careful not to mention any of the psychic phenomena he had witnessed; otherwise it was a complete chronicle of his activities during the past two days. He folded it and put it in the box with the blood and tissue samples that would be delivered to the spaceport in the morning. Someone in the lab would give it to Elissa.

The magic of last night's music was still with Inda, confirmed and strengthened by his experience at the storytelling. He closed his eyes and heard again the gently interwoven notes of harp and shell-pipe. When he leaned back against the wall, his room was transformed into a cave of living stone. He looked at the door with his psychic sight and saw the tree that it had once been. The small iron bar was there in the latch, where Ertis had told him to look for it. It glowed with a soft light, almost like an aura. Inda reached for the bar with his mind, touched it, tried to move it as Ertis had shown him. It felt as if he was trying to lift an impossibly heavy weight.

After a moment he sighed and released the contact. The iron bar was glowing with a brighter light, as if the energy he had used in trying to move it was still there, visible to him.

Sarah Anders had claimed in her journal that she had once created shimmer-light. For the first time, Sinykin Inda believed that he might someday make shimmer-light of his own.

Chapter 7

"It's too dangerous," said Arien. He sat on the edge of the sleeping platform, one hand planted in the furs, the fingers of the other tangled in his hair. Green mist swirled through his aura. "You would have to spend nearly half a day in trance, with your mind far from your body."

Jeryl turned from his friend's concerned gaze, and stared out the window at the bleak morning sky. Gray clouds obscured the dawn. Wind rattled the shutters and piled drifting snow against the inn's door. At his feet sat an ash filled brazier. He pulled his woolen cloak close against the room's chill.

"The guilds' numbers increase from season to season, while the clans' numbers decline. I think the reason is locked inside the crèches. If the guilds have found a way to metamorphose two younglings into Masters at every co-cooning, that method might be adapted to serve us as well." He leaned against the wall. The cold stone chilled his shoulder through the wool. "I must see the inside of that crèche. You know the crèchemaster will not let me enter with you. The only way is the trance drug."

"And you'll see the crèche through my eyes? Why not wait until I return? I can tell you what I see."

"You would be blind to many of the things I can perceive in trance."

Arien rose and came toward him, pleading. "Hanra-bae will be with me. He knows more about this subject than either of us. If there is anything to be learned in the crèche, he will see it."

"I no longer trust this Healer. He twists the truth and hides knowledge the way Terrans sometimes do. The future of Clan Alu may depend on what we learn in that crèche today. I must be there myself.''

"And what if something goes wrong? With no one here to monitor you, you could die!''

Jeryl turned from the window and grasped Arien's shoulder. "Nothing will go wrong. I know the drug; I have done this many times.''

Arien shuddered. "That drug will kill you someday.'' He strode to the doorway between their rooms, pulled the cloth partition aside, and stepped through.

Outside, a flurry of snowflakes blew off the roof and swirled past the window. Jeryl watched the shifting patterns and thought of the dream that had disturbed his sleep for a second night. He had seen Hatar wandering in the mountains, lost and alone, running away from the FreeMasters who offered him warmth and solace. Was it a true vision, or only a dream fabricated from Jeryl's fears and feelings of guilt? The sun rose late and set early at this time of year, making the days short and the nights long and cold, especially in the mountains. Jeryl wanted to ride there and search for his friend Hatar, but his duty to Alu kept him in Berrut. The future of the clan was much more important than the life of a single Master. That knowledge did not lessen Jeryl's pain. If Hatar continued to run and hide in the mountains, he would die there.

Arien spoke from the other room. His words were muffled by the heavy tapestry hanging in the doorway. Jeryl poked his head through and asked, "What did you say?''

"Why do you need my aid? You ride the storms alone. Why not visit the crèche the same way?''

"It is too far to go alone. I could reach the crèche, but the distance would stretch the connection between my mind and body. The more tenuous that becomes, the more difficult it is to maintain a sense of time. All things become immediate. Past and future fall away into fantasy.'' Jeryl shrugged. "It would be easy to forget that I have a body.''

"And you want me to send you back before that happens?''

"Yes.''

"You put me in a difficult position. I am leader of the FreeMasters. We serve clans and guilds alike. If it is learned that I have violated the confidence of a guild by helping you to enter its crèche. . . .''

Jeryl shrugged again. "Then I will go alone, and hope that I return in time. I must get inside that crèche."

Arien's shields came up, glowing translucent white all around his body. "When and where will you meet me? The crèche is at the outskirts of the city, near the stables. I will breakfast with Hanra-bae, and then we will take the red road to the crèche. If you do not want Hanra-bae to know that you are joining me, I cannot delay long on the way."

Jeryl sighed. He would have preferred wholehearted support to grudging acquiescence, but he would take what was offered. Arien had duties and responsibilities of his own. He was risking much in setting them aside to serve the needs of a friend. "I am grateful for your help. Clan Alu owes a great debt to the FreeMasters Guild.

"I will join you before you reach the crèche. Wait for me at the big tea-leaf tree, the one next to the stone wall. Be there just before midmorning, when second-moon is setting. I will find you."

Arien shrugged. "I will be there." He pulled his cloak from a wall peg, swirled it around his back and let it settle on his shoulders, then tugged the hood forward to hide his face. "I must go now."

"Safe journey, my friend." Jeryl spoke to the closing door, but he knew that Arien heard him.

Trance work required careful preparation. Though Arien thought him foolhardy, Jeryl did not enter trance without taking precautions. He cleaned the brazier of ashes, and set it on the stone floor in the center of the room. He shuttered his window to block out light, but opened the one in Arien's room for ventilation. He tied back the tapestry between the rooms, snuffed the wall sconces, and set a bucket of water beside the brazier.

He told the innkeeper he was not to be disturbed, then bribed one of the kitchen attendants to look in on him several times during the day. The youngling was accustomed to the eccentricities of guests; it stashed the coins somewhere under its sash while dipping its eyestalks and waving a reassuring tentacle at Jeryl.

All was ready well before midmorning. Jeryl lit some kindling in the brazier, watched it burst into bright yellow flames. The coals flared briefly, then settled to creeping red as the kindling burned away. After a time, white ash outlined the coals' irregular shapes. Jeryl took the armata pouch from his pack, and chose three large, unblemished leaves. As the leaves began to shrivel and crackle on the coals, he stripped off his cloak and boots. Trance always warmed him.

He settled on the sleeping platform, with his head near the smoking brazier, and began his breathing exercises: draw the smoke in deeply, feel it tickle, hold it until he was ready to choke, then let it out slowly. Again. Again.

By the fourth breath the room was receding. He floated up and out of his body, watched it from the ceiling for a moment, observed the tenuous silver thread that connected the top of his head with the electrical disturbance he thought of as ''himself.'' Then he visualized the street outside, and he was there.

He knew that it was cold. He had left physical sensation behind with his body, but he perceived the chill in other ways: the speed and direction of the wind, the angle of the sunlight passing him on its way to warm the planet. He had no gauge to help him quantify his impressions. He was not even aware that he was measuring. Time and distance had become irrelevant concepts. He had only to think of a place, and he was instantaneously there.

He climbed above the clouds to observe the sun. The orange globe had not yet reached its midmorning position in the sky. S'rea, second-moon, moved slowly westward. It was still too early to meet Arien. Jeryl felt a sudden urge to visit the Healers' library. The information he needed might be there or in the crèche, or perhaps a piece of it was in each place. If he explored the library, he might find a way to get the scrolls Hanra-bae wanted.

He visualized the Healers' library, and was there.

A youngling, tentacles wrapped around a broom handle and eyestalks bent to peer at the floor, swept the room with long, even strokes. Its broom chased puffs of dust across the flagstones, and deposited debris in the cracks between. It did not react to Jeryl's entrance. Like most younglings, it was headblind, insensible to psychic disturbances.

To be unaware of its psychic surroundings, unable to see an aura, set a ward, or conjure shimmer-light, was the blessing (or curse) of a youngling. Jeryl remembered those days with a fondness he knew to be false. Through that long time of servitude, his one wish was to undergo metamorphosis, to become an adult with all the attendant rights and responsibilities.

Now he could not shirk those responsibilities. The Great Sun had laid a heavy burden upon him, and he would not shrink from it.

Martyr! A chuckle of current ran through the energy net of his mind. Sometimes he took himself much too seriously. With a sudden fillip he bounced into existence across the room, then back in the corner, to the window, behind the door. . . . He let the freedom rule him for a moment, reveling in the joy of doing, and being, anything.

There was work to do. He stopped at the door to the chamber where the ancient scrolls were stored. It was harder to enter this chamber, since he had never seen it. Instead of remembering it, he had to build the image in his mind. It took a moment, and then he was inside among the dusty racks and moldering rolls of cloth.

It was not hard to find the scrolls Hanra-bae had been studying. His imprint was on them, clear as brook water in winter. There must be a way to get them out, to take them somewhere safe and translate them. The room had one door and two windows, one facing the compound's outer wall. Jeryl was checking the wards on the latches when he heard voices in the outer chamber.

His first impulse was to flee. If he stayed, he could not hide from Masters for long.

"Here are the texts, GuildMaster. Hanra-bae was examining these, along with some others in the storage room."

Bantu! And the GuildMaster with him! Jeryl's consciousness hovered over the door, hiding in the shadow where wall met ceiling. If they weren't expecting intruders, they might not notice him. He slowed the frantic pulsing of his net, listened carefully to their conversation.

"There is nothing of import in these volumes," said the GuildMaster. "Hanra-bae can examine these whenever he wishes. Show me the others he was interested in seeing."

The door opened. Bantu entered first, his righteous white aura preceding him. With one hand extended, he walked among the storage racks. Unerringly he selected Hanra-bae's scrolls.

"Here they are. Shall I bring them out?"

"No." The GuildMaster strode through the doorway.

From above Jeryl perceived unruly white hair, narrow shoulders and long arms, surrounded by an aura colored gold with concern. He watched as the GuildMaster sent part

of his consciousness ranging about the room, probing for
recent impressions of other occupants. Jeryl stilled the pulsing of his own mind, falling back almost into the stone of
the wall until the danger passed.

Bantu pulled scrolls from the rack and spread them on
the table. The GuildMaster joined him, reaching for the texts
but not quite touching them.

"I cannot tell you which passages interested Hanra-bae,"
said Bantu. He unrolled first one scroll and then another,
skimming the text while the GuildMaster watched over his
shoulder.

A good time to escape, thought Jeryl, preparing to flee
back to the inn. He was about to relocate when the Guild-
Master's exclamation stayed him.

"There! That may be what the fisher seeks." The
GuildMaster took the scroll from Bantu and scanned the
runes. "The common thread in all these texts is reproduction, but none of the information is secret except this account. Here the writer hints at long-forgotten methods of
metamorphosis, at ways of cocooning groups of younglings.
Why should Hanra-bae search for this knowledge?"

Jeryl knew why. He separated from the rock, slipped over
to hover above Bantu's shoulder. He snaked loose a single
thread of his energy net and used it to touch the Healer. He
saw the runes through Bantu's eyes. They had faded on the
ancient cloth, but he could still make them out. It was indeed an account of a mass cocooning, but many of the runes
were obscure and he could not translate them. He recognized a few key words—"larkenleaf," and "sacred moisture"—but the rest was indecipherable. He needed time to
study the scroll, to reveal its secrets. Excitement quickened
the pulsing power of his energy net as he realized that the
knowledge he needed was within his grasp.

"Intruder!" yelled Bantu, dropping the scroll.

Jeryl fled, visualizing the inn as he popped out of, and
into, existence. The cold walls of the library were still
around him. He tried again, this time seeing the street outside the Healers' wall. Still the library enclosed him. Someone was holding him there, preventing his flight in a way
he did not understand. He channeled all his energy into
breaking that hold. For an instant he was free, moving across
the ceiling, but then something imprisoned him again.

This time he saw the GuildMaster's right hand reaching

toward him, all six fingers cupped around the palm. Jeryl felt those fingers grasping him, holding him in the library.

Bantu rushed to join his GuildMaster, extending his own cupped hand to reinforce Jeryl's prison. "It is the one who came with Hanra-bae. Jeryl, of Clan Alu."

"Quiet."

The GuildMaster twisted his arm, and Jeryl felt his prison shrink. Panic quickened the pulsing of his energy net. He pushed against the barrier, seeking a way out. These Healers were skilled. Their powers were almost a match for his own. If they severed the silver filament that connected him to his body, they would kill him. He spun in their grasp, seeking, seeking, and suddenly knew the way to freedom.

He faced them head-on, shot down the lines of force toward their bodies, drawing energy from them and feeding it back transformed into heat. The GuildMaster howled and drew his hand back.

Jeryl was free. Cries of pain still echoed in the library, but Jeryl was outside, hovering above the courtyard. He felt a familiar presence standing just inside the compound's gate. Viela! The Healer seemed unaware of Jeryl's presence. The library door was opening. Jeryl heard the GuildMaster shouting for help. He flitted in the opposite direction, appearing first outside the inn, then on the road to the crèche.

Viela ran to the libary. Kelta, the Healers' GuildMaster, stood in the doorway, holding out his right hand. The skin was gold-red and blistering. Behind him stood his assistant, nursing a similarly burned palm.

"Quickly! To the infirmary!" Viela ushered them out of the library and across the court. "How did you burn yourselves?"

"You should ask who burned us," said Bantu. He cradled his injured hand against his chest. "It was Jeryl, Clan Alu's Mentor."

"That cannot be. I saw no one in the library." Viela opened the infirmary's rear door with a thought. He followed Kelta and Bantu into the cluttered workroom, and thought the door closed behind them. A pair of younglings were standing at a table, sorting and rolling bandages. Viela pointed at the nearest one. "Your GuildMaster and his assistant have been burned. Bring me a pot of salve right away." The youngling trundled away without saying a word.

Bantu swept a pile of herbs from a bench with his good hand. Kelta sat, and rested his burned hand palm-upward in his lap. "It was Jeryl. He was here yesterday, with Hanra-bae. Today his mind returned alone, in trance, to spy on us."

The idea seemed absurd. What could Jeryl possibly want in the library? And why would he have come here with the fisher? "With greatest respect, Kelta, why would Jeryl spy on the Healers Guild? Alu has enemies among the other guilds, but we Healers are neutral. We pose no threat to Alu." Viela extended his own hand, fingers spread, and let it hover just above Kelta's. His Healer's senses explored the injured tissues, assessing the degree of damage. "The burn is not deep. With proper treatment, it will heal in a few days."

"I know," said Kelta. "Psychic burns heal easily—or kill." A youngling brought the GuildMaster a pot of smelly ointment. Kelta spread the salve on the hand himself, then passed the pot to Bantu so that he could treat his own burn.

Viela was still puzzled by Kelta's belief that the intruder had been Jeryl. Perhaps the fisher had influenced Jeryl to spy for him. But Hanra-bae was a Healer, and had access to the library. Why would he want to send Jeryl there to look at things he might easily see for himself? "Do you know where Jeryl is staying? I will go and see him, and confront him about this. I have other news for him, and for you." Viela chose a gauzy bandage from the table, and began to wrap it around Kelta's hand.

"What news do you bring us?" asked Bantu.

Viela tried to keep the anger out of his voice. "The Terran physician, Sinykin Inda, was visiting Alu Keep. He is now on his way to Eiku and Sau. I believe this is a violation of Alu's agreement with the Terrans. He is also making impossible claims. He says he has a potion that will keep our people from succumbing to the plague."

Arien was waiting for Jeryl at the tea-leaf tree. He stood with Hanra-bae, a branch grasped in one hand, examining the bare twigs for insect damage while describing the pests to the impatient Healer. Hanra-bae's aura was a dark and murky green; every third word he took a step toward the crèche but turned back when he realized Arien was not following him.

Jeryl watched the interplay for a moment, then nudged Arien's mind. It opened to him and he slipped in, giving his friend a joyous greeting. Their communication was instantaneous. Arien welcomed him with a caustic remark about the time, which was well past mid-morning. Jeryl replied by sharing his memory of the encounter in the Healer's library. He was amused by Arien's cluck of dismay.

"Arien, the sun approaches midday. We are expected at the crèche," said Hanra-bae, his impatience a gray-green smoke, heavy and acrid, wafting through his aura.

"Yes, I know." Arien released the branch, and it snapped back above his head. "It is not far."

The buildings along the road had given way to orchards and open fields, bordered by low stone walls. They trudged through little drifts of dry snow that squeaked under their feet. Jeryl linked himself to Arien's senses, and through his eyes saw well-tended, happy trees, healthy but dormant; fields plowed in spiral furrows, earth rich with organic matter, autumn-planted seeds sleeping just under the surface; content borras in their stalls in an old stone barn, munching last summer's grain. Here and there he saw a spot of blight, a broken branch, a bruised foot, but no more or less than he would find in any keep.

The crèche was different. Something felt very wrong there. The compound was large and sprawling, two hands of buildings scattered about an open court. There was a huge garden, where last year's stubble was coated with ice, and snow nestled in the furrows. The court was paved with small stones, strewn loose on the ground. Most of the buildings were wooden, constructed with shingled roofs, few windows, and low doors. The largest one was built of stone. It was not dressed and fitted stone like the buildings at Alu Keep, but mortared fieldstone. It looked weather tight, but not as sturdy and certainly not as beautiful as buildings Jeryl was accustomed to seeing in the keeps.

Younglings were working in the stableyard, but they ignored the visitors, and there were no adults in sight. Hanra-bae stepped up onto the flagstone porch, and Arien followed him. The door was an arm's span wide, but barely a Master's height—almost square, with broad leather hinges and a wooden knocker. There was no handle.

"Knock," said Arien, and Hanra-bae did. The thud echoed once, then the door swung inward.

"Greetings," said the smallest Master Jeryl had ever seen. He stared up at the visitors, tiny pale eyes flicking from Hanra-bae's face to Arien's and back again, while one hand tugged at his thinning hair. Suddenly a grin of recognition lit his face and softened his eyes, and he danced out of the way, waving them forward. "Welcome. Reass told me to expect you. I am Kraal, the crèchemaster. You must be the GuildMaster," he said to Arien as he ushered them into the hall. He closed the door and took their cloaks, talking all the while. "You and your guest must come stand near the hearth. You must be chilled from your walk. Can I get you anything?"

Arien took advantage of the opening, and lifted his palm in greeting. "No, nothing right now. Perhaps after we see the crèche, we could share tea. I am Arien of the Free-Masters Guild, and this is Hanra-bae, Master Healer of Port Freewind."

"Good, good. We do not often see fishers in Berrut. Have you been here before, Master Healer? As I said, welcome to the Metalsmiths' crèche. We are happy to show you our facilities. We have more than five hands of Mothers in residence right now, and more younglings than I care to count. Our cocooning-room is empty, though I expect it will be filled again in a few days. I can show you most of the facilities—the outbuildings, the Mothers' quarters, younglings' dormitories, kitchen and weaving-room, gardens, orchards. What would you like to see first? Are you sure I cannot get you some tea? Are the fishers thinking of starting a crèche?" The last was directed at Hanra-bae.

"No, we are not. I studied in Berrut several years ago, and heard much about your crèches. Since the opportunity presents itself, I would like to see this one."

Kraal never stopped moving. His eyes did not settle in one place for more than an instant, and his hands fluttered here and there, brushing at his tunic, tugging his almost nonexistent hair, and pointing in every direction. Even his feet were not still. He shuffled from side to side, sometimes punctuating a sentence with a little hop.

"Could we start by seeing the facilities for Mothers and younglings?" Arien asked, stepping away from the hearth to look about the room. He was acutely aware of Jeryl observing the scene through his eyes. Bare stone walls enclosed them. A single high window provided meager

sunlight, augmented by oil-burning lamps that left smoky
smudges on the ceiling. A wooden bench sat before the
hearth.

"Not a very hospitable greeting-room," thought Jeryl.

"Quiet!" Arien thought back at him. He was angry. "I
cannot converse with you and keep your presence hidden
from Kraal and Hanra-bae. Be silent!"

Kraal crossed the room and pushed open a door. "You
won't need your cloaks. We can see most of the compound
without stepping outdoors. The buildings are connected by
sheltered walkways that can be opened to the breeze in good
weather." He ushered them into a dark, narrow hall. They
passed closed doors on either side. Kraal stopped and
opened one, showed them a small dim chamber with a
sleeping platform, a stool, and some hooks on the wall for
hanging clothing. "These are the chambers where visiting
Masters stay. The quarters are not luxurious, but the Masters are only with us for a day or two. The Mothers' chambers are much nicer."

The guest chambers in Alu's clanhall were opulent
compared with these rooms, thought Jeryl. He saw no sign
of the Metalsmiths' vaunted wealth.

Kraal led them on to the end of the hall, where he pushed
aside a dusty tapestry to enter a bright, sunny room. "This
is our weaving-room." He seemed quite proud of it.

A hand of Mothers worked in the room, three of them at
the looms, pushing shuttles back and forth through forests
of heavy threads. The others sorted and wound great hanks
of yarn, like those that hung from pegs on the wall. One
hank was Metalsmith's red, the rest were dull, dark colors.

"We buy spun wool from Clan Renu," said Kraal, "and
dye it ourselves. The dyeing vats are outside, in the courtyard. We grow deepwhisker root, thorn flower, scarletberry,
and we are experimenting with several mineral dyes."

Hanra-bae approached one of the weavers. "Mother, I
am Master Healer of Port Freewind. Are you feeling un-
well?"

She dropped her shuttle and looked up, startled. Her skin
had a yellow tinge, and there was a dark blot in her aura
near her heart. She flinched as Hanra-bae touched her hand,
and her eyes sought Kraal's.

"Ranii is perfectly healthy," said Kraal, stepping to her

side. "All of our Mothers receive the finest care from the Healers Guild in Berrut."

"Was the crèche troubled by the plague?" asked Arien.

"No, no, not really. A few younglings became ill. . . ."

Ranii spoke. "We lost Allia. She was my friend. When she fell ill, I nursed her. It did no good. She died a hand of days later."

"You do not look well, Mother Ranii. Please let me examine you." Hanra-bae settled her into her chair and stroked her hand.

Kraal took Hanra-bae's arm and tried to lead him toward the door. "Thank you for your offer, Master Healer. You need not trouble yourself. I am sure our Healer will examine Ranii when he makes his regular visit tomorrow. We have much more to see today. Come, let me show you the younglings' quarters."

"I do not care to see the younglings' quarters!" shouted Hanra-bae. "This Mother is ill. I must examine her!"

"Healer!" Arien made the title a rebuke. "We are guests here."

Hanra-bae stared at Arien. Jeryl perceived the ruby gouts of anger erupting from the Healer's aura. "Hanra-bae is correct. The Mother is ill," he thought to Arien. Arien's only reply was a soft warning growl deep in his throat.

"The younglings' dormitory is this way." Kraal opened a door and steered Hanra-bae through it. Arien followed. They were in another long, dark corridor, this one lined with panels that could be removed in nice weather to let in air and sunlight. It was illuminated by one smoky torch.

"We are not concerned with facilities for younglings," said Arien. "We came to see your cocooning-rooms."

"Yes, show us the mating-rooms and the lying-in platforms. And I wish to discuss the mating process with you, or someone else who is knowledgeable," added Hanra-bae.

Kraal's anxiety showed in his dancing fingers and the abrupt movements of his hands. "I am not certain . . . I do not know if I am allowed to show you these things."

Arien turned back the way he had come. "Then there is no point in our visit. If you cannot trust me, leader of the FreeMasters Guild, then I cannot ask my guild members to work for you. The Metalsmiths must find other guides and protectors."

"No, no!" Kraal touched Arien's shoulder. "Please

wait. Let me contact GuildMaster Reass. Could you return tomorrow?''

"Return tomorrow! You have already wasted half of our day!" Hanra-bae shouted, waving his arms and stamping his feet. "We have other business, you know. Yours is not the only guild in Berrut."

"Calm yourself, Healer. If we leave now, we can visit the Merchants Guild this evening. The GuildMaster seemed quite anxious to show us their crèche." Arien had learned how to bluff from a Terran. The FreeMaster did not do it well, but Kraal was so agitated that he did not notice Arien's anxiety.

"Please, if you follow me I will show you a cocooning-chamber. I am certain GuildMaster Reass would approve." Kraal led them back through the corridor to a wide wooden door. Apprehension clouded his aura. He opened the door, ushered them into the dim chamber, then created a ball of shimmer-light.

The chamber was tiny. The mating platform occupied nearly half of the floor space. There was barely enough room for the three Masters to stand beside it.

The chamber had no skylight. Jeryl had seen many co-cooning chambers at Alu Keep, and every one had a sky-light. He thought other keeps were the same. This room was like a cave, close and dark and cold, not warm like a womb. A Mother spent the last days of her life, from mating until the birth of her young, in the cocooning chamber. In Alu she would have sunlight and space and fresh air. Here she would be in a cramped prison.

Arien turned, and Jeryl saw the cocooning grotto through his eyes. It was a shallow indentation in the wall where a youngling or Master would be placed while the silk cocoon was wrapped around him. Arien touched the wall. It was cold and hard, not warm and yielding like the grotto wall he remembered from his own cocooning.

"There are two grottoes," said Hanra-bae, pointing to the second one on the far wall. It looked no more inviting than the first. "Do you cocoon two younglings at the same time?"

"Yes."

"How do you do that? Each Master has only enough silk to cocoon one youngling."

Kraal shrugged. "That is true. We bring in two Masters and two younglings."

"Then when they have completed their metamorphosis, four Masters must mate with a single Mother!" Arien was appalled.

"That is a disgusting perversion!" cried Hanra-bae. "How can your guild perpetuate such a practice?"

"Our guild grows and prospers. We have more Metalsmiths than ever before."

Arien shoved past Kraal to reach the door. "I had not imagined that anyone could condone such a thing. I feel ill just thinking about it."

"The Healers Guild will hear of your perversion," said Hanra-bae, following Arien from the chamber.

"The Healers already know of our practice," said Kraal. "They do not disapprove. In fact, a Healer monitors all of our cocoonings and births."

Hanra-bae turned on the little crèchemaster. Streaks of ruby and topaz flashed through his aura. Kraal backed away, until he reached the mating platform and could go no farther. "If the Healers of Berrut are aiding you, they have lost all sense of decency. I have no respect for them or for you. Port Freewind will no longer deal with the Metalsmiths!"

"Go," thought Jeryl to Arien. "Leave quickly. We have all the information we wanted."

Arien grabbed Hanra-bae's arm, pulled him down the walkway toward the main building. "We will go back to the inn," he thought to Jeryl. "You must return to your body now. You have been gone much too long."

Jeryl needed no further urging. He visualized his room at the inn, and saw his body sprawled on the sleeping platform. Quickly he grasped the silver cord that anchored him to his body, and slipped back along it to hover over the prostrate form. He sensed a presence nearby, a hostile aura moving about in the next room. He loosed the cord, left his body growing cold, and went to investigate.

Someone was going through Arien's things. The contents of the FreeMaster's pack were spread across the sleeping platform, and the intruder was searching the pockets of Arien's spare tunics. The person was tall, and wore a nondescript brown cloak with the hood drawn up to shadow his face. Jeryl could not identify him, nor link him with a clan or a guild.

The intruder was not aware of Jeryl's presence, but in a few moments he would move into the other room, and he would certainly find Jeryl's helpless body. Jeryl could not fight him without first returning to his corporeal form. He sensed his body growing colder, nearing death, and he fled back to the other room and entered it.

His heart was pumping very slowly. His hands and feet tingled and his back ached. He pushed his heart to pump harder, faster, and felt the weird sensation of warm blood moving into chilled arms and legs. His eyelids fluttered open, and he tried to move his head. It ached.

He heard the stranger walking in Arien's room. Jeryl moved first his left hand, then his arm. He tried to sit up but could not lift his head from the pillow. The smell of stale armata smoke gagged him, and he coughed. He wished he could separate his aching head from his body and forget about it for awhile.

The hall door opened. This time Jeryl sat up, despite his pounding head. The youngling he had bribed to check on him said, "Is there anything you need, Mentor?"

"Yes," he croaked. He heard Arien's door open and close, and knew the intruder had fled. "Bring me some tea."

"Certainly, Mentor." The door closed again.

As soon as he could stand, Jeryl stumbled to the window and threw open the shutters. A few breaths of fresh air helped ease his headache. He found some water in a pitcher and poured it over the still-glowing coals in the brazier. They crackled and popped, and sent up a cloud of steam.

Jeryl felt chilled. He pulled his cloak from the wardrobe and settled it across his shoulders like a cape. Then he went into Arien's room.

The door was closed, the window open, and the room was quite cold. Jeryl closed the shutters, and used a flint and knife to start a fire in Arien's brazier. He was too psychically exhausted to conjure shimmer-light or even latch the door. He pushed Arien's things aside and huddled on the sleeping platform, waiting for the youngling to bring his tea.

"Jeryl." Arien's voice woke him from a sound sleep. Shimmer-light blazed in the wall sconces, and the brazier's coals glowed a deep red. The air was warm, and the smell of armata smoke was almost gone.

"Jeryl, what happened here?"

The Mentor threw off his cloak, straightened up, stretched sore and tired muscles. "Someone broke in. I do not know who he was. He was going through your things when I returned."

"He did not harm you?"

"He was frightened off before he saw me." Jeryl reached for Arien's empty pack. "I think we should find another place to stay."

"Arien! Jeryl! Let me in!" Hanra-bae was shouting and pounding on their door. It swung open and he stumbled across the threshold. "Someone has ransacked my chamber. . . ."

Jeryl shrugged. The Healer's mouth stayed open as he stared at Arien's belongings strewn about the room.

"We are planning to leave the inn tonight. Would you like to join us?" asked Arien.

"Where will you go?"

Arien looked at Jeryl. "Do you have any suggestions?"

Jeryl growled. Did Arien expect him to think clearly after spending a day in trance? He had no idea where they might spend the night in safety. "No!" He began stuffing Arien's clothing into his pack.

"Then let us try the Historians' guildhall. My friend Allya should still be there. I think he will welcome us for at least one night. Pack your things," Arien said to the Healer.

They stopped at the desk to settle their account on the way out. The innkeeper gave Jeryl a roll of writing-cloth tied with Healer's cord. Jeryl slipped off the cord and unrolled the cloth. The message was from Viela; he wanted to meet Jeryl at the inn in the morning. Viela wrote that the Terran physician had broken the trade agreement and was traveling with Ertis and some traders, planning to visit Eiku Keep and Sau Keep. Jeryl muttered an oath under his breath. He handed the message to Arien, who read it silently, then rolled the cloth and stuffed it into a pocket in his tunic. "We will have to discuss this later," was his only comment.

Jeryl saw many tunics of Metalsmith's red in the common room. Several of the smiths seemed to be watching him. One of them was tall and slender; he might be the intruder.

When Jeryl glanced back on his way out of the door, the tall one had drained his mug and was rising.

Arien led the way down the road as the sun set. Jeryl's pack was heavy, and he was tired. He lagged behind, watching over his shoulder to see if they were followed. As they turned into a narrow lane, he saw the inn's door open and two cloaked figures emerge.

"Arien, we are being pursued," he called quietly. "They can track us in the snow. Can you find a well-trodden path to confuse them?"

Hanra-bae turned back. "Who are they?"

"Metalsmiths, I think," said Jeryl. Viela was sibling to Reass, GuildMaster of the Metalsmiths. Jeryl wondered whether his loyalties lay with Alu, or with his sibling. What might he have told Reass about Jeryl's trip to Berrut?

They reached the end of the lane, and Arien turned left onto a well-traveled road. "Are they still behind us?"

"They just entered the lane."

"Follow me quickly," said Arien. He stepped between two shops, pushed Hanra-bae and Jeryl past him down the narrow walkway, then stepped back into the road and scuffed the snow across their trail with his feet. "Go," he said, waving them back between the buildings. "The auras of the Masters in these shops will help to hide us. We can follow the cart track to the guildhall."

Jeryl opened the gate to the rutted lane. Hanra-bae followed him through, and Arien closed it behind them.

"Which way?" asked Jeryl. It was dark, and the surface beneath his feet was lumpy and treacherous.

Arien conjured a small ball of shimmer-light. "To the right. Come." He and Hanra-bae moved quickly, and Jeryl lagged behind again.

"How far?"

"Only a hand of gates between here and there. The smiths will not find us."

Jeryl heard a click, looked back over his shoulder to see their pursuers enter the alley. "Run!" he cried. Arien extinguished his shimmer-light.

They found the Historians' gate, and stumbled through into the guildhall's courtyard. Several younglings were stacking wood by the light of a single torch. One of them stopped and addressed Arien.

"May I help you, Master?"

"We are here to see Historian Allya."

"May I tell him your name?"

"Arien of the FreeMasters Guild."

The youngling disappeared into the building.

Jeryl was exhausted. He dropped his pack and leaned against the gate, listening for the sound of the pursuing smiths. Hanra-bae held out his hand, palm forward and fingers spread, offering to transfer some of his own energy to Jeryl's body. Jeryl waved the offer aside. If they had to run again, he would then accept some of the fisher's strength. He heard the crunch of footsteps in snow and felt a presence on the other side of the wall, but no one attempted to breach the gate.

"Arien, welcome!" Allya came out of the guildhall bearing a torch. "You must come inside where it is warm."

"I have brought two friends, the Mentor of Alu Keep and the Master Healer of Port Freewind."

Jeryl held his breath. He was cold and tired and needed a warm, safe place to spend the night. If Allya denied him shelter, he did not know where he would go. The smiths were still on the other side of the gate, waiting.

Allya lifted the torch high and looked first into Jeryl's face, then into Hanra-bae's. "You are shivering. Have you taken a chill? You must all come in and warm yourselves by the hearth. The Historians Guild welcomes you."

Jeryl wondered if Ertis and Inda had found Eiku Keep equally hospitable.

Chapter 8

Sinykin Inda rode beside Ertis, a half-dozen paces behind the Sau traders' wagon. The afternoon sun warmed his shoulders, and helped counteract the pain in his thighs and buttocks. Every little bruise and strain that he had suffered on his ride to Alu was making itself known. He longed to soak in a hot whirlpool bath, and spend the night curled up with Elissa. She would laugh with him, making light of his adventure and his pain.

Instead, he expected to spend this night at Eiku Keep. He looked at the sky, tried to gauge the time from the sun's position, as he had seen Ertis do. The Ardellans measured their day from dawn to dawn, marking midday as the time when the sun was at its zenith, and sunset as the beginning of nighttime. The sun had already moved past its mid-afternoon point, and first-moon Rea was just rising over the eastern mountains. Inda judged the time to be late afternoon, perhaps 16:00 hours by the spaceport clocks. He peered down the road, hoping to see the keep's wall. "I will be glad when we reach Eiku," he said to Ertis.

"Clan Eiku will not welcome us."

Inda was surprised. "Do the Eiku dislike Terrans? Is that why you loaned me this cloak?" Ertis had given him a voluminous brown garment to wear over his parka, to make his alienness less obvious. The camouflage would not hold up under close scrutiny, but from a distance he looked like an Ardellan.

"The Eiku dislike Terrans almost as much as they dislike Alus. They lost a dispute to Alu five summers ago, and are now under our governorship," replied Ertis. "The dispute was instigated by a Terran."

Inda nodded. The dispute must have been the interclan

battle Sarah Anders described in her reports, the contest that occurred when Eiku challenged Alu's right to trade with the Terrans. "How do you want me to behave when we reach the keep? I can wrap myself in the cloak and pull the hood down over my face. Perhaps no one will know that I am not Ardellan."

"Everyone who sees your aura will know who you are, Sinykin. The cloak only makes some of your physical differences less obvious. Clan Eiku will treat us with courtesy. We will be there for only one night, and we will stay at the clanhall with the traders, as members of their party. It would be best if you did not ask to examine anyone, or to take samples for your study. In the morning we will all go on to Clan Sau, where you can continue your work."

"I understand," said Sinykin. He would try to be inconspicuous while they were at Eiku Keep. He was stiff and sore, and would probably spend all his time resting. The road ahead seemed to go on interminably, and Inda was becoming more uncomfortable every minute. He pulled one foot from the stirrup to stretch his leg, and almost fell from the saddle when his thigh cramped. Only Ertis' quick arm steadied him.

"Shall we stop for a rest?" asked the storyteller. "We can rejoin the traders later."

Inda smiled. That would be far worse than continuing to ride. "No. If I get down from this saddle, I may not be able to climb back up. It's best if we keep going."

"Then let me ease your pain. Touch my hand." Ertis reached across the gap between their mounts.

Sinykin caught and held the slender, fragile-seeming fingers. Ertis' aura began to glow with a blue light near the center of his chest. The light slowly spread down the Ardellan's arm to his hand, where it touched Sinykin's fingers. For a moment nothing happened; then Inda felt warmth steal through him, flowing from his fingertips up his arm and into the rest of his body. The blue light came with it, making his aura glow with its sapphire energy. The cramp in his thigh eased, and his bruised muscles stopped aching. He felt pleasantly numb, wrapped in a blanket of warmth. The blue light stayed with him after he released Ertis' hand. "Thank you," he said, knowing that the words were inadequate to express the gratitude and wonder he felt.

As they rode farther from Alu and the spaceport, Inda

saw less snow on the ground. What little had fallen here was dry and powdery, nestled in the fields' deep furrows. The road had been swept clean by wind, but its frozen ruts still made uncertain footing for the aleps. The merchants' cart lumbered along, its wooden wheels bouncing and clattering over the rough ground. The cargo had been covered with a tarp and tied down before they left Alu Keep. The driver nodded as if asleep, while his companions rode ahead.

Though the temperature was below freezing, the day was sunny and without wind. With the pain in his legs eased, Inda could enjoy the ride. He threw back his hood and let his cloak fall open, absently patted the pocket where his notebook and stylus rested. The scrawled notes that filled those clean white pages were his only assurance that he had not imagined Ertis' storytelling of the night before. Just thinking about the experience sent a chill up his spine. He had felt he was witnessing the dispute; yet it had happened many years before his or Ertis' birth. Inda wanted to understand how Ertis involved his audience in the story-telling, and how these vivid memories were passed from one Historian to another. He knew that these secrets might never be revealed to him.

He wondered what other skills these aliens possessed. They created light without fire or fuel, unlatched and opened doors by thought alone, and relieved aches and pains with the touch of a hand. What immense powers and abilities might they be concealing from him?

Inda stared across the fertile fields to the east. Beyond them lay the wasteland and the spaceport, and beyond that loomed red-flecked mountains. Now black clouds hid their summits, and seemed ready to spill down their sides at any moment. In another hour the sun would set and the temperature would drop.

"How much farther is it to Eiku?" he asked, pointing at the approaching storm. The question echoed his son Jaime's impatient inquiries when they traveled together, and that made him smile. This time the answer was a matter of consequence. He was afraid that if the storm caught them on the trail, they might have to spend the night outside the safety of Eiku Keep.

Ertis studied the clouds for a moment, then looked at the trail ahead. Finally he turned to Sinykin. "I think the clouds will bring only a light snow. They are moving quickly, and may reach us soon, but they will not force us to halt. We should still arrive at the keep before nightfall.''

Inda nodded. He eyed the clouds suspiciously, and wished the cart could travel more quickly. A cold wind ruffled the edge of his cloak. He drew the thick wool close about his body and settled the hood over his head. Its weight and warmth were comforting.

In a matter of moments clouds obscured the sun. The wind velocity increased and the temperature plummeted. Sinykin shivered as the cold chilled his fingers. He struggled with his gloves, would have lost one if it had not been clipped to the end of his sleeve. Once he had them on, he activated the chemical heat patches for thirty seconds each. The warmth stopped him from shaking and helped him keep a grip on the rein.

Suddenly Ertis turned his mount off the trail and into the open field. He rode quickly past the cart and the mounted traders, then turned back, waving and shouting.

''Sinykin, come! I can see Eiku Keep!''

Inda needed no more encouragement. He tugged at the rein to turn his mount's head, and squeezed with his knees. The alep plodded into the furrowed field, jostling its rider with every step. Sinykin stared at the horizon, waiting for the keep to appear.

''I don't see anything,'' he complained when he reached Ertis' side.

Ertis pointed to a wavy red line that was barely visible against the distant sky. ''That is the top of Eiku Keep's wall. We are nearly there.'' As he spoke, a big fluffy snowflake landed on the sleeve of his cloak and melted, leaving a damp stain.

More flakes fell as they continued on. The wind died, and the air became warmer. The only sounds were the creaking and jostling of the cart, and the occasional snort of an alep. Soon the snow obscured the horizon, and Inda could see less and less of the trail. He was riding inside a white dome that moved forward with him, so that he was always at its center. The road appeared out of the whiteness ten yards ahead of him and disappeared ten yards behind him.

Suddenly the wall loomed before him. As he moved closer, details became apparent—its red color, like that of

fine granite; the immense size of the cut and dressed stones
that formed it; and the wide wooden doors of its gate.

Ertis knocked at the gate, and one door gaped slowly. A
youngling looked out, saw the cart, and pushed open the
other door. They entered in single file, Inda behind Ertis,
then the traders, and finally the cart. The youngling closed
and barred the heavy doors behind them.

Ertis and the traders dismounted, but Inda clung to the
back of his alep. He stared at the wall, the corral, the stable,
the road, feeling like a child awakened in fairyland. Every
nonliving thing that he saw was made of red stone, and all
of the stone was fantastically carved. The corral's waist-
high wall was a forest of bushes, sculpted with enough detail in leaves, twigs, and berries to look real in the failing
light. The inside of the keep's wall was a seascape, showing
shore and boats, nets drying in the sun, sheds and a short
pier, but no people.

The scene on the stable walls showed neither Masters nor
younglings. Aleps and borras grazed in an open field, and
mountain peaks rose far behind them.

Ertis touched Inda's leg. "You must dismount now. We
will walk to the clanhall."

Sinykin climbed down. The earth felt strange under his
feet, too solid and unmoving after so much time in the saddle. His knees buckled, and he leaned against his mount for
support. The animal was quiet and steady, not at all disturbed by his weight. Inda stretched first one leg, then the
other. When he could stand alone, he unbuckled his pack
from the saddle and slipped the strap over his shoulder.

The youngling led Inda's alep to the stable. The traders'
cart had already been pulled into a shelter and the borras
unhitched from their harness. The others were waiting, their
packs on their shoulders and the hoods of their cloaks drawn
up against the snow and cold. A few big flakes were still
falling, but the storm seemed to be almost over.

They followed another youngling through the streets.
Globes of light, suspended from poles by cables of braided
leather, lit their way. All the structures Inda saw were made
of the same red stone as the wall. Most were carved with
landscapes, or scenes of weird and wondrous animals ca-
vorting in fields or on mountainsides. Where the sun or
moons would be, the artists had carved round windows.
Even the road's cobbles had geometric figures incised into

their surfaces. Nowhere did he see the image of a Master, Mother, or youngling.

The shrubs and trees that lined the streets were not alive but were carved of stone. One tree was so tall that its trunk disappeared into the dark sky before its limbs became visible. Inda stopped to touch it, but Ertis and the others kept moving. Sinykin hurried to rejoin them, stepped on a patch of ice and slipped. His left arm flailed wildly and his pack went flying from his right shoulder as he struck the cobbles. The air in his lungs exited in a single grunt.

"Inda!" Ertis was the only one who turned to see what had happened. He ran back as Sinykin clambered to his feet. Ertis scooped up the pack and offered a hand that the Terran refused with a shake of his head. "Are you hurt?"

"No." Sinykin laughed. He opened his cloak and pointed to his long parka. "I'm wearing so much padding that I don't think I even bruised myself. Give me my pack. I want to find that kitchen and get some hot tea."

The others were climbing the steps of a wide, two-story building. It was also made of red stone, but unlike all the other buildings he had seen, its outer wall was smooth and undecorated. Light shone through the two windows on its front face, and beamed through the opening door. Ertis and Inda followed the traders into the hall, where they were removing their outer garments and hanging them on pegs. The youngling had disappeared.

Inda shrugged off the cloak and hung it by the loop of cloth at its shoulder, as the others had done with theirs. Then he unfastened the velcro at the neck of his parka, and opened the heavy metal zipper.

The traders turned to stare at him. He started to slip off the parka, but Jemma stopped him.

"What was that sound?"

"I don't know what you mean," said Inda.

Jemma stepped closer, backing Inda into the wall. "You made a very strange sound."

All of them except Ertis were looking at him with suspicion. Ertis pointed to Inda's parka, pantomimed the opening of the zipper. Inda fastened the zipper at the bottom, pulled the tab up slowly, and refastened the velcro. "Watch," he said, then pulled the velcro apart. He opened the zipper quickly, this time listening to the sound that was so familiar

to him, but totally alien to the Ardellans. Then he pulled
off the jacket and held it out so they could examine it.

Jemma touched the zipper gingerly. "It is metal! How
wasteful. Ties would be cheaper." He turned and walked
away. The others followed, leaving Ertis and Inda alone in
the hall.

Inda choked back laughter as he hung the parka on a peg.
Then he noticed Ertis' bemused expression. "Have I done
something wrong?"

Ertis shrugged. Inda was not yet able to interpret that
Ardellan gesture, and this encounter did not enlighten him.

"Please, tell me if I have made an error. It is not my
intention to offend anyone."

"You have offended no one," said Ertis. "I was only
wondering why you use metal fasteners on your clothing."

This time Inda's laughter rang in the hallway. "It is no
great mystery. Metal is common on our worlds, and fasteners like these," he touched the zipper, "are often used on
garments. I can get some for you, if you like."

"No! No, that is not necessary. Ties work very well."

"Then let's see if the kitchenmaster has food for us. I'm
famished!"

The hall extended through the building from front to back.
A large, unlit room opened off of it to the left, while on the
right Inda could see two closed doors, and a stairway leading to the second floor. Enticing smells of warm bread and
spice tea greeted them as they passed the stairway. Behind
it they found a short passage that led into the bright, warm
kitchen.

The hearth was in an alcove at the far end of the room,
flanked by clay wall ovens. The crackling fire was being
attended by a youngling. All three traders were already
seated at the long table in the center of the room, with heap-
ing plates of food before them. A fourth Ardellan lounged
on a bench near the door, a mug of tea clasped in one hand.
He wore tanned leather garments, and his long straw-colored
hair was pulled back and tied in a knot at the base of his
skull. His face was tattooed with lines of red dots that
wrapped around his eyes and flowed down his cheeks' natural contours to end on either side of his mouth.

Another youngling approached Ertis. "The kitchenmaster
is not here, but I can offer you food and drink. If you will
sit at the table, we will bring your plates and tea."

"We thank you very much for your consideration. My companion is a Healer, and does not eat flesh. Please bring him bread and fruits."

"We have freshly-baked ground-apples. Shall I bring those also?"

"Yes," said Inda, "please do."

The youngling stared at him as if surprised that he could speak. Ertis cuffed it between the eyestalks and it trundled off to get their food.

As they joined the traders at the table, the other Master rose. He limped across the room, iron rings on his belt clinking, and stood at the end of the table, watching Sinykin.

"You are Terran."

"I am."

The tattooed one turned to Ertis. "And you are a Historian. I bring you greetings from the Historians of the Iron Keep." He offered Ertis his hand, palm up and fingers spread. A blue ceramic tile rested in the center of his palm.

Ertis looked at the tile, but did not touch it. "Extend greetings to my guildmates when next you see them, Messenger. I am Ertis of Clan Alu, and my companion is Sinykin Inda. By what name should we call you?"

"I am Kento of Clan Hai, a resident of the Iron Keep and a friend to the Historians Guild." He slipped the tile into a pocket and lifted both hands in a gesture of greeting. A bracelet of twisted gold ropes gleamed on his right wrist. "I also wish to be a friend to the Terrans."

"I am pleased to accept your offer of friendship, and return it in kind," said Inda, holding out his right hand. Kento let his fingertips brush Sinykin's; the fleeting contact sent a thrill of electricity up Inda's arm. "Isn't the Iron Keep the home of the mining clans? I have been told that they are less than pleased by our presence here."

"That is so," said Kento. "That is part of the message I am carrying to the Historians' guildhall in Berrut."

"You have strayed from your route if you are traveling to the trade city," said Jemma. "Berrut is east of here, and north of the road to the Iron Keep."

Kento shrugged. "I was followed when I left the mountains, so I am taking a roundabout route."

"I would like to know the contents of that message. Can

you share it with me, or is it only for the ears of my GuildMaster?'' asked Ertis.

"It is for all Historians, and for the Terrans also.'' Kento turned to the traders. "It would not hurt for you to carry this message home to your people.'' He closed his eyes, and spoke in a deeper, louder voice.

"Beware the mining clans of the Iron Keep, and the adepts that they have assembled there. Gather your strength to fight them, for they have broken the old laws, and make use of forbidden powers. Their goal is one thing only: to drive the Terrans from Ardel.''

Ertis nodded. "Then the rumors are true? There are weather-workers in the Iron Keep?''

"I cannot say,'' responded Kento. "I suggest you come to the Iron Keep and see for yourselves.''

Inda was both frightened and intrigued by the message. He heard menace in Kento's words, but not in his voice. Could Ertis be right about people in the Iron Keep working the weather? Was such a thing even possible? A week ago Inda would have thought it a fantasy, in spite of the wonders Sarah Anders had described in her journal. The events he had seen and experienced in the last three days made him believe that weather-working might not be beyond the skills of these people. If so, their "forbidden powers'' might have something to do with the electromagnetic disturbances that accompanied the storms and disrupted the navigation systems on the Terran ships. The blizzards would never drive the Terrans from the planet, but the electromagnetic problems might do so. He stared at Kento. "You cannot mean that you want us to go to the Iron Keep.''

"I do mean that. Our Historians would welcome you, and support you in your negotiations with the miners.''

"We thank you for the message, and for the invitation,'' said Ertis. "Our itinerary is planned, and we will not have time to journey into the mountains. I regret that we must decline your kind offer.''

Kento leaned forward and put both palms on the table. He stared into Sinykin's eyes and said, "Do not dismiss this warning. You must come to the Iron Keep. The lives of your people will depend on the knowledge we can impart to you there.''

* * *

Elissa Durant pushed her chair away from the conference table. "We just don't have all the modules we need to generate this kind of shielding," she said.

Tammy Weinberg, the spaceport's chief engineer, nodded. "This project is a little too sophisticated for standard-issue modules. We need some special-order units. Who's going to tell Griswold?"

"I will," said Jeff Grund. "I'll ask her to put in the order tomorrow morning, and to request that it be delivered by a shielded ship. We don't want this shipment delayed by a storm." He rose. "Are we finished for today?"

"I am," said Tammy. She tried to clear the screen of her engineering computer, but it would not accept the command. "Damned antiquated equipment," she muttered, jiggling the interface jack and then keying the save-and-clear sequence again. This time it cleared. She folded the screen down over the keyboard, and unplugged the jack. The entire unit slipped into her overall pocket. "I'm looking forward to a hot meal and a good night's rest. See you in the morning," she called as she left the room.

Grund stood up. "I'll walk you to your quarters," he said to Elissa.

"Thanks, but I have some things to clear up here. I'll stop by and pick up Jaime before supper."

"You could stay and eat with us," offered Jeff.

"Thank you, but no. I want to spend a quiet evening with Jaime. I received a letter from Sinykin today, and I haven't had time to read it yet."

"I'll see you later, then. Let us know if there's anything we can do."

"I will," said Elissa with a smile. She was grateful for the Grunds' friendship, and for their help with Jaime. She knew the offer of dinner was sincere. Perhaps, after she read Sinykin's letter, she would change her mind and spend the evening with them.

"This is not the season for traveling into the mountains," protested Ertis. "We have neither the spare mounts nor the equipment for such a journey."

"Surely Clan Eiku could provide what you need," said Kento. He leaned back as a youngling cleared away his empty plate.

"You could delay your trip to Sau Keep," offered Jemma.

"It takes less than two days to reach the Iron Keep from here. This season there has been little snow on the mountain trails. I would have no qualms about making the journey now, but in a hand of days, that may change."

Sinykin watched Kento. His aura was a soft blue haze about his body. Could he trust this stranger? "What knowledge could have so much value to my people?"

"That you must come and see for yourself."

Ertis was clearly distressed. "This is impossible. We cannot go into the mountains."

Kento raised his left hand and laid it gently on Ertis' shoulder. "There are forces at work here that you cannot command. It is imperative that the Terran come to the mountains, for his sake and the sake of all his people who live on Ardel. It is not necessary that you come with him. Return to Alu, if you wish."

Inda also reached out to Ertis, placing his right hand over the clustered fingers of the Ardellan's left. As their hands touched, Sinykin's fingers began to tingle. The minute hairs on the back of his hand bristled as warmth flowed up his arm. His breath caught in his chest as he experienced a thrill that was almost sexual. Its intensity troubled him, yet he felt a strange reluctance to pull his hand away. He held his breath, and looked into the Historian's eyes.

"I have been charged to guide and protect this Terran while he is outside the spaceport," said Ertis. "He will not travel into the mountains without me, and it is by no means decided that he will journey to your keep. We will retire to our rooms and discuss your proposal in private. We will give you our answer at dawn."

Kento shrugged. "I will be in the kitchen at dawn, waiting for you." He turned and limped from the room.

Ertis slipped his hand from Inda's grasp. Sinykin felt their contact break, but he remained engulfed in tingling warmth.

"Come," whispered Ertis. "We will talk upstairs."

Sinykin and Ertis were shown to a large corner chamber on the second floor. Its walls were hung with threadbare tapestries the color of smoke. The three high windows were shuttered against the cold night air. There was a wooden cabinet for their belongings, and a single wide sleeping platform covered with dusty furs. A small table and two chairs were clustered before a brazier filled with glowing coals; in the corner a crooked stool stood beneath the single burning wall sconce.

Ertis flung his pack into the furs, and a little cloud of dust rose and settled again. "We cannot go into the mountains. I do not think Jeryl would approve of my bringing you this far from Alu; he certainly would forbid a trip to the Iron Keep. We shall travel to Sau Keep with the traders, and in two days we shall return to Alu."

"Why?" Sinykin strode across the room to the brazier and sat on the smaller chair. It creaked ominously when he leaned back.

"I was charged by Jeryl to keep you safe. I do not believe you would long remain so among the miners. They have no love for Terrans."

"Kento made that very clear. He says he is from the Iron Keep, but he speaks as if he is not a miner."

"That is because he is not a miner. He is a member of Clan Hai, the building clan. You must realize that the mountainfolk are not like those of us who live on the plain. They are as different from us as we are from the fisherfolk. Four clans share the Iron Keep, and they have little contact with the outside world. Only a few Masters like Kento ever leave the mountains, and they always return quickly to the keep. Pack trains loaded with copper and iron, silver and gold, come out of the mountains in spring, high summer, and at harvest. They are led by FreeMasters, and return to the Iron Keep loaded with supplies for the winter. No one knows the locations of their mines. They keep secrets and do not trust outsiders."

Inda nodded. "Why do they dislike Terrans?"

"The metals you bring us are better than anything they have produced." Ertis sat on the end of the sleeping platform and began unlacing his boots. "Jeryl says you threaten their livelihood. Already the Metalsmiths prefer Terran iron and copper for making tools, and I have heard they offered the mountainfolk half the usual amount of grain for the summer shipment. The miners did not send a pack train at harvest."

In spite of the coals glowing in the brazier, Inda felt cold. His clothing was damp against his skin. He pulled off his boots and set them near the brazier to dry, then rose and began to undress. "It seems the mountain clans have every reason to wish us gone from Ardel. We have broken their monopoly of the metals trade.''

Ertis brought his own boots over to stand beside Inda's. ''This is not a bad thing. For too long the mountain clans have doled out just enough iron and copper to suit their own purposes.''

''Kento spoke of knowledge that could save the lives of my people. It appeared to me that he was speaking the truth. What is your opinion?''

''He believed that he was speaking the truth. I cannot say whether the knowledge he spoke of would have the value to you that he claims it will. He may be mistaken about its importance. The storms we have experienced this season have been an inconvenience, but they have not cost any lives. If the miners are truly working the weather, they may be spending their time and energy for little more than an early winter.'' Ertis had peeled off tunic and leggings, and was standing in a light shift looking at the sleeping platform. ''I think we shall be a bit crowded.''

Inda heard the sounds of a scuffle outside in the street. He stepped to the window, then pointed to the lighted wall sconce. Ertis extinguished the light with a blink. Inda carefully opened the shutters, and peered down toward the open square in front of the clanhall. Ertis joined him.

Three figures were struggling in the shadows at the foot of the steps. One of them broke free and ran to the middle of the square, where the light of nearly-full Rea illuminated his face. It was Kento. The others quickly followed, catching Kento and holding him by the arms. One of them shouted at him.

''Who have you spoken to here?''

Kento muttered an answer that Inda could not hear.

''Liar!'' One of the black-clad people released Kento's arm and struck him across the face. ''You will return with us to the Iron Keep!'' He pushed Kento toward the stables.

''What can we do to help him?'' whispered Inda.

''Nothing. Those black-clad Masters are from the Iron Keep. This would be considered a clan matter, and it would be wrong for us to intervene.'' Ertis pushed Inda away from the window and closed the shutters. Then he conjured a ball of shimmer-light to light the room.

''I think we must go to the Iron Keep,'' said Inda.

Ertis nodded. "The time has come for me to pay a long overdue visit to the Historians there."

Much heat had escaped through the open window. Sinykin was shivering. He stripped off his clothing, then took a warm robe from his pack and pulled it over his head. It fell in loose folds about his body, the bottom just brushing the floor.

"The trip into the mountains is a long and arduous journey. We must rest and prepare ourselves," said Ertis. He extinguished the shimmer-light with a blink.

"I will join you later." Inda found a match in his pack, and used it to light the candle on the table. Then he pulled out his journal and stylus. "I must make some notes. If the light disturbs you, I can go to the kitchen."

"No, it will not disturb me."

Inda arranged his notebook on the table. He considered meditating, decided to put it off until he had finished his journal entry. He sat down with his feet near the brazier, and opened his notebook.

Recording the day's events took only a few moments and a half-page of paper. Then he pulled a blank sheet from the back and began another letter to Elissa. In the morning he would ask Ertis to find someone who was going to Alu Keep or the FreeMasters' guildhall near the spaceport. The FreeMasters would deliver the letter to Elissa.

Chapter 9

Hatar sat huddled before the tiny fire, trying to absorb every bit of heat that it gave off. He wrapped his cloak close about his lean body and pressed his hands to his chest to keep them from shaking. His mount stamped its feet and nosed around the base of a tree behind him, looking for a few leaves or blades of grass beneath the snow.

The sky above was dark, but dawn would come soon, and he would have to ride again. The FreeMasters had nearly found him yesterday. He had thought about that all night— about how they would take him back to the guildhall and make him live there, far away from Alain and their younglings. He would not let the FreeMasters do that to him. He would kill them first, kill any who tried to capture him. He extended his right hand, fingers pointing at the small woodpile beside his fire. Sparks shot from his fingers, and the wood burst into flames.

He stared at Jeryl across the fire, and reached through the flames with one bare, bony hand. "I can do it, Mentor. I can kill them. Tell them to leave me alone!"

Jeryl sat up and stared across the room. His heart was pounding, and his hands were shaking. The furs slipped off the sleeping platform. He reached for them, and saw Arien sprawled on a blanket on the floor. Jeryl took a deep breath, and smelled the morning smells of tea brewing and fresh bread baking. He was in the Historians' guildhall. The mountainside and Hatar's fire had been part of a dream.

Or had it? Jeryl had experienced the madness of grief when his mate Hladi died. He knew how a FreeMaster could lose control of his newly-acquired psychic powers

and run amok, broadcasting his anguish to all who would
receive it. Jeryl knew firsthand the insanity and despair
that accompanied the awakening of those powers. He
had tried to kill himself, and when that failed, he had
tried to kill those he thought were responsible for Hladi's
death. In the end his thirst for vengeance had been put
to good use on the field of dispute, when he challenged
and killed Eiku's Mentor and saved Clan Alu from Eiku's
greed. The shock of that death had driven out the madness.

Hatar had no convenient channel for his grief. He seemed
to be turning his powers against the FreeMasters who were
trying to help him. Jeryl shuddered. He hoped that he had
merely had a dream, and not received a warning broadcast
from Hatar.

The room was cold, so Jeryl scooped up one of the furs
and spread it over Arien. When they had learned there were
not enough sleeping platforms for everyone, Arien had insisted on taking the floor. He said he was better suited to it
than was Jeryl. Jeryl stepped carefully over his friend. Then
he pulled on boots and slipped a cloak over his sleeping
robe before stepping into the hall.

It was a simple matter to follow the smell of fresh bread
down to the kitchen. The Historians' guildhall was built like
most clanhalls, with sleeping rooms on the second floor and
rooms for meetings and socializing at ground level. Already
a hand of Masters were gathered around the huge table before
the hearth, sharing tea and bread.

"Mentor, come join us," called Arien's friend Allya. "Is
Arien still asleep?"

"He is. Has Hanra-bae come down?"

"Not yet."

Jeryl took a mug of tea and a plate of warm nut bread
from the sideboard, and sat next to Allya. The warmth of
the kitchen and the feeling of companionship helped to dis-
pel the remnants of his dream. He had met most of these
Masters last night, but he could not remember all of their
names. It did not matter. No one seemed to expect a formal
greeting. They treated him as if he was a member of the
household.

"I want to thank you and your guild for your hospitality,"
he said to Allya. "You have been very generous. I wish I
could do something to repay you."

Allya shrugged. "That is not necessary. We Historians depend on the hospitality of the clans and guilds we visit. It is rare that we can offer something more than stories in return."

"You have repaid us well by bringing Hanra-bae to our guildhall," said one of the Historians. "The Healer is already the subject of one story. This visit may become another tale."

"What do you know of the fisher?" asked Jeryl.

Nenno, who was seated at the end of the table, spoke. "I visit Port Freewind often, and I brought back the tale of Hanra-bae's brush with death. His story is well-known among his own people, who consider it a miracle that the youngling Han survived to undergo metamorphosis.

"Han was serving with his siblings on his Master's fishing boat. One day the wind was swift and the sea was rough, and as they returned to the dock, Han was swept overboard. The youngling disappeared from sight, then reappeared, coughing and sputtering. Its siblings shouted for the Master to turn the boat about, for Han was bobbing with the waves, tentacles thrashing and eyestalks waving in the air.

"The boat turned back. The younglings were reaching for Han when one of the ravenous creatures of the deep was seen just below the surface of the water. It was stretching its long tentacles toward Han's body. Han screamed, and reached for the boat.

"The creature grabbed Han's leg and began to drag the youngling under the water. Han's siblings caught his tentacles and pulled. One of them took up the boat's great spear and jabbed it into the eye of the creature. Blood filled the water. Han screamed again, and the injured creature loosed its hold. Han's siblings pulled the thrashing youngling into the boat.

"From that day onward, Han would not return to work on the boat. Han's Mother was indulgent. She apprenticed the youngling to Port Freewind's Healer. Han showed great promise as a Healer, and so was metamorphosed into Master Hanra. He studied long and hard, even coming to Berrut to learn from the Healers here. When he finished his training, he became Hanra-bae, the youngest Master Healer in the guild.

"And he still will not go near the sea."

Jeryl nodded. "Hanra-bae was lucky indeed, and so were the people of Port Freewind. I have watched the Healer work. His skill is great; he certainly earned the title of Master Healer. I do wish that he had spent more time and energy studying his runes. A little more knowledge there would help us out of our current difficulties."

Another Master entered the kitchen. Allya greeted him. "Rissa, what have you learned?"

"There are two Metalsmiths lounging across the lane, watching our front door, and another pair in the cart path in back," he said.

"I fear they are waiting to follow us," commented Jeryl.

"I have no doubt of it," said Allya. "They, or others of their guild, have been outside since you arrived. Are you free to tell us why they are here?"

Jeryl sipped his steaming tea. "There is little to tell. Someone searched our rooms in the inn yesterday, and when we left the inn, two Metalsmiths followed us."

"That they did," said Hanra-bae from the doorway. His hair was disheveled, and the blue tattoos on his face seemed to glow.

At a nod from Allya, most of the Historians rose and took their leave. Only he and Rissa remained at the table with Jeryl, watching Hanra-bae.

"Sit, Healer. I have news for you." Jeryl waited while Hanra-bae fetched a mug of tea and then settled himself on the bench. "Yesterday, while you and Arien walked to the créche, I visited the Healers' library."

Hanra-bae stared at him. "I smelled armata smoke in your rooms last evening. Are you telling me that you went to the library in trance?"

"Yes. Bantu and the GuildMaster were there, examining the scrolls you had asked to see. The information we need is in those scrolls. I saw it through Bantu's eyes before they sensed my presence. They almost trapped me in the library."

Rissa's mouth was hanging open. Allya was less obviously shocked. "Why did you violate the Healers' rules? No outsiders are allowed into the library."

"Hanra-bae and I were there two days ago, searching for some ancient scrolls."

The Healer shrugged. "They let me see the scrolls, but I

cannot read the old runes. Bantu would not let Jeryl translate for me.''

"But what could be so important?'' asked Rissa.

Jeryl slammed his empty mug down on the table. ''The ancient way of creating new Houses! We seek the old knowledge, so that we can reverse the damage the plague has done in the keeps and the fisher towns.''

"A worthy cause,'' said Allya. ''Why should the Healers Guild try to thwart you?''

"I fear this branch of the guild has fallen on hard times, and is now in the pay of the Metalsmiths.'' Hanra-bae tugged at his hair with one hand.

"The Metalsmiths, the merchants, and some of the other trade guilds have little use for those of us who favor limited trade with the Terrans,'' added Jeryl. ''They would like to have open trade. They think they can prosper if they have unlimited supplies of metals from the Terrans.''

Allya shrugged. ''I know the smiths and the merchants seek to undermine Alu. What does that have to do with Healers' secrets?''

"Alu is dying.'' Jeryl's fear and frustration showed in his aura. He tried to temper his feelings, and only succeeded in making himself angry. ''We have lost too many Houses. Another bout with the plague will destroy our clan. The other clans are weakening. The fishers have lost many of their Masters. As we all grow weaker, the Metalsmiths and merchants will take control of the assembly. They will demand free trade with the Terrans. Ardel will change, and the clans will die.''

"Then take the scrolls!'' said Allya. ''Take the information you need.''

"How? I cannot walk out of the compound with the scrolls tucked under my tunic!'' shouted Hanra-bae. His aura was a hazy red cloud that extended a handbreadth from his body in all directions. Jeryl watched it pulse and darken as the Healer's voice dropped. ''The GuildMaster will never allow me to use the library alone.''

"He cannot keep you from using the library, can he? He will not deny you access to the scrolls.'' Jeryl had a plan, but it depended on getting Hanra-bae back into the library.

"I can return and examine the scrolls again, but what will that accomplish?''

Jeryl turned to Rissa. "Do you have some copper wire? An arm's length should be enough."

"Yes."

"Healer, there are two things you must do in the library. You must contrive to open a window in the inner chamber, preferably one that faces the road. And you must wrap a piece of copper wire around each of the scrolls that you want me to borrow."

"Borrow?" Arien stood in the doorway, his eyes on Jeryl. "You should not do this, my friend."

Allya rose, looked from Arien to Jeryl and back again. "Do what?"

"The Mentor plans to use his powers to take the scrolls from the library." Arien's tone made it clear that he condemned the idea. "He will transport them through the window and over the wall by the strength of his mind. How long will it take the Healers to detect your actions and pursue you, Jeryl? I am assuming that you can outwit the Metalsmiths waiting outside this guildhall, and reach the Healers' compound undetected."

"I can do so, if I have your help," said Jeryl. He took his mug to the sideboard and filled it with tea, then poured a second cup and offered it to Arien. "Join us, Arien. It is the only way to save the clans."

Arien came into the kitchen, but he did not take the tea. "And what will you do once you have the secret that you seek? Use multiple matings as the trade guilds do in their créches? Will that help you to create new Houses?"

"No!" Hanra-bae raised both his hands in a warding gesture. "There will be no multiple matings. We seek the formula for the potion that will allow a Healer or a FreeMaster to produce silk and cocoon a second youngling. That youngling will become a Master and witness the mating, but will not take part. It will found a new family line. There will be no matings in the new House until that Master becomes a fertile Mother."

"Then it will be many years before the new House produces younglings," said Arien.

"Yes, it will. And when they are born, they will truly be younglings of that House, not mongrels produced from the mating of four different Masters."

Arien sighed. "I still cannot help you. You have learned

too much from the Terrans. Taking things that belong to others is one of their practices.''

''It is our right to have this information,'' interjected Hanra-bae. ''The Healers are wrongfully withholding it from us.''

''That is Terran reasoning! The fact that they are doing something wrong does not justify what you intend to do. Your actions must be judged on their own merits.''

Jeryl had rarely seen Arien so disturbed. Ruby anger swirled through his aura, which also showed some apprehension and confusion that Jeryl did not hear in Arien's voice. Arien was less certain of his stand than he wanted his companions to believe. Jeryl set down the mugs he was holding, and touched his friend on the arm.

''The very life of Ardel is at stake here,'' he said quietly. ''If we cannot get this information, we might as well close the keeps and the fishers' towns and the Free-Masters' guildhall. Has a FreeMaster ever come to you from the Merchants Guild, or the Metalsmiths Guild? They do not have families, only créches. If a Mother dies before her time, no House is ended. No one suffers the loss of family; no one gains the powers of a FreeMaster. Perhaps their way is better, and we should let the old ways die.''

Arien pulled away from his friend. ''You cannot sway me with that reasoning, Jeryl. I represent the FreeMasters Guild. We serve all clans and guilds equally. I have already helped you more than I should have. Do what you will, and the consequences be on your conscience.'' He pulled a crumpled piece of writing-cloth from his pocket and gave it to Jeryl, then turned and stalked out of the room.

Allya sat with a thud. He stared at Rissa across the table. The other Historian looked back at him, his mouth open but no words coming from it.

''Can you really move the scrolls by mind-power?'' Hanra-bae asked Jeryl.

''I can. The scrolls must be marked so that I can locate them. Will you do that for me?''

''Yes. How will we elude the smiths who await us outside the guildhall?''

Jeryl picked up his mug and gulped the cooling tea. ''We may not have to elude them. I am going to pay a visit to their GuildMaster.'' He glanced at the writing-cloth Arien had given him. It was the message he had received last night from Viela, asking Jeryl to meet him at the inn this morning. He would stop there on his way back from the Metalsmiths' compound.

The Metalsmiths' compound was in red street. One of the smiths followed Jeryl at a discreet distance while the other stayed behind, watching the Historians' guildhall. Jeryl walked briskly, in plain sight, making certain the smith did not lose him in the twisting side streets. The sky was clear and the air cold. The dry snow squeaked under foot. Jeryl's anger kept him warm.

The broad gate of the Metalsmiths' compound was open, and through it Jeryl saw smiths working at the forges. Their only acknowledgment of the season was a peaked wooden roof, supported by six thick poles, to keep the snow from their fires. The Masters wore leather aprons and arm guards, and tied their hair back with thongs or strips of cloth. They worked hot metal on the single iron anvil, taking turns with the hammers. The younglings that assisted them wore nothing at all.

One of the Masters was short and broad, with thick muscles on his arms and thin gray hair captured by a red cloth. Even from the gate Jeryl could see his resemblance to Alu's Healer. Reass, GuildMaster of the Metalsmiths, was Viela's littermate. His body was shaped differently, but his face had the same pointed features, the same determined set, as his sibling's.

Jeryl strode boldly through the gate. "Reass! I would speak with you!"

As one, the smiths stopped working and turned to stare at Jeryl. Their eyes reflected his gray Mentor's cloak. He wore the twin trees medallion of Clan Alu in plain sight. Reass would know with whom he was dealing.

The GuildMaster thrust the blade he was working into a barrel. Water sputtered and steamed. He handed his hammer to another Master and walked out to meet Jeryl.

"You honor us, Mentor," he said, but his aura plainly showed the lie. "What business have you with the Metalsmiths?"

"I have come to warn you, Reass. I know that you are plotting with other GuildMasters to undermine Alu's power in the Assembly. Your guild is withholding iron to help create a false shortage. You hope to cause a crisis that will force the Assembly to end Alu's monopoly of Terran trade, and allow you to trade with the offworlders yourselves. I will not permit it, Reass.''

''You will not permit it? You do not have the power to prevent it, Mentor.'' Reass stripped the cloth from his forehead and shook his hair free. ''The clans are dying. They no longer control the Assembly. Today Mentors and FreeMasters are not the only ones who have power.'' Reass raised his hands high above his head, palms facing Jeryl. Those near him stepped back as his aura changed color; rainbow hues cascaded downward from his hands —amethyst, then sapphire and emerald and topaz, followed by deepest ruby. Sparks flew from the tips of his fingers.

Jeryl was shocked. This was one of the first exercises a FreeMaster learned after he came into his power. Reass was not a FreeMaster. Where had he learned it, and how had he come by the power? Jeryl damped his surprise, pretended to ignore the display.

''Someone entered my room at the Inn of the Blue Door and searched it. Would you know anything about that, GuildMaster?''

Reass answered with another show of power, a single flash that erupted from his palms to reach an arm's length into the air. Though it was a harmless trick, it should have been beyond his capabilities.

Jeryl raised his arms in answer, sending a shower of sparks across the courtyard. These were not harmless. Younglings and Masters yelped, and even Reass dropped his arms in surprise.

''Do not trifle with power,'' called Jeryl as Reass lifted his arms again. ''This is not a game, GuildMaster. If you challenge me, you will die.''

Reass stood very still, watching Jeryl. Finally he let his arms fall back to his sides. ''Do not think you have won, Mentor. This fight is just beginning.''

Jeryl lowered his arms, turned his back on Reass, and was surprised to find Viela standing behind him. ''Well, Healer, what do you think of your sibling's new power? Perhaps you should leave Alu and serve the Metalsmiths Guild,'' said Jeryl as he strode past Viela and out of the compound.

The Healer turned and followed him. "I knew nothing of this, and you can be sure I will question Reass. First there are matters which you and I must discuss."

Jeryl stopped in the center of red street and faced the Healer. He was angry, and he let it show in his aura. "I was on my way to the inn to meet you, but I would as soon transact our business here. What brings you to Berrut when you were told to remain at Alu Keep?"

"There was no reason for me to remain there," replied the Healer. "Sinykin Inda is no longer at the keep. He and Ertis have gone traveling with some traders from Clan Sau."

"Who gave them permission to leave the keep?"

Anger reddened the Healer's aura. "I did not know that they needed permission. They chose to go; no one prevented them."

Jeryl shrugged. "Ertis is an experienced traveler. If they stay with the traders, they should have no problems.

"You still have not told me why you are in Berrut."

"I came to discuss the Terran presence with my GuildMaster, and with some members of the Assembly."

"If you are concerned about the presence of Terrans on Ardel, perhaps you should speak with Reass. He and his guild are campaigning for unrestricted trade with the Terrans. If Reass has his way, there will be Terrans in all our cities and keeps, and their metals and machines will be spread from the mountains to the sea."

"I intend to speak with my sibling about this," said Viela. "First, I have a matter to resolve with you. I arrived at the Healers' guildhall yesterday, just after the GuildMaster and his assistant surprised an intruder in the library. They recognized the intruder and identified him to me as Jeryl, Mentor of Clan Alu!"

Jeryl stared at Viela. "Do you expect me to dignify such an accusation with an answer?"

"I do. Deny it if you can, Mentor."

"I deny nothing."

Ruby rage darkened Viela's aura. "Give me an answer!"

Jeryl would not, for any answer he gave would be an admission of guilt. Viela could identify a lie as easily as any other Master could. "Your rage controls you, Healer. Ask me again when you have your emotions under control." He turned and walked away.

A Master wearing smith's red followed Jeryl all the way to the Historians' guildhall. Twice Jeryl turned and glared at him, with no effect. The smith took up his station across the road when Jeryl entered the guildhall.

"Arien!" called Jeryl as he shed his cloak in the main hall. Allya came in from the kitchen. "Has Arien left yet?"

"No, he is still upstairs."

Jeryl bounded up the steps. The door to the room they had shared was standing open. Arien was inside, fastening the closure on his pack.

"We must talk," said Jeryl from the doorway.

"You cannot convince me to stay."

"I would not try. I respect your right to choose the path that is best for you and your guild. I have other news for you."

"Then come in and close the door."

Jeryl sat on the sleeping platform and tugged off his outer boots. "I have just come from the Metalsmiths' guildhall. Did you know that Reass has power? He channeled energy, and threw sparks from his fingertips. He even sent a blast of power high into the air while I watched. He almost challenged me."

Arien dropped his pack and leaned against the wall. "I did not know. Where did he learn these skills?"

"Where could he learn them, except from a Mentor or a FreeMaster? I am more concerned with how he came by his power. Reass is old, as old as Viela. He should have undergone metamorphosis and become a Mother long ago. I think he owes his power, and the fact that he is still a Master, to the créche. He must have mated at least once. If that Mother—if any of the Mothers with whom he mated—has died, he could have gained some of the power of a Free-Master. With the perverted multiple matings that occur in the créche, it might be possible to build power in an individual Master. Certainly they would choose to empower the GuildMaster. And if the Metalsmiths are doing this, other guilds with créches might be doing it also." Jeryl threw his boots against the wall, watched as they slid to the floor in a tangled mound of leather and laces.

"Are you certain? You were in trance a long time yesterday. Could it still be affecting your perceptions?"

"No, it could not. I saw Reass channel energy. The oth-

ers, the smiths, saw it, too. When he raised his arms, they
drew away from him as if they knew what he intended to
do.''

''If Reass can do this, then some of the other
GuildMasters may have the same power, the same skill.
That is why they are so anxious to have FreeMasters attached to their guilds. They want teachers!'' Arien
slapped the wall with one palm. The sound echoed in the
room; the aura around his hand pulsed gold with pain.
''They want to appropriate our strength and turn it against
us!''

Jeryl shrugged in agreement. Arien's anger touched him,
made him look at the situation from both sides. The
GuildMasters would do what they must to ensure their
guilds' continued existence and prosperity. In that they were
no different from Jeryl. He was fighting for the continuation
of Clan Alu with every weapon he could find.

''Tomorrow I will take the scrolls from the Healers' library,'' he said, watching his friend. ''Hanra-bae and I will
find the key that will make the clans strong again.''

''I hope that you do,'' said Arien. ''I cannot aid you, but
I want you to succeed.'' He pushed himself away from the
wall with one hand, stooped to pick up his pack with the
other.

''Do not go yet. I met Viela on the road. He confirmed
that Sinykin Inda has left Alu Keep, in the company of Ertis
and some traders from Clan Sau.''

''Is this a violation of the trade agreement?'' asked
Arien.

''I do not believe so,'' said Jeryl. ''I did not order them
to remain at Alu Keep. Viela says they plan to go to Eiku
and Sau.''

''Then we need not be concerned. Ertis is a well-known
storyteller, and will be welcomed wherever they travel.''

''That is so.'' Jeryl reached for Arien's hand. Their fingers touched and intertwined. ''We thought Sarah Anders
was safe among us. . . .''

Arien nodded. ''That was a different time, and Sarah
was a different person. Sinykin Inda will not behave as she
did.''

''He has a House, Arien. He has a mate named Elissa,
and a youngling. I would not want to be responsible for the
death of another House, even a Terran House.''

"Something more is troubling you. Why is death so much on your mind?"

Jeryl looked into Arien's eyes. "I have been dreaming of Hatar. I see him, lost and alone, in the mountains. He is running from your FreeMasters and hiding in the ancient forest. His powers have been awakened. I saw him use them. He threatened to kill any FreeMaster who tries to help him."

"We will find him, Jeryl." Arien squeezed his friend's hand. "We will bring him safely to the guildhall."

"Will you send me word when he is there?"

"I will. Let me go now. My mount is saddled and waiting in the cart track."

"Travel safely." Jeryl released Arien's hand, then followed him from the room. They walked down the stairs together, but at the bottom Arien turned toward the courtyard, and Jeryl went into the kitchen.

The sunny room, with its mortared stone walls and huge hearth, felt warm and friendly. Hanra-bae still sat at a table with Allya, talking quietly, a teapot steaming between them. Jeryl grabbed a mug from a shelf and joined them.

"Has Arien gone?" asked Allya.

"He is leaving now." Jeryl looked at Hanra-bae. "He promised to send word of Hatar."

"Good. We have much to do here. I think we can be ready to take the scrolls on the day after tomorrow." Hanra-bae turned his head and a sunbeam brightened his features. His face was still, but the tattoos around his eyes and mouth seemed to dance in the light. He moved again, and the dance ended.

Allya poured tea into Jeryl's mug. "Your mounts are still at the stable. In the morning I will send Rissa to bring them here. We will keep them in the courtyard overnight, with my alep. After you take the scrolls, we can ride down the cart track and get out of the city quickly."

"You intend to come with us?"

"Certainly." Allya laughed. "What kind of Historian would I be if I refused this opportunity to take part in the making of a great tale? I will be able to tell the story of the Mentor of Clan Alu and the Master Healer of Port Freewind, and their quest."

"This is not a game," said the Healer. "We cannot guarantee your safety."

"I have not asked for a guarantee, only for an adventure."

Jeryl gulped his tea, then set the mug aside. "I do not doubt that you will have one. But we must plan it carefully, to make certain that we succeed."

Chapter 10

Inda watched a kite hunting in the distance. It turned above the plain on silent, barely-moving wings, then dove at a target the Terran could not see. A second later it rose, screeching its victory, and circled once before flying toward the mountains. The white body of a coney hung like a trophy from its talons.

"It is getting late. The sun will soon sink behind the mountains," called Ertis. He was riding two meters ahead of Inda, leading a plodding pack animal like the one that trailed behind Sinykin's mount. "We must find a place to camp."

Inda looked around at the snow-covered plain. He saw no shelter nearby, no break in the landscape until they reached the foothills nearly a half-day's ride away. The air was warmer today, though not warm enough to melt the snow, and his legs were not cramping as they had the day before. His mount was tired and tended to lag behind unless Sinykin urged it forward with pressure from his knees and heels.

"I don't think I can reach the hills before nightfall," he commented, his left hand searching the bottom of his pack for a piece of nutbread. "Are there any inns or keeps along the way?"

"No, there is nothing until we reach the FreeMasters' guildhall tomorrow. We will camp on the plain. Watch for a shallow depression that we can clear of snow. That is where we will pitch the tent."

Inda greeted this announcement with skepticism. It suddenly occurred to him that this was not one of the well-provisioned camping trips he had made with Elissa and the children. Ertis had borrowed equipment and food from Eiku

Keep, but Inda was not familiar with any of it. A number of practical questions began to trouble the Terran, and he voiced them. "How will we keep warm? What if it snows? Where will we put the animals?"

"You shall see," replied Ertis. "We will be quite safe." He turned back to the trail, leaving Inda to his own thoughts.

They were not happy thoughts. His current predicament reminded Inda of a lecture his father had given him many years before, on the occasion of his best friend's thirteenth birthday. He and his friend had borrowed a power boat to do some exploring on Lake Havasu. They left the Arizona shore late in the morning, and by mid-afternoon, in the center of the lake, the boat's batteries ran low. They were rowing home when a storm came up. The waves and the wind took them to the California shore before midnight. Both boys were soaked through, and they had no money for food or a recharge. The police called their parents, who drove around the lake to pick them up. The next day Sabri Inda had admonished his son to think carefully and make preparations before taking action in the future. Checking the batteries' charge would have taken only a moment. It was a lesson that Sinykin now wished he had applied to this trip.

The sun had just touched the mountaintops when Ertis pulled his alep up short and pointed off to the right side of the trail. "We camp here."

"I see nothing different about this spot." The snow was as smooth and unblemished as it was on the rest of the plain. There was not even a thornbush to offer them shelter. Inda did not relish spending the night in the open, although he realized that he had no one to blame for it but himself. Ertis had warned him that the trip would be dangerous. Sinykin had expected steep mountain trails and hungry predators. He had not considered the possibility of freezing to death on the open plain.

Ertis dismounted and left his aleps on the trail, reins dangling. They seemed content to stay there when he walked away. The Historian strode through the knee-high snow to a place where the surface dipped to form a shallow dish. He paced a circle around the outside of the low spot. "Come and help," he called to Inda. "We must take the snow from the center of the circle and build a wall around the outside." He began scooping up arm loads of snow and dumping them along the outside of the circle.

Sinykin left his animals on the trail and went to help Ertis. They did not speak as they worked; their breath made puffs of vapor that dispersed quickly in the wind. In a short time they had cleared the space and piled the heavy, wet snow almost to Inda's height on three sides of the circle. The open side faced away from the mountains and the winds. The circle's floor was a thin layer of trampled snow over grass stubble and earth.

The borrowed tent had been loaded on Inda's pack animal. Ertis unpacked the first of its two large rolls, and spread it in the cleared space. It was a circle of thick felted wool that covered almost half the area of their shelter. The second roll was a larger circle of tightly-woven fabric, slit from one edge through to the center. Small loops of cloth were attached to its outer edge. With this was a pole that reached almost to Ertis's shoulder and a bag of stakes.

The Historian spread the second piece of cloth over the first, with the slit facing one of the snow walls. As Inda watched, Ertis walked to the center of the cloth circle, inserted the pole through holes in both cloths, and pounded it into the ground. He folded back the top fabric at the slit, so he was standing only on the felt. Then he raised the fabric and fastened its center to the top of the pole. It formed a limp cone about one and a half meters high at the center.

"Stand here," said Ertis, positioning Inda on one side of the conical tent. He handed the Terran some slender stakes and a small mallet, then went to stand on the opposite side of the tent. "Take a loop and insert a stake, and pound the stake into the ground at the edge of the felt. Draw the tent as tight as you can without pulling the pole over."

They worked on opposite sides of the tent, staking loop after loop until all but the fabric next to the slit was fastened. The walls of the tent were taut, and there was enough fabric left at the slit to form an overlapping door. The tent's diameter was just enough to accommodate Sinykin and Ertis lying side by side in the center. It took them only a moment to stash their food and gear along the inside walls.

It was twilight when they staked the aleps inside the snow wall a few feet from the tent. They unsaddled the animals, brushed the ice from their coats, and watered them. Ertis gave each alep a pile of grain to eat. The animals were sheltered by the walls and could move around a bit, but they could not quite reach the tent.

As the sky darkened, Ertis conjured a ball of shimmer-light that floated above his head and illuminated their little snow fort. The rest of the world disappeared; Sinykin saw only the tent, the animals, the snow, and the dome of black sky above them. First-moon was high above and nearly full, bathing in a river of stars. The quiet blowing of the aleps and the crunch of feet on snow were the only sounds. Inda tried to calculate the time of the smaller moon's rising, but his mind would not bend to the problem. Instead, he asked Ertis.

"When will second-moon rise tonight?"

"Late, just before the night's midpoint. We will be long asleep by then. Come, it is time for us to retire to our tent." He folded the door flap open and gestured for Inda to enter.

The tent was roomy enough to allow Inda to sit comfortably near the pole. Ertis followed him in, holding the shimmer-light in the palm of one hand. He set it in a shallow pottery bowl, and it continued to glow there even when he turned away to tie down the door flap.

Inda rummaged in a saddlebag and pulled out a wrapped package. "Would you like some dried fruit?"

"Yes, I have a good use for that," said Ertis, pulling off his cloak. Then he unwrapped a large package, and set out a bowl, two large beakers, and several stoppered jars. "Would you like red tea, or brown?"

"Red. I think I have some nut bread left in my pack."

Ertis pulled the stopper from the mouth of the largest jar and poured water into each of the beakers. "Save the nut bread for tomorrow. Tonight we will have tea, and porridge cooked with your dried fruit. Will that satisfy you?"

"Oh, yes. I didn't expect hot food on the trail. How will you cook it?" Inda was struggling to remove his cloak and parka in the restricted space.

"Watch and see." Ertis measured crumbled leaves and bark into each of the beakers. Then he took one in each hand, his palms cupped over the open tops and his fingers gripping the sides. He closed his eyes and the ball of shimmer-light shrank until it gave no more illumination than a candle flame.

The tops of the beakers began to glow in the dimness, radiating deep red light between the Ardellan's fingers. Sinykin stared as Ertis swirled the tea. Already he could smell the pungent brew. He extended his hands, carefully touched the beakers with his fingertips. They were warm, and growing warmer.

The shimmer-light returned to its original size as Ertis handed one of the beakers to Inda.

"Drink. It will warm you." Ertis set his own tea aside, and poured water into the bowl. To this he added a small sack of milled grain. Then he dropped in a handful of dried fruit. He picked up the bowl in both hands, palms pressed against opposite sides of the pottery.

Sinykin watched in amazement as the grain and fruit swirled with the water, as if stirred by an unseen spoon. The light dimmed again, and this time Inda did not look away from Ertis. He focused his attention on the bowl and the Ardellan's hands. The pottery began to glow where Ertis touched it, and the redness spread into the porridge. Wisps of vapor rose from the surface and were scattered by Ertis' breath. The mixture thickened, stopped moving, steamed gently. Ertis set the bowl on the felt between them.

"We must eat now, and then sleep. We will break camp at dawn and ride into the mountains."

"How much farther must we travel to reach the Iron Keep?"

"It is less than a day's ride from here. We will eat our evening meal there tomorrow."

They drank their tea and shared the porridge in silence. Afterward Ertis rinsed the beakers and bowl, and tossed the dirty water out into the snow. Then he packed everything away and spread his bedroll beside the center pole.

Inda untied the bedroll he had been given. When he unrolled it he found a rectangular pad of heavy felt, a lightweight woven sheet of the same fabric as Ertis' sleeping shift, and a thick black fur. He spread the felt next to Ertis' bedroll, but on the other side of the pole. Then he covered it with the sheet and the fur. He feared that it would not keep him warm enough, so he spread his cloak over the top.

Ertis had already undressed and crawled beneath the furs. Sinykin thought about making a journal entry, but decided to wait until morning. He stifled a yawn as he stripped, and hurried to get under the covers. The sheet was chilly but warmed quickly, and the felt made a firm, comfortable bed. Sinykin's eyes were already closing as Ertis' shimmer-light flickered and died.

* * *

Something firm hit Inda's left shoulder. He gasped, and his eyes flew open, but he saw nothing in the darkness. One of the aleps had broken loose and was trampling the tent! Sinykin's heart beat fast and hard. He tried to sit up, realized that the thing that had hit him was still resting on his shoulder. It wasn't an alep's foot. He reached up, touched warm fingers. Ertis' hand!

The Ardellan moaned. His fingers twitched beneath Inda's touch. Inda lay still, breathing deeply to calm himself. His companion was restless, that was all. Still, he wished for enough light to see inside the tent.

He felt Ertis' arm begin to shake. Inda rolled over, reached for Ertis' shoulder. It was also shaking. His whole body was shaking! The Ardellan was ill and they were a half-day's ride from the nearest Healer. Sinykin needed light. He sat up, reached for his pack and tried to find his matches and candle-lantern by touch. He would attempt to wake Ertis, and if the Ardellan was able to ride, Inda would bundle him onto one of the aleps and take him back to Alu Keep.

"No!" Ertis sat up, hitting the tent pole with a resounding thump. The fabric fluttered above and around them. Outside, an alep snorted.

Inda found the lantern, pulled it out, and flipped open the compartment in the base where he stored the matches. His hand was shaking. He managed to light a match, and fumbled with the lantern's glass door. The candle lit easily. A puddle of yellow light, reflected downward by the lantern's shade, spread across the floor of the tent.

"Are you hurt?"

Ertis groaned as he rubbed his arm. "No, only bruised a bit. I did not mean to wake you."

"Don't worry about that. You were shaking. Are you feeling ill?" He reached for Ertis' hand, but the Ardellan pulled it away. "I am a Healer. Perhaps I can help you."

"I am not ill. I am having night-starts because I am away from my mate. Do you not miss your mate?"

"Of course I miss her. It doesn't cause me to wake shaking at night."

"You are not an Ardellan." Ertis shivered. He pulled his fur up about his shoulders and sighed. "We both must rest if we are to continue this trip tomorrow. Put out your lantern and go to sleep." He lay down and rolled away from Inda.

Sinykin blew out the candle and lay back down. He stared into the darkness, listening to Ertis' ragged breathing. Sleep did not come to him. Instead he meditated, reaching deep into the earth below for the calming energy he knew the planet could share with him. He drifted on the edge of trance, thinking about his family. Miranda was always close to him when he meditated; tonight he felt very remote from Elissa and Jaime. His reality had separated abruptly from theirs when he went to Alu Keep. Each meter he traveled down this road took them farther apart, physically and psychically. For the first time he began to fear that it was a one-way road, and that he might not be able to return to them. Already he was a different person from the man who had kissed Elissa good-bye. The few phenomena he had seen, like shimmer-light and thought-opened locks and heating water with the palms of one's hands, hinted at many more wonders to be explored. He knew there would come a time when he must choose between his old life and this new one; he only hoped that the time for choices had not already passed.

Elissa sat at the kitchen table, a cup of coffee in her right hand. It was past midnight; she could not sleep. She sipped the coffee. It was cold, and not worth reheating. She set it aside and picked up Sinykin's letter.

"2262:6/29, Eiku Keep

"Dearest Elissa and Jaime,

"The weather is abominable, and riding is more tiring than I expected it to be. We are at Eiku Keep, several kilometers west of Alu, and west and slightly north of the spaceport. The keep is built of wondrously-carved stone. Even the trees and shrubs are cut from rock, so artfully crafted that I expect to hear the leaves rustle. Someday I will bring you both here to see this glorious fairyland.

"Tonight, in the kitchen, a Master from one of the mountain clans approached us. He warned us of problems at the Iron Keep, and invited me to visit him there. He said that Terran lives could depend on the things that I can learn from his people. His manner was brusque and a bit threatening, and I was inclined not to trust him. During the night, I saw him accosted and carried off by two Masters from the Iron Keep. I cannot discount what he told me.

"Ertis has decided that this is a good time to pay a visit

to his guildmates at the Iron Keep. We will go there to talk with the Historians, and see who else contacts us.

"Tomorrow we turn back toward the mountains and the Iron Keep. I have been warned that the journey can be difficult, especially in this season. We will travel with utmost caution. I do not expect to be out of touch with you for more than a six-day.

"Tell Jeff Grund that I have some ideas about the source of those electromagnetic disturbances that accompany the storms. Apparently something or someone at the Iron Keep is affecting the weather, and may be generating the disturbances. I hope to learn more about that when I get there.

"A report for Anna Griswold is enclosed with this letter. If it is delivered to you by mistake, please pass it on to Anna.

"I miss you both. Hug each other for me.

"Love, Sinykin''

The report must have gone straight to Anna. Elissa only had the letter, but it was enough. Sinykin was far away from her, farther than she was prepared to accept. He was journeying into another world, a world where humans too often had died.

Elissa turned and stroked Miranda's urn with her right hand. Her throat felt constricted, her chest tight. A single tear spilled down her left cheek. She had already lost her daughter on Ardel. Suddenly, she was afraid that she would also lose her husband.

Sinykin Inda was dreaming. In his dream he sat cross-legged on a reed mat, a tall white candle in a crystal holder before him. He sat for a long time, staring at the candle. The wick was short and white and bent where it met the candle's tip. It was made of three strands of cord braided together and coated with wax to help it burn. The candle itself was a taper, nearly a third of a meter long and two centimeters in diameter at the base.

Inda was determined to light the candle. That was not such a remarkable feat. It was notable only because he intended to do it without the aid of fire or spark. He would set the wick ablaze by the power of his mind.

He concentrated all his thoughts, all his energy, all his power on that candle wick, heating it up until, with a snap of his fingers, he made it burst into flame.

At that instant someone shook his shoulder. The candle and flame disappeared, and were replaced by the dark reddish glow of bright light passing through closed eyelids. Inda moaned and stretched.

"It snowed during the night," said Ertis in a voice that Inda thought was too cheerful. "We have much to do before we can be on our way. You must rise now."

Sinykin opened his right eye and looked around the tent. A ball of shimmer-light nearly bright enough to blind him floated near the peak, and no light came through the fabric from outside. "How much snow did we get?"

"The *altoara* is half-a-hand deep."

Altoara—that was light, fluffy snow, if he remembered correctly. About six centimeters of it. That explained why no daylight brightened the inside of the tent. They would have to brush off the fabric before they could pack it.

He sat up and began to dress while Ertis untied the door flap. A handful of snow and a blast of cold air entered the tent as he threw back the flap. It encouraged Inda to get into his clothing quickly. They rolled and tied the bedding and set it outside with their packs.

The animals had weathered the night well. They all had snow in their coats, and they were awake and alert. Ertis pointed out a set of fresh tracks near the trail.

"Tol," he said. "Sometimes they hunt at dawn. A big one can take down an alep. We must have frightened this one off with our noise."

Inda looked all around, from the distant foothills to the plain they had crossed the day before, but he could not spot the big silver-furred cat. "Isn't it rather late in the season to see a tol? I thought they followed the grazing herds."

"Some of them do, but the older ones stay on through the winter. I have heard of them coming close to keeps during very hard winters. They have occasionally killed an animal that the stablemaster had taken out for a run."

"Do they ever attack people?"

Ertis walked back to the tent and began brushing the snow off of it. "Rarely. Come, help me with this. We have much to do."

They cleaned and packed the tent, and combed the snow out of the aleps' coats before saddling them. Inda watched Ertis carefully, but could detect no signs of the night's illness. The Ardellan refused to discuss the problem, and insisted that they continue their journey. They breakfasted on cold tea and nut bread before they returned to the trail.

The foothills were not as distant as they appeared to be. Before mid-morning they crossed over a rushing stream and began climbing toward the mountains and the red conifer forests. Inda watched the flora change from snow-covered grasses to thornbushes and leafless shrubs. Beyond the first hill they began to see stubby red-needled bushes decorated with a few clusters of tiny green berries. Small brown birds flitted from branch to branch, pecking at the berries. Coney tracks crisscrossed the trail.

The red conifers were not as tall as Inda had imagined. Only a few exceeded ten meters in height. Their needled branches were weighed down by heavy blankets of snow, and Inda saw only a few of the thumb-sized brown cones. He pulled one from a branch as he passed and put it in his pocket for Jaime.

The trail twisted and turned between the trees, then dipped to cross an open valley. On the other side they climbed again, first through conifers, later past an orchard guarded by a low stone wall. Ertis pointed out the mark of the FreeMasters Guild carved into the stone. They followed the wall as it turned to the left, away from the main trail. Soon Inda saw a gate, and beyond it, several buildings gathered around a courtyard planted with trees and shrubs. Winding paths, carefully cleared of snow, led between the buildings and around a bubbling pool fed by a warm spring. An alep was tied at a post beside the largest building, and several Masters were working in the yard. One was carrying a saddle into what appeared to be a barn, while two others were splitting and stacking firewood in the far corner.

The main building was two stories high, constructed of gray stone. A flagstone veranda roofed with wooden shakes extended along its entire front. The wide wooden door was flanked on either side by rectangular windows, larger than the ones on the second floor.

As they entered the yard the door opened and another Master appeared. Ertis rode toward him and raised a hand in greeting.

"GuildMaster! I did not expect to see you here!"

Inda stared as the Ardellan looked up. He recognized Arien, leader of the FreeMasters Guild, from several conferences at the spaceport. The GuildMaster had always been polite and cooperative, but Sinykin sensed that he was not comfortable dealing with Terrans. The way he looked at Inda seemed to confirm that.

"I just returned from Berrut," said Arien. "Viela was there; he told Jeryl that you and Sinykin Inda were going to Sau Keep. What are you doing in the mountains?"

Ertis dismounted. "The Historians of the Iron Keep have invited us to visit there. We can only make a short stop here; we intend to reach the keep by nightfall. Did Jeryl return with you from Berrut?"

"No, he did not. He stayed in the city with Hanra-bae."

"May the great sun smile on you," said Inda to Arien, lifting his hand and spreading his fingers in the best approximation of the Ardellan greeting that he could manage.

"And you also," replied Arien. "You may dismount and come inside. I will send one of the younglings to water your aleps."

A huge hearth filled one wall of the guildhall's main room. Inda shucked his parka and stood by the fire, warming his hands as he listened to Ertis and Arien talk.

"We could have ridden straight through to the miners' keep," explained Ertis, "but I wanted to stop and speak with Hatar. Jeryl took him from Alu before I was able to see him."

"He is not here," said Arien quietly. "He took an alep and left the guildhall the day after he joined us. Several of my FreeMasters are still searching the mountainside for him. He seems to be hiding from them, running farther down the mountain toward the wasteland."

A youngling brought in a tray of cups and set it on the hearth. It struggled to lift the heavy tea kettle from the fire with three of its four healthy tentacles, and yelped when the hot liquid splashed it. Inda grabbed the kettle and set it down, then bent to examine the scalded youngling.

"Hatar and his mate were very happy together. He will not easily adjust to life without her." Ertis walked to the hearth, picked up a cup and poured himself some tea. He ignored Inda and the youngling. "Will you keep searching for him?"

"Of course," said Arien.

Sinykin looked at Arien. "Is there a Healer here? This youngling's burn needs attention."

"One of the other younglings was apprenticed to a Healer.

It can put some salve on this one." Arien tapped the youngling between the eyestalks to get its attention. "Find naPelit
and show it your injury. It will help you. Do not trouble our
guest any longer."

"It was not disturbing me," protested Sinykin. "I, too,
am a Healer. I only wished to help the youngling." He
watched the youngling leave the room. "I noticed its deformed tentacles. Did it contract the plague?"

Arien strode to the hearth and poured two cups of tea.
He handed one to Inda and sipped from the other himself
as he looked into the Terran's eyes. "Most of the younglings
who come to us were born with deformities. This year,
though, we have received many who were damaged by the
plague. That was one of them.

"Jeryl told me that you are looking for a way to keep the
plague from killing and damaging our people. Why are you
doing this?"

Inda met Arien's gaze with a steady stare. "I cannot tolerate needless death and suffering. I shall do everything I
can to prevent that, among both our peoples."

Arien shrugged and looked away. "I hope you are successful," he said quietly. "Now tell me, why do you wish
to go to the Iron Keep?"

"Master Kento of Clan Hai invited me to visit the keep.
He told me that I would learn things there that could affect
the lives of my people. His manner was strange and threatening. I did not trust him."

"Kento also carried a token and a message from the Historians of the Iron Keep," said Ertis. "He told us, 'Beware
the mining clans of the Iron Keep, and the adepts that they
have assembled there. Gather your strength to fight them,
for they have broken the old laws, and make use of forbidden powers. Their goal is one thing only: to drive the Terrans from Ardel.' "

"It is not wise for you to go into the mountains. I know
Jeryl would forbid it," said Arien.

Ertis shrugged. "Kento was not lying. He believes the
warning he gave Sinykin, and I believe the message from
the Historians."

Arien put down his tea. "Be very careful when you are
among the mountain clans. I have heard reports that they
practice the ancient rituals. A Historian told us that he saw

a weather-working circle when he was there a few days ago."

"Weather-working?" asked Inda. "Ertis also mentioned that. I thought it was myth, invented by a storyteller to enthrall his audience."

"Weather-working is not a myth," Arien assured him. "It is a skill that was used long ago to channel violent storms away from keeps and settlements. In time the Mentors learned that moving a storm increased its ferocity. The storm caused more damage at the next keep it encountered. A minor thunderstorm would grow each time it was channeled around a keep, until at last it would be so large and violent that it could not be diverted."

Inda stared at the tea in his cup. He no longer wanted to drink it. "What happened then?"

"The winds lifted Houses from their foundations; cattle drowned or were struck by lightning in the fields; snow obliterated the roads. Many Mothers and younglings died. Finally the Assembly forbade any further weather-working. I had thought the skill was lost lifetimes ago."

"Until this year, when the winter storms came early and centered around the spaceport. I think I know why Kento invited me to the Iron Keep." Inda set his mug down and reached for his parka. "Thank you for your hospitality and the information. I really must leave now."

"You and Ertis will not go alone." Arien gestured at the FreeMasters sitting at a nearby table. "Lemki, go out to the stable and saddle a mount. Carra, pack your pouch. Quickly! You are riding to the Iron Keep!"

Carra, a tall, slender FreeMaster, quickly climbed the stairs to the second floor. A moment later he came back down, his cloak in his right hand and his saddle pouch in his left. Arien introduced him to Ertis and Inda.

"This is Carra, one of my best riders. He will guide you to the Iron Keep and back. He is personable and efficient, although he talks little. Keep him with you in the Iron Keep. It may help you to have the protection of a FreeMaster."

"I understand," said Ertis. "Thank you."

Beyond the FreeMasters' guildhall the trail was steep and slick. It switched back and forth across the mountainside, through forest and meadow. The aleps trod carefully, all six legs extended for better footing on the snow and ice. They climbed steadily until midafternoon, when Carra called a halt to rest the animals. They all dismounted and shared a flask of hot tea that Arien had sent with them.

Inda looked around at the snow-covered conifers. Something moved at the top of one of the white-draped red trees. He pointed it out to Ertis. "What is that?"

"A fuzzbird. They lose their dark feathers in the fall and grow new white ones for winter. Have you ever heard one screech?"

The bird took off from the treetop, screaming raucously. It circled, flapping its broad wings, then tucked them in and dove at one of the pack animals. The alep ducked its head and jumped, twisting its body. It landed with its two front feet on a patch of ice and fell, squealing. The other animals snorted and tugged at their reins.

Carra dropped his tea and ran to the animal's aid. Ertis followed, shouting for Inda to bring his pack. The Terran Healer pulled the pack from behind Ertis' saddle, stopped to give his mount a reassuring pat, then ran to Carra's side. The fuzzbird circled once more before returning to its perch, squawking occasionally.

"How badly is it hurt?" asked Inda as he knelt beside the alep.

"I do not think it is seriously injured," said Carra as he stroked one of the animal's front legs. He ran his hands down each leg in turn, then felt each of the shoulder joints. He reached under the alep and it flinched and squealed. When he pulled back his hand it was red with blood. The other aleps smelled it and snorted.

"We need to get it back on its feet so that I can see the wound. Help me unload the packs." Carra wiped his hand in the snow to remove the blood. Ertis had already unstrapped the saddle, and together he and Inda pulled it off the alep's back and dumped it, packs and all, at the side of the trail.

The fuzzbird squawked again. All the animals were restless. Inda looked up, saw a silver-gray animal streaking from the woods toward them. "Ertis!" he shouted, pointing.

"Tol!" yelled Ertis. It was heading for the injured alep. Ertis stepped in front of the animal, raised his dagger and slashed as the tol leapt for the alep's shoulder. The tol screamed and twisted as the knife entered its chest. Razor-sharp claws raked downward as the beast fell, one paw tear-ing at the alep's shoulder, and the other at Ertis. Its blood poured onto the snow, and it screamed once more before it died.

The alep collapsed, blood gushing from its shoulder. Inda took one look at it and knew he could not save the animal. Carra grabbed Ertis' bloody dagger and used it to slash the alep's throat. Inda put an arm around Ertis and helped him to the side of the trail. He sat Ertis on the pack saddle, then ran to his own mount for his medical bag. All the aleps were trying to tug their reins free. They looked back at the bloody corpses and snorted in fear.

"Hit them between the ears," called Carra. "It will distract them." He knelt beside Ertis, who sat rocking and holding his shoulder. Drops of blood welled between his fingers.

Inda smacked each of the frightened animals on the head. Carra joined him, and began petting and soothing the aleps. Inda took his bag and went to tend Ertis' shoulder.

The Historian flinched when Inda cut away his ruined cloak and tunic. Both were soaked with blood. Sinykin searched through his bag for alcohol, the only disinfectant he was sure he could use on an Ardellan.

"This will hurt," he warned Ertis as he poured alcohol onto a cotton pad. He cleaned the blood away and found that the tol's claws had caught the top of Ertis' shoulder, then cut downward almost eight centimeters. The gashes were jagged and shallow, not more than a centimeter deep. Sinykin was amazed to see that they had almost stopped bleeding.

The longest cut just nicked the top of a lumpy node on Ertis' chest. Sinykin probed it gently, and Ertis gasped.

"The dormant tentacle is not damaged," he whispered. "I can feel a nick in the sheath, but it was not opened. It will heal."

Inda nodded. He pulled a package of suture tape from his pack and began to tape the wounds closed.

"What are you doing?"

"Closing the wounds so that they will heal properly."

Ertis tried to shrug, and winced instead. "It is not necessary. They will heal from the inside out. There will not be a scar."

Sinykin shrugged and kept taping. When he was done, he put a gauze pad over the wounds and taped it down. He made a sling for Ertis' arm, then went back to his mount for the heavy brown cloak Ertis had loaned him. He wrapped it around the Historian.

Carra was already loading the dead alep's packs onto the other animals. "If we leave now, we can still reach the Iron Keep before dark," he said.

"I thought we would take Ertis back to the FreeMasters' guildhall."

"The Iron Keep is closer than the guildhall." Carra tore a scrap of cloth from Ertis' ruined cloak and tied it over the eyes of the Historian's alep. Then he led the animal to Ertis' side. He helped Ertis rise, and lifted him into the saddle.

Ertis took the rein in his left hand. "I can ride. Take the blindfold off this animal."

"When we are away from the carcasses. I do not want your mount to bolt. Wait here while we get the other aleps," said Carra.

Inda helped him load the last of the gear onto the remaining pack animal. Then they both mounted, and turned their animals away from the carnage. Inda led the pack animal, and Carra led Ertis' mount.

In a short time they left the forest behind. They moved through barren fields dotted with red boulders and twisted, uprooted trees. The trail became a ruined road between two ancient stone walls. There were no gates or openings in the walls; whoever followed that road was meant to stay on it from beginning to end. Ertis and Inda rode abreast, following Carra upward toward the Iron Keep.

They passed a crumbling tower that might once have housed guards. One side of it had been torn away, from peak down to middle, and the stones had been scattered about the field. A kite rose from the top of the desolate ruin and circled twice, then silently returned to its perch.

"Look ahead," said Ertis. "The keep is above us."

Inda looked up; he saw four black towers that disappeared into low-hanging clouds. Below them, a forbidding black wall stretched across the mountainside. Shuttered windows dotted its sheer face.

The road turned sharply to the right, then left, then right again to bring them to the foot of a tall wooden gate.

A guard in a black cloak stood on top of the wall beside a burning torch. He leaned forward and glared down at them. "Who seeks to enter the Iron Keep?"

Ertis straightened in his saddle. "We are Ertis, Historian of Clan Alu; Sinykin Inda, Terran Healer; and Carra, of the FreeMasters Guild. We come at the invitation of your Historians, to visit with them and share tales!"

"Wait," shouted the guard. He disappeared from sight. When he returned a moment later, he pointed to Carra. "The FreeMaster is not welcome here. You others may enter, but he must return the way he came."

"Why is the FreeMaster banned from your keep?" called Ertis.

"The council has said that no FreeMasters may enter the Iron Keep. You may enter alone or turn back. Which do you choose?"

Inda looked over his shoulder at the setting sun. The trail back to the guildhall was steep and icy, and would be treacherous in darkness. Before them was the grim face of the mysterious Iron Keep. If they entered there, would they ever leave? He glanced at Ertis. The Historian's face was pale, and his hand was trembling.

"Carra, Ertis cannot ride back to the guildhall tonight. He must rest so that his wounds may begin to heal."

"I understand," said Carra, turning his mount to face back down the trail. "I will tell Arien."

"We will enter alone!" called Inda.

The guard waved, and the gate slowly opened.

Chapter 11

Hanra-bae wrapped the coil of flat copper wire around his wrist. It hugged his skin, snug under the sleeve of his borrowed tunic. He wore the copper and gold colors of a Historian under his familiar Healer's cloak, but the wire was not part of his costume.

Jeryl was also dressed as a Historian. His usual gray cloak and blue tunic were hidden in his pack, and he wore his Mentor's wristband tucked under a long copper-shaded sleeve. Superficially, he was an ordinary member of the guild, but anyone who looked closely at his aura would recognize his power and know that he was not meant to wear the copper tunic. Jeryl sighed. The disguise would have to do. He looked out of the window at the clear sky and cursed under his breath.

"Is something wrong?" asked the Healer.

"I was hoping for a storm to hide us, but it is a sunny day. We will be seen and identified, and even a youngling will be able to follow our tracks in the snow."

"Then we must confuse our tracks and make things more difficult for our pursuers."

"How do you propose to do that?" asked Jeryl.

"Tonight is Festival. There will be many Masters in the streets today, preparing for the celebration. They will be preoccupied; Allya has promised that some of the Historians will be among them, dressed in the colors we are wearing." Hanra-bae lifted his pack, slung it over his shoulder. "When the Historians see us fleeing with the scrolls, they will distract our pursuers by drawing attention to themselves. If they can confuse even a few of the Healers, we will have a better chance of escaping."

Jeryl shrugged. "Their strategy may help us, but it will

not be as effective as a storm. If Arien was here to aid me, I might be able to call down snow from the mountains." He turned away from the window and picked up his pack. "No, I suppose I would not interfere with the weather. In the end such meddling could cause more problems than it would solve.

"Come, Rissa has brought our mounts. They are waiting for us in the courtyard."

Hanra-bae followed Jeryl down the stairs and out the guildhall's back door. They found Allya in the courtyard with Rissa, holding the reins of two aleps. Rissa held the other two. Allya greeted Jeryl with a dour look.

"We have a pair of problems, or perhaps I should say 'two pair.' The smiths have returned; two are watching the cart path in back, and the other two are waiting for us near the front door. It is impossible for us to leave the guildhall without being seen and followed. Rissa and I have been discussing strategies for dealing with them." One of the aleps nipped at Allya's shoulder. He turned and smacked it between the eyes with his palm. "I think some of my guild-mates can distract the pair in front, and keep them occupied until Hanra-bae and I reach the Healers' compound. You and Rissa must deal with the other two yourselves."

Jeryl buckled his pack to his alep's saddle. "We will find a way to get past the smiths," he said, tugging at the ani-mal's ears. It pressed its nose against his shoulder and snuf-fled affectionately. He stroked its long neck and patted its rump, then bent to check the saddle girth.

"I am anxious to reach the library," said Hanra-bae as he fought with the fasteners on his pack. "I want to finish this as quickly as possible. Can we leave now?"

Jeryl stared at the Healer. Sickly green streaks of fear shot through Hanra-bae's aura. Anyone passing him on the street would know that something was very wrong. Jeryl reached for the Healer with both hands, fingers extended and palms almost touching Hanra-bae's chest. "Calm your-self. You cannot hope to deceive the Healers if you show fear. Touch your palms to mine and I will help you to center."

Hanra-bae's hands pressed against Jeryl's. The Healer's palms were cold and dry, his fingers stiff as they clutched Jeryl's hands. Jeryl felt the fisher's apprehension; it slipped down Jeryl's arms and into his chest, tightening the muscles, stiffening his back and clenching his throat. Jeryl took a deep breath, then another, and released the tension into the ground. Hanra-bae's fingers relaxed.

"Breathe!" Jeryl said, and listened as the Healer inhaled. "Again!" With each exhalation he felt the other's fear recede. "Enough."

Their hands separated. He checked Hanra-bae's aura, found it clear and bright. The Healer could go now, without danger. "Keep your cloak fastened; no one must see the tunic you are wearing until you are finished at the Healers' compound. I will meet you outside their gate. You can change cloaks then."

"Come," said Allya. "Rissa will stay with the mounts until Jeryl is ready to ride. Hanra-bae and I must leave for the Healers' compound. Jeryl, come with us for a moment. I want you to help my guildmates distract the smiths."

They walked back through the guildhall toward the main entrance. Two young Historians, one tall and the other short and slight, were waiting in the big chamber. Jeryl did not know their names. They rose and followed when Allya beckoned to them.

The group stopped just inside the open portal. Jeryl saw the pair of smiths lounging against a wall across the street, watching the doorway. If Allya and Hanra-bae left the building now, at least one of the smiths would follow them to the Healers' compound.

Allya pointed to the smiths. "Keep them occupied," he said to his guildmates. "Recount a story for them, so that their minds will be occupied and they will pay less attention to the guildhall and the road. Jeryl, you must erect a shield between us and the smiths, so that they will not notice us leaving the guildhall. Can you do that?"

"Easily," said Jeryl. He felt out of place as he followed the Historians across the graveled road. Any passersby would think they were all guildmates, in their identical cloaks and tunics. He was discomfited by the deception and knew that it showed in his aura. Perhaps that would help to disguise his power. He took a deep breath and steeled himself to face the smiths.

"May the sun smile on you today," said the taller Historian, one hand raised, his fingers cupped in greeting. "It is cold even in the sun. May we bring you some hot tea?"

The older smith returned the greeting. "Thank you for

your generosity. We have a flask of tea, and there is nothing else we need.''

"Then let us amaze you with a tale. You must be bored standing here in the cold," said the shorter Historian.

"We shall recount the story of Nirra, the first Mother who ever took a seat on a clan's council," added his tall guildmate.

"That is not necessary," said the old smith. The younger one was silent, watching.

"Of course it is not necessary," agreed the tall Historian. "We wish to do it. Do you refuse the gift of a Historian's tale?"

"No, no! Certainly not. We do not wish to offend you or your guild. It is just that we have duties. . . ."

The Historians manipulated the smiths well. Managing the emotions of their audiences was a skill required by their profession. Jeryl had never before observed this control objectively. He was dismayed to see the ease with which they maneuvered the smiths. They controlled their audience in much the same way that he had seen humans interact with and attempt to control each other. Ardellans were perhaps not as different from Terrans as he had thought.

Jeryl stood to one side, where he could watch both the smiths and the guildhall. He extended his right hand behind the tall Historian's back, and created a ball of shimmerlight. Then he spread it upward and outward into a thin haze that provided a backdrop for the visions produced by the storytellers. The shield hid nothing, but it distracted the smiths' eyes and blurred their perceptions of the buildings and objects across the street.

"It is a short tale," said the tall storyteller. "It begins, as many stories do, with a death. In the cold winter of the great snows, after the summer of little rain, in the year we number 4212 by the old scrolls, the mate of Nirra died. His name has long been lost, but it is known that he was Master of one of the original houses of Clan Renu, which sits at the foot of Dark Winter Mountain. He was a member of the clan's ruling council. No one remembers how he died; it is not important. What matters is that Nirra did not die with him.''

The shorter historian took up the tale. Jeryl looked away from him, trying to watch the guildhall's door through the shield and only half listening, so that he would not become caught up in the visions of the tale.

"Nirra wanted to die. Her younglings were grown, fostered out to other Houses, and she was nearing her time of fertility. When she felt her mate's death cry, she tore at her own tentacles, trying to rip them from her body. She hoped to bleed enough to follow her mate into oblivion. But the clan's Healer was visiting her at the time, and he restrained her. He would not allow her to die.

"And so she survived, filled with anger and pain. She would not leave her House and would allow no one but the Healer to see her. One day, as the weather warmed toward spring, he came and told her that the council was abandoning the seat that had belonged to her House. The empty chair had been turned away from the council table and would remain that way until a new House was chosen to fill it."

When his short guildmate paused for breath, the taller began to speak. "This angered Nirra even more. In her years as a Master, she had sat at that council table and helped decide the course of Clan Renu. She could not bear that her House should lose the seat it had held since the founding of Renu Keep. She rose from her platform and dressed in her finest robe and cloak, and then walked through the muddy streets to the clanhall, the Healer by her side."

The smiths seemed to be enthralled by the story. Jeryl was still watching the guildhall; he thought he saw the door open and two blurred figures slip out. Neither of the smiths noticed them.

"The council was thrown into an uproar when Nirra entered the chamber. No Mother had ever interrupted the Masters' deliberations. Nirra demanded that she be allowed to take her mate's seat. The Healer supported her claim, but the entire council was against her. The Mentor was strangely silent."

The shorter storyteller shrugged. "What she asked was unprecedented. No Mother had ever been allowed to sit on the council. This intrusion could not be permitted. The council's leader, an old Master whose name has been forgotten, called the younglings in to remove Nirra from the chamber. He wished to continue with the selection of the new council member.

"Nirra refused to leave. She stood at the foot of the long

table, arms extended and tentacles decently shrouded, and she began to speak. She talked of her time on the council, when she was Master Nirra. Most of those who sat at the table had been younglings then. Only the council leader and the Master who sat at his right remembered. And, of course, the Healer and the Mentor, for they were both very old. She told them of how she had guided the council in important decisions, of her wisdom and experience. Still, they would not be swayed.''

"They would not be swayed," repeated the taller historian as he took up the story. "They did not believe that a Mother possessed the strength of will, the intelligence, the power to make the choices they were faced with every day. They all shouted for her to leave the chamber.

"Then the Mentor rose and called for silence. He sent for his apprentice, and when the apprentice came, the Mentor whispered something to him and sent him out again. The Mentor called upon each of the council members in turn, and asked each one how long he had served on the council. None had served for as many seasons as Nirra had. Then he asked them to consider the wisdom of Mothers, who must guard and protect the lives of their younglings and the sanctity of their homes. Could any at that table truly say that Nirra was not wise and intelligent?

"No one answered him. Then the leader rose and faced the Mentor.

" 'We all know that Mothers are weak,' he said. 'She does not have the strength to be one of us!'

"At that moment the apprentice returned, bearing a bowl of sand and a small wooden box. He set these on the table before the Mentor.''

Jeryl tried to watch Hanra-bae and Allya as they strode down the road. They stayed close to the walls and buildings, blending in with the distorted objects he saw through the shield. They seemed to be moving as quickly as they could without running. The smiths made no move to follow them.

The short historian began again. "The Mentor proposed a test. He smoothed the sand in the bowl, then opened the wooden box and extracted a small square ceramic tile. He held it up for all to see. On it was the symbol of Nirra's House.

" 'We came here today to destroy this tile, for it is our law that, with the death of the Master, the House is dead.'

He laid the tile face up on the sand. 'Nirra feels that she can fulfill the duties of her House. Let her prove it by preventing the destruction of this tile.'

'' 'She cannot possibly keep you from annihilating the tile,' said the council leader.

''The Mentor looked at the Masters one by one. 'I will not destroy this tile,' he said. 'Nirra challenges all of you. You must destroy it.'

''The Mentor carried the bowl of sand with the tile in it to the other end of the table, and set it before Nirra. All the council members joined hands to combine their power, and they concentrated on turning the tile to vapor. A slender tendril of smoke drifted up from the dish, twisting and twining before it vanished in the air currents.''

''Nirra held her palms toward the bowl, and focused her energy into a tiny shield to cover and protect the tile. This little piece of fired clay had been the symbol of her House through all the history of Clan Renu. She must protect it, she must save it, she must keep it intact. This was her only purpose now. She built a shining blue dome of power over the tile, felt the energy of the Masters as they tried to pierce the shield. Working together, they were very strong. She faltered, thinking she could not hold the shield against them, and the shield slipped.''

Jeryl watched as first one, and then the other, blurred figure turned a corner and stepped out of sight. He saw no one behind them, following. The street was deserted, and Allya and Hanra-bae were safely away. Jeryl turned back and pretended to listen to the story as he began gathering the shimmering shield back into his palm.

''Another wisp of smoke rose from the tile. Nirra was afraid now. She thrust all of her power into the little protective dome, and made it grow, expand, until it reached the edges of the table and began to push outward against the Masters. She pushed and pushed until, one by one, they dropped their hands and shoved their chairs away from the table.

''The council leader was the last to rise. He accepted defeat with dignity and welcomed Nirra to the council. And when it was time for him to step down as leader, Nirra, being the eldest, took that place. She led the council of Clan Renu until she died.''

Jeryl pulled the last of the shimmer-light into a tight ball in the palm of his hand and extinguished it with a blink. He could feel the Historians' control of their audience slipping away. The older smith straightened, the younger one stretched. They glanced up and down the street as if they were confused.

"We hope the tale was to your liking," said the tall Historian. "Your enjoyment is our payment. We will leave you now, for we have duties of our own to attend to." He lifted his hand in a parting gesture and walked back to the guildhall, his guildmate and Jeryl trailing after him.

Rissa was waiting in the courtyard with the four aleps, one each for himself and Jeryl, and the other two for Hanra-bae and Allya. They had all been saddled and were ready to travel. Jeryl walked to the open gate at the back of the yard, and peered down the narrow cart track toward Berrut's trade district. Merchants used the walled road to transport goods and supplies to their shops near the city's center. The track was often crowded with borras and carts, but this was a festival day and the roadway was empty, except for the two smiths lounging against the stone wall. They stood between Jeryl and his destination near the city's central circle.

Most of the walls that bordered the cart track were built of stone, and were at least a hand's span taller than Jeryl. The gates were set flush with the walls. The track was wide enough for two small carts to pass each other, if their drivers were skilled. Four aleps running abreast would fill the narrow road.

Jeryl mounted his alep and took the rein of Hanra-bae's mount in his right hand. Rissa led Allya's alep and rode his own.

"We ride abreast," said Jeryl, turning his mount toward the gate. "If we move quickly and keep all four aleps together, the smiths will run from us. They will fear being trampled."

Rissa's aura clouded. "I would prefer not to injure them. '

"I agree. Perhaps we can force them to take refuge behind one of the gates, and we can be gone from the road before they can follow us."

"Where do we go?"

"To the yard of Ismal the tapestry merchant. He buys many tapestries from Clan Alu. He will help us." Jeryl was saddened as he remembered his last visit with Ismal. He and Hatar had come to Berrut to sell some of the weaver's works. If Arien's FreeMasters succeeded in finding Hatar and bringing him out of the forest alive, there might someday be more of his beautiful tapestries to sell in Ismal's shop.

Jeryl kneed his mount forward. It lumbered along on all six legs—this track was too rutted for a four-legged run. He passed through the wide gate. Rissa followed. Jeryl turned his mount to the left so that he hugged the far wall, and waited for Rissa to maneuver into position at the other side of the road. The spare mounts ran between them, pulled up on short leads.

The smiths stepped away from the wall and stared at Jeryl and Rissa.

"Start," said Jeryl, kneeing his alep again. The animal began walking slowly down the road.

The smiths backed away, hugging the wall and watching the approaching aleps. Their formerly brilliant white auras were tinged with green, the color becoming more evident with each backward step they took.

Jeryl pressed his knees harder into his mount's ribs. "Faster," he shouted. He felt every bump and jolt as the alep picked its way over the rough ground. The other mount tugged at its lead. Jeryl pulled it forward. The animals' flanks brushed one another and they both snorted; they did not like these close quarters.

The smiths had stopped watching. They turned and ran down the track, stumbling in the ruts. One fell, and the other bent to help him up. Their auras were brilliant green now, and fear pulsed about them.

Jeryl slowed his mount just a little. He wanted the smiths to find a refuge. One of them stopped to pound on a gate, but it did not open. They ran on, and Jeryl and Rissa pursued them at a steady pace.

Jeryl's mount stumbled. The Mentor gasped as his thigh, recently bruised and torn by the river rocks, scraped against the rough stone wall. His trance journeys had drained his physical resources and kept the wound from healing completely. Pain ran down his leg; he clenched the pads of his foot as new skin tore and bled. Jeryl flinched away from the wall, felt his other leg pressed between the alep's flanks. He feared he would be trampled if either alep stumbled. Then Rissa pulled ahead, giving him room to maneuver.

Jeryl lost sight of the smiths. He followed Rissa blindly, guiding his mount to the smoother parts of the road as they moved faster. Something ahead banged loudly. A moment later Jeryl passed an open gate. The smiths were sprawled in the dirt just inside the courtyard, and a confused merchant stood at the gatepost. Jeryl waved to him as he rode past.

They passed a dozen more gates before Jeryl called to Rissa to turn. Ismal's gate was open, his courtyard empty. Jeryl slid from his mount's back, grunting when his foot hit the ground and jarred his injured leg. He looked down, saw blood seeping through his legging. The cloth was already tugging at the wound. The scrape would have to be soaked with wet compresses to loosen the stuck fabric, and the legging would have to be cut away.

Rissa had already closed the gate behind them. The sweating aleps blew little puffs of moisture into the cold air. Their heavy odor filled the yard, mixing with the smells of compost and borra dung. Jeryl patted his animal's shoulder, then opened one of the packs and pulled out a copper cloak to exchange for Hanra-bae's Healer's cloak when they met outside the library. He folded it carefully and draped it over one arm.

There were only two routes out of the court—through the gate in back or through the shop in front. The back wall of the shop was featureless except for a tall double-width door in its center. Suddenly this door swung open. A young Master stepped into the yard.

"I did not expect you so soon," he said, lifting one hand in a half hearted greeting.

"Ismal," called Jeryl as he handed the aleps' reins to Rissa. He limped over to greet the merchant. "Thank you so much for the use of your yard. Rissa will stay with the animals while I conclude my business. We should be leaving Berrut before midday."

"You have been injured!" Ismal stared at the spreading stain on Jeryl's legging. "Shall I call a Healer?"

"It is just a scrape. It looks much worse than it feels." Jeryl touched the merchant's arm, turned him away from Rissa and the animals. Ismal led the way into the shop, and a youngling shut the big door behind them.

"Best keep your younglings out of the yard until we have gone," said Jeryl. "They are not accustomed to aleps."

"I will. Why are you wearing Historian's garb?"

"They were very kind to loan it to me." Jeryl's aura showed he was being evasive. He knew that courtesy would keep Ismal from probing further. "I must be on my way. Again I offer my appreciation for the use of your yard."

The shop opened onto gray street, three buildings away from Berrut's central circle. The Healers' library was almost straight across the circle, which meant that Jeryl had to skirt the assembly hall in its center. Allya had been correct; the streets were crowded with Masters freed from their workshops for the holiday. Most were dressed in their Festival finery—bright cloaks and tunics over dark leggings and soft boots. They strolled through the streets, talking and staring into shop windows.

Jeryl tried to hurry. The faster he moved, the more he limped. His leg ached from hip to knee, and his blood-soaked legging was beginning to freeze in the cold. He pulled his cloak closed in front, to keep the wind away from his leg.

He saw no familiar faces. No one seemed to pay attention to him as he threaded his way around the crowded circle. He was close to the library when he suddenly felt a familiar, and unwelcome, presence nearby. Viela was somewhere between Jeryl and his goal.

Jeryl tugged his hood forward to hide his face, knowing that it was a futile gesture. Viela would recognize him as easily as he had recognized the Healer. The only way to avoid this encounter was to keep moving.

Viela crossed the street, and stopped in front of Jeryl. Jeryl tried to step around him, but Viela moved to the right to block his path. Jeryl's cloak fell open, and the Healer saw the copper tunic beneath it.

"Why are you wearing Historian's garb?"

Jeryl flipped back his hood and glared at Viela. "Why does my clothing concern you, Healer?"

"It does not," said Viela as he stared at the stain on Jeryl's legging. He reached toward it with his right hand, to sense the extent of the damage. "Your injury concerns me. Come with me to the compound. I will clean the wound and bandage it for you."

"There is no need," said Jeryl.

"There is indeed a need," replied Viela, reaching for Jeryl's thigh. "Your leg is bleeding."

"Do not touch it!" Jeryl stepped back, letting the anger he felt redden his aura. "I will tend to it later. Tell me, did you speak with Reass yesterday? What did your sibling tell you about his newly acquired powers?"

Viela looked up; his eyes locked on Jeryl's. "That is not your affair. You did not answer my question yesterday. I ask you again, Jeryl, were you in the Healers' library two days ago, unescorted and without permission?"

"If I was, what would you do about it?" Jeryl glanced over Viela's shoulder; across the road, the gate to the Healers' compound was opening. Hanra-bae should have finished marking the scrolls, and would be expecting Jeryl to meet him at the gate in a moment.

"It is not up to me to punish you." Jeryl stared into Viela's eyes. They were dark with anger, but the Healer's aura was brilliant white. Jeryl could feel his righteous rage across the arm's length of space that separated them. "The Assembly will demand reparations in the name of the Healers Guild."

"Then let them do so," said Jeryl. He could see Hanra-bae and Bantu standing at the Healer's gate. They were having an animated discussion. "This is your third day in Berrut, is it not? You should be on your way back to Alu Keep. How long have you been absent from your duties?"

A ruby flush darkened Viela's aura. "I have an appointment today. When my business is completed, I will be leaving for Alu."

Jeryl looked across the way. He saw Hanra-bae give Bantu a parting nod and step out of the Healers' compound. Bantu closed the gate behind him. Hanra-bae stood for a moment, scanning the crowd. His Healer's cloak was still fastened, and his medallion shone proudly on its breast. He saw Jeryl and started to cross the road toward him.

Where was Allya? Jeryl did not want Hanra-bae and Viela to meet. He turned back to the Healer. "Then I suggest you go about your business!"

"I shall! See that you have someone attend to that leg!" Viela stalked off in the direction of red street and the Metalsmiths' guildhall.

Jeryl sighed. What else could go wrong? No, do not think such thoughts, he told himself. They always seemed to invite disaster. He went forward to meet Hanra-bae.

"Where is Allya?"

Hanra-bae pointed to a bench across from the Healers' gate, under the eave of the assembly hall. Allya sat there, arms folded and robe wrapped about him like a cocoon. He seemed to be meditating, but he acknowledged Jeryl's nod with a dip of his head.

Jeryl and Hanra-bae walked to the wall of the Healers' compound, to the place closest to the open library window. There, Hanra-bae exchanged his Healer's cloak for the copper one Jeryl had brought, and tucked his medallion inside his tunic. Jeryl leaned against the wall, and the fisher stood before him, pretending to converse. They looked like a pair of Historians out for a holiday stroll.

"I marked the scrolls with copper wire as you asked," said Hanra-bae quietly. "Bantu left me for only a moment, so I had to work quickly. There are five scrolls in all. I left the window open a hand's span, with a scroll rack partially hiding the opening."

"Keep talking," said Jeryl. More Historians had appeared in the circle, walking and talking together. They formed a kind of vanguard around Jeryl and Hanra-bae, moving others away without seeming to do so.

Jeryl ignored Hanra-bae's words. He pressed his back against the wall, leaned his head back to touch the stone, and flattened both palms against the wall at his sides. The rock was old and tired, fatigued in a way that made it weak. He felt through it for the library wall, the little room, the racks and piles of scrolls. In a few places he touched bright copper. With his mind's eye he saw the shape of the room, the table just under the open window, the rack of scrolls pulled partway across the opening. The room was empty of life.

He reached for one of the copper-tagged scrolls. He imagined himself lifting it, carrying it to the table. It was heavier than he remembered, and he knew that this was because he was lifting it with his mind rather than his hand. He settled the scroll carefully before the open window, then crossed the room to get the second.

He was sweating when he put the third scroll on the table. He was halfway to the fourth when he sensed a presence at the door of the little room. Surprise sent his mind straight back to join his body.

". . . and we shall overcome it." Hanra-bae was mumbling nonsense.

Jeryl sagged forward, losing much of his contact with the wall. He tried to straighten up, took a deep breath and was surprised at how cold his body felt. His fingers were stiff, his legs shaking, and beads of sweat were freezing on his brow. He wiped his face with a corner of his cloak.

"Where are the scrolls?" asked Hanra-bae quietly.

"They are still in the library," said Jeryl. "I was startled by someone moving about in there. I must go back for the scrolls."

"You are exhausted!"

"The shield I made to help you escape from the smiths took more energy than I expected it would." Jeryl shivered.

Hanra-bae pressed his right palm against the center of Jeryl's chest. "Close your eyes," he whispered. "I will give you some of my energy."

The Healer twisted his hand, and Jeryl felt warmth and power flood into his body. He breathed deeply and let the energy flow into his back, his legs, his arms, and fingers. His whole body tingled with renewed strength. Jeryl stopped trembling, and Hanra-bae removed his hand.

Jeryl did not want to return to that dark and musty library, but there was no other way to get the scrolls. He pressed his body back against the wall, and cautiously let his mind slip through. He paused at the window and scanned the library for changes.

The door between the main room and the one containing his scrolls was standing open. Bantu sat at a table in the outer room, reading. Jeryl watched and waited, hoping he would leave. Bantu set aside the scroll he was studying and reached for another.

Three of Jeryl's scrolls were just inside the window, close enough that he could lift them and carry them through the window without disturbing Bantu. The other two were on a table across the room. There was no way to move them without risking discovery, yet Hanra-bae said he needed all of the scrolls. Jeryl dare not leave those two behind.

Jeryl reached for the fourth scroll. He imagined himself moving stealthily, cloaked in an aura of invisibility. He crept across the room, keeping his imagined body bent low and the scroll near the floor. It was difficult, and used more energy than moving all the other scrolls.

He went back across the room for the last one. He was tired, and this was more work than he had thought it would be. He wanted to be done with it. He picked up the heavy scroll and started toward the window. The imaginary hand that held the scroll was shaking. Jeryl steadied his thoughts, moved more slowly. It was not enough. He felt the soft thud as the scroll bumped the edge of a wooden rack.

Bantu turned to look into the little room. Jeryl tried to be very still. Bantu pushed back his chair, rose, and walked toward the doorway.

Jeryl's mind flew across the room, gathered up all five scrolls, and levitated them through the window. He knew Bantu was watching; Jeryl could hear him shouting for assistance. The scrolls were outside, between the building and the wall. Jeryl lifted them high, higher, over the top of the wall, and with a sigh of relief let them fall.

He heard Hanra-bae's exclamation of surprise, heard him scrambling to pick up the scattered scrolls. He sensed much activity behind the wall. Bantu was running and shouting, organizing pursuit. They dared not stay here any longer. Jeryl opened his eyes.

There were many Masters near them, and at least half of them were Historians. They had miraculously cleared a path around the assembly hall toward gray street. Allya was walking toward them. Hanra-bae held up the last scroll.

"Run!" shouted Jeryl. Bantu would be coming through the gate in a moment. Allya turned and raced across the circle. Hanra-bae stuffed the scroll into a pocket in his cloak. Jeryl waved him on ahead. The gate was opening, the Historians beginning to close in around it. Jeryl knew that they would block the path behind him.

He ran. It was a relief to stretch muscles that had stiffened from standing in the cold. The energy Hanra-bae had shared with him still coursed through his body, powering his legs as he ran. He was hungry and thirsty, but he must wait to satisfy those needs. Every stride jarred his body, hurt his chilled feet, and tore the frozen legging from his thigh even as the movement warmed him. He felt damp stickiness on his leg as the scrape began to ooze blood again. There was shouting behind him, and he ran faster, following Allya and Hanra-bae around the turn into gray street.

They had counted on having more time before they were pursued. Hanra-bae ran with the gait of a lame wool-deer, his cloak and its burden of hidden scrolls flapping and tangling about his legs. Even limping, Jeryl passed him. He could see the front of Ismal's shop; several Masters were looking in through the window. Allya slowed his pace, passed the Masters, and strolled sedately into the shop.

Jeryl stopped running. He grabbed Hanra-bae's arm as the Healer came abreast of him. "Walk," he said quietly. "We must go through the tapestry shop to reach our mounts."

The Masters had turned away from the window, and were walking toward Hanra-bae and Jeryl. Two of them wore Metalsmiths' colors. Jeryl looked at the ground at his feet. He wished he could hide his face with his hood, but running had thrown it back over his shoulders. If the smiths recognized him there would be trouble.

They passed without incident. Jeryl led Hanra-bae into the shop. He waved a greeting to Ismal, who was busy with a customer, and followed Allya to the courtyard.

Rissa had turned the aleps to face the open gate. He was already scrambling into his saddle. Jeryl ran to his mount, swung up on its back despite the pain in his thigh. "Move," he shouted, waving for the others to precede him. He heard shouting at the front of the shop.

Running footfalls thudded on the shop's wooden floor. Jeryl followed the others through the gate, turned to grasp the handle, and saw Bantu and some other Healers run from the shop. The smiths were behind them. Jeryl pulled the gate shut, and kneed his mount to a run. The others were already flying down the cart track toward the edge of the city. He hoped none of the animals tripped in the ruts.

There was more shouting behind him, in the cart track this time. The words echoed from wall to wall; their sense was lost before they reached Jeryl. He knew the Healers could not catch him on foot, but they were not giving up pursuit.

Because of the holiday, the merchants were not transporting goods. The track seemed clear ahead. Allya and Rissa rode abreast, leading Jeryl and Hanra-bae quickly away from the center of Berrut. They passed the Historians' gate; it was tightly closed. Then Allya shouted in anger.

"Let us pass!"

Rissa dropped back, and Jeryl could see a team of borras on the path several lengths ahead of Allya. They were wearing harness and pulling out into the track from a wide gate. Allya was almost upon them when the cart appeared, carrying a load so wide that it blocked their path. Allya's mount was nose-to-nose with the borras. Allya turned his alep sharply to the side, and disappeared through the open gate into a courtyard. The startled merchant stared after him.

Jeryl slowed his alep's pace and followed the others into the courtyard. A glance back down the track told him that their pursuers were gaining ground.

"Go!" Allya shouted at the merchant. "Move your cart forward! We want to get around you!"

The merchant just stared at him. Jeryl heard Bantu shouting, telling the merchant to stay where he was. They would be trapped here!

Rissa rode to the gate, leaned out and tugged the reins away from the merchant. He dropped them and slapped one of the borras hard on its rump. The animal brayed and started forward, forcing its partner to move. Still the merchant said nothing.

The cart moved forward. Allya squeezed his mount between it and the far side of the gate. Hanra-bae followed. Jeryl looked back, saw Bantu and a pair of smiths trying to clamber over the cart, which was still moving forward. He kneed his mount, followed Rissa through the widening opening.

The track ahead was again clear. They rode quickly and soon lost their pursuers. Jeryl wondered idly if Bantu had recognized him. It did not matter. He had the scrolls.

They stopped in a grove of fruit trees outside Berrut. Jeryl and Hanra-bae dismounted, hid the scrolls in one of Jeryl's packs, and returned their borrowed cloaks and tunics to Rissa.

"Thank you for your help." Jeryl pulled on his familiar Alu tunic. "The Healers will be very angry with your guild."

"There is little they can do against us," said Allya. "They know that two Masters wearing Historians' garb took the scrolls, but we can truthfully say that they are not members of our guild. We have much support among the clans and guilds; the Healers will not challenge us."

"I hope that you are correct," said Hanra-bae. "Jeryl, let me see your leg."

"There is no time for that, Healer. We must ride now if we hope to reach our destination before dark." Jeryl tried not to wince as he swung up into the saddle.

Hanra-bae started to protest, but a sharp glance from Jeryl stopped him. He tucked up his Healer's cloak and re-mounted. "May the sun smile on you and your guild," he said to Allya and Rissa.

"And on you." The Historians turned their aleps back toward the city and the stables.

"Come," said Jeryl. "We have far to go." He led the way toward the mountains.

Chapter 12

"Aboard *Manatee?*" Jeff Grund threw up his hands. "Why did the Trade Commission put those modules on *Manatee?* That's an unshielded ship. It won't be able to land if there's a storm. And we can't get our shields up and running to protect the ship's navigation systems until we have those modules!"

Anna Griswold nodded. She looked around the conference table at the rest of her staff. "I requested that they ship the modules aboard a shielded military craft. Sandsmark's office reports that there's some sort of disturbance on Heller's World, and most unassigned military ships have been diverted to sector eight until it's resolved. There won't be a shielded transport available for at least twenty days. They decided not to wait, and sent a shuttle out to intercept *Manatee*. Now we have to hope for good weather. What's the forecast?"

"More storms are coming," said Grund. "We have a slight chance of snow flurries tomorrow, and a chance of heavier snowfall the day after. There's a storm front gathering force up in the mountains. We should have three or four days before it moves down to the plain. Then we'll have another blizzard, probably accompanied by electromagnetic disturbances."

"*Manatee* may be able to land before that happens. If she can't, she'll leave the modules at her next stop, and the next ship through will bring them to us. That may take a few weeks. Marta, what's our supply situation if *Manatee* doesn't land?" asked Griswold.

"We're almost out of diet supplements for the chickens. I recommend slaughtering three-quarters of the flock. That way we'll have enough supplements to keep the rest of them healthy until we can get the shield working and start receiving our regular supply shipments." Marta Grund punched a key and checked the screen of her inventory computer. "We can freeze most of the meat, and what we can't freeze, we can eat. The flock will still be large enough to be genetically viable."

"All right," said Griswold. "Are there any other shortages at this time?"

Marta shook her head. "Nothing critical. We may have to open some of our emergency stores if *Manatee* can't land. We're running low on paper, detergent, and some minor maintenance components. I've checked with Medical Services; they're still well-stocked. My staff will post a conservation bulletin on line to all computer terminals this afternoon."

"Then let's move on to Security. Alec, yesterday I received this report from Sinykin Inda." Griswold handed a sheet of paper to Security Chief Harwood. "He has abandoned his original mission, and is heading into the mountains in the company of a native 'Historian' named Ertis."

Elissa stared at the Administrator. What was Griswold doing? When had Sinykin's activities outside the compound become a subject of concern to spaceport security, or even a topic of discussion at the morning staff meeting? Elissa knew the answer: when Sinykin had left the compound against Griswold's wishes. Sinykin was head of the Science Division, and as such Secretary Sandsmark had granted him limited freedom to act outside the stated policies of the administration. It seemed that Griswold was about to curtail that freedom.

"I believe Dr. Inda's actions may be in violation of our trade agreement with the Ardellans. His actions may have jeopardized our position on this world. He has almost certainly placed himself in danger by traveling outside Alu Keep. I hope that he will not share Sarah Anders' fate." Griswold looked at Elissa, and sighed. "I am considering filing a petition with the Trade Commission to have Dr. Inda recalled from Ardel. I will delay making a decision on that matter until we have resolved the present crisis. Meanwhile, I have sent a message to Inda, requesting that he immediately return to the spaceport. The FreeMaster who took the message told me it might be several days before it can be delivered.

"I want an additional security guard stationed at the gate pending Inda's return. The spaceport grounds are now closed. No one will be allowed to leave the compound."

Recall! Elissa clenched her hands under the table. Griswold could request that Sinykin be recalled, but Secretary Sandsmark would never agree to it. Sandsmark had chosen Sinykin for this posting and had promised him the position of envoy. He wouldn't go back on his word. Would he?

A beam of light struck Sinykin Inda's face. His eyelids popped open, then closed tightly against the brightness of the morning. He yawned, stretched, and opened his right eye just far enough to peer around the unfamiliar room. He could see little of the far wall. Sunlight streamed in through cracks around the shutters, blinding him when he looked in that direction. The walls near his bed were dismal gray stone, adorned by neither tapestries nor carvings. The floor was made of the same stone, smoothed by the steps of many feet. Smoky black circles marred the uniform gray of the high ceiling. There was no brazier, no hearth, no warmth. Sinykin shivered.

The sleeping platform was broad enough for two people to share it in comfort. Sinykin remembered wandering into the room in darkness, after he and Ertis had eaten and Ertis had been settled in his own bed. Inda had collapsed on the right side of the platform, on top of the furs. He was still wearing his clothes, except for the heavy parka that he had stripped off after they entered the clanhall.

His chronometer told him that he had slept until nearly mid-morning. Inda sat up, saw the mess his muddy boots had made on the furs. He smelled of blood and stale sweat and dried earth. He wanted to strip, wash, and put on clean clothing, but his packs were not in the room, and he saw no sanitary facilities. Instead he rose and walked to the door that joined his and Ertis' rooms.

Sinykin knocked twice.

"Enter," called Ertis. The latch clicked and the door swung slowly inward.

Ertis was sitting at the head of his sleeping platform, leaning back against the wall. The bandages that Sinykin had applied to his shoulder were strewn across the floor. A stranger stood beside Ertis, examining his wounds. As

Sinykin watched, the stranger removed one of the suture tapes and dropped it next to the bandages.

"Don't do that!" cried Inda as he ran toward Ertis. "The gashes will reopen if you remove the sutures."

"Do not be concerned," said Ertis. "The skin has already closed."

Sinykin stopped beside the bed and stared at Ertis' shoulder. The smooth skin was marred by four thin, jagged red lines, the only visible evidence of yesterday's injury. He touched the shoulder gently, and when Ertis did not flinch, ran an index finger over the red welts. The wounds were healing cleanly, without puckering. The injured tentacle nodule was neither enlarged nor tender.

The stranger pulled off the last piece of tape before turning to look at Inda. "You cleaned and bandaged the wounds very well. Have you been trained as a Healer?"

"Yes, I am a Healer. My name is Sinykin Inda."

"I am Satto, Healer of the smelting clan. I hope you spent a restful night. Had we known you were coming, we would have brought in a brazier and heated the rooms."

Inda shrugged. "The room is fine," he said. He was thinking of Sarah Anders' journal. In several passages she described the Ardellans' miraculous ability to recover quickly from burns and other injuries. He had believed her claims were exaggerations. She was not a physician and could not judge the true extent of a wound. Now he knew that she had not overestimated the power of these people to heal themselves.

"Our trip was arranged rather suddenly," said Ertis, reaching for a robe. "I received a message from your Historians and decided to visit them. Are either Perli or Vaant available?"

"I do not know." Satto gathered his tools and ointment jars and placed them into a stiff leather bag. "I have not seen either of them for several days."

Ertis wrapped the robe around his bare shoulders. "We will check later at the clanhalls of the builders and the herders."

"That is a beautiful wristband," said Inda. "Are you free to tell me if it has a significance other than ornamentation?"

Satto pulled back the sleeve on his right arm to show a wristband of twisted silver and copper wires. "This is the emblem of the smelting clan. Members of each of the Iron Keep's four clans wear a different type of wristband. That of the builders is made of thick gold wires, twisted together."

"I once met a builder," said Ertis. "His name was Kento. He said he was a member of Clan Hai. Can you tell me where to find his clanhall?"

"It is in the northwestern corner of the keep. You might find him there."

"Thank you for the information and for attending to my wounds. Your help is much appreciated." Ertis rose and walked Satto to the door. They were still a few strides away when something clattered in the hall. The door swung inward to reveal a pair of younglings stooping before the threshold. A wooden tray lay on the floor between them, and cups, bowls, and utensils were scattered across the flagstones.

One youngling scooped up a rolling bowl with one tentacle, a mug with another, and deposited both on the tray. The other, its eyestalks crossed, appealed to Satto. "It was an accident, Master. The tray slipped."

Sinykin could not hide his amusement. A laugh burst from his mouth and rolled out to echo from the walls. The others turned to stare at him. He pointed to the younglings. "They look so . . . so . . ." he did not know the Ardellan word, so he used a Terran one, "silly!" He succumbed to a giggling fit, as much a response to the tensions of the past few days as to the younglings' antics. Wrapping his arms across his chest, he held his sides and bent almost double as tears welled in his eyes. He gasped and choked, unable to catch his breath.

"Are you hurt?" Satto sounded alarmed.

Ertis took Inda's arm and led him to a chair. "He is well. He finds the younglings humorous."

"They are incompetent bunglers, fit only for cleaning stables. They will be dismissed!"

"No." Sinykin straightened up and drew a long, shuddering breath. "Please do not dismiss them. I am sorry that my outburst disturbed you."

The younglings finished collecting the utensils and stacked them neatly on the tray. They lifted it together, carried it into the room, and set it on the table. Satto watched disapprovingly as they gathered the dirty plates and mugs from last night's meal.

"These two are called naReina and naLeera. They are littermates born to Clan Hai, and have been in service here for several seasons. They each wear the circle of twisted gold. Perhaps they can lead you to Master Kento." Satto nodded to Sinykin and Ertis, then left the room.

Sinykin glanced at Ertis, wondering if the Historian was angry with him for creating such a scene. "I shouldn't have upset the Healer," he began, but Ertis cut him off.

"That one could find offense in an alep's sneeze! Do not be concerned about his sensibilities. We have more important things to deal with, such as breakfast."

The younglings had put all of the dirty dishes on their tray, and were carefully wiping and setting out the clean bowls and utensils. One of them paused and looked at Ertis. "We will bring your breakfast from the kitchen."

"I hope you will be more careful with it than you were with this tray!" said Ertis.

"Yes! Yes!" said the younglings in unison. They picked up the laden tray and trundled toward the door. A cup slipped off a pile of plates and rolled across the tray. One of the younglings squealed and grabbed the cup with a tentacle, and they scurried over the threshold and down the hall.

Sinykin laughed again. This time he managed not to lose his breath. "My bladder is bursting."

"Behind the curtain," said Ertis, pointing. "And in the communal room beyond that there is even a pool. The water is very cold. Perhaps the younglings will bring us a brazier, and we can heat some water."

Inda pushed aside the curtain and found a primitive sanitary facility. He hoped the chute didn't empty too near the keep's kitchens. The next room held a sunken stone pool a meter deep and nearly two meters square. It was filled with clear water that flowed in through a shallow trench in the stone floor. On the other side of the pool, water spilled out into a deeper trench that disappeared into the wall. The system was too primitive to be called plumbing. The water was ice cold, and appeared to have been diverted from a mountain stream.

Three doors opened into the room. None of them had handles or visible latches. Sinykin stared at one of them, trying to visualize the latching mechanism. He closed his eyes, and sensed the tiny iron bar within the latch. He imagined it tilting, turning clockwise. It seemed to move, and then his stomach growled loudly, breaking his concentration. He went back to Ertis' room.

"What shall we do after breakfast?"

"I want to bathe," called Ertis. "The pool can accommodate both of us. We can search for Kento and the Historians when we are clean."

Sharing an Ardellan's bath was something Sinykin had never contemplated. He considered the idea while he washed his hands at the basin. It appeared from the size of the pool that Ardellans were accustomed to communal baths. Four, or perhaps even six, of the slender Masters could comfortably share this pool. Ertis seemed to be unconcerned about their physical differences. This would give Inda his first opportunity to see a Master's unclothed form.

"The water's not much warmer than ice. I'll bathe with you if we can heat the water. Could you heat it the way you heated water on the trail?"

"No. I must put my energy into healing my wounds. Today I have none to spare for things that can be done as well with coal and flame."

Sinykin pulled out a chair and sat at the table with Ertis. "Then it takes power to accomplish the healing?"

"Oh, yes. Minor wounds like mine can be healed almost overnight. Serious wounds require the expenditure of more power to repair the damage, and complete healing takes even more time."

Sinykin heard the clink of pottery in the hall. He turned, and saw the younglings reappear in the open doorway. This time each of them bore a smaller wooden tray laden with covered bowls and steaming pots. "Masters, we have brought your breakfast," said the one on the right. At Ertis' nod they brought the trays to the table.

Inda cut the crusty loaf of nut bread. Fragrant vapors curled up from the warm slices as Ertis spooned a dollop of fruit preserves onto each one. One of the younglings poured them each a cup of steaming tea, while the other lifted lids to reveal bowls of stewed fruit, hot porridge, and fried nuts mixed with tubers.

"We thank you, naReina and naLeera, for your kind attentions," said Ertis. "We have one more favor to ask of you. We would like to bathe, but the water is too cold for comfort. Can you bring a brazier and heat some water for us?''

The younglings looked at each other. One dipped an eyestalk and the other echoed the gesture, as if they were engaged in some silent form of communication. Inda could not tell them apart. They wore identical gold hoops that pierced the loose skin beneath one tentacle, and no other adornment. Their bodies were rounder than those of the younglings he had seen on the plain, with chubbier legs and thicker tentacles. They probably had an extra layer of fat to help protect them from the cold weather. Since they were members of the builders' clan, Inda wondered, might they know Kento?

The younglings turned back to face Ertis, and the one on the right spoke again. ''My sibling and I will be happy to serve you. We will bring a brazier, some coal, and a large pot for heating the water. Do you require anything else?''

''Not at this time,'' said Ertis as he held out a pair of small iron rings. The younglings each extended a tentacle and scooped up a ring before they left the room.

Inda swallowed a mouthful of bread and jam. ''This tastes good. I didn't realize that I was this hungry. I must have been too tired to eat very much last night.''

''I am also very hungry. Do you want some sweetener for your tea?'' Ertis held out a pot of sticky green liquid.

''No, thank you. I will have some of the fruit, though.''

Ertis passed the fruit to Inda, then picked up the bowl of porridge and scooped a huge spoonful onto his plate. He tasted it, then covered the bowl and set it on the far side of the table. ''Do not try the porridge,'' he said to Sinykin. ''They have included a grain that made Sarah Anders ill. I do not think it would be wise for you to eat it. The fruit and the tubers should not give you any trouble.''

Inda stared at the piece of nut bread he held in his hand. He had eaten almost half of it. ''What about the bread? Would they have put that grain in the bread?''

''It is never used in bread. The grain has a bitter flavor when it is ground.''

''Good.'' He set the bread down, and ladled thinly-sliced fried tubers onto his plate beside a helping of stewed fruit. Inda suddenly realized that his fork and spoon were in his pack. ''Ertis, do you know where they put our packs?''

"I think someone would have brought them up during the night. They may have left them in the hall, to avoid disturbing us. Look outside the door."

Sinykin pushed his chair back, rose, and strode toward the open door. The heels of his boots clicked on the stone floor. He walked out into the hall, looked to the right and then to the left. "The packs are here," he said as he bent over. He returned to the table with his pack.

"There was someone in the hall," Sinykin said quietly. "I saw someone dressed in black step around the corner just as I walked out there. He was watching me."

"Did you expect that we would not be watched?" asked Ertis through a mouthful of porridge. "We are strangers here, and probably unwelcome visitors. They undoubtedly searched our belongings last night."

Sinykin unzipped the front compartment of his pack. His eating utensils had been removed from their pouch and were scattered among his notebooks, pens, and other gear. He wondered what kind of a mess the searchers had made of his medical bag and sample case. There was nothing he could do about it now. His breakfast was getting cold, and he was still hungry. He fished out his fork, set his pack on the floor, and attacked the fruit and tubers on his plate.

Ertis was scraping the last of the porridge from the bottom of the bowl when the younglings appeared at the door.One of them carried a large brazier filled with charcoal, and the other held a huge glazed ceramic pot. At Ertis' nod they trundled through the room with their burdens, and ducked behind the curtain. Inda heard much thumping, splashing, and mumbling coming from the bath.

"I think they may drown one another," he said to Ertis as he poured more tea.

"They are not as incompetent as they appear to be. We will shortly be able to enjoy a fine, warm bath. Do you want the last piece of bread?"

"No, thank you. I've had quite enough." Sinykin leaned back in his chair and sipped his cooling tea. "How shall we go about looking for Kento? These two younglings are from his clan. Do you think they might be able to help us?"

"Perhaps. We can certainly ask them if they know him. If they cannot help us, we shall go to the builders' clanhall and ask for Master Kento. Someone there must know where to find him."

There was another huge splash in the bathroom. One of
the younglings peered around the curtain. Water dripped
from its tentacles. "Masters, your bath is ready. The water
is warm now. Come quickly, before it cools."

Inda watched Ertis. The Ardellan rose and slipped off his
robe, folded it neatly and left it on his chair. As Ertis bent
to remove his leggings, Inda stood and skinned out of his
filthy tunic. He stripped off muddy boots and stained slacks,
and was left standing in his underwear.

"Come," said Ertis, who by this time was naked. His
body was thin and pale and hairless, with long slender legs
and arms; aside from the tentacle nodules on the chest and
back, it was smooth and unblemished, and showed no evidence of external genitalia. He looked like a youngling
thinned down, with two of its tentacles turned to arms and
its legs grown long, and a proper head instead of a lump
with mouth and eyestalks. Ertis walked over to a cabinet,
pulled out a thick, rough towel, and tossed it to Sinykin.
After choosing a towel for himself, he led the way into the
bath.

The glowing coals in the brazier had warmed the room.
Beside the pool the younglings had set two small bundles
of dried grass tied with blue cords, and a pot of thick white
rancid-smelling goo. "What is that?" asked Sinykin, pointing to the pot.

"You rub it on your skin, Master, and scrub with the
grass to clean yourself," said one of the drenched younglings.

"I have Terran soap in my pack. Would you like to try
some, Ertis?"

"Certainly. One of the younglings can fetch it."

"No, I'll go. Get into the water; I'll join you in a moment." Inda put the lid on the pot of evil-smelling stuff
before he backed out of the room and let the curtain fall
across the door. He took a deep breath, hoping to clear the
stink from his nostrils, but the smell lingered. He found his
pack, pulled out the plastic box with its sage-scented soap,
flipped the lid and sniffed the clean, fresh scent. Then he
tugged off his underwear and draped his towel casually over
one shoulder before he returned to the bath.

Ertis was already in the pool, water lapping at his chin.

"Catch," called Sinykin, tossing him the bar of soap. He

dropped his towel away from the pool's edge and stepped cautiously into the water. "The water's not very warm."

"It is as warm as we are likely to find here. This water comes from a mountain stream. It is cold even at midsummer." He sniffed the soap. "I like this smell. What is the scent?"

"It is an herb native to Earth. We use it for seasoning food, too." Sinykin eased down into the water. It felt cool and refreshing on his skin, though it was too cold to ease the aches in his muscles. He stretched his arms and legs and let the water loosen the dirt that streaked his body.

The younglings were still standing beside the pool, and now one of them reached down and touched Ertis' shoulder with the tip of a tentacle. "We have other duties, Master. If you have no further need of us, we will go."

"We do have a question for you. Do you know where we might find Master Kento of the builders' clan?"

"No, no, Master," said first youngling, backing toward the door.

"We have other work to do, Master," said the second. "We must go now." It and its companion slipped around the curtain and were gone.

"What do you think?" asked Sinykin. "Were they telling the truth?"

"Oh, yes. Younglings are very literal. They meant exactly what they said. My question did upset them, though."

"Is that significant?"

"Perhaps. We may not know for certain until we find Kento." Ertis picked up the bar of soap and held it out to Inda. "How do I use this?"

They scrubbed and rinsed and rinsed and scrubbed until the water grew cold. Then they climbed out of the pool and dried themselves beside the warm brazier. The outer chamber was cold, and Inda, wrapped in a damp towel, shivered as he searched his pack for clean clothing. He found a black sweater and yellow coveralls, and donned them quickly. While Ertis did up the intricate lacings on his Ardellan footgear, Sinykin wiped his own boots clean with a scrap of cloth. He pulled them on, then slipped his journal and pen into a capacious pocket. He was ready to explore the Iron Keep.

Ertis threw open the shutters and leaned out of the narrow window. "Look!"

Inda joined him, squinting in the bright sunlight. Looking down, he saw a maze of narrow streets wrapped around squat stone buildings. The roofs were gardens, with neat rows of vegetables planted between miniature fruit trees, or lush green sod on which tethered goats were feeding. Younglings in leather ponchos worked everywhere, milking goats, chopping wood, and gathering the last of the harvest into huge baskets. In the distance he saw two towers, one on each side of the keep.

The maze ended abruptly at the keep's wall, which abutted the tower to the left of their window and blocked their view of the mountainside. There was a window on that side of the room, and Inda ran to it and flung open the shutters. His breath caught in his throat as he gazed out at the mountainside. To the east he could see the mountain rising until the red conifers grew sparse and snow streaked the barren earth. A stream rushed down the mountainside toward the western valleys, passing within a few hundred meters of the keep. Sinykin leaned out and looked straight down, and saw that the tower's walls were part of the keep's outer wall. Scrub and tall grass grew right up to the wall's base, making it almost impossible for anyone to walk along this side of the keep. For a moment he felt like a prisoner in a castle tower; his life with Elissa and Jaime seemed very remote, almost like something he had but dreamed. The thumb of his left hand stroked his wedding ring, turning it on his finger and reminding him of the reality of that other world.

The hallway was faced with the same gray stone that lined the walls of their chambers, with a window at either end casting sparse sunbeams into its gloom. All the junctures where walls met floor and ceiling were shadowed, as if someone had spread soot over them. The flagstone floor was worn smooth in the center by the passage of many feet, but near the walls it was uneven. They passed a half-dozen closed doors, evenly-spaced on either side of the corridor, before they reached the end of the hallway.

The stairway was on the right, perpendicular to the hallway. It ran downward only; apparently they were on the building's top floor. Inda looked down, saw someone dressed in black turn the corner on the landing below and disappear from sight.

"Is he a guard?" he asked Ertis, pointing.

"Possibly."

"Let's find out!" Sinykin ran down the stairs, his heels clattering on the dressed stone. His feet hit the landing with a crash. He grabbed the end of the wall with his right hand, swung around the corner, and peered down at the next landing. No one was there. Inda ran again, down a dozen more steps, glanced down the empty hallway, then turned the corner and stared at another empty staircase. His quarry was gone.

Ertis came down the stairs behind him. "Have you captured him?"

"I only wanted to ask him some questions."

"Whoever he is, he remains hidden for his own reasons. You may ask your questions when he reveals himself to us."

Inda shrugged. "I just want to know why Kento insisted that I come here. Why is everyone so secretive?"

"That we shall also learn in good time. Impatience will gain us nothing. We can stay here and chase shadows, or go out and see the rest of the Iron Keep."

Inda smiled. A tour of the Iron Keep would be more than enough adventure for one day. He was the first Terran ever to walk the streets here, the first to see these secretive people go about their daily lives. Even Sarah Anders had never come this far. He would send a detailed report to Secretary Sandsmark as soon as he returned to the spaceport.

Had it only been six days since he left Jaime and Elissa at the Terran compound? It seemed like another lifetime. He slipped his right hand into the pocket of his parka and held the spiral cone he had picked for Jaime. Delivering that cone to his son was as important as sending the report to Sandsmark.

He followed Ertis down the last flight of stairs and into a wide, sunny room that extended all the way across the front of the clanhall. The room was empty except for a bench along the back wall. Ertis went straight to the door, which opened before he reached it. A set of narrow steps led down to a street that was barely wide enough for three adults to walk abreast. It paralleled the keep's eastern wall to their right, then bent ninety degrees in front of the clanhall and wound downslope between the buildings. The houses were crowded side by side, their stoops extending into the street to trip an unwary walker. Many of them had rough stone stairways built into their front walls. These stairways led to the roofs. Looking up, Inda could see leaves and flowers and occasionally the face of a goat looking down at him.

A narrow trench ran down the center of the road, covered here and there by rough planking. Foul-smelling liquid trickled through it, making its slow way down the mountainside. A youngling was sweeping the street clean of goat pellets while another shoveled the little piles into a pushcart. Farther down the street, two younglings tended sweet-smelling plants that grew in window boxes.

The street turned sharply to the left around a goat pen, although the trench passed under the fence and through the pen and came out on the other side. The goats were woolly, black, and six-legged, with curved horns set just above their red eyes. Most of them stood sedately munching the grass or basking in the sun as Ertis and Inda walked past. One of the smaller goats loped to the fence and followed them around, sticking its narrow muzzle between the fence rails and sniffing at Inda's parka.

The day was bright and sunny, with only a few wispy clouds in the sky. Although the air was cold, Inda walked with his parka unzipped. He breathed deeply of the crisp mountain air, despite the putrid-smelling trench and the musky odor of the goats. He and Ertis continued to walk westward, past more goat pens and haystacks and working younglings. Inda was surprised that he saw no adults about, either supervising the work or walking through the streets. He heard no shouting, no laughter, not even the low murmur of conversation. The Iron Keep might have been deserted by everyone but younglings and goats and two confused guests.

Ertis walked up to one of the younglings who was grooming a goat. "Is the herders' clanhall near?"

"Oh, yes, Master. Just follow the road around the next bend and you will see it." It pointed in the direction with one tentacle.

The herders' clanhall occupied the southwest corner of the keep. It sprawled there, its second story almost reaching the top of the wall, its roof terraced and planted with berry bushes and spreading plants. Red-leafed vines, dripping clusters of purple berries, trailed down the facade. Many younglings were working outside the clanhall, cleaning the goat paddocks and tending the gardens. Inda saw no Masters.

Three broad steps led up to the clanhall's double doors. Inda and Ertis climbed them together, and Ertis lifted, then dropped, the heavy stone knocker. An instant later the right-hand door swung open, and a youngling faced them.

"How can I help?" it asked.

"We would like to speak with Perli the Historian. If he is not available, we would speak with the Elder of your clan's council," replied Ertis.

"Neither can speak with you today. They are both occupied." The youngling began to close the door.

Sinykin stopped the door with his booted foot. He held it open and peered into the gloom inside while Ertis continued to talk with the youngling.

"Is there someone else in authority with whom we might speak? Is the Mentor free?"

"The herders have no Mentor. Everyone is busy with festival preparations today. Come back tomorrow. Someone will speak with you then."

"Thank you," said Ertis. He looked at Inda, and the Terran released his grip on the door. They both stepped back as the youngling pulled it closed.

"This doesn't feel right," said Inda. He walked down the steps to the street and stopped there, staring back the way they had come. "Some people are following us."

"I know that." Ertis took Sinykin's arm and began walking northward, toward the keep's main gate. "You cannot confront them. They will disappear into a building or an alleyway before you reach them. It is best that we go on about our business and leave them to theirs."

Inda shrugged. He knew that Ertis was right, but he still wanted to run back and face those black-clad Masters. His intuition told him that they could lead him to the mysterious Kento.

In the bright light of day the gate was smaller and less menacing than it had seemed in last night's darkness. The adult guards had been replaced by a crew of younglings in leather ponchos. Two of them sat on top of the wall, looking down at the twisting road, while four others stood ready to pull open the massive wooden gates if anyone should approach.

The stable where they had left their aleps was just inside the gate. Ertis led Inda into its darkened recesses. "I want to check on our mounts,'' he said, walking toward the first occupied stall.

This building was made of stone, like all the others in the keep. It was long and narrow, with three walls and a row of pillars supporting the low roof. Beyond the pillars was a courtyard filled with watering troughs and haystacks and manure piles. There were many narrow stalls along the wall, about half of them occupied. Inda saw a few pack animals, some riding aleps, and many of the stocky borras that were used for pulling carts.

Harnesses hung from hooks on the pillars, and saddles were flung over stall dividers. The animals seemed content to rest and munch the grain in their feed pails. Only a few of them turned their heads to look at Inda as he followed Ertis through the stable.

Their animals were in the last stalls at the far end. They had been brushed and fed, the pack saddles cleaned, and the bridles hung neatly beside them. Ertis slipped into the stall with his mount, rubbed its head, and spoke quietly to it. Inda stayed in the open and patted his alep's rump.

''Do you see our saddles?'' asked Ertis. He backed out of the stall and joined Inda.

''I saw the pack saddles, but not our riding saddles.''

Ertis strode back past the pack animals and checked the next few empty stalls. ''They are not here. Look behind the pillars.''

''Nothing,'' called Inda. ''Perhaps we should ask the stablemaster about them.''

''We certainly shall speak with the stablemaster. I do not intend to become a prisoner in the Iron Keep. I will have my saddle with my alep, where it belongs.''

Sinykin stared at Ertis. The Historian's anger was a fine red mist all around his body. It looked much like the auras Inda could see around humans, auras that most people saw only in Kirlian photographs. Usually he had to close his eyes and concentrate to see the faintly-colored emanations that surrounded all living things; this was the first time such a vision had come to him unbidden. He watched the mist darken and swirl about Ertis as the Historian stalked across the courtyard.

''You, youngling!'' Ertis called to one of the workers sweeping the cobblestones. It looked up at him, startled.

''What may I do for you, Master?''

"Where is the stablemaster?"

"Gone, Master. He will not return until tomorrow morning."

Gouts of orange mist erupted like flames from Ertis's aura. "Who is in charge of the stable during his absence?"

The youngling dropped its broom. Its eyestalks quivered as it spoke. "There is no one here, Master. You must return tomorrow."

"I want my saddles. They are the property of Clan Alu, and they mistakenly have been removed from the stalls of our mounts. They will be returned immediately!"

"Certainly, Master. I will place them in the stalls as soon as I can find them." The youngling bent to retrieve its broom, and as it straightened Ertis rapped it between the eyestalks.

"See that you do," he said.

Sinykin blinked, and the aura that had surrounded Ertis disappeared from his perception. His skill at seeing auras was increasing, but sustained perception required intense concentration. He could not keep that up for long. He strode after Ertis and touched him on the arm. "Why are you so concerned about our saddles? What did you mean about being a prisoner here?"

"We cannot leave without our saddles. We cannot ride without them, and we certainly cannot walk down the mountain in the winter season."

"But there were many saddles in the stable," protested Sinykin. "We could take any of them. If someone wanted to keep us here, he need only bar the gate."

"My mind can open any gate. I cannot ride an alep without a saddle, and I will not take another's saddle without the owner's permission. Either the stablemaster has committed a grave discourtesy, or someone wants to be certain we cannot leave the Iron Keep."

"I think you misread the stablemaster's actions. He has probably sent the saddles to be cleaned and repaired. Even if, as you claim, he is motivated by some sinister intent, a missing saddle will not keep me in the Iron Keep against my will." Inda stared intently at Ertis. He did not understand the Historian's reasoning at all. "Chains can bind me and locked rooms can hold me, but lack of a saddle would never deter me."

Ertis sighed and walked on, toward the northwest corner

of the keep. Inda followed him to the builders' clanhall, and waited as Ertis climbed the stairs and knocked on the narrow door.

The door opened a hand's span wide, and a youngling's eyes peered out. "May I help you?"

"I would like to speak with Master Kento."

"He is not here," replied the youngling. It started to close the door.

Ertis put his hands on the door and held it open. "Where can we find him? We must speak with him."

"Master Kento has not been here for at least a hand of days. I do not know where he is." The youngling's eyestalks quivered as it spoke.

"Let me speak with Historian Vaant, then."

"He is not here."

"Your clan's elder?"

"There is no one here now. Come back tomorrow." The youngling pushed the door again, and this time Ertis let it close.

"I feel weary," the Historian said as he returned to Inda's side.

Sinykin was immediately concerned. "We should return to our rooms so that you can rest."

"I would prefer to continue our walk around the keep. We should visit the miners' clanhall. We might learn something about Kento there."

"We can visit the miners tomorrow." Sinykin took Ertis' arm and turned down one of the diagonal streets that would lead them back to the smelters' clanhall. Ertis did not resist his guidance. "I am tired, too. We could both nap this afternoon."

They walked slowly through the winding streets, treading uphill between the stone walls of buildings. Here there were no goats, and no younglings worked in the street. They passed many closed doors and shuttered windows. A red lizard basking on a sunny stoop scuttled away at their approach, disappearing into a dark passage between two walls. As he passed the spot, Inda looked back and saw the pair of black-clad Masters behind him. They noticed Sinykin watching them and stepped into the shadows until he turned away. Inda shrugged. He could not force them to reveal their secrets.

It was well past midday when they reached the steps of

the smelters' clanhall. As Inda followed Ertis up the stairs, he was thinking about a mug of hot, fragrant tea and a chance to remove his boots. He could feel a blister forming on his right heel. He needed to apply antibiotic ointment and bandage it before he developed an infection.

The clanhall's door swung inward, and a short, well-muscled Master appeared in the opening. He looked down at Ertis and Inda. His eyes were dark, nearly black. Inda stared into them and felt fear tighten his chest. The Master raised his right hand in greeting and spoke.

"Master Ertis, Master Inda, we have been waiting for you to return. We have many questions to ask you."

Chapter 13

"Come in," said the dark-eyed Master. He stepped aside so that Ertis could enter the clanhall. Inda followed, and was surprised to find the room crowded with Ardellans. All of the Masters he had expected to see throughout the keep seemed to be gathered here. They stood at the far end of the room and all along the front wall, watching the door. Most of them were dressed in leather garments like the ones Kento had worn, and many of their faces were decorated with tattooed lines of red, blue, or green ink. All of them had dark eyes.

Inda stepped farther into the room, into the tension created by those staring eyes. He felt them probing his aura, pressing to learn more about him, and he tried not to cringe. There were footsteps on the stoop behind him. He turned to see the black-clad Masters who had followed them throughout the keep. The pair entered the clanhall together and the door closed behind them. They ignored Inda and Ertis, quickly removing their black cloaks and hanging them on pegs near the door before they joined the other Masters.

'I am Matri," said the Master who had opened the door. "I am leader of the smelting clan. I offer you the hospitality of our clanhall, such as it is, and I apologize for not being here to greet you when you arrived last night. Please come and be seated. We have tea for you."

Inda felt an instant dislike for Matri. His pinched features and narrow eyes gave him a sinister look, and his words did not seem sincere. His gestures were abrupt, and the imperious tilt of his head was vaguely threatening. When he pointed toward an empty bench, Ertis and Inda walked to it and sat.

"Master Ertis needs to rest," said Inda. "He is recovering from a serious shoulder wound. We returned to the clan-hall because he is weary. He should go to his room and sleep.'' Inda searched fruitlessly among the alien faces for Satto the Healer. Satto would certainly be concerned about Ertis and insist that he be allowed to go upstairs and rest.

Matri shrugged. He addressed Ertis with deference. ''We are sorry to trouble you, Historian. Unfortunately, it is imperative that we have your answers to these questions now.''

''Please send for Satto,'' Inda urged Matri. ''I will answer your questions if you will get the Healer for Ertis.''

Matri stared at the Terran. His dark eyes seemed to bore into Inda's soul. Inda stared back, trying to remain calm despite the thudding of his heart. He knew that Matri would read his fear in his aura. At last the Ardellan looked away.

''Why have you come to the Iron Keep?''

Ertis sat with his back to the wall, his right leg outstretched and his left tucked under the bench. He lifted one hand, then let it drop back into his lap as he answered the question. ''An invitation to visit your keep and exchange stories with your Historians was conveyed to us by Master Kento of the builders' clan.''

A youngling came in with two mugs of hot tea and offered one to Ertis and the other to Inda. The cup warmed Inda's hands and the fragrant steam was enticing. He sipped, watching the Masters over the rim of his mug. Three who had stood at the back of the crowd were moving forward. Their faces, like Kento's, were tattooed with swirling red lines that ended at the corners of their mouths. The tallest wore leathers, and the others were dressed in black. Could they have been the Masters who watched his room and followed him through the keep? Inda looked for their bracelets to see if they were builders, but he could not make out the patterns from across the room. He half-closed his eyes and tried to separate their auras from those of the Masters around them. He could not do it; only Matri's greenish-gold aura was distinct.

''Where did you meet Master Kento?'' asked Matri.

Inda replied. ''At Eiku Keep.''

''You are a Terran. What were you doing at Eiku Keep?''

''I am a Healer. I was traveling to Sau Keep to interview survivors of the plague that has killed so many among the clans.''

''For what reason?''

"I am searching for a way to keep the plague from killing and maiming so many of your people."

"Then why did you come here? We have not been troubled by the plague."

"Master Kento said that it was important for me to come to the Iron Keep. He said that the Historians would welcome us." What right did these unpleasant Masters have to interrogate him? Inda was beginning to see that there might be dangerous secrets hidden in the Iron Keep.

"Where are Historians Perli and Vaant? Where is Master Kento? When we inquired at Kento's clanhall, we were told that he had not been seen in many days. The herders say Perli is 'occupied.' Historian Vaant is not at his clanhall. We are tired of this secrecy, this mystery. Please produce Master Kento now, or we shall leave the Iron Keep as soon as Historian Ertis is fit to travel."

Matri's face twisted into an expression that Inda could not read. "You will not leave the Iron Keep. You have come here without our leave, and here you shall remain until we choose to let you go."

"Then the disappearance of our saddles was intentional!" Ertis rose and advanced toward Matri, right hand raised, his fingers spread and curved like talons. "I remind you that you are dealing with an important member of the Historians Guild. Your discourtesy shall be long remembered. You will return our saddles to us immediately, and my companion and I will be allowed to come and go as we please, or the Iron Keep will be put under interdict. The Historians who live among you will cease to tell their stories. No other Historians will come here to bring you news. You will disappear from our histories, until you are remembered by no one outside your keep. It has been many lifetimes since we laid such a prohibition on any keep or guild. We have not lost the ability to do so."

A murmur ran through the watching crowd. Matri stepped back, raising his hands to ward off Ertis' approach. "We would not think of interfering with the wishes of such a prominent Historian. I misspoke myself in the heat of the moment. I am not accustomed to being challenged by one such as your companion. The stablemaster informed me that your saddles needed mending; they will be in the stalls with your mounts tomorrow."

"Good." Ertis dropped his hands. "If you are finished

with us, I would like to return to my room and rest. I am also hungry. Please have the kitchen send up fresh tea and bread." He handed his still-steaming mug to Matri, then turned and walked toward the stairs. Inda followed slowly, wondering if Matri would stop him. At the bottom of the steps, Ertis turned back and spoke to the gathered Masters. "Any of you who wish to speak with us are welcome to join us at our evening meal."

Their rooms had not been disturbed. The breakfast dishes were still on the table. Housekeeping in this clanhall seemed to be lax; the younglings should have come and cleared the dishes away before midday. The bedding had not been straightened, and the now cold brazier still stood in the bath. Inda moved it aside so that he could use the facilities.

"Would you rather eat or sleep?" he called to Ertis, who had sprawled on his bed.

"I am too hungry to sleep. After I have eaten, I will rest."

Sinykin came out and sat at the table. He pushed aside a dirty plate, then set down his journal and pen. He wanted to record as much as he remembered of the smelter's threats. "I do not think Matri was speaking the truth when he said that our saddles were being mended and would be returned to us tomorrow."

"Why do you say that?"

"I was watching his aura. As he spoke, it became hazy and changed from gold to a vile, muddy green color."

Ertis sat up and leaned his head back against the wall. "You read auras well. Sarah Anders claimed that she could not see them. She told us that Terrans are head-blind, like younglings.

"Most of us are head-blind. Many Terrans refuse to acknowledge the existence of psychic phenomena like auras. I have been able to see auras since I was a child, but I am only now learning to interpret them."

"Then remember that a person's aura is a psychic manifestation of his emotional and physical state. The shifting colors correspond to the changing flow of energy within the body and mind." Ertis leaned forward, resting his hands on his thighs. "It is impossible to hide an untruth from anyone who can read an aura. Only younglings and head-blind Terrans can be fooled by lies."

Inda nodded. "If Matri knew that you would see his lie, why did he not tell the truth? What purpose did the lie serve?"

"He probably believes that you are head-blind and would not see his lie. He might be testing the bond between us, trying to learn how much you know about my people and how much I tell you. And it is possible that he did not want to speak the truth. Sometimes the truth is more incriminating than an acknowledged lie."

Someone tapped at their door. The noise surprised Inda; he turned with a start.

"Come in," called Ertis.

The youngling naReina pushed open the door for naLeera, who was carrying a tray laden with food. Inda saw a loaf of steaming bread, and pots of preserves and bowls of nuts. The inviting aroma reminded him of his hunger. He stood up and helped to stack the dirty dishes on a corner of the table. That cleared enough space for the tray. naReina brought in a pot of tea and closed the door.

"Did you find Master Kento?" the youngling asked as it poured the tea into two huge mugs.

"No, we did not," said Ertis. He walked to the table and picked up one of the mugs. "No one seems to know where he is."

"It grieves me that we could not be of more help." naLeera set out clean plates and removed the tops from the pots. "Will this be enough food, or should we bring some roast fowl from the kitchen?"

"This is fine." Ertis watched as Inda spooned purple preserves onto a thick slab of bread. "I have invited the other Masters to join us for dinner this evening, and if they do, we will need extra tables and chairs. Are there some available in the clanhall?"

"We can bring some from the other rooms on this floor if you need them. I do not think that you will because most of the Masters are with Master Matri. I think they will be busy for most of the night."

Ertis shrugged. "Come check with us just before dinner. We can decide then."

The tea was hot and cinnamony. Inda sipped slowly as he watched the younglings gather up the breakfast dishes. Ertis was shelling nuts with a dagger, slipping its tip between the shell halves and prying them apart. He popped the green nutmeats into his mouth and crunched them noisily between his teeth. Inda reached for a nut, and Ertis gently touched his hand with the tip of his dagger.

"Do not eat those. They made Sarah Anders ill. Roundnuts and fir nuts are safe for Terrans to eat, and these green nuts are all right after they have been roasted. These are raw. They might make your stomach hurt."

"Thank you for telling me," said Inda. He smiled and cut another slab of bread. The younglings finished clearing the table and trundled off with a tray full of dirty plates.

The Ardellan leaned back in his chair, pushing aside the plate of empty nutshells. "I am tired. I will sleep now."

"Have you finished your tea?" asked Inda.

Ertis lifted the mug to his lips and drained it. "Do you have any other orders, Healer?"

"No, Historian. Sleep well." Inda refilled his own mug and carried it to the door. Ertis was already stripping off his tunic. "I'm going to explore the clanhall. I'll be back before dark."

"Mom! Are you home?" called Jaime. The front door slammed.

"I'm in the kitchen." Elissa finished slicing a tomato, then set aside her knife and wiped her hands on a towel. "How was class today?"

"May I have some hot chocolate?" Jaime came in, pulled off his coat, and dropped it on a chair. "It's cold outside. Tommy and I went out behind the landing field and built a snow keep on the hill. Then Security came by and told us to go home. They said the compound's been closed, and we shouldn't play back there any more."

"That's right," said Elissa as she put a mug into the heating unit. "You should stay closer to the apartment. What is a 'snow keep'?"

"Like Alu, or the Iron Keep, Mom. We built a wall around the top of the hill, and then we made little snow houses, and streets, and corrals for the aleps. I wanted to call it the Iron Keep, because that's where Dad is." The heating unit's timer beeped. Jaime opened the door and removed his hot chocolate. "Why did they close the compound?"

"Administrator Griswold is worried about the storms. She doesn't want anyone to leave the spaceport right now."

"But Dad's already gone. How is he going to get back in if the gate is locked? When is he coming back?"

Elissa reached down and brushed Jaime's tousled hair into place with her fingers. "The gate won't be locked, honey. Security will have guards there to make sure no one leaves. They'll let your father back into the compound." She smiled. "I don't know when he'll be coming home, though. We have to wait for his next letter. Now hang up your coat, and wash your hands before dinner."

Jaime grabbed his coat and dragged it into the other room. Elissa's smile was replaced by a worried frown as she watched him go.

Sinykin cleaned and bandaged his sore heel before he left the room. Then he took the narrow service stairs down to the kitchen, following the aroma of roasting meat. He stood in the doorway, drinking his tea and watching the plump kitchenmaster lay seedcakes out to bake on the hot hearthstone. The kitchenmaster was nearly bald. Two thin white wisps of hair stood straight up from his gleaming scalp, like strands of monofilament. He was intent on his work, and did not notice when Inda set his empty mug on the table and left.

The main hall where Matri had confronted them was empty. Inda wandered through it, gazing out of the window at the deserted streets. He did not see even a single youngling. Had everyone been ordered to avoid him? That would not be surprising, considering Matri's anger. Did Matri have that much power over the residents of the Iron Keep?

At the far end of the hall Sinykin found a narrow, dark passageway. He peered down it, and saw a patch of light at the far end. Sunbeams streamed in through a high window and illuminated a rectangle of the stone floor. As he watched, a small gray animal scurried through the light, its slender tail extending straight upward. It looked much like a mouse, with larger ears and a more well-defined head. Inda scuffed the toe of his boot on the stone floor, and the animal stopped and looked at him, then ran quickly to a shadowed corner and disappeared.

The passageway was dirty. Dust and grit had gathered at the seams where walls and floor met, and smoke had blackened the ceiling. Inda saw no cobwebs, and no insects scuttled away at his approach. A single tiny lizard, less than ten centimeters long, basked on the windowsill. Its long tongue suddenly flicked from its mouth and captured an unidentifiable morsel. The lizard slowly closed its eyes and settled silently back onto its perch.

Just past the sunbeam, the passageway turned sharply to the left. It went on into darkness, nearly twice as far as had the first section. Inda wished for a lamp before he had taken three steps. He walked slowly, feeling along the wall with his right hand. The stone was rough, like the wall of a cave, but the floor had been worn smooth and slick by the passage of many feet. The sound of his heels clicking on the stone echoed up and down the corridor.

An imposing door blocked the end of the passage. Its wood was smooth as satin under Inda's hands. He felt up and down both sides of it and found no knob or handle. He sensed the latch, with its tiny iron bar, set in the left side of the door. Placing his palms carefully over the latch, he visualized the bar moving, tilting, opening the latch. He pushed against the door. Nothing happened. He sighed and began to turn away. Then he heard a noise from the other side of the door.

Again Inda located the iron bar. With his eyes closed, he reached for the bar with his mind. He imagined it slowly turning clockwise while he listened for the click the latch would make as it opened. Suddenly he heard it. His breath caught in his throat. His heart beat faster. He pushed hard against the door. It was heavy, but he managed to open it a hand's span. He had tripped the latch with his mind! He was so excited, he almost let the door close again.

Sinykin heard the sound of distant chanting. Bracing his feet firmly, he put his shoulder to the door and pushed harder. It opened wider, and the sound of chanting was more distinct. Sinykin slipped through the opening and let the door close behind him. He was standing at the base of a narrow staircase that spiraled upward in a clockwise direction. The tiny room had no other outlet. He could only climb, or go back the way he had come.

The chanting was growing louder. A jumble of undifferentiable syllables flowed down the staircase to echo in the bottom chamber. Inda did not want to climb toward the source of that noise. He turned back to the door and ran his palms over its surface, searching for a handhold by which to pull it open. The wood was smooth, and the door had been cut to perfectly fit its frame. He could not get even his fingernails into the crack between door and wall. He could release the latch with his mind, but he could not open the heavy door from this side. That left him with only two choices—he could cower in the darkness and wait for someone to find him, or he could go upward.

Sinykin stayed close to the outer wall of the staircase and climbed the steps as silently as he could. He kept his left palm against the wall, carefully feeling for a hidden door or passage, and he counted the steps as he climbed. At the fifteenth step he began to see glimmers of light coming from above, jumping and flickering like the flames of candles.

On the twenty-third step he saw the shadow of a person. Inda stopped moving. He pressed his back against the wall. The fingertips of his left hand slipped into a crack and gripped the stone. The chanting was louder, the syllables more distinct if still indecipherable. His heart was beating to the chant's rhythm—bah-boom, bah-boom—one double beat for each syllable. He took a shallow breath and held it as he inched up the staircase toward the shadow's source.

A Master was standing near the top of the stairs, looking upward. A tiny flame flickered in the wall sconce above him, making his shadow jump and dance on the steps below. He was dressed in black leggings and tunic and his feet were hidden in the shadows, but Inda could see the six opposable fingers of his left hand.

The Master turned to look at Inda. His facial tattoos showed him to be a member of Kento's clan. He nodded and motioned for Inda to stay where he was. The rhythm of the chant was speeding up. Sinykin took a deep breath, slowly released it through his mouth, then took another as he tried to slow the beating of his heart. He watched as the Master came silently down the stairs to join him.

"You have come too soon. You should not be here," he whispered. "Kento will come for you and your companion tomorrow. All will be ready then. Now you must go back the way you came."

"I cannot," said Inda softly. "The door is closed."

The Master put a hand on Sinykin's shoulder and gently pushed him. "Go back down the stairs. There is danger here."

"I can't open the door." The chanters were shouting now,

and the sound that they produced cascaded down around Inda until he feared that he would drown in it.

"Go! Now!" shouted the Master. This time he shoved Sinykin.

Inda stumbled down the stairs, barely staying on his feet. He lost count of the steps, and reached the bottom sooner than he had expected. Momentum tumbled him across the little chamber and into the wall. He sat in the darkness, breathing hard.

Something creaked. Sinykin heard the unmistakable sound of squeaking hinges, and wood scraping on stone. The door was opening! He crawled to it, wedged a hand between the door and its frame, and pulled. The door swung open. He crawled through to the outer passage and let the door slam shut behind him. At the far end of the empty hallway he could just see the edge of the sunlit window.

He found Ertis pacing back and forth in their rooms, his heavy cloak wrapped tightly around him. Both windows were shuttered and the wall sconces had been lit. By their feeble glow, Sinykin saw sleeping furs heaped on the floor and clothing scattered about the room.

"Are you ill?" he asked, closing the door behind him.

"I am cold," replied Ertis. In the dim light his face was a flat, pasty-looking mask, with black holes for eyes. His normally wild hair was stuck to his scalp, and beads of sweat glistened on his forehead. He looked as if he was in shock.

Sinykin threw the thickest fur across the bed. "You should lie down," he said, taking Ertis' hand. The Ardellan's fingers felt cold and clammy. Inda led him to the bed and helped him recline, then covered him with another fur. "I think there are some coals left in the brazier. I'll see if I can get a fire going."

He brought the brazier in from the bath. Using matches from his pack and some crumpled paper torn from his journal, he managed to relight the charcoal. Then he examined one of the sconces, found the control that increased the height of the wick, and turned up all of the lamps. He opened the shutters in his room for ventilation, and left the door between the rooms open. In ten minutes the chamber was warmer and much more cheery.

Ertis' skin still looked pasty. Sinykin pulled his medical

kit from his pack and took it over to the bed, where he sat beside Ertis.

"Are you feeling any warmer now?"

"Yes."

"I'd like to examine your shoulder."

Ertis wiggled under the fur. "My shoulder is fine. There is no need for you to trouble yourself with it."

"I think you might have an infection," said Inda, turning back the fur.

"There is nothing wrong with my shoulder!"

Sinykin shrugged. "You are not well. If you will not let me examine you, I will send for Healer Satto and he can examine you."

"You need not disturb Satto." Ertis sat up, dropped his cloak from his shoulders, and struggled out of his tunic. He moved his arm easily, showing no sign that it gave him pain.

Inda could see only faint scars on the shoulder. The skin was white and clear and showed no sign of infection. The tentacle nodule below the shoulder was red and puffy, and Ertis pulled away when Sinykin touched it. It felt hot under his fingertips.

Sinykin closed his eyes, and held the palm of his hand flat above the swollen nodule. He sensed that the tissues were inflamed and painful.

"I must get Satto," said Inda, rising. "Your tentacle nodule has become infected."

Ertis grabbed his hand. "There is no need to send for the Healer. The nodule is not infected."

"Its condition has changed since this morning. I think it would be best if Satto examined you."

"No!" Ertis bared the other side of his chest and showed Inda a second nodule which was also enlarged and inflamed. "This has nothing to do with my injury. It is something that all Masters experience at some time in their lives. The tentacles are growing faster than the nodule can accommodate them. The problem will subside in a few days."

Inda could see that Ertis was speaking the truth, but he still was not convinced that these inflammations were benign. "You should be examined by one of your own Healers. I can't judge the severity of this problem. The nodules might need to be opened to relieve the pressure."

"Please do not be so concerned. The problem will resolve on its own." Ertis slipped into his tunic and pulled the cloak back around his shoulders. "Thank you for warming the room. I am already feeling much better. Now tell me, what did you learn from your exploration of the clanhall?"

Sinykin sighed. He had often wondered what law of nature made patients uncooperative. He felt no better learning that Ardellan patients were much like human patients in that respect. He tucked the fur in close to Ertis' body. "I opened a latch with my mind today! It was very difficult." He began describing the passage and the hidden staircase.

"A Master was standing near the top of the staircase. He was dressed in black, and his face bore tattoos very like Kento's. I think he was watching the chanters. When he saw me, he said that I had come too soon. He told me that Kento will come for us tomorrow.

"Then he told me to go back down the stairs. I knew that the door was closed tightly and that I could not open it. I would be trapped. He pushed me down, and when I reached the bottom the door opened, even though there was no one there to do it. He must have opened it with his mind, from the top of the staircase."

"Did he tell you his name?"

"No, he said nothing more to me. He did not follow me down the staircase. He may still be up there, listening to the others chant."

Ertis put his hand on Inda's and curled his fingers around to touch the Terran's palm. "I am pleased that you were able to open the latch. Keep practicing; in time it will become easier. Now tell me, could you understand the words of the chants? Did anything that was said make sense to you?"

The Historian's soft, dry touch was pleasant. Sinykin felt an unexpected pride when Ertis praised him. "I couldn't understand any of it. The chanting echoed in the stairwell and the sounds became confused. The syllables were too jumbled and distorted to identify."

"Then we are forced to wait for Kento's appearance tomorrow. He will certainly explain this mystery to us." Ertis squeezed Inda's hand lightly, then released it. "We can share a good supper. Perhaps some of the other Masters will join us."

Inda watched as Ertis stripped the last bit of meat from a wingbone. The Ardellan tossed the bone into a bowl beside his plate, where it joined half a dozen others, and licked the grease from his fingers. Although the younglings had brought up huge trays of roast fowl and baked tubers, enough to feed at least six people, Inda and Ertis ate alone. None of the Masters had accepted Ertis' invitation to sup with them, and neither of the Historians had appeared.

"Did you have enough to eat?" asked Ertis.

"Oh, yes." Inda looked down at his empty plate. He had eaten two large tubers, a heap of roasted nuts, and a whole bowl of stewed fruit. He sighed contentedly and poured hot tea into his mug. "What shall we do with all the extra food?"

"The younglings will take it back to the kitchen after they bring fuel for the brazier." Ertis shivered. "It is growing cold in here."

Sinykin was immediately concerned. "You must go back to bed and wrap yourself in the furs. I will find the younglings and have them bring the charcoal right now."

"There is no need to rush off. Sit and enjoy your tea, as I am enjoying mine." Ertis patted Sinykin's hand. "I am not ill. Soon we will have a fire, and the room will grow hot and stuffy. Enjoy the chill while you can."

"Then let me put a fur around your shoulders." Inda brought one of the lighter furs from the bed and draped it around the Historian. He felt more than a physician's concern for his patient. In the past few days he had come to think of Ertis as a friend. "That should keep you from getting too chilled."

"I feel invigorated. I would like to tell a story. Do you still want to hear of the death of Sarah Anders?"

"I do," said Sinykin.

"I must warn you that with such a small audience, the effect of this story-telling will not be as all-encompassing as the first one you heard me tell. The tale builds and resonates in the psyches of my listeners."

"No matter. I want the sense of the tale, the truth of the events," said Sinykin. "My people would like to know how and why Anders died. Your explanations of the event have never been understood."

The younglings came in to clear the table. They dropped a bag of charcoal at Sinykin's feet, took away the trays of food, and left the dirty dishes stacked on a corner of the table.

"The habits of this clanhall are rather slovenly."

"They are," agreed Ertis, settling onto the sleeping platform. "We would not be so careless on the plain. Our clanhall would soon be infested with all manner of pests."

"I saw a small lizard today, basking on a windowsill." Inda took the charcoal to the brazier. He lifted off the pierced clay top and piled the burning coals together, then placed more lumps of charcoal on the sand around the edge of the pile.

"Lizards are common in the mountain keeps. They eat the insects that manage to survive the cold winters by coming indoors. The lizards that live near our keeps prefer the freedom of the open plain to the shelter of our buildings. Instead of lizards, we have night mice eating our crumbs."

Sinykin closed the brazier and set the extra charcoal well away from its heat. Then he settled into a chair, his journal and pen in hand. "I'm ready."

Ertis leaned back and pressed the fingertips of one hand against the fingertips of the other, making a circular cage between his palms. He stared into its center. "Jeryl was newly-made Mentor of Clan Alu, and Arien was FreeMaster and had been guide to the Terran Captain Nicholas Durrow, and Sarah Anders was Terran Attaché.

"Durrow had been trying to make a trade agreement. He wanted titanium for his employers. Alu would not trade with him, so he went to Clan Eiku. He convinced Eiku to challenge Alu for the trade rights. Eiku and Alu fought a ritual battle. Durrow's mercenaries tried to interfere. One of them was killed and the others were captured. Durrow and the rest of his crew escaped.

"Jeryl and Arien and Sarah Anders helped the FreeMasters to capture Durrow and his spacecraft. Both Jeryl and Arien believed that Durrow owed them a life-debt. They all went to the city of Berrut so that Arien could testify before the Assembly. While Arien was locked in the assembly chamber, Jeryl killed Durrow," recounted Ertis.

"When Arien learned of this, he was very angry. He hated all Terrans and wanted them to leave Ardel forever. Some members of the Assembly agreed with him, but others believed that trade with the Terrans would be beneficial for Ardel, and they approved of the trade agreement that Sarah Anders had negotiated with Clan Alu.

"In his anger, Arien called out challenge against Jeryl as

Mentor of Alu and thief of a life-debt. The stakes were this: victory for Jeryl would mean trade with the Terrans, governed by Clan Alu; victory for Arien would mean that Sarah Anders and all Terrans would be banned from Ardel forever.

"Sarah Anders attempted to stop the dispute. She offered to have Ardel placed under interdict, so that Terrans would be forbidden to come here. She said she would leave with her captives and never return. This offer was a great personal sacrifice, for any who saw her knew that she felt toward Jeryl as one feels toward a beloved sibling or a mate of many years standing.

"Jeryl refused to stop the dispute. At dawn of the next day he met Arien in the park opposite the Inn of the Blue Door. Sarah came to watch, as did the Healer Viela, and the leaders of many of the clans and guilds. Starm of the Messengers Guild brought a moss-green funeral urn and placed it in the center of the park. Then he confronted Sarah and tried to send her away. Arien and Jeryl stopped him, and insisted that she be allowed to stay. For Jeryl this was a point of honor. Arien only wanted the Terran to see her ally defeated.

"Jeryl wore a deep blue tunic bound by a leather girdle, and his gray Mentor's cloak. Arien wore a white robe. Neither wore boots or slippers. Sarah offered Jeryl the patterned sash that she often wore around her waist, and he wrapped it around his own over the girdle. Then he joined Arien in the center of the garden."

Ertis paused to sip tea from his mug, then leaned his head back against the wall before continuing. "They took their time setting the wards on the gates and building the dome of protection. Their auras shone bright and clear, for they were both righteous.

"The first strike was Jeryl's, and it was ineffectual. Arien countered with a flash that burned Jeryl's left hand. Sarah Anders cried out, as if she shared his agony.

"Jeryl attacked again and severely burned Arien's leg. That did not stop the FreeMaster. He struck Jeryl down with a blow to his side that left him in agony from his shoulder to his knee. Sarah sat on a bench, holding her left side and gasping as she watched.

"The dispute was nearly over. Neither Arien nor Jeryl

could survive another blow. They were both weak and sorely
injured. Yet each was still trying to hurt the other.

"Sarah Anders could not bear to watch any longer. She
entered the circle and stood between Jeryl and Arien, the
funeral urn at her feet. She intercepted Arien's attack and
channeled it harmlessly into the ground. Then she turned to
Jeryl, her arms extended in victory, and found herself facing
a blow intended for Arien. She could have stepped aside
and let the power destroy him, but she did not. She reached
for the energy, accepted it. It engulfed her fingers, her
hands, seared the nerves in her arms, burned its way through
her body until it reached the earth."

Ertis swallowed the last of his tea before he looked at
Sinykin. "Jeryl killed her. He did not mean to do it. The
horror of her death put an end to the dispute. Jeryl and
Arien took Sarah's body back to Clan Alu. They cremated
her and put her ashes in the moss-green urn. Jeryl still wears
the sash that she gave him. Arien reveres her memory and
no longer hates Terrans, for he has seen Terran honor."

Inda's hand trembled as he put down his pen. He reached
into his pack and brought out Sarah Anders' journal. The
journal and an urn on Alu Keep's mourning wall were all
that remained of that idealistic woman who had unwittingly
sacrificed her life. Yet she would live in story and memory
as long as the Ardellan people survived. Inda sighed and
wondered if he would ever earn such immortality, and what
it would cost him.

Chapter 14

Jeryl turned his mount sharply and rode through the gate and down the narrow path to the FreeMasters' mountain compound. The guildhall loomed out of the darkness to his right. He rode past it into the stableyard, and began to dismount near the stable's wide door. Pain jarred the pads of his right foot as they touched the frozen ground. His sudden exhalation created a cloud of steam before his face.

Hanra-bae stopped his alep near Jeryl's and dismounted with a grunt. "I shall never become accustomed to this cold weather," he complained quietly.

"You need not stay in the mountains. You can return to your warm and sunny seaside at any time."

"I cannot!" Ruby anger flashed in the Healer's aura. "I have a mission, just as do you. I will not return to my people until I can bring them the potion that will let us create new Houses."

Jeryl offered one hand palm-upward in a gesture of apology. "I am sorry, Healer. My comment was cruel. This weather is uncomfortable even for those of us who are accustomed to it." He shifted more of his weight onto his right foot. The pads had stopped hurting. They tingled now, and the joints ached. Jeryl's leg was numb from the cold. He knew it would throb as it warmed. He pulled his left foot from the stirrup and lowered it to the ground. Dizziness washed over him. He leaned against his alep.

"Jeryl." He felt Hanra-bae's hand on his shoulder. "Are you ill?"

He breathed deeply and opened his eyes. The stable had stopped moving. "I was dizzy. I am fine now. We should stable our mounts."

"I can get help from the guildhall. Wait here while I find some younglings to feed and water the aleps."

"Do not disturb the FreeMasters," said Jeryl. "We will exchange our mounts for two fresh aleps and be on our way."

A third voice came from behind them. "That is best. I would offer you the hospitality of our guildhall, but doing so would sully the reputation of the FreeMasters Guild. You are, after all, a pair of thieves."

Jeryl stared back over his shoulder. Arien stepped from the shadows and took the rein from Jeryl's limp hand. His fingers touched Jeryl's for a moment. Energy surged through the contact, climbing Jeryl's arm and moving to the center of his chest. Jeryl was grateful for the gift.

"Did you believe that you could pass me without my knowing it?" Arien conjured a ball of shimmer-light and led the way into the stable. "Your mounts deserve a chance to eat and rest. I will shelter them here and give you fresh aleps so that you may continue your journey."

"I had hoped for a meal and a night's lodging in your guildhall," said Hanra-bae as he followed Jeryl. "We have been riding most of the day."

"With angry Healers in pursuit, no doubt. You cannot stay here."

"I know," said Jeryl. An instant later he stumbled against a bale of hay and, gasping, fell headlong to the wooden floor. The others immediately left the aleps and came to kneel by his side. He pushed their hands away and struggled to untangle his body from his heavy cloak, then sat up and leaned against the bale.

"I do not believe that the Mentor can ride anymore tonight," said Hanra-bae. "I think he has injured his leg again. I will need a lantern, clean rags, and some hot water to clean the wound."

"I will have a pair of younglings bring those things to you," said Arien. "They will also bring some hot cider and bread. I will tell them to switch your packs and saddles to fresh mounts."

"The Mentor is injured. We will not refuse him shelter!" Three FreeMasters stood in the stable's doorway. Jeryl recognized his old friends, Carra and Lemki, although the speaker was a stranger.

"The Mentor and his companion have stolen several documents from the Healers' library in Berrut.'' Arien rose. "The Healers are pursuing them. If we give them shelter, we will be knowingly aiding thieves. The Assembly will not treat us kindly if the Healers bring a complaint against our guild.''

"A plague on the Assembly, and on the Healers!'' The stranger came forward and offered his arm to Jeryl. "We will not allow the Mentor of Clan Alu to ride while he is injured, or to spend a night in our stable. There is a bed for him in the guildhall.''

Arien shrugged. "All of the FreeMasters must know of this and agree before these two can be allowed to enter the guildhall.''

"Then go and talk with them, GuildMaster. We will stay with the Mentor,'' said the stranger. Carra and Lemki were already unsaddling the aleps.

Arien returned to the stable a few moments later.

"What have your FreeMasters decided?'' asked Jeryl. He was cold and tired, and he desperately wanted to sleep. Yet if the FreeMasters denied him shelter, he would ride away from the guildhall without complaint.

"They are readying your rooms now,'' said Arien. Jeryl knew that Arien feared the consequences of sheltering him. He also sensed the pride Arien felt in his FreeMasters. "Come, let me help you into the kitchen. The Healer will examine you there.''

One of the older FreeMasters was putting an extra log on the fire when they brought Jeryl into the guildhall. Arien and the stranger supported Jeryl between them, his arms thrown over their shoulders and theirs wrapped around his back. Carra and Lemki brought the packs, and Hanra-bae carried his bag of herbs and potions.

They propped Jeryl on a bench before the fire, where he could warm himself and watch the bustle. It seemed that every FreeMaster in the hall was awake and dressed. Two of them held a whispered conversation with Arien before donning riding cloaks and leaving through the front door. Another put a pot of water on to boil, while a fourth brought a tray of bread and cold fowl from the larder.

"I must cut away your legging,'' said Hanra-bae, looking down at Jeryl's thigh. "It looks as if you were bleeding most of the day.''

"It is only a scrape," protested Jeryl. He winced as Hanra-bae prodded the crusted legging with a finger.

"You lost too much blood. It is no wonder you were dizzy." The Healer looked at Carra. "Bring the Mentor some broth. Just warm it a little and put it in a mug. He should drink at least two mugs full." He searched through his bag, then handed Carra a packet of green powder. "Put a spoonful of this into the broth after it is heated."

"It is not necessary to trouble yourselves. . . ."

"Yes, it is necessary, Mentor!" Another of Jeryl's old friends was descending the stairs, bringing a tray of cloths and bandages. He nodded to Hanra-bae. "Welcome to our guildhall, Healer. I am Lissa, Healer to the FreeMasters Guild. May I be of assistance?"

The fisher was already cutting the legging with tiny scissors. "I welcome your help. I need some wet compresses to soak the cloth from the Mentor's wound. He bled through his legging all day, and the fabric is stuck tight to his thigh."

Lissa folded a length of cloth into a pad, dipped it into the steaming water, and laid it, dripping, on Jeryl's leg. The Mentor smothered a gasp. Carra brought Jeryl the broth, frothy and green with Hanra-bae's powder. Jeryl drank it down despite the bitter taste, and asked for more. The Healers peeled away his blood-soaked legging to reveal the scraped patch on his thigh. It was longer than his hand and just as broad, and it burned as they cleaned it with soft cloths and potions. Blood welled in two spots, and Hanra-bae dabbed those with a white paste before he and Lissa bandaged the wound.

"You should not ride for at least a day," advised Lissa as he wrapped the gauze around Jeryl's thigh.

Jeryl shrugged. "I do not wish to trouble the FreeMasters Guild more than I already have. We should leave tomorrow."

"That is not necessary," said Arien, joining them at the hearth. "My FreeMasters are offering you shelter for as long as you need it. I warned them that they may someday regret that decision. They chose to not heed my advice."

Jeryl laughed. "Such is the lot of a Mentor or a GuildMaster. We are appointed to advise and guide our clans or guilds because they consider us to be wise and powerful. Then they choose not to listen to us."

"Yes." Arien shrugged. "Perhaps the trade guilds have

a better system. Their GuildMasters rule all the guilds' activities without question, without opposition.''

"You and I would not be happy leading wool-deer," said Jeryl. "Opposition keeps our minds sharp and our skills polished. Convey my thanks to all the members of your guild. Their hospitality is appreciated. Now tell me, is there any word of Hatar?''

"We are still tracking him. He has moved down the mountain and is hiding in the forests. Every time we approach him, he slips away. He does not want to be found." Arien squeezed Jeryl's shoulder with his right hand. "He is still alive, my friend, and he may yet come to his senses and return to us.

"I have other news which you may not receive so well. Ertis and Sinykin Inda stopped here yesterday. They were journeying to the Iron Keep.''

Jeryl struggled to his feet. "What nonsense is this? I did not give Inda permission to go beyond Alu Keep!" He leaned too heavily on his right leg and felt the bandage grow damp as blood began to seep from the wound again. "Viela said that they had gone off with some traders from Sau Keep, but he said nothing about a trip up the mountain. Ertis is not a fool. Why would he take the Terran to the Iron Keep?''

"Sit, Jeryl. There is nothing you can do to stop them now." Arien pushed him back down on the bench. "They did travel to Eiku Keep with the Sau traders. There they met a Master from the Iron Keep. They said his name was Kento, and he carried a message from the Historians of the Iron Keep. He told Ertis and Inda that the Historians would welcome a visit from them. He also told Inda that he should go to the keep because he would learn something important there.

"They left the traders and continued on their own. When they stopped here, I told them of the reports we had heard, that someone at the Iron Keep is working the weather. Ertis said that Kento's message hinted at the same thing.''

"Ertis had received other messages from his Guild-Master, reports of weather-working in the mountains," said Jeryl. "We discussed them before I left for Berrut.''

"I tried to dissuade them from continuing the journey, to no effect.''

"Like most of the Terrans I have met, Inda is headstrong

and will have his own way. Ertis should have been more sensible.''

"Sense seemed to have little to do with this journey. Inda seemed convinced that his people are in danger. I sent Carra with them, to act as their guide and stay with them in the keep. He returned late that night. The guards at the Iron Keep refused to admit him. Inda and Ertis would have returned with him, but Ertis was injured on the trail and could ride no further. They decided to stay at the keep.''

Jeryl slapped the bench with his palm as he quoted an old proverb. "He is a fool who walks into the mouth of a hungry tol hoping that his sacrifice will keep it from feasting on his wool-deer tomorrow! The Terran is my responsibility. I must ride to the Iron Keep and bring them back.''

"You will do no such thing!" Hanra-bae strode to Jeryl's side and stared down at him. "You have ridden much too far with that wound. Now you must sleep and recover your strength. Tomorrow we will discuss what to do about the Terran.''

"You know that the Healer is right, Jeryl," said Arien. "You must rest now. I will show you to your room.''

Jeryl knew that further argument would accomplish nothing. He was exhausted, and if he tried to walk out to the stable and saddle a mount, Hanra-bae and the others could easily stop him. Instead he grabbed his pack and followed Arien up the stairs to one of the last rooms opening on the long balcony. He sat on the sleeping platform, and Arien helped him remove his boots and what was left of his leggings. Jeryl skinned off his tunic, then crawled into the furs.

"Sleep well, my friend." Arien paused at the door. "Tomorrow we will discuss getting the Terran out of the Iron Keep and returning the stolen scrolls to the Healers' library. For now, you must rest." The door shut quietly behind him.

Jeryl burrowed deeper into the warm furs. In the morning he would see about Sinykin Inda, and then he would begin searching the old texts for the information Hanra-bae needed. Once he had found it, he would consider returning the scrolls to the Healers.

A door slammed. Jeryl's eyes opened suddenly, then closed again when light, streaming in through the cracks around the shutters, jarred them. Jeryl sat up, squinting, and listened to the shouting downstairs.

"Yes, thieves! We are following the trail of two thieves who stole some scrolls from the Healers' library in Berrut. The tracks show that they turned into your compound, and rode out again on a different pair of aleps."

Jeryl could not hear the reply. He crept to the door and opened it a crack, peered out over the balcony rail into the main hall. Arien was standing near the door, speaking with someone wearing Healer's colors.

". . . voice down. There is an injured FreeMaster sleeping upstairs. Are you certain that the Masters you followed were the thieves?"

"There is no doubt," replied the other, waving his left arm. "They rode directly to your stable."

"And you think we gave them fresh mounts and sent them on their way?"

The Healer shrugged. "Another set of tracks left the stable and continued up the mountain trail. I suggest that your guild provided the thieves with fresh mounts!"

Arien was angry. His ruby aura billowed toward the Healer, and his words were quiet and forceful. "We did not knowingly provide mounts for any thieves! You insult me and my guild with your charges. I will not tolerate your accusations any longer. Please leave my guildhall, now!" He stepped forward, forcing the Healer to back toward the door.

"You are not telling the whole truth, GuildMaster," cried the Healer. "We will find the thieves, and we will learn the truth. There will be retribution if your guild has given them aid or shelter. We can withdraw the FreeMasters' Healer from your service. How long would your guild prosper without a Healer?"

The door was opening behind the Healer. Arien backed him out into the yard and let the door slam shut behind them.

Jeryl could still hear muffled shouting. He straightened up and gasped. Pain spread across his thigh like flames licking at skin. He could feel each thread of the bandage as it scraped his raw flesh and tugged at growing scabs. Moisture seeped from the wound, oozing through the newly-cracked incrustations and wetting the gauze as he moved.

Jeryl realized that he could not ride today. His leg had

been injured and irritated too often during the past few days. He would have to rest and let it heal. Tomorrow morning the scabs would be gone, and new skin would protect his tortured thigh.

He limped across the floor to the window and threw open the shutters. Three Masters in Healer's colors were riding from the stableyard as Arien, his feet lost in a snowdrift, watched them. The GuildMaster's aura was still red with anger. Jeryl knew that Arien's wrath had been misdirected at the Healers. Soon the GuildMaster would come to Jeryl's room and vent his ire. Jeryl hoped that that encounter would not mean the end of their friendship.

Younglings were already at work hauling the day's water and chopping wood for the kitchen. The thought of food made Jeryl salivate. He considered the long climb down to the common room, realized he had best wait for someone to bring him bread and tea. His leg was already throbbing.

Jeryl stopped beside the sleeping platform and bent to retrieve the Healers' scrolls from his pack. He tucked them among the furs, along with a blank scroll and a stylus, then climbed up and sat on the platform with his back to the wall. He wrapped one fur around his shoulders and covered his legs with another. His feet were cold, but he could not bend to put on his boots. The furs would have to do.

He had no idea which of the scrolls contained the information for which he and Hanra-bae were searching. All five were made in the old style, with a long, three-hands wide strip of writing-cloth stretched between two ornate wooden dowels. The cloth was yellowing and brittle with age, and the ends of the dowels had been darkened and worn smooth by the touch of many hands.

The runes were also of the old style, ornate and complex, which made them difficult to read. Modern writing was simpler, due to the work of the great teacher Hakai a hand of generations ago. Few Masters, other than those who made caring for the libraries their life's work, were taught to read the old runes now. Jeryl knew some of them, but not all; his education had been interrupted by the untimely death of his mate. He had become Alu's Mentor within a hand of days after that awful event and never returned to his studies.

He knew the old rune for cocooning, with its vertical bar wrapped by three horizontal loops and capped by an arc. "Larkenleaf" and "sacred moisture" were also mentioned in the passage he sought. He took up the most worn of the scrolls and began skimming the text an arm's length at a time, watching for those runes.

He soon realized that this would be a monumental task. The runes had been drawn from left to right across the end of the scroll, small and close together, and the nutshell ink had faded to taupe. It blended well with the age-darkened cloth. Jeryl conjured a small ball of shimmer-light to glow above his head and illuminate the figures.

He had skimmed nearly a sixth of the text when someone knocked on his door. He tucked the scroll under the furs with the others before calling, "Come!" and unlatching the door with a thought.

Arien entered the room. "The Healers were here. They were looking for you and your companion."

"And you lied and told them I was not here?"

"They never asked me where you were. They accused me of giving you fresh mounts and sending you on your way."

Jeryl shrugged. "Whose trail are they following?"

"Trinn and Eblar came to me last night, shortly after you arrived, and asked my permission to travel to Sau Keep. They both have siblings there. It will not be long before the Healers learn that they are following the wrong Masters and come back here to search for you."

"The ride to Sau Keep will take more than a day, and then they will be another day returning. We have some time."

"I think it will not take them that long to learn the truth. Healers are not stupid. They will soon return here and demand to know where you are hiding." Arien touched his friend's shoulder. "They threatened to remove Lissa from the FreeMasters' service."

"They are not so powerful that they can force me to withdraw from my post!" Lissa stood in the open doorway. A morning sunbeam touched his feet and legs, but the rest of his body remained in shadow. "I would not leave here unless the FreeMasters dismissed me. May I enter?"

"Certainly, Healer," said Jeryl. "Thank you for your

ministrations last night. My leg is healing well, although it is very stiff today."

"I would like to change the dressing on your wound," said Lissa. A youngling followed him into the room, carrying a tray laden with bandages and salve pots. "Hanra-bae sends his greetings and will bring you tea and bread shortly. He is warming himself at the hearth downstairs."

"That fisher will never become accustomed to our cold weather. He complained all the while we were in Berrut."

"You should be more charitable, Jeryl," chided Arien. "You have dragged that poor fisher into a mountain winter. Would you fare any better in the heat of the seaside at high summer?"

Lissa nodded. "The fishers cannot tolerate cold weather. Their bodies are not used to it. Hanra-bae has done well to travel this far without becoming ill."

"He came willingly! Do not lay the blame for his discomfort on me." Jeryl was not ready to admit that he had grown to like the fisher.

Jeryl slipped his injured leg out from under the furs so that Lissa could examine it. A scroll tumbled out of its hiding place, and he scooped it up and tucked it under the edge of his robe.

Arien reached for the scroll. "I will take that and return it to the Healers. I can take back all of the scrolls for you."

"No!" Jeryl pushed Arien's hand away. He and the fisher had risked much to get the ancient texts. "These scrolls will go back when we have finished with them. After Hanra-bae and I have found the information we are seeking, we will give the scrolls to you. You may return them to the Healers yourself or send them to Berrut with one of your Free-Masters."

"You are being foolish, Mentor. Little useful information can be garnered from those ancient scrolls. You will only jeopardize the standing of Clan Alu and the FreeMasters in the Assembly. You are giving Reass and the others another excuse to challenge Alu."

"Perhaps so, GuildMaster." Jeryl tried to remain detached, despite the hurt he felt. He wanted Arien to accept and support his actions. "You need not worry about the standing of your guild. I will make it clear that your

FreeMasters did not know about the scrolls, and that you did not willingly grant us hospitality."

Arien's aura reddened quickly from top to bottom. As long as Jeryl had known him, he had had a short temper. This flash of anger came as no surprise. Suddenly Jeryl felt remorse for deliberately provoking his friend; he could not even look up as Arien left the room.

Lissa said nothing. He unwrapped the bandage from Jeryl's thigh and exposed the scabbing wound. Clear fluid was oozing in several spots where the scabs had torn away. The Healer swabbed these areas with a ball of cloth dipped in green liquid. Jeryl gasped as the solution touched raw flesh. He closed his eyes and held his breath until Lissa was done. Then the Healer spread white salve over the whole area and wrapped it with clean gauze.

"You cannot ride until tomorrow," he told Jeryl as he closed his pots and jars.

"I know. I intend to stay here until tomorrow morning."

The Healer shrugged. "I will inform the GuildMaster." He handed the tray back to the youngling and followed it out of the room.

Jeryl had just found his place in the text of the first scroll when Hanra-bae appeared in the doorway, carrying a tray of food.

"Good morning, Mentor. I have tea, bread, and fruit for you."

"Come in. The food is most welcome. How did you spend the night?"

Hanra-bae entered and set the tray on the small table beside the sleeping platform. Another Master followed him into the room. Jeryl looked closely, recognized the stranger who had come to their aid in the stable last night.

The fisher poured three cups of steaming tea, handed one to Jeryl and another to the stranger. "I slept well, although I was cold. Even the hearth-fire could not warm me this morning. This is Aakar, from Clan Rais. He is newly-made a FreeMaster and has offered to aid us in our task."

"Greetings, Aakar. I am Jeryl, Mentor of Clan Alu. It seemed last night that you knew me, although I do not know you."

"That is so, Mentor. I had never met you, but I knew you through stories told by the Historians. The tale of the dispute between Alu and Eiku has seen many tellings at Rais Keep."

Jeryl dismissed that statement with the wave of a hand. He had never set out to become a living legend. He had done only what was necessary to preserve Clan Alu. "You have me at a disadvantage, FreeMaster. Tell me about yourself."

"He has been here less than a season," said Hanra-bae.

"Hanra-bae is correct. My mate was one of the first to die of the plague. It reached the northern keeps at the end of high summer, before the second harvest. Metar died quickly, the younglings were fostered, and I was left foundering in the clanhall. After the last harvest, our Mentor brought me here. Now I am trying to make a place for myself in the FreeMasters Guild, which has no need of a librarian."

"Librarian!" Jeryl held out the scroll he had been studying. "Then you can read the old runes? Can you translate these passages?"

Aakar took the scroll and studied it for a moment. "Yes, I know these old runes. It would take me some time to translate the entire text into modern script."

"We need only a small portion translated," said Hanra-bae. "We are searching for some very specific information."

"Then perhaps I can be of help. Tell me what you are seeking."

Hanra-bae pulled up a chair for the librarian and a little stool for himself, and they sat beside Jeryl's sleeping platform, sipped their tea, and listened as Jeryl ate and talked.

"Too many of our Mothers have died during this plague. All of the clans, and the fishers, and even the guilds have lost Mothers. It does not affect the future of the guilds, for they use perverted mating practices to increase their populations. The clans and the fisher settlements are in danger. More than half of the Houses in Clan Alu stand empty, their lines ended, and we have no way to replace them. A few more plague seasons will wipe out Clan Alu, and several of the other clans as well. The guilds will continue to grow and prosper, and any clans that survive will live under their rule."

"It is the same for the fishers," said Hanra-bae. "Port Freewind's council of Mothers was decimated by the plague. We lost some of our elders, some of our most experienced leaders."

"Yet you send no mateless Masters to join the Free-Masters Guild," said Jeryl. "I have never seen a fisher among the FreeMasters."

"There are no FreeMasters among the fishers. If a Master's mate dies, the Master throws himself into the sea with her body, to drown or be devoured by the creatures of the deep. If a Master is lost at sea or suffers an accidental death, his mate throws herself into the water to die."

"It was once so among the people of the keeps. Mothers tore their tentacles out and bled to death when their mates died; Masters wandered into the wilderness and were never seen again. Our population is now too small to allow those unnecessary deaths to continue. We need the strength and the power of the FreeMasters."

Hanra-bae nodded. "We cannot long survive as fishers unless we find a way to create new family lines to replace those that have been lost. The council of Mothers sent me out to search for the old knowledge, the ancient method of creating new Houses."

Jeryl shrugged in agreement. "My quest is the same. Long ago it was common to cocoon two younglings together, one to become Master of the existing House, the other to begin a new line. The method was lost, or so we were told by the Healers. I thought that it might be recorded in some of the ancient texts, so Hanra-bae and I went to the Healers' library in Berrut. We asked to see the oldest scrolls."

"They would permit only me to see the scrolls. Jeryl was barred from the library. I have great difficulty with the ancient runes and need the help of a translator."

"It was obvious that they did not want us to read and understand the ancient texts. Since they would not give us free access to the scrolls, we borrowed them." Jeryl swept back the fur to show Aakar the other scrolls. "We know that there is a passage in one of these texts that gives instructions for cocooning two younglings. That is what we need to have translated."

"And the Healers who came this morning . . . ."

The Mentor leaned forward and touched Aakar's arm. "They are searching for us. When they learn that they are following the wrong people, they will come back here. They will ask us for the scrolls, and when we refuse to give them up, they will try to take them, even if they must kill us to do it."

Chapter 15

Sinykin Inda completed his meditation, rose and stretched, and checked his chronometer. Although his room was dark, the hour was well past dawn. He walked to the window and threw open the shutters. Heavy gray clouds hung low over the Iron Keep, blocking out the sunshine that brightened the distant valley. At least Jaime and Elissa would have a sunny day. Sinykin shivered and pulled his borrowed cloak closer about his shoulders.

He had slept late and poorly. Most of the long night he had lain awake, thinking about the story Ertis had told him. He had recorded the tale of Arien's dispute with Jeryl and its tragic outcome in his journal. Inda was not certain how the Terran authorities would react to this account of Sarah Anders' death. They had discounted her reports of the Ardellans' psychokinetic powers. Perhaps they would also doubt this story.

At the moment it was an academic question. Sinykin and his journal were many kilometers from ships and transmitters. He would decide what to do with the report when he returned to the spaceport. He closed the journal and slipped it into the innermost pocket of his pack. With the velcro pressed closed, it was well hidden.

Ertis always woke early. Inda knocked lightly on the connecting door and waited for the Historian's invitation to enter. There was no reply. He knocked again, louder, thinking that Ertis might be in the bath. That reminded him of his own body's needs. When there still was no answer, he pushed the door open and peered into the dimness.

Sinykin blinked twice as his eyes adjusted to the lack of light. He saw the Historian sprawled on the sleeping platform, right hand flung across his face, left arm hanging off the bed, hand twitching.

"Ertis."

The Ardellan did not react. Inda padded across the room and ducked behind the curtain to use the facilities. When he was finished, he came out and opened both sets of shutters. The clouds seemed darker and lower than they had a few minutes earlier.

Ertis' position had not changed. Sinykin bent down, touched the Ardellan's shoulder. Ertis gasped and began to shudder. His right arm swept up and out, his fingers missing Inda's eyes by centimeters. His chest lifted from the platform, back arching, head thrown back, eyes still closed and mouth now gaping. Tremors ran through every visible part of his body.

Inda knelt beside the bed, scooped up a discarded tunic, rolled one edge into a thick pad and thrust it into Ertis' mouth just before his jaws clamped shut. Ertis' head jerked from side to side, his neck cracking and snapping with the sudden movements. Sinykin tried to hold him still. He placed one hand on either side of Ertis' face and pressed his forearms and elbows against the Historian's chest.

"Ertis! Wake up, Ertis!"

The Historian's legs thrashed. The furs slid away and puddled on the floor. Ertis twisted nearer to the edge of the platform. Sinykin feared he would fling himself onto the stone floor. The Terran pressed his body against the side of the bed, and tried to keep Ertis from rolling off.

"Master!" Someone knocked at the door.

"Enter!" called Inda, and he was surprised by the panic in his voice. He took a deep breath. A youngling looked in and squeaked in dismay. "Get the Healer! The Historian is having convulsions. I need help!"

"I go!" cried the youngling. It left the door open. Inda could hear its frantic footfalls echoing down the corridor.

Ertis' body relaxed, settled back onto the stone platform. Sinykin dared not release his grip of the Ardellan, instead shifting his legs around to make his knees more comfortable on the hard floor. His cloak had slipped off and he shivered from cold and apprehension. He could find no obvious cause for the convulsion, no head wound or concussion. Might it be related to the night-starts Ertis had experienced on the trail? Ertis had never made an adequate explanation of those mysterious bouts of shuddering. Perhaps the Healer would be able to enlighten Inda.

He felt Ertis' muscles growing rigid again and braced himself for another convulsion. This one was stronger than the first. The Historian's arms flailed about, striking Inda first on the left side of his head and then on the right, while Ertis' legs kicked against the stone platform. Sinykin tucked his own head between his arms, nestling his face on Ertis' chest. He felt the fluttering of the Ardellan's heart and knew from his research that it was beating in an abnormal rhythm. He wished for a cardiac crashkit and the knowledge to use it on this alien body. Where was that Healer?

Ertis arched away from the bed, forcing Inda upward. The Historian's neck bent backward until the top of his head touched the stone. Sinykin readied for a final burst of energy, a thrashing of limbs and tossing of head. It never came.

With a great exhalation, Ertis relaxed. His body flattened against the stone of the platform, arms and legs extended. His head would have flopped to the right if Inda had not supported it. Ertis spat out the roll of cloth and sighed.

And opened his eyes.

"Ertis?" Sinykin tried to slow the frantic beating of his own heart.

Ertis blinked. "Yes?"

"How do you feel?"

He did not even pause to think. "Alone."

Inda lifted his arm from the other's chest. His wrists ached from the strain of holding Ertis' head still. "You don't feel ill?"

"No. I feel alone. I want to go home."

"That is not an impossibility," said someone near the door.

Sinykin looked over his shoulder to see who had spoken. Satto was standing in the doorway, with naLeera and another youngling. "I was told that you needed my help, but you seem to have managed on your own."

"Not well," replied Sinykin. "Ertis is very ill and needs your attention."

The Healer strode to the sleeping platform, beckoning the younglings to follow with their burdens. He looked down at Ertis and Inda and the scattered furs and clothing, and shrugged. "What is wrong?"

Sinykin described the trembling, the seizure, the sudden relaxation and waking. Satto's expression did not change.

Finally the Healer took his bag from naLeera. "I must examine Ertis," he said. "This is best done in private. Go into the other room for a moment, please. I will call you when I am finished."

Inda rose. He did not wish to leave Ertis, but he would not argue with this Healer. He walked into his own room and closed the connecting door.

If Ertis wanted to return to Alu Keep, they would go as soon as Satto said he was able to travel. Sinykin did not want to leave the Iron Keep before he could speak with Kento, before the builder could explain why he thought it necessary for Inda to come here. So far Sinykin had found nothing that might endanger his people. Matri had made vague threats, but they were directed at Sinykin personally, not at the whole Terran population.

Sinykin began folding his soiled clothing and stuffing it into the bottom of his pack. His stomach growled, and he pulled out a small ration bar and nibbled at it while he waited for Satto to call him back into the room. He was concerned that Ertis' thrashing might have reopened his shoulder wound. That would mean another delay before they could travel, and he was beginning to feel that the Historian's need to return home was genuine and urgent.

Satto came for him before he had finished his ration bar. He folded the plastic wrapper around the remaining few bites and stuffed it into his pocket as he followed the Healer into Ertis' room. The Historian was sitting on the edge of the sleeping platform, pulling on clean leggings. He wore only an undertunic, and through its thin fabric, Inda could see that his shoulder was perfectly healed.

"Ertis must return to Clan Alu immediately," said Satto. "I would like him to leave here before midday."

"What about the convulsions?" asked Sinykin. "Surely he should not be riding while he is ill?"

Ertis finished with his leggings and reached for his boots. "I am not ill, Sinykin. My mating time has come early. I must return to Poola and House Actaan."

"The convulsions, and the night-starts Ertis tells me he experienced on the trail, are caused by his separation from his mate at this very important time. They will cease as

soon as he returns to her.'' Satto shrugged. ''Will you travel
with him?''

''Certainly,'' said Inda. ''I would not allow him to go
alone.'' Ertis looked up, met Sinykin's gaze, and nodded.

''Then I will send someone to the stable to have your
mounts readied.'' Satto handed his pack to one of the younglings. They both followed him to the door. ''I wish you
clear skies and fast travel.''

''Thank you for your help,'' Ertis called after him. He
struggled into a clean tunic and then began throwing clothing into his pack.

Inda finished gathering his own things and brought his
packs into Ertis' room. He was feeling troubled and guilty
as he dropped the packs beside the open door and turned to
watch Ertis. ''Why did you agree to make this journey, if
your mating time was so near?''

Ertis folded his spare boots and tucked them into his pack
before closing it. ''I did not know that Poola was ready to
mate. We should have had at least two more winters before
she matured. Her time has come early.'' He shrugged.
''Nothing is the same for us since the plague came.''

''Masters!'' naLeera was standing in the doorway, a pot
of tea swinging from one tentacle and a small tray of mugs
and bread held in three others. ''I have brought you food.''

''Thank you,'' said Inda, clearing space on the table. The
tantalizing odors made his stomach rumble. ''You are very
kind.''

''Master Matri is coming to see you,'' offered naLeera
as he set down the teapot, tipping it just enough to send a
thin red stream splashing onto the table. ''Ooh! I am sorry!''
In his agitation he dropped the tray. It landed upright on the
table, and nothing was damaged except the top of the jam
jar, which bounced off the pot and shattered. ''Oh, no!''

Sinykin could see that the youngling was distressed, so
he swallowed a laugh and tried to reassure it. ''Tell the
kitchenmaster that I broke it, naLeera. It was not your
fault.''

''Why is Matri coming to visit us?'' asked Ertis.

naLeera shifted his weight from right leg to left with little, agitated jumps. ''The Healer told him that you are leaving the Iron Keep.''

''Does he propose to stop us?''

naLeera looked at Inda. ''Only one of you.''

Ertis dismissed the youngling with a wave. "Thank you for your help. We can serve ourselves." He closed the door as naLeera left the room.

"Well," said Inda. He pulled out a chair and sat, reaching for a cup. "Tea?"

"Certainly," said Ertis. He sat across the table from Sinykin and picked up the knife. "Bread?"

Without speaking, they ate thick slabs of warm bread slathered with jam, and each drank two cups of tea. Sinykin stared out the window at the lowering clouds. It was not a good day to begin a journey, but staying alone at the Iron Keep was a more intimidating prospect than traveling through a snowstorm. Inda knew better than to trust nature, which could be blindly malevolent. Matri had been even more threatening. Without Ertis' protection, Sinykin would be at the smelter's mercy. He was afraid that he might never leave the Iron Keep.

Ertis set his mug aside and stacked the empty plates. "You should not stay here, even if Matri invites you to do so. I do not trust him. I think you would be in danger."

"I agree," said Inda, wondering if Ertis had read his mind. He drained his mug and handed it to the Historian. "I do not intend to let you ride those mountain trails alone."

The door's latch clicked, and the door swung open on creaky hinges. Sinykin turned quickly and watched Matri walk in, uninvited. Another Master and a youngling followed him.

"The Iron Keep's council would never allow the Historian to travel alone at this time of year. An escort is already waiting at the stable," said Matri. "Please excuse my forwardness. I wanted to speak with you both before Ertis leaves us."

"I am grateful for your concern," said Ertis, rising. "Sinykin and I will not need an escort. We have packed our things and are ready to leave now. If you will send a pair of younglings to carry our packs, we will be on our way."

"Certainly you can spare us a few moments." Matri gestured to the other Master. "I have been remiss. Please let me introduce my companion. This is Sanid, leader of the miners' clan. Sanid, this is Ertis, Historian to Clan Alu, and Sinykin Inda, from the Terran Spaceport."

Sanid nodded in Inda's direction. "Greetings from the miners of the Iron Keep. Master Ertis, I congratulate you

on the fecundity of your House. I certainly understand your
eagerness to return to Alu Keep for your metamorphosis.
The Historians Guild will not be pleased to lose one of its
most accomplished members.

"Master Inda, I asked to see you as soon as I learned of
your presence here. I offer you guest quarters at the miners'
clanhall."

Sinykin trusted Sanid no more than he did Matri. The
miner was short, squat, and heavily muscled. Black leggings were stretched taut across his thick thighs, a sleeve-
less leather tunic covered his substantial gut, and his dirty
gray hair was tied back with a thong. His black eyes rarely
blinked.

"Your offer is most kind. Why do you request my presence?" asked Sinykin.

"We should like to talk with you about Terran methods
for mining metals. Perhaps we could make arrangements
for some of your miners to visit us."

Inda nodded. "I would like to help you, but I know nothing of mining. I am a Healer. At this time we have no mining specialists at the spaceport. They are not scheduled to
arrive until spring."

"Still, I am certain you can answer some of our questions. Our methods are very simple; perhaps you could suggest ways we can improve them."

"Your confidence in me is misplaced. I am no engineer.
Perhaps my mate would be able to help you. I suggest you
send a representative to the spaceport to talk with her in the
spring, when the weather is better. She is quite accomplished in the field of maintenance engineering and knows
a bit about our mining methods."

Sanid looked at Matri, who shrugged. He turned back to
Inda. "We are not accustomed to dealing with Mothers in
such matters."

"Terran customs are quite different from ours," said Ertis. "Perhaps you should withhold judgment until you learn
more about them."

"This learning is something we should like to do," replied Matri. "For this purpose we would encourage Master
Inda to stay with us awhile."

Sinykin still did not trust them. "I thank you again for
the invitation, but I must refuse. I will be leaving with Master Ertis."

Matri's dark eyes clouded. "I am very sorry that you will not stay with us. There is much we could teach each other." He beckoned to Sanid. "We will send younglings to carry your packs."

The miner raised one hand in farewell. "I hope we shall meet again. Good journey to you, Historian." He and Matri left the room, the silent youngling trailing behind them.

"What did he mean about the Historian Guild losing one of its most accomplished members?" asked Sinykin. "What will happen when you go home to mate with Poola?"

Ertis sat down again and reached across the table to place his right hand on Sinykin's. Inda felt a tingling rush through his fingers and up his arm; he almost pulled his hand away. Instead he tried to relax, and waited for Ertis to speak.

"I will return to House Actaan, and there Poola and I will cocoon a youngling. I will put my affairs in order and tell my last few stories. When the new Master of House Actaan has completed his metamorphosis and emerged from his cocoon, it will be my turn to be bound. In a few hands of days, by the time the younglings have left Poola's body, I will emerge a Mother and begin my new work of raising the younglings."

"But you can still tell stories. . . ."

"A Mother cannot be a Historian, Sinykin. Nor can she be a merchant, or keep an inn or a stable. She can be only what she is—a Mother." He pressed Inda's hand. "Do not be troubled by it. It is our way."

Ertis rose and walked to the window. "There are other things with which we must concern ourselves. Matri and Sanid were lying."

"I know." Inda followed him to the window. The sky was looking more threatening with each passing hour. "Their auras were murky and greenish. I do not trust either of them."

"They want very much to keep you here," said Ertis. "Perhaps they will try to prevent your leaving with me."

An unfamiliar voice replied. "They will do worse than that." Inda spun around, saw a stranger standing in the doorway that connected Sinykin's room to Ertis'. He was wrapped in a long black cloak, its hood pulled forward to hide his face. "They will try to kill both of you on the trail."

"Who are you? How did you get in here?" asked Inda, walking toward the stranger.

The black-cloaked master threw back his hood.

"Kento?" Ertis came closer, too.

Inda studied the leather tunic and leggings, the straw-colored hair pulled tightly back, the builder's bracelet. Everything fit his memory of Kento, even the red dots tattooed from his eyes to the corners of his mouth. Still, Sinykin was skeptical. Why had Kento waited so long to reveal himself?

"Master Inda, you must not travel with the Historian. It would bring death to you both. Stay at the Iron Keep, for the danger of which I warned you is at hand. Matri and Sanid are planning to attack the spaceport tomorrow."

Sinykin almost laughed. He imagined an army of miners and smelters mounted on aleps, brandishing daggers as they rode across the spaceport's landing field. How much harm could they do? Then he remembered Ertis' stories, remembered the flashing power, remembered the image of Sarah Anders' burnt body. If Sanid and Matri controlled that kind of power, they could indeed harm the Terrans.

"What are they planning to do?" asked Ertis.

Kento looked behind him, then stepped into the room and closed the connecting door. "Please latch and ward your door," he said to Ertis. "For your sakes, I must not be found here. Matri would surely imprison us all.

"The smelters and the miners have taken control of the Iron Keep. Builders and herders are treated as slaves now, working to support the rest of the keep but given no voice in the governing of it. The keep's council has been disbanded. All decisions come from Matri and Sanid.

"Many of the builders are discontented. Together we searched out the secret places where Matri and his people are working, and we learned some of their secrets. We tried to stop the weather-working, and for that, some of us were killed. Most of the others have returned to the clanhall, and now do as Matri instructs them. The Historians helped me to escape, and I rode down the mountain to deliver their message to their GuildMaster. I was followed, so I rode to Eiku Keep, and there I found you."

"How can we help you? How does all this endanger the spaceport?" asked Inda. Kento's story was a moving one.

The builder's aura was a halo of white light around his body. Sinykin trusted him.

The door latch rattled. Kento rushed to the connecting door and opened it slowly, peering into the room beyond. Then he looked back over his shoulder at Ertis.

"Who disturbs my door?" called Ertis.

"It is me, Master. naLeera! naReina and I have come to carry your things to the stable."

"Wait a moment, then. We shall be ready shortly."

Sinykin and Ertis joined Kento at the connecting door. They stood, heads close together, and whispered to one another.

"What has happened to Historians Perli and Vaant?" asked Ertis. "We have not been allowed to see them."

"They fled the keep a few days ago, in fear for their lives."

"What is Matri planning to do?" asked Sinykin. "Will his people be riding down the mountain tomorrow?"

"Oh, no. They will work the storms from here. Already the clouds are forming at the mountaintop. Soon they will spill down toward the valleys, and tomorrow a blizzard will close all the trails."

Ertis stared at the builder. "This is the danger you see? A blizzard? The spaceport is built to withstand snowstorms."

"This will be much more than a snowstorm. Matri's people are using the forbidden secrets of weather-working. They will make winds blow harder, snow fall more heavily, ice coat every surface, and they will concentrate all of their power on the spaceport." Kento gripped Sinykin's shoulder. "If you go with the Historian, they will surely kill you both in order to keep their secrets. If you stay here, we can try to stop the ceremony. If we disrupt the ritual, we can lessen the fury of the storm."

"And if we do, what then?" Sinykin looked out the window at the heavy gray clouds. The spaceport had been built to withstand severe weather. High winds and ice might damage a building or send one of the towers crashing down, but that would not drive the Terrans from Ardel. They would rebuild and continue with their plans to mine titanium. They would find a way to shield incoming ships from the electromagnetic disturbances that disrupted their navigation systems. They would live with the storms. Sinykin was more concerned that the Ardellan miners and smelters were angry and desperate enough to resort to forbidden magic in an attempt to rid their planet of the Terrans.

Kento shrugged. "If we can stop them, even temporarily, we will win time for the FreeMasters and the Assembly to act. Weather-working is forbidden. Matri and those who help him will be punished."

Ertis was not satisfied. "I think you can disrupt this ceremony yourself. You do not need Sinykin to help you. Nor do I believe that Matri would try to have us killed. Such a crime could not go undiscovered for long. My death cry would bring the Masters of Alu Keep and the Historians Guild swarming up the mountain, and they would soon discover the Iron Keep's part in our deaths."

"They would," said Kento, "but not until the storm had destroyed the spaceport."

"The storm will not destroy the spaceport," said Inda. "What good will it do for Matri to keep me here, if he allows Ertis to leave? Ertis will surely tell the FreeMasters where I am, and they will come to get me. Won't they?"

"Perhaps." Kento grasped Ertis' forearm, lifted it to show Inda the Historian's trembling hand. "See how he shivers? Examine his eyes. He already has trouble focusing. He is being drawn back to his House and his mate. Soon he will forget about you and your problems. By the time he reaches the FreeMasters' guildhall, he will be able to think of nothing but the mating."

Sinykin looked at Ertis' shaking fingers, at the unaccustomed flush on his face and hands, at the sluggish movements of his eyes. What if Kento was right?

"You exaggerate!" exclaimed Ertis, pulling his arm from Kento's grip. "I will be home with my mate before that happens to me. I will listen to you no more. Go now and send up some younglings to carry our packs."

"The younglings are here, Ertis," said Sinykin. "Remember? They wait outside the door."

"Then let us go now." Ertis scooped up his cloak and settled it on his shoulders. "Leave us, Kento, or I shall call Matri and tell him that you are here."

Kento stared into Sinykin's eyes. "Be careful. Think about what I have told you."

"I will." Sinykin watched as Kento stepped back into the adjoining room. The door swung shut behind him.

"Come, come," said Ertis, tugging at Inda's arm. "We have a long journey ahead of us."

Two Masters were waiting for them at the bottom of the stairs. Neither said a word. They walked to the door, donned voluminous black cloaks that were hanging on pegs there, and led the way out into the street. Sinykin and Ertis followed, and the younglings trailed behind, complaining quietly to each other about the weight of the baggage.

The sky was even darker than it had seemed from the window. Inda looked up toward the top of the mountain and found it hidden by heavy black clouds. They were moving slowly outward toward the plain, blown by winds he could not feel inside the keep's high walls. The temperature of the air around him was cool but seemed to be well above freezing. Sinykin was beginning to sweat inside his silk thermals, coveralls, parka, and cloak. Beside him, Ertis shivered.

"Are you feeling chilled?" Inda asked.

"Oh, yes. It is very cold today." Ertis pulled his cloak in close to his body. "I cannot seem to keep my chest warm."

Sinykin took off his cloak and draped it over Ertis' shoulders. "This should help warm you," he said as he tugged the sides around and fastened the front clasp. Inda was still warm, so he unzipped his parka and let it hang open. Both members of their escort jumped when they heard the sound of the zipper and turned to stare at Sinykin. Neither said a word, but one of them dropped back to walk behind Ertis and Inda, where he could watch them.

They would be riding ahead of the storm. Sinykin believed they could reach Alu in just over a day if they rode quickly and made only a short stop at the FreeMasters' guildhall. He might spend tomorrow night in his own bed at the spaceport, with Elissa beside him and Jaime asleep in the next room. That thought made him smile. He missed his family, and Jeff Grund, and even Anna Griswold. It would be good to put the mountains and the sinister people of the Iron Keep behind him and return to the safety of Alu and the Terran compound.

The Historian was still shivering when they reached the stable. Another escort was awaiting them there—four stocky Masters dressed in stained leathers, all with their hair pulled

severely back and knotted, the blades of long knives showing beneath their wide belts. Six aleps, including the two
that Ertis and Inda had ridden into the keep, were saddled
and waiting.

For the first time since landing on Ardel, Sinykin wished
for a stunner. He could not forget Kento's warning. The
sight of these sinister guards was enough to make him believe that Kento was telling him the truth, that he and Ertis
would not reach the foot of the mountain alive.

Ertis looked as if he would die from the cold even before
he could mount his alep. The second cloak had not warmed
him. "Take off your cloaks," suggested Inda, slipping out
of his parka. "I want you to wear this for a while. It will
be warmer than the cloaks." While their escort watched, he
helped Ertis struggle into the heavy coat, then taught him
how to operate the zipper. He wrapped one cloak over the
parka, then tossed the other over his own shoulders.

It took him only a moment to fasten their packs to the
saddles and to help Ertis onto his mount. Sinykin was ready
to swing his own leg up and over the back of his alep when
he heard shouting behind him. He dropped back to the
ground and turned to find Matri and Sanid hurrying down
the road toward the stable.

"Master Inda, you cannot leave. There have been some
irregularities. . . ." shouted Sanid.

Matri waved to the two Masters in black cloaks. "Bring
the Terran to me. He will not be leaving with the Historian."

Sinykin turned and tried to mount his alep. He had just
gotten his foot in the stirrup when a Master grabbed his
right arm and pulled him away from the animal's side. He
struggled and tried to push the Master away. The other Master seized his left arm. They dragged him up the street away
from Ertis and the gate.

"Take the Historian as far as the FreeMasters' guildhall,
and take the Terran's mount with him," Matri shouted to
Ertis' escort. "Go now!"

"No!" Inda kicked the Master on his right, who howled
but did not relax his grip on Inda's arm. "Ertis is ill! I must
ride with him!"

The sinister Masters mounted quickly. One of them
tugged the rein from Ertis' hand, and another grabbed Siny-

kin's alep by the halter and led it away. Ertis turned in his saddle, struggling to dismount, but the riders closed in around him and forced him and his alep through the gate. Inda could hear Ertis shouting as the heavy doors closed behind him.

"Come," said Matri. "Your struggles accomplish nothing. You can walk or be carried to the smelter's clanhall."

Sinykin began to protest. "You cannot force me to stay here," he said, and felt the tightening grip of the Masters' hands on his arms. Apprehension choked back the rest of his angry words. These Ardellans could easily make him a prisoner in their keep. He wondered if he would ever see Elissa and Jaime again.

Matri and Sanid stared at Sinykin for a moment, then turned their backs and marched toward the clanhall. The escort forced Inda to keep up with their pace.

Sinykin was shivering now, and it was not from the cold.

Chapter 16

"Jeryl!" Hanra-bae was waving one end of a partially-unrolled scroll in the air. "This is the passage!"

"Put that down," said Jeryl. The rebuke was sharper than he had intended to make it. He softened his voice. "These scrolls are old and brittle. You will tear the cloth if you are not more careful."

"What matter, since I have found the formula we seek? Come, read this."

"Bring it to me."

Hanra-bae rose from his chair near the window and carried the scroll to the sleeping platform. He held one ornate wooden rod in each hand. A loop of cloth hung almost to the floor and crinkled as he walked. He spread the cloth on the furs so that Jeryl and Aakar could examine it. "Here is the rune for cocooning," he said, pointing to a pair of vertical lines wrapped by a pair of loops.

"You are translating that incorrectly!" said Aakar. He showed Hanra-bae a rune in the scroll he had been reading. "Cocooning is a single line with three loops wrapped around it and an arc over the top. What you point out is the rune for mating."

Jeryl sighed. He would probably spend the evening reviewing Hanra-bae's scroll, unless they found the information they sought in one of the other manuscripts. Jeryl shifted his sore leg carefully under the furs. Why had he ever believed that the Healer would be able to help with this search? He had known that Hanra-bae could not read the ancient runes.

"Forgive me." The fisher rerolled one end of the scroll before picking it up. "The runes are similar. I was just confused."

"Yes," replied Aakar, "they are similar, but there is enough difference that you should be able to identify them. I can draw them on a piece of writing-cloth for you and put the modern equivalent next to each one."

"Do not take time for that just now," said Jeryl. He could not take his eyes from the scroll spread across his lap. "Get your writing-cloth and stylus and help me translate this passage. I think I have found what we seek."

Aakar handed his scroll to Hanra-bae. "Roll this for me and store it with the others." He grabbed a blank roll of writing-cloth and a stylus and sat beside Jeryl on the sleeping platform.

"It begins here, with the rune for cocooning." Jeryl pointed to a large, ornate rendering of the rune. "Bantu identified this passage as information the Healers had been keeping secret for generations."

"Why would they do such a thing?" asked Aakar as he bent close to examine the faded runes.

"Because the Healers Guild has allied itself with the trade guilds of the cities. They have reverted to primitive methods of mating, have abandoned the higher system of Clan and House in favor of the perversion of indiscriminate group matings. Their Mothers are treated as breeding animals." Jeryl shuddered.

Aakar looked up, his eyes showing Jeryl his disbelief. "The Healers would not condone such actions."

"The leaders of the guildhall in Berrut have done so." Hanra-bae's words sounded bitter. "Their fortunes have declined, and now they deny their oaths and corrupt the guild's teachings in an attempt to regain their lost power. I studied there not so many seasons ago; I did not recognize the aura of the guildhall when I returned to it. Greed and fear blanket the buildings and the students now, and the teachers I knew have become cynical and closed. I do not trust them."

"Then we must bare their secrets and use them to strengthen the clans." Aakar handed the blank cloth and stylus to Jeryl. "I will translate. Write down everything I say, using the modern runes. Sometimes there will be more than one interpretation of a phrase. We can sort them out later and decide which translations are most appropriate."

Aakar began. "A hand of days plus three have passed

since the beginning of the planting season. Three Mothers of Clan Renu become fertile today. This is a boon like none I have seen since I became Healer to Clan Renu. The council I approach, and tell that we must use this boon to all advantage. Three Houses in the Keep stand empty, now to be filled.'' The manuscript was a Healer's diary. Aakar read on through the details of the council meeting, Jeryl sometimes asking him to repeat phrases so that he could inscribe the runes accurately.

''Mentor Illar, apprentice Morta, and FreeMaster Srack will aid me in the cocooning. A hand of younglings the council has chosen to be cocooned at dawn tomorrow. Preparations I must make today. Larkenleaf and windwort to gather and brew.''

Jeryl's heart beat faster. This was it—the actual method, the procedures they needed to learn in order to create new Houses within the clans. Would all of the instructions be here, down to the smallest detail? He drew as quickly as he could, watching the brown runes march row by row across the cloth.

''Smaller than last season was the windwort patch; smaller it grows each time I visit it. I know not what is killing the plants. A few I have uprooted and moved to new locations. They only die. I have sent the younglings to search out a new patch, but they find none.

''The tea I make with three parts larkenleaf and one part windwort, ground to a fine powder and steeped until the water is dark green. The FreeMasters drink this before sleep; in the morning they will be ready to produce silk for the cocooning.''

There it was, the secret for which he had been searching. Jeryl clutched the stylus tightly between his fingers. He was shaking with excitement; he could barely shape the runes. The FreeMasters become surrogates to cocoon the extra younglings! He thought of the vow he had made nine days ago, when he brought Hatar and the others to the Free-Masters' guildhall. He had promised to come to the mountain on midsummer day and make a blood sacrifice, a gift of thanksgiving for this knowledge. His heart was full as he realized that he might be able to cocoon a youngling and start a new House before midsummer.

So easy, once he knew the secrets. There was more, much more. Some of it was very confusing. He kept on writing, putting down everything Aakar said. Hanra-bae sat near the window, watching the darkening clouds and listening, the fingers of his right hand tapping out patterns on the sill. Jeryl made Aakar stop once for tea, then let him resume the dictation.

It was mid-afternoon before they finished. Aakar had just rerolled the scroll and set it with the others when Hanra-bae spoke.

"Someone is coming down from the Iron Keep."

"Who?" asked Jeryl.

"I do not know. Three Masters, mounted on aleps. Two of them are wearing black cloaks. The third is riding between them, wearing Historians' colors. He looks ill." The Healer rose and walked to the door.

Jeryl dropped his stylus. "If they are coming from the Iron Keep, the Historian could be Ertis. Is one of the other riders Sinykin Inda? Quickly," he said, turning to Aakar, "help me up."

"You are to remain in bed, Mentor. The Healer ordered it."

"My leg is much better now." Jeryl scooted to the edge of the platform, reached down to retrieve his scattered leggings. He bent the injured leg, felt the scabs pull. This time there was no cracking, no bleeding. The scabs would last through the night; by morning they would drop away and new skin would cover the thigh. He pulled up the leggings, then reached for his boots. "Go on ahead, Healer. You may be needed downstairs."

The sickly rider was indeed Ertis. When Jeryl reached the common room, Hanra-bae was settling the Historian on a bench before the hearth. He removed Ertis' cloak, and beneath it found a strange garment that Jeryl recognized.

"That is the Terran's parka!" Jeryl limped across the room, showed Hanra-bae how to unfasten the velcro closures and the zipper. They struggled together, trying to take Ertis' arms out of the sleeves, but gave up when he continued to clutch at the fabric with his fingers and refused to straighten his elbows. Ertis muttered something unintelligible and hugged the parka close across his chest.

Ertis' companions were no help. One had guided Ertis

into the guildhall while the other stayed outside with the mounts. The one who had come in stayed near the door, and when Jeryl turned to ask him about Ertis and Sinykin Inda he said, "I cannot answer your questions. We were charged to deliver the Historian here and are expected to return immediately to the Iron Keep." Then he backed out of the door, and before anyone could stop him, he and his companion mounted and rode away.

Lissa brought a restorative tea from the kitchen. He sat beside Ertis and began feeding it to him in little sips, all the while glaring at Jeryl over the rim of the cup. It seemed he did not approve of the Mentor being up and about. Arien joined them also, standing near the hearth and watching Jeryl and the Historian.

Jeryl was concerned with other things. Where was Sinykin Inda, and why was Ertis wearing Sinykin's parka? Might the Terran be dead? Terrans made no death cry; Sarah Anders had died in silence. Perhaps something or someone in the Iron Keep had killed Sinykin Inda. That would explain Ertis' shocked state, and the parka.

And if that had happened, how would Jeryl explain it to the Terrans?

Ertis had taken almost half of the tea, and now he refused to drink any more of it. Jeryl went over and knelt before him, ignoring the sudden pain in his thigh. He settled with his back to the hearth and his right hand on the Historian's leg. The contact sent a jolt up the Mentor's arm; his fingers tingled and his wrist ached.

"Leave us," Jeryl said softly to Lissa, and the Healer rose and walked away.

Ertis' aura was murky, gray-green, dense and lifeless. He had been staring at the hearth, but now he looked into Jeryl's eyes, acknowledging the gift of energy Jeryl offered with his touch. Jeryl felt power flowing down his arm and through his fingers, draining into Ertis' body.

"Sinykin gave me this," Ertis said, running his hands over the parka.

"Why did he give it to you?" the Mentor asked quietly. "Cold."

"Cold weather? You were cold?" What did he mean? Ertis shivered. "Cold."

He had been cold, and Inda had given him the parka to

warm him. That was simple enough. "Where is Sinykin now?"

"They kept him."

"Who kept him?" That worried Jeryl.

"Smelters."

What could they hope to gain by detaining the Terran Healer? Jeryl believed that the people of the Iron Keep wanted only one thing from the Terrans—that they leave Ardel. Would the smelters try to use Sinykin Inda as leverage to force his people off the planet? What about the rumors of weather-working? Those also centered on the Iron Keep. What was going on up there?

Jeryl patted Ertis comfortingly, then rose and walked over to join Arien. Lissa returned with Hanra-bae, and they attended to Ertis.

"I must go to the Iron Keep," said Jeryl. "Sinykin Inda is still there, perhaps detained against his will."

Arien stared at him. "Have you ever visited the Iron Keep? Would you know where to begin looking for Inda? The guards at the keep turned away Carra; they are not likely to let you enter by the front gate."

"Then I will find another way in. A keep is a keep. The Iron Keep cannot be so different from others I have visited."

"It is very different, and I think right now it is very dangerous. Carra and I have been there several times to make arrangements for the caravans. The people are not friendly at the best of times."

"The Terran is my responsibility." Jeryl closed his eyes and tried to block out the memory of seeing Sarah Anders' body engulfed in flames. She had trusted him, and he had killed her.

Arien touched Jeryl's shoulder. "The Terran's welfare is *our* responsibility, just as Sarah's death was the result of *our* actions. I allowed the Terran to go to the Iron Keep. I should have stopped him or gone with him myself. My guild has been charged to stand between our people and the Terrans, to protect each from the other.

"Carra and I will go to the Iron Keep. I know how to enter and leave it in secret. We will find Sinykin Inda. I do not like to think of him alone among the miners and smelters who have professed hatred for everything Terran.''

"Nor do I," said Lissa, joining them, "even though he brought this on himself. Arien tried to convince him not to go up there, but he would not be dissuaded. I am certain Ertis would not have left him alone at the Iron Keep, except that his own situation is so grave. He must be taken down to Alu Keep immediately. His mate is fertile; a youngling must be chosen and cocooned within a few days, or his mate will pass out of the fertile stage and Alu will lose another House.''

"What do you mean?" asked Jeryl. "Ertis should have had two more winters before Poola became fertile."

"So he tells me. Did Poola contract the plague?"

"No. All of the Mothers who were ill died. Poola never became sick.''

"And what about Ertis and the younglings?"

Jeryl knew that Ertis had not been sick. "I think one or two of their younglings were ill. I remember some deformities.''

Lissa shrugged. He looked at Hanra-bae, who nodded. "Then Poola was exposed to the plague. It probably affected her body's cycles. We have had reports from other clans of Mothers becoming fertile before their time, and always it is in a House that was touched by plague.''

Jeryl looked at the Historian. "Someone will have to take Ertis down to Alu Keep today. My apprentice must be told to convene the council tomorrow morning so that a youngling may be selected for cocooning.''

"Or two younglings," suggested Hanra-bae.

Arien stared at him. "What do you mean?"

The fisher pointed to Jeryl. "We know how to cocoon a second youngling. Pick windwort and larkenleaf at the right times, grind them and mix them in the proper proportions, and brew a potion. A FreeMaster must drink it before he sleeps, and in the morning, he will produce silk. Ertis' mating might be the first in many generations to begin a new House.''

"Then you found the information you needed in the scrolls?" asked Arien.

"We did." Jeryl could not stop looking at Ertis. "With the help of Aakar, I have copied out an account of a multiple cocooning. All of the instructions are there. The next co-cooning at Alu could begin a new House.''

"What of the scrolls? Who will return them to the Healers?''

"Aakar volunteered to do so. After all, he is a trained librarian. The Healers cannot fault his handling of the scrolls. He will be our emissary.''

"Then you must return to Alu Keep with Ertis," said Arien.

Jeryl shook his head. "I must go to the Iron Keep with you.''

"No.'' Arien reached for Jeryl's hand. "I will see to the Terran. You must go with Ertis. Cocoon a youngling for me, Jeryl. Start a new line—for both of us.''

"We should take a tent," said Hanra-bae, looking through the window. "There is a storm coming. We may have to stop and camp until it blows over.''

"Three pack animals, then—one for each of us.'' Jeryl let his fingers intertwine with Arien's. "Can you supply us with storm gear?''

Jeryl's gear, and Hanra-bae's, was quickly gathered. Jeryl refused to pack his transcript of the old scroll—that he wrapped carefully and placed in the pocket of his tunic. Hanra-bae laced his boots for him, because Jeryl grimaced with pain when he tried to do it himself. The kitchen filled their journey bags with dried meat and fruit, and fresh nut-bread, and flasks of steaming tea for them to drink on the trail.

Arien had six of his freshest aleps brought around, three saddled and three ready to carry their packs. The sky was dark with the promise of snow.

Jeryl and Hanra-bae came back down to the common room, the five "borrowed" scrolls in Jeryl's hands. He presented them to Aakar.

"My thanks cannot repay you for the help you gave me today. Clan Alu owes you a life-debt. When you have finished your training here, we would welcome you at Alu Keep. I can promise you a free hand with the Alu library, which has been sadly neglected.''

"I will consider it, Mentor." Aakar took the scrolls with gentle hands. "You will receive word from me after the scrolls have been safely returned to the Healers.''

"Which may be sooner than you think!" said a Free-Master standing near the window. "Carra signals—the Healers are returning!"

"Go now." Arien helped Lissa get Ertis to his feet. They fastened his parka and settled a cloak over it as Jeryl and Hanra-bae donned their own cloaks. "Go out the back way. I will have Lemki bring your mounts around. Take the back trail out to the main road. We will invite the Healers in and keep them occupied for a time."

"My thanks," said Jeryl, touching Arien's shoulder as he passed him. "Take care at the Iron Keep."

Ertis seemed to become more alert when they left the guildhall. Perhaps the cold air, or the fact that he was moving closer to Poola, revived him. Jeryl held Ertis' alep while Hanra-bae helped him mount and settled him in the saddle. Then the Healer helped Jeryl up. The scabs on his thigh pulled tight as his leg bent around the alep's chest, but nothing tore, no blood seeped onto the bandages. Jeryl sighed and patted the pocket where he had stashed the transcript. It made a comforting bulge in his tunic.

They rode out quickly, Jeryl leading the way down the trail that skirted behind the stable then climbed the hill to join the main road. The last section was icy and steep, and here they rode slowly, letting the aleps pick their six-legged way up the slope. The clouds obscured most of the mountain behind them, looking as though they would spill down and engulf the travelers at any moment. Somewhere in those clouds was the Iron Keep, and Sinykin Inda.

"Ah!" exclaimed Arien as he opened the guildhall's door. "Welcome, Healers. We did not expect you to return to our guildhall so soon. Have you come to apologize for your ill-mannered behavior of this morning?"

"Of course not," cried Bantu. "We have come back to search your guildhall for a pair of thieves!"

"You will find no thieves here. Come in and search the hall if you wish. We will be happy to cooperate with the Healers Guild." Arien ushered the three Healers into the main hall. He clapped his hands, and a pair of younglings trundled out from the kitchen. "Take the Healers' cloaks and hang them by the fire to dry," he said to the first youngling. He sent the second back to the kitchen. "Bring mugs and a pot of hot spiced cider for the Healers."

Bantu refused to remove his cloak. "We would like to see Jeryl, Mentor of Clan Alu."

"Then I suggest you ride to Alu Keep. The Mentor is not here."

"His trail ends at your stable door."

Arien lifted his hands in a gesture of apology. "You may search the stable, the guildhalls, and the grounds. You will not find Jeryl."

Bantu turned to his companions. "Search the stable. Check the grounds. The thieves must be here!"

"Healer, do not waste your time and energy." Aakar stepped forward, holding the scrolls in his hands. "I am Aakar, formerly librarian of Clan Rais and now a member of this guild. I have a message for you from the Mentor of Clan Alu. He returns these scrolls to you, and thanks you for your generosity in allowing him to borrow them from your library." He offered the scrolls to the astonished Bantu. "Alu will repay the debt. You can expect a shipment of grain and tapestries, dyed wool, and leathers. It will be delivered to your guildhall in Berrut at winter's end. I hope you will accept the shipment, and the thanks of Jeryl and Alu's council."

"That will not compensate our guild for the insult and injury we have suffered at the hands of Alu."

"It is all you will receive," said Arien. "I suggest that you accept it with grace."

Rage flashed in Bantu's aura. "We shall lodge a complaint with the Assembly and demand additional reparations!"

Arien turned his hands, transforming his gesture of apology into one of power. "You may certainly do that. Think carefully on the repercussions of such an action. The Healers Guild is not blameless. Would you have the Assembly know what you concealed in your library, and why you concealed it?"

Bantu gathered up the scrolls and tucked them inside his cloak. "I am certain the scrolls have been damaged by mishandling. They will need to be recopied or restored. Alu must reimburse us for the cost."

"The scrolls are in excellent condition, considering their age and the way they were stored," said Aakar. "Your librarian needs more training. Scrolls of such antiquity should be stored upright, in cloth bags to protect them from dust and insects.''

Bantu ignored him. ''Our GuildMaster will contact Alu to discuss appropriate compensation. Come,'' he said to his companions. ''If we ride quickly we can reach the guildhall before dark.''

Chapter 17

"Jaime!" Elissa Durant called to her son as she opened the door of their apartment. "Put on your coat. Let's walk over to Supply and get something special for dinner."

There was no reply. Elissa stepped inside and closed the door. "Jaime?" The lights were on, and the entertainment screen in the living area was playing the introductory sequence of Jaime's favorite game. His pack and his parka were not where he usually dropped them.

Elissa checked the kitchen, the bedrooms, the bath. Jaime was not in the apartment. There was no message telling her where he had gone. She found Sinykin's last letter on the table beside a half-empty mug of chocolate milk.

He must be at Tommy's, she thought, grabbing the vidphone and punching up the Grunds' number. Her finger struck a wrong button; she canceled and began again. The line clicked once, then buzzed to let her know the connection was made. She waited impatiently for someone to answer the call.

"Grunds'."

"Marta, this is Elissa. Is Jaime there?"

"No, he's not. What's wrong?"

"He's not at home. Have you seen him today?"

"He came by this morning and walked to class with Tommy. I haven't seen him since then. He's probably playing with another friend."

"He always leaves a note telling me where to find him." Elissa strained to keep the panic out of her voice. "Can I speak with Tommy?"

Tommy looked scared when he faced Elissa. "Did Jaime go?" he asked.

"Go where?" Elissa was suddenly frightened.

"He made me promise not to tell."

"It's all right to tell Elissa, honey," said Marta, hugging her son. "Jaime may be hurt or in trouble. She only wants to help him."

"He went to the Iron Keep to see his father."

"Thank you, Tommy. Marta, I'll call you back." Elissa broke the connection. Her hands shook as she punched up Security.

Sinykin Inda shivered. He sat on a narrow stone shelf, his back pressed against one wall of a narrow room, and stared at a narrow strip of cloudy sky through the single window slit. There was no sunshine, no light but what the clouds reflected, to illuminate the room.

A fierce storm was gathering above the Iron Keep. By now, Jeff Grund would have seen it coming and posted warnings to all the department supervisors. Elissa would be preparing her maintenance crew and their heavy machinery to deal with the high winds and snow. During the blizzard the crew would be clearing ice and snow from the landing field and roadways and keeping the generators running, the water pumps working, and other essential services operating. Elissa would be with them, meeting every emergency head-on. It had always been Sinykin's place to stay with the children during such times, to take them with him to the infirmary, give them work to occupy their hands and minds until Elissa came safely home.

Jaime was probably at the Grunds' quarters today, playing with Tommy. He had never been afraid of storms; Miranda had been the child who was easily frightened. Thunder and lightning had always sent her scurrying to her parents' bed, to climb between them and huddle under the covers.

Yet when the family had faced the crisis of her illness, Miranda had been the strongest of them all. While Sinykin and Elissa had sent frantic messages to specialists who treated rare blood disorders, Miranda had endured frequent blood tests and transfusions with quiet trust. Her love had kept the family together, even when she had been deemed too weak to survive a proposed trip back to Earth for experimental treatment.

Miranda's death had been hardest on Elissa. Before they had reached Ardel she had had a premonition that this new world would change her family forever. When Miranda be-

came ill she was frantic with fear and guilt, and angry with
Sinykin for bringing them all to Ardel. After Miranda's
death, Elissa had withdrawn from Sinykin and thrown herself into her work; Sinykin and Jaime had waited patiently
for weeks and then months, until she had worked through
her anger and forgiven Sinykin. When she returned to them,
they were able to grieve together. Since then, they had been
closer than ever.

Watching the storm clouds move swiftly across his narrow field of vision, Inda considered what his disappearance
might do to Jaime and Elissa. Would they ever know what
had become of him?

His trip to Alu Keep had not been a mistake. Nor had he
made an error in undertaking the journey to Eiku Keep. His
judgment had become faulty only when he insisted on traveling up the mountain to this misnamed stronghold: the Iron
Keep, where he had seen much stone and no metal. He had
been foolishly headstrong, disregarding the advice of Ertis
and Arien when they were only concerned about his safety.
Now he was paying for his stubbornness.

He looked around the room, at the blank stone wall opposite his shelf, the shadowed corners, the heavy door.
Would he spend the rest of his life here? Would he ever see
Elissa and Jaime again? After the Iron Keep's gates had
closed behind Ertis, Sinykin had seen no one but Matri and
a few of his black-cloaked Masters. Everyone else had
seemed to be in hiding, or gone from the keep. Even the
younglings had disappeared. There had been black-clad
Masters stationed on either side of the clanhall's front door
and at each landing of the main staircase. No one else had
seen Matri take Inda into the clanhall and imprison him.

Certainly no one would come to rescue him. Griswold
had warned him not to leave the spaceport; she would not
risk the lives of other Terrans in what she would see as an
effort doomed to fail. His fate was in his own hands, as it
always had been. He rose and went to the door, pressed one
ear against the wood and listened for noise in the hall. He
heard nothing.

He had tried unsuccessfully to unlatch the door moments
after Matri had locked him in the room. Now he was feeling
angry and frustrated, and he was determined to try once
more. His hands explored the door's surface, fingers pressing along the crack that separated door and frame, searching

for hinges, lock, and handle. The door had been cut from a single slab of wood, its surface planed smooth. It turned on recessed hinges, set well out of his reach. There was no knob, no latch handle, nothing which he could grab or twist or pull.

When he closed his eyes, he saw the latch with its tiny iron bar. The bar glowed with an eerie green light. Inda concentrated on the metal, reaching for it with his mind and trying to move it. The light repelled him, kept him from making contact with the bar. Inda set his shoulder against the door and pushed, but it did not move.

If he could not open the door, perhaps the window would offer more possibilities. He climbed up on the shelf, leaned over to touch the clear crystal pane. It felt cold under his fingers, smooth, and very hard. The crystal was set directly into the stone and could be removed only by breaking it. He set the heel of his hand against it and pushed, to no effect. Bending down, he pulled off his right boot. The sole was hard, and clattered when it hit the pane, but did no damage. He swung the boot again, and again, until the noise of heel striking crystal filled the little room.

"It will not break."

Inda dropped the boot and swung around to stare at the door, mouth open, right hand grabbing at the wall, left arm flailing in the air. He lost his balance and fell from the shelf, landing on his one bare foot with a grunt of pain, never taking his eyes off the figure silhouetted in the open doorway.

"Put on your boot and come with me."

"Kento?" Inda was incredulous.

"Yes, Master Inda. Was I not correct when I told you Matri would not allow you to leave the keep and live? It pleases me that he did not have you killed. I have come to take you to the tower and show you the weather-workers. We must go now, very quietly."

Inda sat on the bench and pulled on his boot, then gathered up his cloak and put it on. Kento handed him a dark, heavy bundle.

"Wear this over your clothing and keep the hood pulled up."

It was a cloak of thick wool, black like the ones worn by many of the miners and smelters, like the one Kento was wearing now.

"Will this be enough to disguise me?" asked Sinykin. "Won't they recognize me by my aura?"

"Few of the Masters have seen a Terran. We will avoid the main floors where they may be gathered and take the back halls and staircases instead. Those who see us will know that you are different, but they will not know why, or who you are."

Inda had doubts about that. He settled the cloak over his shoulders and pulled the hood up and forward. The hem nearly touched the floor, hiding his boots and trousers, and his face was obscured by the deep shadows of the hood. He might fool some of the less observant Masters, and at least he would be out of this tiny room. "Let's go," he said, nodding to Kento.

In the corridor, hidden in the shadow where floor met wall, a prostrate form lay wrapped in a black cloak like the ones worn by Inda and Kento. Kento led Sinykin quickly past the disabled guard, down the hallway to the narrow service staircase at the far end. The stairs, lit by a single sconce on each landing, were uneven, the walls rough and cold. Kento made a little ball of shimmer-light that floated just behind him, illuminating the steps for Inda. At ground level, the staircase ended in a short hall. This opened into a kitchen on the right and a courtyard on the left. Kento extinguished the shimmer-light. He leaned forward, peered around the end of the wall and into the kitchen for a long moment, then crossed the hall and checked the open court. He motioned for Sinykin to follow, stepped out and walked quickly across the yard toward a door on the other side.

Inda took a deep breath and strode after Kento, keeping his head bowed so that the cloak's hood hid his features. He walked quickly, watching the path and the Ardellan's feet. Another pair of black boots, protruding from beneath the hem of a black cloak, appeared to his right. Sinykin's breath caught in his throat. One of the feet moved as he passed; he held his breath and listened for footsteps behind him. He reached a stoop, stepped up through an open door, passed Kento, and moved into another hall. The guard had not followed.

They were in the forbidden tower. A narrow staircase led upward into darkness. Kento climbed to the first landing, carefully looked around, then motioned for Inda to join him. Sinykin followed as quietly as he could, lifting the front of his cloak so that the hem did not trip him. His heart was racing when he reached the landing. The sound of chanting drifted down the stairwell, muffled by the twists and turns above them.

"The circle is working," whispered Kento, leaning close to Inda's ear. "Sanid and the others are calling the storm, changing its direction to send it against the spaceport. I will take you up and show you their gathering."

"Is it safe?"

Kento paused. "You are no longer safe anywhere in the Iron Keep." He led the way up two more flights of stairs, moving slowly and quietly, carefully checking each landing and corridor they passed.

They crawled up the last flight on hands and knees, stopping three steps below the landing. Kento crept upward on his belly, right side pressed to the wall, left hand level with his face. He peeked over the edge of the top step, then waved for Inda to follow.

Sinykin's hands shook as he reached upward, searching for a handhold by which to pull himself to the next step. The heavy cloak was flung back from his shoulders and his knees scraped along the cold stone. He breathed dust and stifled a sneeze. One more step, then another, and he was sprawled beside Kento, peering into a huge round room.

The group of Masters (Sinykin counted fifteen, but he wasn't sure he had seen them all) were gathered in a circle in the room's center. They sat in a circle, holding hands and chanting, watching a single Master who stood in the center of the circle, arms upraised, turning slowly as he stared at the sky through the open windows that ringed the room. Cold air and flakes of snow swirled around him. Inda waited and watched as the Master's face, Sanid's face, came into view. The leader of the mining clan was the chief weatherworker!

Inda closed his eyes and concentrated on his psychic perceptions of the room. He could feel the power gathering there, spinning about the edge of the circle, creating a vortex like the eye of a tornado in the center of the room. The chanting washed over him, enticing him to rise and join the circle, to lend his own energy to their working.

Kento touched Sinykin's arm, then pointed at a guard who had entered the room through a doorway on the other side. Inda let his body slide quietly back down the steps, keeping out of the guard's sight. Kento crawled down beside him and slipped carefully across the landing and around the corner. The sound of chanting diminished.

Inda sat beside Kento on the dusty stairs. He took a deep breath, held it for a moment, then released it slowly. The frantic beating of his heart slowed a little. Another deep breath, then a third, and his hands stopped shaking.

"My own people are gathering to try to counteract the weather-working." Kento rose. "Come, I will take you to our circle."

By the time they reached the third floor landing, they could hear footsteps and shouting in the stairwell above them. Kento grabbed Inda's hand and began running down the stairs, pulling the Terran behind him. Sinykin gathered the front of his cloak in his other hand, lifting the hem so that he would not trip, and flew down the steps two at a time. He was afraid that he would stumble at any moment, fall against Kento and they would roll and bounce down the rough stone to their deaths. The thought did not make him more cautious; if the shouting guards caught him, Matri and Sanid would probably have him killed. Running seemed to be the best course.

Kento stopped suddenly on the second floor landing. Inda ran into him and they both stumbled, then Kento recovered and led him into the hallway. They heard shouting below now, guards gathering at the courtyard door. Their escape down the service stairs had been cut off.

The hallway was empty. They strolled quickly toward the wide staircase at the other end, their black cloaks wrapped close about them and the hoods up. If most of the guards were pursuing them on the service stairs, they might yet escape through the front door. Inda kept his head down, and tried to control his fear. It would be a bright beacon to any Ardellan who looked at him.

The shouting behind them grew louder. They reached the landing, which miraculously was unguarded, and turned left. Sinykin risked a quick glance down the hall and wished he had not looked. Three Masters were running toward them, cloaks flying from their shoulders, feet slapping the stone. Inda suddenly remembered the story of Sarah Anders' death and realized that these people would not need to use weapons to stop him. He turned and fled.

He reached the first floor in a few seconds and stopped.

Kento was gone! He looked in the main hall, and then back up the stairway. Kento had disappeared. Their pursuers were already at the top of the stairs. Inda ran to the door, tugged it open, and found himself looking into Matri's forbidding eyes.

"Ah, Master Inda! I was just coming to visit you. We have much to discuss," said Matri, grasping Inda's upper arm tightly and forcing him backward, into the hall. Someone ran down the staircase behind him and stopped. "I am surprised to see you wandering about our clanhall without an escort. You would have been wiser to stay in your room until we sent for you."

Three black-cloaked guards followed Matri into the hall. They gathered around Sinykin, boxing him in so that he could not escape. Only then did Matri release Inda's arm. Two other guards were waiting at the foot of the stairs, breathing hard from the chase. Matri ignored them.

Sinykin decided to try a bluff. "Someone did come for me, Matri. I thought you had sent him."

"I sent no one. What name did this person give?"

"Kento." Inda knew better than to lie to an Ardellan. "He was with me just a few moments ago. Those two were chasing us," he pointed to the breathless guards, "and Kento ran down the stairs and disappeared. I was trying to find him."

Matri shrugged. "I think it would be to your advantage to avoid this Kento in the future. Come, let us go up to your room where we can talk."

"We can talk here. This hall is much more pleasant than that tiny room." Sinykin tried to break away from the guards, but they herded him toward the stairway. He considered sitting on the bottom step and refusing to move. They would probably pick him up and carry him to his prison. He began to climb slowly, wondering if he could outrun them when he reached the second floor. They looked fresh, and he was tired from the chase. He glanced back and saw Matri talking quietly with the two guards who had pursued him. Then they went off, probably to search for Kento, and Matri joined Inda on the stairs.

"Are you hungry, Master Inda? I can have tea brought to your room."

"That would be very kind," said Sinykin. Perhaps with more people coming and going from that little room, there would be another chance to escape. First he would listen to Matri and try to learn more about what was going on at the top of the tower.

Elissa paced across the kitchen, reached the sink, and turned back. "I should be out there myself, looking for Jaime! I could take one of the ATVs. . . ."

"Don't be silly," said Marta Grund. "You have to stay here in case Security calls. Anyway, they'll have taken all the ATVs out to patrol the compound's perimeter. The Security team will find Jaime. They're trained to find people. After all, he's only a little boy. How far can he have gone in an hour?"

"It's nearly dark, and it's snowing again." Elissa stopped pacing and looked out through the kitchen window. Her left hand stroked Miranda's urn; when she turned back to look at Marta she had tears in her eyes. "I can't bear the thought of losing him, too."

Marta walked over and hugged Elissa. "Sit down, Lissie. Let me make you some tea. I'm sure Security will call any minute and tell you that they've found him."

Elissa sat with her hands folded in her lap and stared at Inda's letter. "Jaime was afraid Sinykin wouldn't be allowed back into the spaceport. He thought that Griswold's order to close the compound was meant to keep his dad out."

"Griswold dislikes Sinykin because he challenges her authority, but she'd never do anything to hurt him."

"I know. I told Jaime that the guards would open the gate for his dad." She sighed. "He misses Sinykin so much. They became very close after Miranda died."

"I wish Tommy and his dad got along that well."

Not at such cost, Elissa thought.

The vid-phone's buzzer sounded. Elissa jumped to her feet and reached for the keypad. Her shaking hand hovered there for a moment. The phone buzzed again. She tapped the accept key.

Alec Harwood, the spaceport's Security Chief, smiled at her. "We found him, Elissa. Jaime was out behind the landing field, halfway to the perimeter fence. Joswyn is bringing him in now. You can meet them at the infirmary, if you want to. He's not injured; they just want to check him over before you take him home."

Elissa smiled and nodded. The tears she had been holding back spilled down her cheeks.

Inda looked for the prostrate guard, but he was gone from the shadowed corridor. Either he had awakened and wandered away, or someone had carried him to another part of the clanhall. The wall sconces had been lit, for it was nearly dusk, and the door to Inda's prison stood open. Matri followed Sinykin into the room, conjuring a ball of shimmerlight to float near the ceiling. The guards stayed outside.

"You know that we are working the weather." Matri said it quietly, standing while Inda sat on the narrow shelf.

"I know that you are doing something in the tower room. Kento told me that you are weather-workers. I do not know what that means."

"It means that we can control the storms. We can direct them from one area to another, gather them together to increase their fury, cause them to move quickly or slowly."

Inda nodded. That fit with the details Kento had given him. "You are directing this blizzard against the spaceport."

"More than one storm," said Matri, looking at the darkness outside the window. "Sanid will bring together three storm clouds, and hold them over your settlement until their fury is spent. There will be high winds and much falling snow and ice coating buildings and trails. Your people will be trapped until the blizzard is over, and it will take them days to clear away the snow and ice. Before they can do that, other clouds will come. This is only the beginning of storm season. There will be many more blizzards gathering at the top of this mountain, and each one will spill down to trouble the spaceport. Your ships will be unable to land. Your homes and your people will be in danger."

"We are not unfamiliar with snow and cold weather. Our buildings are built to withstand blizzards, and we have equipment to deal with the snow. You will find that we are resourceful people." He tried to sound more confident than he felt. He was thinking of all the things that could be damaged by high winds and ice: the communication towers, the windmills, the power lines they had not yet found time to bury, and the temporary housing. These installations were always built on a meager budget. Cutting corners was expected, and Griswold had cut many in her rush to complete the spaceport. Now it might cost them equipment and time.

Matri shrugged. "In time you will deplete your supplies. There are things that must be brought to you by your ships, and the ships will not be able to land. Your food-birds will die, and you will consume all of the herbs that allow you to eat our foods. You will use up the fuel for your power machines, and the storms will tear apart your wind catchers. How resourceful will your people be when they are cold and hungry?"

As if in response to his question, a youngling appeared in the doorway with a pot of tea and a tray of mugs and plates. Matri watched silently as the youngling set the tray on the shelf beside Inda, unwrapped a loaf of warm bread, and poured two cups of tea.

"What do you want of me?" asked Inda, cradling a mug in his hands and inhaling the fragrant steam. He was impatient with this catalog of threats.

Matri sipped his tea, then set the mug aside and sliced the bread. It looked heavy and dark, dotted with some greenish fruits or nuts. He passed a slice to Inda, spread sweetener on one for himself, and took a large bite. Sinykin balancd his slice on his thigh and watched Matri expectantly.

"We want all Terrans to leave Ardel. We want the spaceport closed, the buildings destroyed, the Terran metals gone. We want no more trade with your people."

"What will happen if I give my word that we will leave?"

"We shall turn the storm away. We shall keep the skies clear so that your ships can come and remove your people from our land."

"And if I refuse?"

"Then the winter winds will destroy your spaceport, and snow will bury your homes. It may take one night, or a hand or hands of days, but it will happen. Be wise and go."

"We will not," said Sinykin. His hands were shaking; he did not know whether from fear or anger.

Matri stared at him for a long time. Then he picked up his mug and drained it with one long swallow. He set it on the tray and walked to the door, the shimmer-light bobbing above his head. Left hand braced against the doorjamb, he looked back over his right shoulder at Inda.

"You will not leave the Iron Keep alive."

He extinguished the shimmer-light, stepped into the corridor, and let the door close behind him.

Inda sat in the darkness of the cold room, hands clasped tightly around his cooling mug of tea. He was frightened, he was hungry, and most of all he was angry. He was angry with Matri's unreasonable demands, and he was angry with his own stupidity. He had walked into the Iron Keep with his eyes wide open, and he had refused to see the possible dangers.

At this moment he could do nothing about the anger or the fear, but he could relieve the hunger. He reached for the piece of bread Matri had given him. It had grown cold, but it was comfortingly heavy. He bit into it, enjoying the firm texture. Its taste was not so pleasant. It was bitter, like the gruel Ertis had warned him against eating. He finished only the one bite, set the rest aside and fumbled for the teapot. He managed to refill his mug, spilling only a little despite his shaking hands. Then he remembered the half-eaten ration bar stuffed into his pocket. It had crumbled, and he chewed the pieces and washed them down with the rest of the tea.

His whole body was beginning to tremble. At first he blamed it on the cold, but when nausea doubled him over he could no longer deny that he had been poisoned. The bread had contained something bitter, perhaps the grain that Ertis said had made Sarah Anders ill. Inda huddled in a corner, legs pulled up to his chest, arms wrapped around his knees, and passed out.

Chapter 18

The ball of shimmer-light bobbed and weaved above Ertis' head as he led the way too quickly down the trail. Jeryl kicked his own mount to greater speed, letting his shimmer-light hover behind as he chased the Historian. He knew that Hanra-bae would follow more slowly, guiding his mount carefully over the frozen earth. The Healer was always a cautious rider, and there was nothing but the cold to hurry him tonight.

They had entered Alu lands before dark, and in good weather they would already have reached the keep. Tonight the weather was not good. Heavy clouds obscured the moon and stars, making the shimmer-light necessary, and snow and ice made the trail treacherous. Jeryl felt the cold most acutely in his fingers and toes, and down the length of his healing thigh. The new skin itched despite the chill, and he longed to scratch it.

He caught up with Ertis at the top of a rise. Ahead were the fields and vineyards that surrounded Alu Keep. Ertis was staring forward into the darkness. He mumbled a few words; their sense was obscured by the blowing of their mounts.

"What did you say?" asked Jeryl, leaning toward Ertis.

"Poola is waiting for me. Everything will be fine now. There is enough time."

"Time for what?"

"For the cocooning. We can select a youngling in the morning and have the cocooning in the afternoon, or on the next day." Ertis turned to look at him. "This is all happening much too soon."

"We can discuss that when we are safe and warm at the keep." Jeryl looked back, saw Hanra-bae's alep beginning the short climb up the rise. "We are nearly there. Will you lead, or shall I?"

Ertis nosed his alep forward more slowly on the down-slope, letting it choose carefully where to put each of its six feet. Jeryl followed a length behind, with Hanra-bae an-other length behind him. They reached the keep in that or-der, well before the middle of the night. The main gate was closed, so Jeryl dismounted and banged on the night-gate. The tiny window opened slowly and a single eye, perched on a stalk, peered out at him.

"Open the gate for the Mentor and his party," said Jeryl. He raised his wrist and let the sleeve of his cloak slide back. Shimmer-light reflected from the wristband that denoted his office.

The eye disappeared, the shutter slid closed, and the small gate was opened. Jeryl led his mount into the stableyard.

The creaking of the gate's hinges brought a hand of young-lings scurrying from the stable. They took the travelers' aleps and began to unload the pack saddles. The stablemas-ter's apprentice followed the other younglings out, its eye-stalks drawn back against the lantern light.

"Do you wish to have the packs taken to the clanhall?" it asked.

"No, they should all go to House Actaan. We will sort them there," said Jeryl. "Also, send a youngling to the Healers' quarters. Viela is needed immediately at House Actaan."

The apprentice blinked. "The Healer is not in his quar-ters, Mentor."

"Then send to the clanhall, or wherever he is!" Jeryl stalked toward the apprentice. It backed away from him, its tentacles fluttering ineffectually. Jeryl was surprised by the intensity of his feelings; the ride and the cold had left him short-tempered. He swallowed, tried to damp the ruby flare of his aura, and explained, "He must come and examine Poola and Ertis."

The youngling crossed its eyestalks and took a step away from Jeryl, into the shadows. "The Healer is already at House Actaan, Mentor. He has been there most of the day."

"Then we should waste no more time," said Jeryl. "Er-tis, Hanra-bae, come!" He started off down the graveled roadway.

* * *

Septi greeted Ertis and his companions at House Actaan. He waited in silence while Jeryl and Hanra-bae removed their cloaks and Ertis struggled out of Sinykin Inda's parka. Then Septi led them into the main room, where the fire in the hearth already had been banked for the night. It took him only a moment to rouse the younglings and send them for more wood.

When the fire had been fed and its orange flames were dancing under the teapot, Septi spoke.

"I am pleased by your safe return, my friend," he said to Ertis. "Your mate will also be pleased. You should go to her now; she has news for you."

"I already know the news. It is the reason I made such a precipitous return to Alu Keep," replied Ertis. "Poola is fertile."

Jeryl sat on the hearthstone and let the fire's heat warm his back. "The gatekeeper told me that Viela is here. Is he with Poola?"

"He has been here most of the day," said Septi. "He said he would not leave her until Ertis returned."

"And you?"

"Poola sent one of the younglings to fetch me this morning. She did not feel ill; she was only concerned that Ertis might not return in time to perform a successful cocooning. I sent for Viela."

"I should examine her now and consult with Viela," said Hanra-bae. "I will be able to tell you how soon we must cocoon a youngling."

"There is no need for you to examine Poola," said Viela from the hallway to the Mother's chamber. "She is fertile. A youngling should be chosen and cocooned as soon as possible. I suggest that the council convene at dawn tomorrow."

"Thank you for your advice, Healer," said Jeryl. "I think it would be polite for us to allow Master Healer Hanra-bae to see Poola."

"Yes, please examine her." Ertis was pacing back and forth before the hearth. "Tell her that I will come and see her when you have finished. Jeryl and I must discuss the arrangements for the cocooning."

Viela offered up one palm in an insincere apology. "Come with me, Master Healer. I will show you to the Mother's chamber." He led Hanra-bae down the dark corridor and through a doorway.

"If only we had more time," said Jeryl. His back had become too warm. He moved to one of the benches beside the hearth, and he watched Septi add powdered bark and leaves to the steaming water. "If we had a hand of days, we could cocoon two younglings instead of one."

"Two younglings!" Ertis spun around and stared at Jeryl. "You found the method for creating new Houses!"

"We did. I have the notes right here." Jeryl patted his tunic pocket. "I had hoped that we would arrive here in time to make the necessary preparations for cocooning a second youngling."

"How much time do you need?" asked Septi.

"Two days, perhaps three. We must search out a patch of windwort and gather fresh larkenleaf and several other herbs. Hanra-bae has the skill to brew the potion. I must drink it before I sleep, and in the morning I will be able to cocoon a youngling." Jeryl wanted to postpone this cocooning until the potion could be prepared. He knew that might not be possible; his desire to create a new House was overwhelmed by his fear that the delay would destroy House Actaan. Surely, there would be another cocooning before the winter was over.

Septi took the pot from the fire and poured fragrant tea for Ertis and Jeryl. The Mentor sipped quietly, enjoying the warmth of the flames and the comfort of being home in Alu Keep. Ertis gulped his tea and resumed pacing. His aura reflected a jumble of emotions—excitement, apprehension, and concern—all normal for a Master about to experience mating and metamorphosis.

"How soon can we call the council together?" asked Ertis.

"If we send out runners now, the council can meet at dawn," replied Jeryl. "Will that be soon enough?"

Ertis shrugged. "If it cannot be done any sooner. Septi, would you send the younglings out to inform the council members of the meeting?"

"Certainly. Is there anything I can get for you while I am in the kitchen?"

"Could you bring a bowl of nut meats?" asked Jeryl. He was feeling tired and hungry after the long ride, and he would not have time for sleep until after the council meeting. The tea was invigorating, but it did nothing to assuage his hunger. Ertis would probably not eat or sleep until after the cocooning, but that was no reason for Jeryl to deny himself those comforts.

While Septi was gone, a pair of younglings trundled into the room and dropped several packs beside Jeryl's bench. The younglings left and returned a moment later with more packs, which they set beside the first group. "Are there any more?" asked Jeryl as the younglings backed away.

"No, Mentor," said the larger one before they retreated toward the kitchen.

Ertis stopped at the hearth and refilled his mug with tea, then watched as Jeryl sorted the packs. "That one is mine," he said, pointing to a small bag made of iridescent blue leather, "and those two belong to Sinykin Inda."

Jeryl was surprised. He opened the larger pack, saw the boxes and jars of the Terran's sampling equipment. The smaller pack contained clothing, and tucked beside that was a bound volume that looked familiar. Jeryl touched it and instantly recognized that it was Sarah Anders' journal. He had held it before, when they had traveled together, and again when he had returned it to her people after Sarah's death. He had not expected it to find its way back into his hands.

He opened it and stared at the strange runes Sarah had inscribed on its smooth, white pages. Sorrow filled his heart, followed quickly by fear. Was this an omen of Sinykin Inda's death? "How is it that you have the Terran's gear, when he is still in the Iron Keep?"

"We were planning to leave the keep together. When the Healer told me that I must return immediately to Alu, Inda insisted that he would accompany me. We packed our gear, and while we waited for the escort to take us to the stable, a builder named Kento came and spoke with us. He is the Master who brought us the message from the Iron Keep's Historians and insisted that Sinykin should visit the Iron Keep. Kento wanted Inda to stay; he warned us that the Iron Keep's leaders would not let Sinykin live to leave the mountain. Kento claimed that there were weather-workers practicing in the Iron Keep, and that they were gathering a great blizzard to attack and destroy the spaceport. Kento said that his people would try to stop the working, and he wanted Inda to help him. Sinykin chose to go with me.

"We set out for the stable together. Matri of the smelting clan had promised us that our saddles would be mended and our aleps waiting, ready for the trip. They had even promised us an escort as far as the FreeMasters guildhall." Ertis had slipped into his storyteller's voice, and the scene at the stable became clearly visible to Jeryl.

"I was shivering from the cold. I could not seem to get warm, although I was wearing two cloaks. Sinykin could not bear to see me suffer. When we reached the stable, he stripped off his parka and dressed me in it and took my spare cloak for himself. I was so preoccupied with thoughts of Poola that I did not thank him.

"I remember that he helped me to mount my alep. He was getting ready to mount his own animal when Matri and Sanid appeared with some guards. They were shouting that Sinykin must not leave the Iron Keep. My escort mounted, and one of the Masters grabbed the rein from my hand. They led my alep out through the gate. I was shouting and straining to break away, but the gate closed behind me. I could not see what happened to Inda."

"This is another good reason to force the Terrans to leave our planet!" said Viela. He walked to the hearth, followed by Hanra-bae. "Discord and discontentment follow them wherever they go. They disrupt the lives of our keeps and cities and interfere with our patterns of trade. They do not belong here!"

"Perhaps not," said Jeryl. The scene Ertis had projected was fading, but Jeryl still felt the Historian's concern for his Terran companion. Jeryl hoped that Arien would be able to find Sinykin Inda and bring him safely out of the Iron Keep. If the weather-working tale was true, their escape from the keep would not be easy. Clouds, heavy with snow and the promise of cold temperatures and high winds, had been rolling down from the mountains most of the day. A light snow was already falling.

Jeryl tucked Sarah's journal back into Inda's pack. He set both of the packs with his own belongings, to be taken to the clanhall. Then he returned to the hearth and poured tea for Viela and Hanra-bae. Septi brought in a large tray of fruits and nuts, which he set on the end of the bench.

"Poola is healthy." Hanra-bae took the mug that Jeryl offered him. "She has come early to her fertile time, probably as a result of exposure to the plague. This will not complicate the mating. There is still some time—a young-ling should be cocooned within three days.''

"It is senseless to wait," said Viela. "Select the young-ling tomorrow morning and cocoon it tomorrow after-noon.''

"Three days might be enough time." Ertis looked from Hanra-bae to Jeryl. "We could try to cocoon two youn-glings. Do you think you could find the botanicals you need within three days?''

The fisher shrugged. "We could try. I can make no guar-antees. I know of a patch of windwort, but it is nearly a day's ride from here, and it already may have been frozen out. The other herbs are not as difficult to locate.''

Viela stared at them. "Cocoon two younglings? What nonsense are you suggesting now? It is not possible to co-coon more than one youngling at a time.''

"It is possible," said Hanra-bae. "We found the method in an old text in the library in Berrut. I need to find the nearest patch of windwort. Where do you gather yours?''

"I will not be a party to this folly. You would gamble the future of House Actaan on an uncertain translation of an ancient text you stole from the Healers' library?'' Ruby streaks of anger flashed in Viela's aura as he confronted Jeryl. "You are not fit to serve as Mentor of Clan Alu.''

Jeryl raised his hands and showed the scarred palms to Viela. "Would you challenge me, Healer? I have defeated challengers who were much more powerful than you are. Let us put an end to this argument now. Gather your power and face me.''

"No!" Ertis stepped between them. "You will not do this in my House.''

"Apologies, Historian. I did not mean to disrupt the peace of your House," said Jeryl.

Viela backed toward the door. "I will see you in council tomorrow, Mentor.'' He turned and strode out of the room.

Jeryl turned to Ertis. "I will not postpone this cocooning if it risks House Actaan.''

"But we have time," pleaded Ertis. "I would not endan-ger Poola or the House by delaying the cocooning too long. The Master Healer says we can wait three days. If you can-not gather the necessary herbs and prepare the potion before the second day is over, I will cocoon a single youngling on the third day. House Actaan will continue.''

"This is the task for which you and I risked our reputations and our lives, Jeryl," said Hanra-bae. "Let us at least attempt to gather what we need. Poola is in no immediate danger."

"We may have difficulty reaching the windwort. There is a blizzard coming, and if Ertis' report is correct, its center will be the spaceport. Alu Keep will be well within its range."

Hanra-bae took a handful of nut meats. "I have seen more than enough snow on this trip. If Viela will not tell me where he gathers his windwort, we will ride westward, toward the waters and away from the storm. I know of a patch that is less than a day's ride away."

"All right. In the morning, the council shall choose two younglings. They are to stay here with you, Ertis. You must not leave the House until at least one of them is cocooned."

Ertis made a gesture of acceptance. "I agree, Mentor."

Jeryl laid his hand on the Historian's shoulder and looked beyond him into the fire. In the flames he saw the image of Sarah Anders, smiling and reaching for him. He hoped that he was not making another mistake.

Chapter 19

Arien could see nothing of the Iron Keep except the small patch of wall directly before him. Heavy clouds hung all around the top of the mountain, enveloping trees and trails and interlopers alike in fog. It was a mixed blessing. Arien's cloak was damp, and the cold had penetrated his leggings, but he was grateful for the mist's concealment. An alep snorted behind him. He turned to look for his companion, Carra. Only darkness and fog were visible until Carra was close enough for Arien to reach out and touch him. Behind Carra, he heard the muffled crunch of gravel under the spare alep's feet.

They stayed away from the main gate and instead followed the wall around to the south. Arien knew of several doors scattered along the keep's imposing wall. They were difficult to reach unless one knew the way. Each door led directly into one of the clanhalls. Arien searched for the door nearest the southwest corner of the keep, the one used by the FreeMasters' caravans for making deliveries to the smelters' kitchens. It was surrounded by scrub and thornbushes and was usually warded but never guarded.

He reached the end of the west wall and turned the corner, waiting a moment to make certain that Carra was still behind him. Then he urged his mount forward, letting the animal pick its way between the stone wall and the brambles. During each growing season the crew of the year's first caravan hacked away at these bushes to clear the trail, and by winter the bushes almost obscured the path again. Arien struggled through, wishing he had brought a branch-cutter. A long thorn tore his legging and scratched his calf just above the boot. He winced and swept his cloak forward to cover his legs.

They rode on for much longer than he thought necessary. The door was disguised to look like part of the wall, but Arien had always found it before without difficulty. This time he must have missed it. He could feel the Terran's presence behind him, high in the smelters' clanhall. He must turn back.

He stopped and waited for Carra. They dismounted and turned the mounts carefully, one at a time, then tied their reins to the brambles and left them contentedly munching the few leaves that autumn winds had not stripped from the bushes. Arien bundled his cloak and left it on the saddle, taking only his ropes with him.

This time Arien walked along the wall, left hand pressed to the stone at shoulder level, right hand trailing against the wall near his hip. Carra followed closely, touching neither his GuildMaster nor the wall.

Arien sensed many presences in the clanhall, most of them gathered on the upper floor of the big tower. The rest were scattered throughout the building, several in the general vicinity of the Terran.

Was the Terran whose presence he sensed Sinykin Inda? Arien could feel no other Terran in the Iron Keep. Of all Ardellans, he had had the most contact with Terrans. He had on occasion thought that, given a large enough circle of Masters to channel power to him, he could locate every one of the invaders on his planet.

And since he still thought of them as invaders, why was he here, risking his life to rescue one of them? They had caused so many problems for him and for his people. How many Ardellans had died at the hands of Terrans? But that was unfair—as many Terrans had lost their lives to Ardellan madnesses. And some of the Terrans possessed a nobility that had shocked Arien the first time he saw it in Sarah Anders. It still surprised him when he found it in others of her kind. It was the potential for that nobility, he realized, that had brought him to the Iron Keep to rescue Sinykin Inda and return him to the spaceport.

His fingers found a wider crack between the stones, and beside it, a panel of rock veneer over wood. The door! He traced out its edges with both hands, probed with his mind to locate the lock and hinges. Then he stood back and beckoned Carra close.

"I will need to draw power from you to overcome the

warding on this latch,'' he whispered. ''Once I am inside, I will close the door, but I will not latch it. I will try to bring the Terran out this way. Stay with the mounts. We will meet you here.''

Carra grasped Arien's upper arm tightly. ''I am coming with you.''

''No!'' Arien pulled his arm away, then grabbed Carra by the shoulders. ''I will not risk both of us. You will wait here, and if I am not back by dawn, you will return to the guildhall and get help.''

Carra just stared at him.

''If both of us enter the keep, we will increase our chances of being discovered. You will serve me best if you stay here and see that the mounts are ready and waiting when I bring the Terran out.''

''Yes, GuildMaster.'' Carra touched Arien's hands, then pushed him toward the door. ''I will be here, and the aleps will be ready.''

''Good. Now help me open this door.'' Arien visualized the latch, and its iron bar glowing with the soft light of a ward. He tried to move the bar, could not even touch it. The ward repelled his mind.

He grasped Carra's hand, drew power from the Free-Master's body, and approached the latch again. This time he concentrated on dimming the glow of the ward. If he could extinguish the light, he could then easily open the door.

Each approach he tried made the bar glow more brightly. This was not an ordinary ward. It was feeding on Arien's energy, growing stronger each time he tried to break it. Someone in the Iron Keep had expected a surreptitious visit from a FreeMaster and had very carefully warded the door.

Suddenly Carra's mind was inside the latch with Arien's. *Here,* thought Carra, *and here, these are the ward's weakest points. You attack it there, and I will attack it here, and perhaps we can break it.*

They each poked and pried and prodded, and the light grew brighter, until the whole latch began to glow. They pushed and pulled, and the iron bar grew warm, and then hot, with the power that they poured into it. A tendril of smoke escaped the narrow crack where the door met the stone wall. The hot iron bar expanded within the scorching wood. It tripped the latch, and the door opened.

''Many thanks,'' whispered Arien. ''I will return before dawn.''

The kitchen was dark except for the glow of the carefully banked hearth-fire. It warmed the room and the stone ovens, and its meager light made the kitchen seem much brighter than the foggy outdoors. Arien peered around the door's edge, checking the hearth and the benches for sleeping younglings. The smelters' kitchenmaster kept a disciplined scullery; none of his assistants had crept back to spend the night in the kitchen's warmth. The room was deserted.

Arien opened the door a little wider and slipped into the kitchen. He knelt and felt along the juncture where wall met floor, touched the oblong rock that he had expected to find there. It slipped easily between door and jamb, preventing the latch from locking.

He climbed the narrow back staircase slowly, his left arm extended, hand flattened against the inner wall, feet carefully exploring each step. Once away from the kitchen's dim light, he moved in total darkness. Eleven steps, and he could feel where the wall ended at the landing. He leaned forward, peered into the corridor, saw nothing in the blackness. Reaching out with his other sight, he searched for auras. There was no one on this floor. Arien stepped up to the landing, turned, and began climbing toward the third floor.

He could see a faint glow at the top of the staircase. By the time he had climbed a hand of steps, he could hear the whisper of hushed voices coming from above. Five more steps and he stood just below the landing, barely outside the bright arc of light cast by a glowing wall sconce in the corridor. Holding his breath, standing very still, Arien listened to the Masters conversing quietly in the hall.

''How many guards did you see?''

''Only two, and they were nearly asleep.''

''Good. We must surprise them and knock them unconscious before they can cry out. It is certainly convenient that they put him back in the same room.''

''They must be expecting us, Kento. It will not be so easy to free him this time.''

''If they were expecting us, there would be more guards, more Masters scattered throughout these corridors. They are more concerned with the weather-working than with this

lone Terran. Matri has called most of the Masters into the
tower room.''

Kento! That was the name of the Master who had invited
Sinykin Inda to visit the Iron Keep. Had he and his companion also come to free the Terran? Arien heard them
walking toward the stairs. He stepped back into the shadows
and waited. They entered the stairwell and climbed to the
next floor. Arien followed quietly.

Before he reached the landing he heard more conversation. It began with a low-voiced command, certainly from
one of the guards.

"Go back to the stairwell. No one is allowed on this
floor."

"We came to check on the prisoner. Is he well?"

"He sleeps."

"I see that you have a pot of tea. Might we share it? The
kitchenmaster has banked his fires and gone to bed."

Arien risked a quick glance around the corner. Kento and
his companion were striding down the corridor, had nearly
reached the guards.

"We have no extra mugs. You must go now. Please return
to your rooms."

"We shall take the main stairs," said Kento, pointing
down the hall past the guards. As Arien watched, Kento
passed the first guard and stopped before the second. He
reached out with both hands, struck the guard first on the
right temple, then on the left. The Master crumpled to
the floor, where he was joined an instant later by his companion. They were unconscious, not dead—Arien had felt
no death cries.

Kento and his friend dragged the guards across the hall
and left them in the shadows. Then they walked back and
began to examine the door to the Terran's prison.

"It is warded," whispered Kento's companion.

Kento extended his right palm toward the latch. A blue
spark jumped from his hand to the door. Arien watched in
amazement. No ordinary Master could generate such power.
Kento must be a FreeMaster!

The door opened, and Kento and his companion stepped
into the Terran's room. The clanhall had become very quiet
except for the sound of shuffling feet far below in the stairwell. Arien looked down and suddenly realized that someone was climbing the stairs from the kitchen. It was probably

a guard, perhaps two, coming to check on the prisoner or relieve the first set of guards. Arien no longer had time to spare for cautious action. He must get Inda out of the building now.

Arien stepped into the corridor, keeping to the shadows as he moved down the hall. He pressed his back against the stone wall and inched toward the doorway.

"Why will he not awaken?"

"Perhaps Matri drugged him. We must get him out of here quickly."

"We can carry him."

The footsteps on the stairs were much closer now. Arien's heart lurched in his chest, began to beat rapidly. Sweat dripped from his tentacle nodules. He was so close to his goal. The circumstances called for a bold move. Arien took a deep breath, turned, and stepped into the doorway.

Sinykin Inda was sprawled on a platform, unconscious. Kento, shimmer-light floating above his head, bent over the Terran. Kento's companion stood just inside the door. Arien touched his shoulder, then pointed at Kento.

"Tell him to get away from the Terran."

The reaction was instantaneous. Kento took a step back and turned to stare at Arien. His companion tried to slip from the room. Arien lifted his arms, let his aura spread to fill the doorway with its pure white glow.

"I have come for Sinykin Inda," said Arien, resisting the urge to look back down the hall at the stairway. His heart was beating so loudly that he could no longer hear the footsteps. "I intend to take him out of the Iron Keep."

Kento answered him with uplifted arms and a show of sparks from his palms. "I will not allow you to harm this Terran."

"I am Arien, leader of the FreeMasters Guild. I intend to take the Terran safely back to his people" He could hear footsteps now, running toward him down the corridor. Stepping back into the hall, he lifted his arms higher and turned to face the two newcomers. "Stay where you are," he said in his most commanding tone. "I have come from the FreeMasters Guild to take the Terran. You will not interfere with me."

"You have no rights here," shouted a black-cloaked Master, still running toward Arien. "Step away from that door!"

The shouting would bring more guards in a few moments. Arien spread his legs, braced his feet against the stone floor, turned his palms toward the approaching pair. He felt a presence beside him, turned, and saw Kento also standing ready to challenge the newcomers. "Take the second one," said Arien.

Arien cupped his fingers to channel power, concentrated, loosed a stunning charge that struck the first Master's shoulders and dropped him in his tracks. Kento stunned the second Master an instant later. Little curls of smoke rose from the burnt spots on their cloaks. Arien rushed forward, bent over each one to assess the damage, decided that they would live even if they did not receive immediate attention. He turned back to Sinykin Inda's prison.

"Move!" shouted Arien. He grabbed Kento's companion by the arm, pulled him from the room. "Others will be coming in just a moment. We must get Inda out of here."

"He is not conscious," said Kento. "He lives but we cannot wake him."

Arien touched Inda's chest, felt the slow rise and fall of his breathing. He stroked the Terran's forehead. It was damp with sweat. "He is either ill or drugged. I think I can wake him." *But I will need someone to guard the door while I do it*, thought Arien. He looked at Kento, wondering how much he dared trust this stranger. "You are a FreeMaster. Why have you not come to the guild?"

Kento shrugged. "I was needed here. I tried to jump from the tower after my mate died last year. Historian Perli stopped me. He gave me a place to live, and I sometimes carried messages for him. Then Matri and Sanid began experimenting with weather-working. Since I no longer had a House and a mate to protect, I chose to stay here and fight them."

"The rumors are true, then? Your people are using the ancient powers?"

"Not my people. The miners and the smelters are violating the laws. We builders and the herders have shared the Iron Keep with them from the beginning, but the four clans have often been at odds. We are trying to stop the weather-working, trying to keep them from harming the Terrans."

"And why do you love Terrans so much that you would turn against your own keep to help them?"

"We do not love Terrans. We hate the miners and the

smelters, who have oppressed us for generations. When they no longer control the metals trade, we will once again be their equals." Kento stepped forward, helped Arien to lift the Terran into a sitting position. "If the Iron Keep is poor, we will all need to work together to survive."

There was no guile to Kento's aura. He spoke the truth as he knew it. Arien's intuition told him to trust this FreeMaster.

"I need to wake Inda. Guard the corridor; this will take several moments." He turned his back on Kento and placed his right hand on Inda's forehead.

Mist flowed around him. It was suffused with a soft light that guided him forward, toward the sound of a Terran voice. He walked past dark eddies that threatened to suck him in and whirl him away to another existence. Breezes touched him, blew oppressive patches of fog across his path. He walked on.

The voice became louder. It was answered by another voice, a familiar voice. A gust of wind swept away the mist, and he saw before him—

Sarah Anders standing in a circle of light, facing Sinykin Inda across a narrow chasm. Her right hand was reaching toward him. A ball of shimmer-light glowed above her head.

"Join us," she pleaded. "Miranda is with me. She misses you."

Inda stared at Sarah, "How do you know of my daughter?"

"I told you, she is with me. She is waiting for you to join her. All you have to do is cross the chasm."

"No!" Arien stepped to the edge of the circle. "It is not your time. You are needed here."

Inda was gazing at Sarah's shimmer-light. "Can you teach me?" he asked, reaching for her hand.

Arien leaned forward, grabbed Inda's hand and turned him away from Sarah. "Come with me!"

"I don't want to," said Inda, looking over his shoulder at Sarah.

"Elissa waits for you. Jaime waits for you. I will take you to them."

"Elissa . . . is far away."

The vision of Sarah Anders was receding into the mist. Arien pulled Inda away from the chasm. "Elissa is at the

spaceport. We will go there." He led the Terran into the
mist.

With a start, Arien separated from Inda. The Ardellan's
palm tingled and his fingers were numb, the inevitable outcome of mind-to-mind contact. He opened his eyes slowly,
looked into Sinykin Inda's still face. Drops of liquid seeped
from the Terran's eyes, ran down his cheeks in tiny rivulets.

Arien watched as Sinykin opened his eyes. The Terran
blinked rapidly, twice, then reached up to wipe the wetness
from his face. "It was only a dream," he whispered. "Let's
get out of here."

"They are coming," said Kento from the corridor. "You
must leave now."

Arien rose, grasped Sinykin's hand. "Which staircase?"

Kento looked from one end of the hall to the other.
"Both. At least a hand of Masters on each one."

"Then we need another way out." Arien fingered the coil
of rope he wore across his chest. "Is there a window that
opens on the outer wall?"

"Come," said Kento. He and his companion led them
back to the narrow service stairs. A recessed window, tall
and narrow, looked out on the night's darkness. Kento
touched the crystal pane and it swung aside, letting in a
chilling breeze.

Arien lifted the rope over his head, dropped the coil to
the floor. He handed one end to Kento. "Tie this to something secure. It must hold my weight, and the Terran's."
He could hear running feet and shouting in the stairwell.

"There is nowhere to tie it. We will hold it for you,"
suggested Kento. "You must go down one at a time."

The guards were close now. They would be here in a
moment. Arien could hold them off for a time, but he did
not have the power to defeat so many, even with Kento's
help. Their only choice was to take the rope down three
stories to the ground. He leaned out the window, made a
ball of shimmer-light to brighten the scene. Carra was waiting below with the mounts. Arien waved, and Carra waved
back. If they could reach him quickly, they might escape.

Kento knotted one end of the rope around his companion's waist. Arien showed them how to hold it so that their
hands would not be cut. Then he tied the other end under
the unresisting Inda's arms.

"You must climb down," Arien said, leading Inda to the window. "Carra is waiting for us. He will help you. I will guide the rope, then I will climb down and join you." Arien looked to the side, saw the head and shoulders of a guard appear in the stairwell. "Go!" He pushed Inda over the sill, watched as the Terran twisted to put hands and feet against the wall.

Arien played out the rope quickly. Kento was guarding his back. He could feel the FreeMaster gathering power and sending out blasts of energy to keep their attackers at bay.

Inda managed to keep his feet turned toward the wall and used them to push his body away from it as he fell. His rope ran out before he hit the ground, and he came to rest against the wall and struggled to free himself. With Carra's help, he untied the rope. Arien watched, kneeling on the window-sill.

"Go now!" shouted Kento. "I cannot hold them!"

Arien looked back, saw angry eyes in the tattooed face of an approaching guard. He wrapped the rope around his forearm, pushed away from the sill, and tumbled out of the window.

The descent was fast and bruising. Arien's shoulder and upper arm hit the wall before he could bring his feet up to take the blow. He slid down nearly a story, the rope twisting around his sleeve, cutting off circulation in his forearm. His hands burned. Then his feet caught the wall, and he used it to slow his fall. He pushed off, dropped an arm's length, then touched the wall again. He could hear much shouting up above, and several times the rope jerked ominously.

An alep snorted. The sound was comfortingly close. Arien looked down, saw Carra waiting. He pushed away from the wall again, and suddenly he was falling. Someone had untied the other end of the rope. Arien landed on his back, heard the sound of frozen branches breaking. Carra ran toward Arien as he rolled out of the thornbush. The rope fell in a heap beside him.

"Are you injured?" asked Carra.

"No." Arien rose, settled his tunic, and bent to gather up the rope. He winced as pain shot through his back. The ride down the mountain would be painful, and he would be stiff and sore tomorrow. He wondered how Kento and his companion were faring. "We must go now. Is the Terran ready?"

"He is mounted. Let me bring your alep."

"Quickly, quickly!" Arien looked up, saw a tattooed face peering down from the window. Guards would be running back down the stairs to the kitchen door. Arien remembered leaving the door propped open. He ran to it, pulled out the stone and let the door close. The latch clicked home, and the ward snapped back into place. That would slow the pursuit.

"Here you are, GuildMaster." Carra had brought Arien's alep. "Let me help you mount."

Arien did not protest. He held his breath as he swung his right leg up and over the alep's back, then settled into the saddle with a sigh. He looked over at Inda, who sat his mount with the careful posture of a bruised rider. This trip would be painful for both of them, but hot baths and healing herbs awaited them at the guildhall. Arien sniffed. The air was still heavy with the promise of snow. They must ride quickly or be caught on the mountainside in the storm.

Chapter 20

Hatar stared at Jeryl over the great ball of shimmer-light that hovered between them. He lifted his right hand, fingers spread and palm exposed. "I challenge!" he cried. "You have taken Alain and hidden her from me. I will fight you for her return. Come, accept my challenge!"

"I will not fight you. Alain is dead! The plague took her from you," said Jeryl. He saw the frozen carcass of Hatar's mount, partially covered by ice and snow, on the ground behind the FreeMaster. It still wore its saddle.

"She is not dead! If Alain had died, I would have died with her. You must have her. You must!"

Jeryl could see the madness in Hatar's eyes. They glowed with the red light of rage and grief. Hatar raised his other hand, threw back his head, and opened his mouth to scream. Ruby sparks danced up his arms to gather at the tips of his fingers. He fashioned them into an incandescent ball and hurled it at Jeryl.

Jeryl sat up. The sleeping furs slid away from his body. He shivered as the cold air touched his skin. His heart was beating fast and hard. He took a deep breath, blinked, and a ball of shimmer-light appeared in the wall sconce. His cloak was folded on a nearby chair; he rose and wrapped the heavy wool fabric around his slender body. It was not yet dawn.

He remembered his own days of madness after his mate's death, when the only thing that had mattered to him was vengeance. Like Hatar, he had lost the ability to reason. Sarah Anders had forced him to face reality and to accept the responsibility of leading his clan.

Hatar had no one to help him. He was wandering alone in the wilderness, descending into insanity.

Jeryl stood at one of the council chamber's tall windows, watching snow swirl in the darkness outside. He shivered. Heavy clouds obscured the rising sun. Behind him, wooden chairs scraped across the stone floor. The council members were gathering at the table.

The Mentor's chair was at the foot of the table, opposite that of the council's leader. Jeryl waited until the shuffling and scraping stopped, then turned, stepped behind his empty chair, and lifted a hand in greeting. Oreyn, Master of House Natuaa, stablemaster and leader of Clan Alu's council, replied in kind.

There were twelve seats on either side of the long table. Most of them were occupied by Masters Jeryl had known all his life. To his left, in the Healer's chair, sat Viela. Beside him was Jeryl's apprentice, Secko. Hanra-bae, wearing his guild's colors and the medallion of a Master Healer, sat to Jeryl's right.

Oreyn clapped his hands to call the meeting to order. "We, who are twenty-one of the original twenty-four Houses that formed Clan Alu, are gathered this morning to ensure the continuance of one of our filial Houses," he said. "Poola of House Actaan is fertile. A youngling must be chosen for metamorphosis. Mentor, have you the list of candidates?"

"I do," replied Jeryl, still standing behind the high-backed Mentor's chair. He dropped a small roll of writing-cloth on the table. "Eight candidates are offered at this time. One is to be chosen for Actaan, and a second is to be chosen, provisionally, for House Ratrou."

Viela slapped the table with both palms. "No. I will not permit it."

Hanra-bae stared at him. His left hand touched the copper medallion that hung from a leather thong about his neck. He spoke in a cold, carefully measured voice. "Healer, obey the laws of your guild. You serve Alu. The clan's council must decide this matter."

Viela pushed his chair back from the table and stood. "I am Healer here. You have no say in the governing of Alu. Go back to the fishers and leave us in peace!"

There were murmured protests up and down the table.

Oreyn raised both hands, clapped again. "Sit, Healer. Let the Mentor speak."

Jeryl acknowledged Oreyn with a nod. "This is Hanra-bae, Master Healer of Port Freewind. He traveled with me to Berrut, and took me with him into the Healers' library. Together we searched the ancient scrolls and found a way to create new family lines. We know how to cocoon two younglings at the same time."

"You stole those scrolls," said Viela, rising again. He challenged Hanra-bae. "You violated the sanctity of your Healers' oath!"

Hanra-bae rose and faced him. "The guild makes a mockery of that oath. It sells its secrets and its loyalty to the trade guilds and denies the rest of us the knowledge that is our right."

"Stop it, both of you!" Jeryl ordered. "The scrolls have been returned, and the leaders of the Healers Guild will be well paid for the inconvenience we caused them. Now sit and hear me out.

"To cocoon two younglings, Hanra-bae needs certain rare herbs that he may not be able to obtain in this season. Ertis has offered to delay the cocooning of his successor to the last possible moment, while we search for the necessary plants. Therefore I ask you to choose two younglings, that all may be ready when we return with the herbs."

"That is a reasonable proposal," said Oreyn. "Are there any objections?"

"What foolishness is this?" Viela was on his feet again, his palms pressed to the tabletop and his face turned toward Oreyn. "You gamble the future of House Actaan on a strange Healer and an untried potion. I will not stand by and allow this to happen in my keep!"

Jeryl touched Viela's shoulder. "This is not your keep. If you will not cooperate with us, you may leave the council chamber."

Viela stared at him.

"The Mentor is correct," said Hanra-bae. He rose and walked around the table to stand beside Viela. "This is not your keep. You are here by the grace of this council and of your guild. Since you do not approve of what we intend to do, we will not require your participation."

"I will send a complete report to my GuildMaster!" cried Viela as he stalked from the room.

Hanra-bae sat in the Healer's chair.

"I object," said Kalou, acerbic Master of House Baator. "This fisher is usurping Viela's responsibilities."

"I agree. Viela has been Clan Alu's Healer for many years. The council should carefully consider his advice," suggested Secko. He would not look at the Mentor.

Jeryl let a ruby streak of anger show in his aura. "Viela has chosen to absent himself from his duties. If he returns, the Master Healer will certainly teach him all he wishes to learn about cocooning pairs of younglings. Until that time, Viela does not concern us. A qualified Healer is seated at the council table."

Kalou would not be put off so easily. "Why have you chosen to create a new line for House Ratrou? There are other empty Houses in Alu Keep. Surely the council should be allowed to choose which House will be renewed first."

The ruby light of Jeryl's ire spread through the rest of his aura. He opened his mouth to speak, closed it again when he saw Oreyn rise.

"Master Kalou has raised an objection to the choice of House Ratrou," said the council leader. "Is there any support for this objection? It is known to all of you that Ratrou was Jeryl's House. Do you deny his right to restore Ratrou first? If so, speak now." Oreyn began to circle the council table, walking behind the members' chairs, waiting for one of them to stop him with a wave or a nod.

Jeryl stared straight ahead while Oreyn completed his first circuit without interruption. By the ancient laws, the council leader was required to circle the table twice more, giving each Master ample opportunity to voice an opinion. This time Jeryl watched Oreyn's progress, staring at each of the council members in turn. None spoke or even raised a hand, and only Kalou would not meet Jeryl's eyes.

Oreyn finished the ritual in silence and returned to his chair. "Give me the list of candidates. We will choose one among them to become the new Master of House Actaan, and one who may become Master of House Ratrou." He unrolled the writing-cloth and began reading the names and qualifications aloud.

The council had no further need of Jeryl. He turned back to the window, saw the first big crystals of *ranaia*, "ice snow," lifted on the wind. The sky had lightened and the clouds above were colored deep purple to slate gray. Jeryl

leaned closer to the window and looked to the east, into the
sunrise and the coming storm. The keep's high wall was a
shadow in the distance, and beyond it he could see only the
white *ranaia*.

The crystals struck the windowpane with a clicking sound.
The first few melted and slid down to the sill before the
chill air could freeze their trails. They were followed by
many more, blown almost horizontally by the howling wind.
The crystals gathered and melted and were frozen into ice
on nearby roofs. They clung to windward walls, piled on
steps, and spread across the streets. Walking immediately
became treacherous. Jeryl lost sight of the keep's wall, of
the buildings two streets over. The storm was quickly becoming a whiteout, that dangerous condition where one
could not see things even an arm's length away.

The wind rattled the windowpane and flung up another
fistful of snow. Jeryl shivered, reached for the shutters, and
pulled them closed. Behind him, the wind howled down the
chimney, carrying a few snow crystals across the room in
its cold draft. A fire had been laid on the hearth but not lit.
Jeryl closed his eyes and willed a flame to ignite the little
pile of cloth scraps and kindling beneath the logs. The
flames consumed the tinder quickly, lit the dry bark and
then the wood of the larger pieces. The smoke and heated
air fought for supremacy against the cold wind, forcing it
back up the chimney.

"Mentor, we are ready to proceed," said Oreyn. "The
younglings have been chosen. You may have your apprentice
bring Ertis into the council chamber."

Jeryl nodded to Secko, who walked to the doorway,
opened it, and looked out into the corridor. The Historian
was waiting there, sitting on a bench. "Come," said Secko.
He stepped aside and closed the door behind Ertis.

Hanra-bae rose from his place in the Healer's chair. Before him, on the table, were an empty bowl and a footed
plate of glossy black ceramic. Three pieces of charcoal
rested on the plate. The Healer leaned forward, held his
hands over the charcoal, muttered something under his
breath, then blinked as the black lumps began to glow red.
He picked up a stick of blue smokewood, pulled his dagger
from its sheath, and carefully scraped wood shavings onto
the charcoal. Tendrils of gray smoke and the fragrant scent
of the wood filled the chamber.

"Ertis, Master of House Actaan, join me here before the council of Clan Alu," said Hanra-bae. "It has been reported that your mate is fertile. The time has come to add a new Master to the line of House Actaan. Has a successor been chosen?"

Ertis stepped forward and accepted the small scroll Oreyn offered to him. He read it quickly, then rerolled it and dropped it on the table. "The youngling naOflea will come to Actaan."

"Have you brought the symbol of your House?" asked Hanra-bae.

Ertis offered him a silver ring with the sign of House Actaan, scarletberries on an amethyst background, executed in enamel on its face. Hanra-bae accepted the ring and placed it in the bottom of the black bowl. Then he picked up the bowl and handed it to Ertis.

Jeryl watched closely as Ertis stared into the bowl. The time had come for the Historian to give up his House. He must do so willingly, without reservation, and Jeryl was not certain that Ertis could do that. Poola's fertile time had come upon them too soon. It had cut short Ertis' career, changed his plans for the next few years. Had he been able to come to terms with those changes?

The ring in the bottom of the bowl was beginning to glow. The scarletberry design brightened, the silver shone, the amethyst enamel was transformed to a deep, translucent purple. Slowly the bowl filled with shimmer-light, and in the center of the light, the image of the scarletberries grew. It expanded until it half-filled the bowl, turning slowly in the midst of the shimmer-light. Ertis sighed, and the image began to shrink. It became smaller and smaller, until it disappeared from sight. He returned the bowl to Hanra-bae.

The Healer lifted the bowl and presented it to the council. "Actaan rests in this dish, awaiting the emergence of Oflea from his cocoon." He set the bowl on the table beside the plate of smokewood.

Oreyn looked around the table. "We have concluded our business this morning. Many of us have duties to see to before the storm worsens. The council is dismissed."

"No." Jeryl returned to the Mentor's chair and sat. "I have need of the council's energy. This storm that assaults our Houses and chills our bodies is not a natural storm. There are weather-workers in the mountains, guiding and reinforcing it. They are hoping to damage the spaceport and trouble the Terrans."

There were incredulous murmurs from around the table. The Masters could all see by Jeryl's aura that he was telling the truth as he knew it. Still, Jeryl knew that some of them would believe he was mistaken.

"The miners and smelters freely admit that they have revived the craft of weather-working," said Ertis. "They are trying to drive the Terrans from Ardel."

"Impossible," said Oreyn. "A single storm would not make them leave."

Jeryl shrugged. "I do not think that storms alone would discourage the Terrans. Yet the storms are the reason we have had so few shipments of metal. Sinykin Inda has told me that the great ships have not been able to land during even a mild storm.

"Listen to the fury of the wind, and remember that this blizzard has just begun. Think of the tales we have heard, of how the storms grew more powerful and more dangerous as they were directed from one place to another. The Historians tell us that weather-working was banned because it destroyed the balance of nature. It took many seasons before the weather returned to its normal patterns."

"What can we do?" asked Kalou. "We know nothing of weather-working."

"There is no need for you to know or do anything, other than to lend me your power. I have ridden the storms before. Controlling the weather may be beyond my power, but I will learn who directs these storms. We can take that knowledge to the Assembly in Berrut." Jeryl held out his left hand, fingers spread in a sunburst, and joined it palm-to-palm with the right hand of Hanra-bae. As their palms touched, their fingers curled around to lock their hands together. Then the Healer offered his left hand to the Master beside him. One by one, the Masters entered the circle. Only Kalou hesitated for an instant before joining his hand to Oreyn's.

The circle was nearly complete. Jeryl reached into his pocket and brought out a handful of dried armata leaves. Leaning forward, he crumpled them onto the plate of smoking charcoal. Then he grasped the proffered hand of the Master to his right and completed the link.

* * *

Elissa Durant stared at the photo on the wall behind Jeff
Grund's head. It showed the landing field at dusk, with a
huge freighter parked in its center. She wondered when she
would again see a ship on that field.

"The electromagnetic disturbances resumed just after
midnight," said Jeff. "The storm moved swiftly down from
the mountains. Its leading edge touched us just before dawn.
We already had three centimeters of snow on the landing
field when *Manatee* asked for clearance to touch down."

Anna Griswold nodded. Her short gray hair was disheveled, her tunic was rumpled, and there seemed to be some
new lines on her forehead and around her eyes. She looked
as if she had not slept well. "You advised them that their
navigation equipment might be damaged?"

"Certainly. Captain Hilton elected not to land at this
time. He can hold in parking orbit for eight hours; if he
can't land by then, he'll have to move on to his next stop."

"Taking our shielding modules with him," said Griswold. "How long do you think the storm will last?"

Grund shrugged. "This one is a blizzard. It could last
eight hours, or twelve, or twenty-four. We may get as much
as forty centimeters of snow, and if the storm follows the
usual pattern, we'll get some sleet."

"Elissa?"

"We've already got the trucks out on the landing field,
Anna. We plan on keeping the field clear so that *Manatee*
can land as soon as the atmospheric disturbance ends."

"Fine," said Anna. "Contact Security if you need more
people. Now let's all get back to work."

Elissa rose and grabbed her parka from the back of her
chair. She stood at the wide window and looked out at the
spaceport as she slipped her arms into the parka's insulated
sleeves. Snow covered the ground, the roofs, and part of
the landing field. The snow was now twelve or fifteen centimeters deep, blowing into knee-high drifts where the wind
could reach it. The huge windmills had been disconnected
last night; snow and ice were building up on their blades,
which spun freely in the wind. Shiny ice coated the pipes
of the landing field's towers and the windward side of the
buildings.

Jaime was safe and warm at the Grunds', playing with
Tommy under the watchful eyes of his mother. Sinykin was
in a keep that had withstood hundreds of years of storms.

There was nothing more Elissa could do to protect either of them; her immediate concern was the spaceport. Her crew's trucks were moving down one side of the landing field in a neat diagonal line. Her own vehicle, the largest of the maintenance trucks, was parked downstairs. Elissa grabbed her thermal gloves, nodded to Jeff and Anna, and headed out to join her crew.

Palm touched palm, and Jeryl dropped into the net of power created by the council. He breathed deeply of the armata smoke, held it in his lungs until his body forced him to release it and breathe again. His blood quickened. The smoke filled him until he feared he would burst. Jeryl closed his eyes and saw the circle of Masters as a ring of energy, each individual a node of pulsing light. Together they formed a web of power, a reservoir from which he could draw the strength he needed.

Above and around the clanhall, the storm controlled the atmosphere. It did not rage; rage is swiftly spent. The storm was dynamic, powerful, a living, growing disturbance that seemed to be settling in for a long siege.

The armata smoke changed Jeryl's perceptions, until the energy patterns of the blizzard were more real to him than the touch of the Masters whose hands he held. He was being drawn into that other world of swiftly-moving air currents, of clashing temperature gradients and wind-tossed snow crystals. Jeryl made the mental adjustment, the twist of thought that freed him from his body, and his mind soared upward, out of the clanhall and into the storm.

Where his eyes had seen only whiteness, his discorporate mind perceived many things. The falling snow no longer blinded him. He tracked back along its downward path, climbing toward the storm's center through buffeting winds. He found the curving plane where cold air clashed with warm, releasing energy that fueled the blizzard. As the storm flowed over and through him, its power disturbed the silver thread that connected Jeryl's mind to his body, reminding him that should he stray too far, he might never be able to return.

He reached the storm's center and climbed above it, into warmer, calmer air. From this vantage he could see two other, larger storm cells, each producing a full-blown blizzard. One of the storms had reached the spaceport; the other was moving quickly across the plain toward it.

Jeryl followed the air currents across the plain and into the storm that threatened the spaceport. There he sensed pockets of warm air within the clouds, where the falling snow was melting. The moisture formed into droplets, then froze into pellets of ice when it reached the colder air near the ground. Some of the water did not freeze until it touched branches, roofs, wires, anything solid and cold. Jeryl had seen orchards ruined by such ice storms, branches broken and trees torn asunder.

Another mind brushed against Jeryl, tangling for an instant in the fringes of his perceptions. The fleeting contact was threatening, hostile enough to make Jeryl draw away quickly. Could it have been one of the weather-workers?

The mind had disturbed the energy patterns of the storm, leaving an indistinct trail through the clouds. Jeryl followed cautiously along this pathway. Gusting winds blew snow around and through him; the white crystals were unchanged by his presence. He passed from cold air into warm and back to cold again, through damp places where snow crystallized and fell away from him, around spots where energy was discharging like tiny lightning bolts. He was greedy, absorbing the power when he could. The storm ignored him.

The trail led through the clouds to a place in the high atmosphere, into the frigid peace above the storm. There Jeryl encountered the mind again. He touched a single tendril of the other's awareness. The tendril curled rapidly away from him, withdrawing toward a place above the storm's center. Jeryl followed, reaching out with tendrils of his own to try to locate and identify this being.

One tendril brushed against the silver cord that connected this being's mind and body. Jeryl could name his enemy now: Sanid, leader of the mining clan, the oldest and most powerful Master in the Iron Keep. A circle of Masters worked with him, supporting him as Alu's council supported Jeryl.

Jeryl sensed another presence above the storm. A cautious touch alarmed him, and he fled into the clouds. The mind followed, reached for him, touched him again.

I am an ally. I am Kento.

Knowledge flooded into Jeryl. He saw visions of a dying Mother, a desperate FreeMaster, fleeing Historians, and a weather-working circle, all in an instant. He knew that Siny-kin Inda had escaped from the Iron Keep, and that Sanid and his circle were trying to destroy the spaceport.

We can help one another, thought Kento. *If we work to-gether, we can turn the storm away from the spaceport.*

To what purpose? The storm will not destroy the space-port or drive the Terrans from Ardel. Once its fury is spent, all will return to normal.

Sanid is mad with greed. He will continue working the weather, sending storm after storm against the Terrans, with no regard for the consequences. You have heard the stories; you know what harm comes from meddling with natural forces. We will all pay a high price for Sanid's folly.

Jeryl feared that Kento was correct. *Then we should stop Sanid. Let the storm run its course; we will fight the weather-workers.*

No! They have gathered enough energy in their tower to ravage a city. If we try to destroy them, we may demolish the entire keep. We should turn the storm away from the spaceport and prove to Sanid that we are as strong as he is. Then he may stop this madness. His followers will surely desert him.

And if we do not succeed?

There will be time then to consider alternatives.

Together they faced the storm that menaced the space-port. Kento showed Jeryl how to conjure a wind; they di-rected its force and began to move the storm toward the unoccupied wasteland. Jeryl pressed forward, drawing power from Clan Alu's council as Kento drew energy from his own supporters.

They felt immediate resistance. Sanid fought the wind, driving the storm back toward the spaceport. He pushed hard, focusing the strength of his circle on guiding and maintaining the storm. Jeryl and Kento pushed back.

With each interference, the ferocity of the storm in-creased. It absorbed the energy that Jeryl and Kento and Sanid expended in moving it and grew more powerful and more unstable with each passing moment. Lightning flashed among the upper clouds, and heavy, wet flakes of snow fell on the land below, sticking to already icy surfaces and weighing them down.

With strength born of desperation, Jeryl and Kento gath-ered more wind from the open plain and tried again to direct the storm. The air through which they moved was becoming colder, more energetic, harder to control. The wind began to quarrel with Jeryl. It blew first one way and then another, teasing him with its power. He was no longer its master.

Elissa settled into the cabin of the big maintenance vehicle and plugged her headset into the control panel's jack. Discordant voices vied with one another for her attention. Long practice had taught her how to separate the important information from the meaningless chatter.

She pushed the starter, switched to manual control, and guided the vehicle along the main road to the landing field. She lowered the plow. Snow curled up and away from it to pile up at the edge of the road. Defrosters kept the windows clear, but gusting winds and blowing snow sometimes cut her visibility to less than five meters.

There were ice crystals mixed with the snow. She could hear them hit the windshield.

"Residential units fourteen through twenty are reporting a power outage."

Elissa reacted immediately. "All right, cut the chatter. Umbala, take Dickson and start checking for downed wires."

"Sure thing, Chief."

A gust of wind shook the truck and splattered wet snow across the windshield.

"Oh, shit! The antenna's coming down!"

That was Sobsczyk, leading the "conga line" on the landing field.

"Which antenna?" queried Elissa. "I can see the weather station. Everything there looks fine."

"Behind you, Chief. The microwave dish!"

Elissa stopped her vehicle and looked over her shoulder just as the microwave antenna atop the administration building tore loose from its anchors. It cartwheeled across the roof and over the edge and landed with a crunch on the pavement. Wind and gravity had combined to turn it into useless junk. It had torn a substantial hole in the roof.

"Elwood, get a repair crew over to patch that hole. Work on it from the inside. I don't want you up on the roof!" Elissa turned back and put the truck into gear. This storm was worse than any of the others they'd faced this season;

the high winds would cause more damage than snow ever did.

She drove down the plowed side of the field, toward the first of the windmills. *We should have taken the blades off last night when we disconnected everything,* she thought, as she watched them spin crazily. Wind buffeted the big truck, catching at the plow. Elissa decelerated and steered with a light hand.

The tower just ahead began to sway to and fro. Elissa quickly turned the wheel and felt her rear tires begin to skid as they lost traction on the ice. She changed gears and straightened the wheel, trying to bring the vehicle back under control.

With a groan, the network of steel tubing that supported the windmill tore free of its pad. The wind caught at the spinning blades and pushed the tower over. It crashed down across the huge truck's cab, shattering windows and crushing steel.

Elissa screamed.

Jeryl and Kento climbed above the clouds and looked down on the stormscape below. The second storm cell had reached the spaceport. It touched the first cell and began to merge with it. Lightning flashed, passing energy from cloud to cloud. The thunder swept through Jeryl. He watched as the two storms coalesced into one swirling, devastating blizzard centered over the spaceport.

Sanid controlled the winds that no longer would obey Kento and Jeryl. He directed the storm as he pleased, changing snow to sleet, and then to ice. Jeryl moved above the clouds, sensing Sanid's activities below. He did not know how to wrest control of this storm from Sanid, but he did know how to curtail Sanid's power.

Jeryl led Kento back down into the storm. They followed Sanid through the clouds, seeking the threads of power that connected him with his circle of weather-workers.

The slender, delicate filaments were as strong as copper wire. Jeryl tugged at one, tried to break it, and only succeeded in attracting Sanid's attention. Kento grasped another thread and sent a jolt of power down it toward the Iron Keep. The thread vibrated for a moment, then dissolved into bits of energy that were scattered by the wind.

Jeryl tried the same tactic, sensed the shriek of pain as

his jolt of energy burned the weather-worker on the other end of the thread. Sanid recoiled with shock. His control of the storm slipped. The winds slowed as Sanid reached for one of the filaments that connected Jeryl to Alu's council. Jeryl fled but not fast enough. He felt Sanid's touch.

Kento wrapped a tendril around another of Sanid's filaments. *I challenge you! Release the other. Fight me. I am one of your kind!*

He was too late. Jeryl felt Kalou scream, felt their bond dissolve. Then someone tugged on the delicate silver thread that connected Jeryl's mind to his body. It pulled him inexorably back to the clanhall.

Jeryl opened his eyes. He took a deep, shuddering breath, felt sweat trickle down his chest and dampen his back. There were hands on his shoulders. He leaned back, looked up into Secko's face.

"Why did you call me back?" he whispered, his voice cracking in the middle of the question. He cleared his throat, longed for a drink of water. Cramps twisted his palms. He stretched them, spreading his fingers.

"The Masters were afraid," said Hanra-bae. He was spreading salve on Kalou's burned hands.

Oreyn shrugged. "Kalou is badly hurt."

"I must return to the storm. Come with me or not, as you choose." Jeryl's voice was stronger, but scratchy. He felt warm, and wished that the hearth fire was smaller.

Behind him the shutters rattled. The wind whistled outside the clanhall, sending a draft through the stifling room. The fire flared, then a gust of wind blew smoke back into the room. Jeryl's eyes stung. He coughed. So did the others. The fire sputtered and sizzled and steam billowed out of the hearth as ice and snow cascaded down the chimney. The flames died, and the hearthstone split with a resounding crack. It was an ominous sign.

Kalou left the table. Secko took Jeryl's right hand. Hanra-bae took his left. One by one the others joined the circle. Jeryl sprinkled another handful of armata leaves on the charcoal and once again breathed deeply of the smoke.

Jeryl returned to the upper atmosphere, seeking Sanid and Kento. He found them within the storm.

Sanid's rage was a ruby light that flashed like lightning

within the clouds. Wind swirled around him. He answered Kento's challenge.

Flee from me. I will break the silver cord that connects you to your body, and you will be forever lost. Your body will die, and your spirit will travel the winds until it dissipates and becomes one with the planet and the elements.

Look to your own body, Sanid! If it dies, you will die with it! Kento reached for Sanid's silver cord. He brushed against it, and Sanid fled into the clouds.

Kento and Jeryl stalked him through the storm. He led them from cloud to cloud, through snow and ice and lightning. They followed, seeking that elusive silver cord. Jeryl brushed against one of the fine threads that connected Sanid with his weather-workers. He severed it, thinking of Kalou's burned hands when he sensed the weather-worker's scream.

In the midst of a dark cloud, the trail disappeared. Kento and Jeryl swept quickly through the surrounding atmosphere, searching for Sanid. They found no sign of him. Kento looked above the clouds, and Jeryl looked below, seeking evidence of Sanid's influence upon the storm.

Here, thought Kento.

Jeryl rose through the clouds to join them. Kento was exploring a strange pattern of energy. His silver cord extended back through the clouds toward the Iron Keep. Jeryl scanned its length, sensed the place where it was attenuated and about to break. Sanid had wrapped a tendril of power around it!

No! Here, thought Jeryl. He attacked Sanid, extending tendrils of his own to grapple with the weather-worker and drain his energy.

Kento slipped down the cord and strengthened it, then wrested it free of Sanid's grip. Ruby lightning flashed. Sanid was no longer controlling the storm. It began to follow its natural pattern of movement away from the spaceport, taking its wind and snow out over the uncharted wasteland.

Sanid fled high into the atmosphere, into a cold, calm place above the mountains. Jeryl and Kento followed him, faced him with all their power and strength. Energy flowed through them, sparkling like bits of ruby and topaz light. They waited, watching to see what Sanid would do.

He attacked. He struck at Jeryl, absorbed power from him and severed another of the fine threads that connected him to Alu's council. Jeryl felt Oreyn's scream cut short as the filament that bound them dissolved.

Jeryl backed away. Sanid stalked him, severed another thread, and another. Jeryl could not bear the screams. He was unshielded for the first time since he had become Mentor. He felt exposed and knew he was jeopardizing the lives of the Masters in Alu's council chamber. Sanid reached for him again, and Jeryl fled toward the mountains below.

Sanid followed. He had grown strong feasting on Jeryl's energy. He spread himself to attack once more. Jeryl fled lower, until he sensed the Iron Keep just beneath him. Kento was already there, waiting above the weather-workers' tower.

The tower room sparkled with the energy Sanid had gathered. Kento challenged him. *Come, face me here.*

It is too dangerous, warned Jeryl. *There is too much power here!*

It is the only way!

Jeryl was frightened. *You will die! You cannot control this much power!*

Then we shall all die together!

Kento struck at Sanid. The air was filled with lightning and streaks of power. Jeryl fled again, upward this time. Beneath him, the tower room disappeared in a brilliant flash. The tower collapsed, taking half the wall with it.

Sanid's death cry passed through Jeryl first. Kento's touched him next. The death cries of many strangers followed, sweeping down the mountain to tell the plains dwellers of the tragedy at the Iron Keep.

There was nothing Jeryl could do for the dead or the injured, or for the living who scrambled through the ruins of their keep. His energy was nearly depleted. He wanted to rest. He reached for the thread that would guide him home.

The silver cord that connected him to his body had been severed!

Jeryl tried to envision his body, to see the place where he had left it. He could not remember! Nothing existed except the air through which he moved, the wind and snow. . . .

No! There were things he must do. What were they?

He tried to remember his home. A keep . . . rambling . . . walled . . . Alu? Where was it? Everything seemed strange. Only the clouds were familiar.

He began spreading out into the clouds. The air felt com-

fortable, like a new kind of home. He would exist here for a while, slowly extending himself farther, becoming thinner and thinner. The others no longer needed him. He could rest now. . . .

Someone touched him. Memories of death, of eyes shining with ruby madness, a torn cloak, and a challenge. . . .

Hatar! Hatar was below, on the solidness beneath the air. Jeryl floated down to touch his friend. Hatar was cold. The heart within his body barely beat. Jeryl settled into Hatar's mind, touched his grief, and absorbed it. He spread himself throughout Hatar's body, willing warmth and strength into the cold tissues.

He was too late. Hatar sighed and his heart stopped beating. His essence, that which was mind and soul, rose out of his body. Jeryl went with it, clinging to this one familiar thing in a strange new world. Together they soared through the air, seeking Hatar's mate and siblings, to touch them one last time before they spread themselves to the four winds.

They went to a familiar place, to a wall lined with stone urns, and to a crowded room and another cold body very near death. They hovered there, thinking of clouds and winds and freedom. They could dissipate now and have the peace they had been seeking ever since their mates' deaths.

Chapter 21

Sinykin Inda stood at the wide front window of the FreeMasters Guildhall and stared across the snow-covered orchards in the direction of the spaceport. The clouds were gone, and the larger moon would rise soon; it was a crisp, clear night.

Inda heard a soft footstep. He turned and found GuildMaster Arien standing behind him.

"We are almost ready to leave," said Arien. "Come, there is still time for you to share our meal. You will travel more comfortably if you have eaten."

"I can't have anything but tea. My stomach is queasy from the drugged bread they gave me in the Iron Keep. If I eat now, I'll be ill." Inda turned back to the window. He had slept through the storm because of that drugged bread and had lost an entire day of travel. "The snow doesn't look too deep. We should be able to make good time."

Arien pointed in the direction of the spaceport. "We were on the edge of the storm. There is probably much more snow down on the plain. We must be prepared to dig our way through drifts once we leave the mountains."

Inda shivered. He reached into his pocket and pulled out the message that had been waiting for him when he had arrived at the guildhall last night. He read it through, then crumpled it and stuffed it back in his pocket. "Are the aleps already saddled?"

"The younglings will prepare the mounts as soon as they finish loading the cart."

"A cart? Won't that slow us down?"

"It is necessary," said Arien. "Drifts on the plain can reach well above the height of a Master. We must take a crew of younglings with us to clear the trail. They will need shovels and picks to move the snow and break the ice. You do not expect them to walk and carry their tools, do you?''

''No. That would slow us down even more.'' Sinykin sighed. ''I've been ordered to return to the spaceport immediately. The Administrator is closing the compound. She won't let any Terrans leave the grounds.''

''Why would she do that?''

''She says I violated the trade agreement by traveling beyond Alu Keep.''

Arien touched Sinykin's arm. ''Do not be concerned about it. Jeryl does not think you violated the agreement. You did what you felt was needful. Come, drink some tea with us; we will be mounted and ready to travel by the time the moon rises.''

Sinykin followed Arien to the table and accepted a mug of steaming tea. He wrapped both hands around the cup and let its warmth soak into his chilled fingers, but he did not drink. The smell of food upset his stomach. His medicines, all his gear, even his journal had gone down the mountain to Alu Keep with Ertis. He did not even have an antacid tablet in his pocket. He clenched his teeth and watched the FreeMasters eat, willing them to finish quickly. For a moment, he thought they heard his silent plea. Several pushed aside half-empty plates and drained their mugs.

''It is time,'' said Arien. ''The younglings have finished preparing our mounts.''

Across the room, the wide door opened. A blast of cold air made Sinykin shiver. The hearth fire flared. A single youngling shook the snow from its poncho, entered the room, and pushed the door closed. Its one healthy eyestalk swiveled to look at Arien.

''GuildMaster, the cart is ready and your mounts are saddled. How many younglings do you want to take with you?''

''Two hands of you, if you will all fit in the cart. You must all have ponchos and slippers.''

''I will tell them,'' said the youngling. He went out again.

More FreeMasters were pushing away their plates and rising. Sinykin set down his mug and took a deep breath. Soon he would return to the spaceport. That should have pleased him; instead, he felt his stomach twist into tighter knots. He walked to the hearth and took his borrowed cloak from a peg at its side. The cloak was warm and dry. He slipped his arms into its too-large sleeves and let its folds

settle around his body. He missed the close-fitting parka
that he had lent to Ertis. That day seemed so long ago.
Sinykin turned and followed the FreeMasters out into the
courtyard.

Burning torches had been jammed in holders beside the
barn doors. The flames flared in the wind, making the snow-
covered earth a place of bright reflections and deep shadows.
In the center of the court, a dozen younglings clambered into the little cart that was hooked behind a pair of
long-haired borras. The front of the cart was loaded with
wide, flat-bladed shovels and assorted picks and scrapers.
More younglings held the reins of eight aleps. Each of the
big animals was saddled and standing placidly on six legs.

Inda walked over to the largest alep. Its back reached
nearly to his shoulder. He fitted his left foot into the too-
wide stirrup, then swung his right leg up and over the animal's back. He groaned as his buttocks settled onto the
broad saddle. The muscles on the insides of his thighs ached
from too many days spent riding. He was in pain from knees
to crotch. He took a deep breath, straightened his knees and
pushed his feet out to either side to stretch the sore muscles.
After a moment he relaxed, and the pain became a dull
ache.

The small moon rose as Sinykin rode through the gate
and out onto the trail. He looked back over his shoulder at
the FreeMasters' mountain compound, and wondered if he
would ever see it again.

By midnight they had left the mountains and passed
through the foothills. The large moon was high in the sky
when they reached the stream that separated the hills from
the plain. The snow was deeper here, reaching above the
alep's ankles, and the air was just cold enough to keep it
from melting. A smooth crust of ice reflected moonlight
from the surface of the stream.

The cart stopped just before it reached the wooden bridge
that crossed the water. Arien rode forward and examined the
timbers by shimmer-light.

"The bridge is treacherous," he called back. "It must
be cleared of snow and ice before we can cross it."

Inda sighed as he watched the younglings snatch up tools
and jump from the cart. This was only the first of many
delays he expected to experience before they reached the

spaceport. If the snow continued to grow deeper with each passing kilometer, the drifts on the plain would be high indeed. Elissa and her crew were probably clearing the spaceport's walks and landing field right now, sitting warm and snug in the cabs of their heavy trucks. He hoped so.

The younglings all stripped off their ponchos and left them in the cart. Each one tied a length of rope around its bulbous middle and fastened the free end to the railing before it ventured onto the bridge. Inda dismounted, clenching his teeth as he straightened bruised thighs and aching hips, and followed them to the stream. He stood well back from the bank and looked down at the water. The reason for the safety lines was immediately obvious. The ice was very thin, and under it cold water moved swiftly. Somewhere in the mountains, snow was melting.

The aleps snuffled and snorted, but the borras stood silently in their harnesses. Sinykin walked back and forth to ease his aching legs and listened to the younglings' chatter.

"Too much snow to leave on the bridge. Dump it in the stream."

"Will crack the ice!"

"No matter. Scrape away this hard stuff. The aleps will slide on it."

"I will chop!"

The last comment was followed by rhythmic pounding that resonated through the bridge's timbers.

"Quickly!" called Arien. "We must hurry."

A shout made Inda turn back to look at the bridge. A youngling had slipped over the side and was swinging at the end of its tether, squealing and waving its tentacles. It kicked and broke through the ice with one foot. The water swept away its slipper, which made it squeal even louder. The other younglings dropped their shovels and picks and ran to its aid. Several grabbed the rope and in a moment they had pulled the frightened youngling back onto the bridge.

Sinykin joined Arien at the foot of the bridge. "Let me take that youngling back to the cart and dry it off before it gets frostbite."

"Quickly, then. The bridge is almost clear. We will be ready to cross it soon."

"It will only take a moment," said Sinykin. He called to the youngling. "Come, let me help you."

The youngling was warm and dry, huddling under its poncho in a corner of the cart, by the time Arien declared the bridge safe to cross. Inda mounted his alep, winced as he settled into the saddle. It would take more than a warm bath to ease the cramps in his thighs. He checked his chronometer—they had been on the trail for over four hours. He had hoped to reach the spaceport by dawn, but now he knew that was impossible. Mid-morning would be a more realistic guess. He looked back over his shoulder, and saw that the mountaintops were once again obscured by clouds. Were they a natural formation, or one gathered by Sanid and his circle? Despite Arien's assurances, he did not believe the weather-workers were dead. When he closed his eyes he could see them gathered in the tower room and hear their chants.

They traveled more slowly now. Snow-filled ruts caught at the cart's wheels, and the drifts were sometimes as high as its axles. When the borras balked before a high drift, the younglings would jump down, carrying their shovels, and scurry up to clear the trail. The aleps, snorting their displeasure, plodded through without trouble. Each kilometer brought deeper snow, until Arien sent the younglings ahead to clear the trail.

By dawn, the second FreeMasters' compound was in sight. The clouds cleared away, and the rising sun brought warmer air. Sinykin no longer feared another storm. He had other worries. He saw bent and broken saplings, snow-covered roofs, and windows half-hidden by drifts. The windmill had been stripped of its blades, before the storm, he hoped. Its supports were coated with ice. It would be useless until the weather warmed enough to melt the ice.

Had Elissa been able to dismantle the spaceport's much larger windmills before the storm hit? And would the towers stand under the weight of so much ice and snow?

"We will rest our aleps here," called Arien, leading the way into the compound. "The younglings will go on ahead and clear the way to the spaceport."

Inda and Arien had just begun to dismount when Ramis came out to greet them. He brought along several younglings, who took charge of the aleps.

"Greetings, Master Inda. May the great sun smile on you today." Ramis offered Sinykin the open-palmed greeting before he turned to Arien. "GuildMaster, it is good to see you. We have unexpected guests in the guildhall. Reass of the Metalsmiths Guild is here with a delegation of merchants and GuildMasters from Berrut.''

Arien muttered something that Sinykin could not translate. ''What are they doing here?''

''They were on their way to the spaceport when the storm trapped them here yesterday.'' Ramis shrugged. ''We delayed clearing the trail this morning, hoping they would become discouraged and return to Berrut. Now they will probably want to travel with you.''

''I am not likely to allow that,'' said Arien. He strode into the guildhall, with Ramis and Inda following close behind.

''Ah, GuildMaster! We did not expect to see you here,'' said a small, well-muscled Master. He wore a red tunic and leggings, and high black boots, and his gray hair was bound with a red thong. ''And you have a Terran with you. Greetings, Master, from the Metalsmiths Guild and the other trade guilds of Berrut.''

Arien lifted a hand in formal greeting. ''Nor did I expect to see you, Reass. What brings you to our guildhall?''

''We are here by an accident of the weather, Arien. We had planned on riding straight through to the spaceport, but the storms stopped us. Your FreeMasters offered us the hospitality of your guildhall for the night. We are grateful and are now ready to resume our journey.''

''It is forbidden for anyone to go to the spaceport without the permission of Jeryl or Clan Alu's council,'' said Arien, walking past Reass to the hearth. A youngling took Arien's cloak and gave him a steaming mug of tea. ''Do you carry a token from Jeryl or the council?''

Reass shrugged. ''The Terrans can make their own choices in these matters. If they do not wish to speak with us, they will send us away.''

Inda had intended to stay out of this discussion, but now he stepped forward. ''I am the spaceport's Assistant Administrator. I can tell you that we will not receive visitors who have not been approved by the representatives of Clan Alu.''

''We are here to challenge the authority of Alu,'' said Reass. ''We are not pleased with the way Alu is handling the trade agreement, and we would offer your people an alternative.''

"My people have a binding contract with Clan Alu. We cannot entertain other offers at this time. Any changes in the contract must be negotiated through Clan Alu." Inda followed Arien to the hearth.

"I suggest that you and your delegation return to Berrut," said Arien.

"Do not instruct us, GuildMaster. You have no authority over the trade guilds." A red flush of anger spread slowly downward from the top of Reass' aura.

"I have the power to decide who travels the road from here to the spaceport, and I say that you will not pass beyond this guildhall. Go home, Reass. State your challenge before the Assembly, and let it judge your claim." Arien turned to watch the fire.

"You cannot dismiss me. I challenge you, GuildMaster!" Reass lifted his hands, palms turned toward Arien and fingers arched. A shower of sparks flew from his fingertips.

Arien dropped his mug, spun around, raised his own hands. The pottery struck the hearthstone and shattered, and tea splashed Inda's boots. An arc of power flashed like lightning from Arien's fingers, grounding an arm's length in front of Reass. The threat left a scorched and smoking scar on the floorboards.

Reass did not move. His companions rose, backed toward the wall, said nothing. Inda's heart was beating wildly. This was how Sarah Anders had died. He wanted to step away from Arien, yet he could not move. He watched, horrified, as streams of white energy arced from Reass' hands toward Arien.

Arien's answering charge caught the Metalsmith's attack in mid-flight. The sudden release of power produced a blinding fireball that sent most of the audience diving under tables and benches. It dissipated quickly, leaving another scar on the floor. Inda blinked away the bright afterimage, saw Reass raise his hands once more. Arien shouted a warning, then sent a smaller fireball spinning across the room. Reass howled in pain as it engulfed his hands.

Inda saw the burning flesh, swallowed his fear, and ran to Reass. He reached for the Metalsmith's hands, expecting to see charred and flaking skin. The palms were only reddened, the fingers swelling but not blistered. Inda touched the skin, felt its unnatural heat. Then one of the Free-Masters pushed him aside and took Reass' hands in his own.

Inda knew that his Terran healing skills were neither needed nor wanted. He returned to Arien's side.

The other members of the delegation crawled out of their hiding places and approached Arien. The tallest spoke.

"I am Harra, GuildMaster of the Innkeepers. I offer apologies. As soon as Reass is ready to travel, we will return to Berrut."

"See that you do. Now, please leave us." Arien took Sinykin by the arm and led him to the window. They stood side by side, watching the younglings working in the courtyard.

"I knew you were foolhardy when I learned that you had gone to the Iron Keep," said Arien. "It is a characteristic common to most of the Terrans I have met. Today it could have cost you your life. Heed my warning, Terran. Never step between fighting Ardellans."

Sinykin pressed his right palm to the windowpane and spread his fingers. "That is how Sarah Anders died. She stepped between you and Jeryl, to keep you from killing one another. She was not foolhardy. I have read her journal; I know that she came to love your people. She would not have been able to stand aside and watch you hurt each other."

"She was an honorable person." Arien set his circular palm beside Inda's rectangular one. Where the Terran's fingers stretched up and out, the Ardellan's extended in all directions. They were different, yet they served the same purpose.

"I am a Healer, GuildMaster. I could not stand by and watch someone suffer pain, even if it meant putting myself in danger."

Inda turned his hand palm-upward, and offered it to Arien. The Ardellan laid his palm on Inda's.

"You also have honor. It is time that I return you to your people. The aleps are rested, and the younglings will have cleared a good part of the trail by now. Come." Arien led the way past Reass and his delegation without acknowledging their presence. At the door, a youngling helped him into his cloak.

Inda gathered his own things and followed Arien. Outside, he stared down the trail toward the spaceport. On either side of the narrow path, snow was piled to the height of his alep's shoulders. The trail curved, so that it looked like they would be traveling into a blind canyon of snow. He could no longer see the younglings who were clearing the way. The blades of their shovels occasionally appeared above the distant drifts, trailing plumes of snow.

Sinykin mounted and turned his alep to follow Arien. He held the animal's rein tightly in his right hand and pressed his left against his thigh to still his twitching fingers. Adrenalin was still pumping into his bloodstream. The extra meter's height gave him a better view of the surrounding drifts, but he could see nothing of the Terran compound.

The snowdrifts sometimes reached to his shoulder. There was little wind. His black cloak soaked up the sunlight until the warmth and his fear made sweat run down his spine. The wasteland's features were disguised by the snow. Sinykin had no idea how the younglings were navigating across this white plain. The trail twisted and turned, but the sun was always at his back.

He passed through a huge drift, and at last he could see the top of one of the spaceport's great windmills in the distance. Its blades were missing, but the tower seemed undamaged. He pressed his mount forward, passed Arien, and rode more quickly toward the compound. The top of the administration building came into view. A maintenance crew, easily identifiable in their bright orange jackets, was repairing the roof. Inda could hear vehicles, probably the heavy plows out clearing snow from the landing field.

He saw the second tower when he reached the compound's gate. It had been torn from its pad and dropped on one of the huge maintenance trucks. The tower was broken, and the cab and the side of the truck, Elissa's truck, were crushed.

Inda forgot his debt to Arien, forgot the rituals of diplomacy as fear seized him. He vaulted from his alep's back and began to run as if his—or Elissa's—life depended on it.

Chapter 22

Sinykin flung open the door to the quarters he shared with his family. "Elissa!" he shouted. "Jaime!" Heart pounding, he ran from room to room. No one was there. Clothing was strewn across the floor of Jaime's room, and some of Elissa's belongings had been tossed carelessly on their bed. Where were Elissa and Jaime?

Inda took a deep breath and tried to suppress the panic that had tightened his chest. If Elissa had been in that truck when the tower fell on it, they would have taken her to the infirmary. He ran from the apartment, letting the door slam shut behind him.

The roadway was slippery with hard-packed snow. His left foot hit an icy patch and slid out from under him, pitching him headfirst into a snowbank. The cold wetness touched the skin of his face and shocked him into an instant's stillness. He could do nothing for Elissa if fear and panic controlled him. He struggled free of the snow and walked toward the medical complex.

The road took him past the battered truck. His heart began to pound as he stared at the crumpled metal and shattered glass. The falling tower had crushed one side of the truck and most of the cab. Could the driver have survived the impact? He tore his eyes away and ran across the square to the infirmary.

Ice coated the roof and the windward side of the building, down to the top of the drift that buried the first-floor windows. A narrow path had been cleared to the door. The plastiglass and steel panel did not slide as he approached. Inda grabbed the emergency handle and pushed. The door opened, and he stepped into the vestibule. The inner doors parted automatically.

The odors of disinfectants and medications filled his nostrils. They seemed harsh and alien after the earthy smells of the keeps. Inda stood before the open doors, poised between two very different worlds. With his second breath, the smells became familiar, welcoming. He stepped into the waiting room, stripped off his Ardellan cloak, and dropped it on a low table.

His stomach knotted when he saw Jaime sitting with Marta Grund and her son Tommy. Jaime jumped up and ran toward him.

"Dad!"

Sinykin bent and caught his son in both arms, lifted him and hugged him close. He saw no bandages; Jaime appeared to have survived the storm unscathed. "Is your mom here?"

"They operated on her arm!" cried Jaime.

"She's in the recovery room, Sinykin," said Marta. She gave him what he interpreted as a reassuring smile. "Jaime wanted to see her, but they won't let him go back yet."

"I'll take him back," said Sinykin. "Did they tell you anything about her injuries?"

Marta shook her head. "Dr. Addami just said that he was going to put pins in the bones of her left arm. They were broken in several places."

Relief made Inda smile. He hugged Jaime once more, then set him down. "Let's go see your mom."

"I'm glad you came home," said Jaime, reaching for his father's hand. "You were gone a long time."

"I know," said Sinykin. "I'm glad to be back."

Elissa was sitting up, her forearm in its green fiberglass cast propped on a ceramic tabletop. The orange dot of a pain-blocker patch showed on her upper arm. A healing lamp was suspended above the cast. Its bulb glowed with an eerie blue light. Elissa smiled when she saw Sinykin and reached for him with her good arm. "When did you get back?" she asked, giving him an awkward hug.

"Just now." He kissed the top of her ear, breathed in the sweet scent of her hair. "I missed you."

"I missed you, too. I was worried about you." She kissed him.

Jaime tugged on his mom's good hand. "Can you come home now?"

"Soon," said Elissa. "My arm has to stay under the

healing lamp a little while longer. Dr. Addami wants the bones to begin knitting before I leave the infirmary. Go out and tell Marta that I'll be ready in fifteen minutes.''

''All right.'' Jaime ran out of the room.

Inda tried to swallow. His mouth was suddenly very dry. ''Were you in the truck when the tower fell on it?''

Elissa nodded. ''It was a close thing. The truck went into a skid just before the tower came down. My arm was pinned in the wreckage. Sobsczyk was plowing the landing field. He saw the tower fall. His crew had me out of that truck in less than ten minutes. I'm afraid they wrecked the cab.''

''It looked like the tower did that for them.''

She hugged him again. ''It scared me,'' she whispered. ''I thought I was going to die.''

''When I saw the truck I was afraid that I'd lost you.''

''Remember that when you get tired of seeing me sitting around the house. Addami won't let me work for at least ten days.'' She laughed. ''I suppose I can still go to the staff meetings. I'll have to explain why I didn't have the field cleared in time for *Manatee* to land.''

Sinykin brushed a stray hair from her forehead. ''Was Griswold tough on you while I was gone?''

Elissa nodded. ''Anna Griswold is so angry with you that she's threatening to have you recalled.''

''I got that impression from her message.'' He saw concern in Elissa's face. They were settled here; Jaime had friends and they both had good jobs. If the Trade Commission removed him from his post, Elissa would have to resign from her job. They'd have to move again, start over somewhere else. He wanted to tell her that it wouldn't happen, but he couldn't be sure. ''I don't think Sandsmark will recall me just because Anna requests it. He won't make a judgment until he receives my report of the trip.''

''You should go and talk to Anna. She wanted to see you as soon as you returned.''

''It can wait until I get you home and settled,'' said Sinykin. He twined his fingers in the soft curls of her hair.

Elissa pushed his hand away. ''You should go now. If you can placate her, she may change her mind about the recall petition. Marta will see that Jaime and I get home.''

He looked down at her face, saw that her chin was thrust

forward and her lips were pressed tightly together. It would be foolish to argue with her. He would speak to Griswold and then meet Elissa at home. She and Jaime were the center of his life; keeping them safe and happy was all that mattered.

"I love you," he said. He kissed her once more. "I'll see you at home."

Most of the mural on the front of the administration building was obscured by snow. Inda stopped to look at it, pulling his borrowed cloak close against the cold. The mural seemed silly, a poor rendering of one of human-kind's dubious accomplishments. The building itself was ugly and impermanent when compared with the artistry and enduring construction he had seen in the Ardellan keeps.

Perhaps Viela was correct when he said that Terrans did not belong on this world. But that was no longer a matter open to negotiation. Terrans had come here and had already changed this land and its people beyond reckoning.

A gust of wind blew Inda's hood back. He felt the chill on his ears and neck. Shoulders hunched and head down, he went into the building.

"Dr. Inda!" Anna Griswold was standing at the top of the staircase. "What an unexpected pleasure. When did you return to the compound?"

"An hour ago, Anna. I've been at the infirmary, checking on Elissa. She said that you wanted to see me."

"Indeed. Come up to my office. We'll have something warm to drink and discuss the outcome of your trip." It was a command, not an invitation. "Your journey must have been chilling. That cloak doesn't look very warm. Did you lose your parka?"

Inda shook his head. "I loaned it to someone."

In her office, Griswold filled two mugs with hot water from the dispenser. "Synthetic coffee or herbal tea?" she asked.

"Tea," said Inda. He never drank coffee, not even synthetic coffee. Anna knew that.

She dropped a perforated plastic sphere filled with herbs into one mug, spooned brown crystals into the other and stirred it. She brought both to the desk and set Inda's on the low table between the two chairs that faced it. "Sit down, Doctor." She took her own seat behind the broad desk.

Sinykin chose the left-hand chair. He arranged his Ardellan cloak carefully as he sat, then picked up the mug and held it close to his chest. The fragrant steam warmed his face. The odor was light and sweet, very different from the heavy Ardellan brews he had been drinking. He sipped the tea, enjoyed its heat and its familiar flavor.

"There have been some changes while you were away," said Griswold. "Jeff Grund has replaced you as Assistant Administrator. He'll be staying on in that post, and heading the Science Division. You have been relieved of all administrative duties, pending review of your recent activities."

Sinykin stared at her. "Has the change in my status been approved by Sandsmark?"

His question angered Griswold. She slammed her palm down on the desk. "You received your assignment from Secretary Sandsmark, but while you are working at this facility you are under my jurisdiction and required to abide by my policies. Personnel changes are my decision. You may file a grievance if you so choose."

"I don't intend to fight you, Anna. I never wanted to be your enemy. Right now what I want to do is get this vaccine ready. This plague deforms and kills the Ardellans, and they can do little to treat it. I have enough blood and tissue samples to thoroughly test the vaccine. I should know in a few weeks if it's safe to administer to the Ardellans. My gear came down the mountain before the storm. It should be at Alu Keep. I'll go get it tomorrow and start my research right away."

Griswold stared out the window. "I have closed the compound, Dr. Inda. No one will be allowed to leave the spaceport grounds, not even you."

"You cannot justify completely isolating us."

"The trade agreement isolates us. No Terran is allowed to travel beyond the spaceport grounds without the permission of Clan Alu's council, as expressed by the clan's Mentor. You broke that agreement, Dr. Inda. You did not have permission to travel beyond Alu Keep. We cannot let anyone leave the compound until we understand the consequences of your trip.

"We continue to have contact with the FreeMasters at the gate. Messages come and go as always." She turned back to face him. "Ardellans will be allowed to visit the compound as long as they apply for permission three days in advance. All passes onto the grounds must be reviewed and approved by my office. But none of my people will leave the compound."

"Why, Anna?" Inda was certain Sandsmark and the Trade Commission would not approve of this.

Lines that he had never noticed before furrowed her brow. She gazed at the alien cloak that was draped around him, then looked into his face. "Too many Terrans have died during their dealings with the Ardellans. Sarah Anders, and Nicholas Durrow and two members of his crew—all dead in ways that we don't understand, with only their ashes returned to us, and in Anders case not even that. I think it is too dangerous for us to travel freely among these aliens. I feared for your life, Sinykin, and I feared the consequences of another unexplained death."

He knew that her fear was justified. His life had been threatened more than once on this trip. Despite that, Terrans and Ardellans could not remain isolated from one another, not if the spaceport was to remain on Ardel. Even if they demolished the compound and evacuated all the humans, what good would it do? He had seen the weather-workers; he knew some of the powers that these people wielded. If they could gather storms and move them about their planet, might they not also learn to reach into space, to manipulate other worlds and other races now that they knew of their existence? If Griswold was right, if Ardellans were to be feared rather than trusted, there was no place to hide from them.

Inda set his mug aside and rose. "All right, Anna. I'll send for my packs. Jeryl will have one of the FreeMasters bring them to the gate."

Griswold nodded. "There's a message from Sandsmark waiting for you. I think it's under personal seal. And I'd like to see your report before you transmit it."

"I'm sorry, Anna. I don't think that will be possible." He had no intention of letting her read his report. He would tell no one but Sandsmark of the things he had witnessed in the mountains.

Jeff Grund's office was on the first floor of the administration building. Inda stopped before the open door. Dr.

Grund was seated at his terminal, feet tucked under his chair and ankles crossed, shoulders hunched forward, right hand clutching a stylus and scribbling notes on a slate. At his left was a short stack of printouts. Hard copy was rarely generated at the spaceport; all the paper had to be shipped in from off-planet.

"Jeff," said Inda quietly, wondering how often he had warned Grund that his favorite working posture would harm his spine and give him headaches.

"Be right with you," said Grund without looking up. He dropped his stylus and entered a command at his keyboard. Slowly his back straightened and his ankles uncrossed. His fingers were still tapping keys as he peered back over his shoulder. "Sinykin?"

"Yes, Jeff."

Although he did not take his eyes off Inda, Grund finished the command string and lifted his hands from the keyboard before he turned away from his terminal. His look of wonderment slowly changed to a broad grin that Inda could not help returning.

"When did you get back?" asked Grund. "Have you seen Elissa?"

"An hour ago; and, yes, I just came from the infirmary. She has multiple fractures of her left forearm; otherwise she and Jaime are fine."

"Come in and close the door." Jeff pointed to the extra chair at the end of the table. "Did Elissa tell you that Griswold is thinking of having you recalled?"

Sinykin nodded. "I just came from Anna's office. She told me that she's closed the compound. No one goes out, and no one comes in without her permission." He heard in his voice the anger that he had kept so tightly controlled in Griswold's office. His jaw was tight, his face flushed. He laid his right hand down, palm flat on the table and fingers spread. He stared at it, remembering the touch of Arien's palm at the guildhall a few hours ago. They had begun to forge a bond, between two individuals and between two peoples. He would not let Griswold destroy that. He would not defy her, but he would use his knowledge and his influence to open the compound again.

"It doesn't matter to most of us. We never planned on leaving the spaceport," said Grund. "What did you see out there?"

What could he say? That he had met people who wanted to drive the Terrans from Ardel, who believed they could destroy the spaceport with storms? That he had seen one Ardellan burn another with a power born of thought? Would Jeff understand? Sinykin looked away. "I saw a lot of snow. I'll tell you about it sometime." He slipped off his cloak. "I heard that I have a sealed message from Sandsmark. Can I access it on your terminal?"

"Certainly. Just let me save this," said Grund, tapping a few keys. Then he rose and walked to the door. "I'll be back in about twenty minutes."

"Thank you," said Inda. He had already seated himself at the terminal and keyed in his private code. The message from Sandsmark was fifth in his mail queue, the only one under security seal. He entered the three codes that broke the seal, then watched as the message scrolled onto the screen.

It was filled with questions about the Ardellans' psychic abilities, about the Healers and the Mentors and the way Sarah Anders died. Had he gained the trust of the Ardellans? Would he be allowed to move freely among them? If their psychic "tricks" were real, would he be allowed to study them, to learn how to perform them? Sandsmark wanted explanations and answers.

And there, in the last paragraph, was the offer Sinykin had been waiting for. He could have the post of envoy, if he still wanted it. His heartbeat quickened, not with excitement but with fear. Faced with the realization of his ambition, he had a sudden desire to turn and run away.

The envoy's job would not be easy or safe. He must stand between the Terrans and the Ardellans, protecting each group from the other. Already he was facing some difficult decisions—should he confirm the truth of Anders' journal entries or hide the reality of the Ardellan's powers from Sandsmark and the other Terrans? Should he tell Grund of the weather-workers? How much could each side safely know about the other?

He knew he could trust no one else to make these decisions. The job of envoy was his. And for the safety of both Ardellans and Terrans, some things must remain secret. He pressed two keys to scramble Sandsmark's message, then touched a third to send it into oblivion.

It might be weeks, or even months, before official confirmation of his appointment as envoy was received at the spaceport. Until then he would abide by Griswold's rules. He would work on the vaccine, and watch, and wait.

He touched a key to clear the screen, pressed several more to engage his security seal and the automatic scrambler, and began composing his report.

Chapter 23

Cold . . . Hatar was very cold. And stiff. His body was stiff, chilled, near death. His heart beat very slowly, his lungs barely breathed. Stillness threatened to pervade his form. He welcomed it, prepared to let his spirit drift toward oblivion.

He drifted out of his body and touched a familiar mind. It was Jeryl, and he was lost, confused, and helpless. Jeryl clung to Hatar's spirit, became part of Hatar's death cry. Together they rode the wind to Alu Keep and the mourning wall.

Hatar found many familiar urns there, and bits of the spirits of many lost friends. He caressed the spark that was all that remained of Alain. He was ready to join her in death.

Then Jeryl was summoned into a warm place. Hatar tried to separate from Jeryl. He wanted to stay with Alain, but he could not disentangle all of his spirit. Part of him went with Jeryl, into the chilled body that waited in that warm room.

Jeryl opened his left eye, closed it again quickly. His head ached. Sunlight filled the room; it made dappled golden patterns on his closed eyelids. Something heavy was covering his body, pressing him against the sleeping platform. He moved one arm, felt cloth and fur and warmth.

He stretched and opened both eyes slowly. Mid-afternoon sunlight streamed in through the window of his room in Alu's clanhall. Beside the sleeping platform, a cheery brazier warmed the air. He was safe in Alu Keep, and Sanid and the other weather-workers were dead, destroyed by their own power. He remembered the explosion, the death cries flowing past him to oblivion.

He also remembered Hatar's death cry. He reached inward, and touched the spark of Hatar's spirit that now lived in him. *I hope you have at last found peace, my friend,* he thought.

Jeryl struggled against the heavy furs. He had no time to lie abed. He had much to do. There was windwort to gather, and a cocooning to perform.

"Be still," said Septi from the corner. "Hanra-bae made me promise to give you this potion before I let you rise." He set a small teapot on the brazier to heat and put a mug and a packet of herbs on the table.

"Where is Hanra-bae?" asked Jeryl.

"He and Secko went out to gather windwort. The fisher asked me to tell you that he will return before this afternoon to prepare you for the cocooning."

A lump of charcoal popped in the brazier, sending up a flurry of sparks. Jeryl watched the red line of fire devour it, leaving behind gray ash. Steam rose from the spout of the teapot. Septi poured hot water into the mug, then added some green powder from the packet and stirred. He offered it to Jeryl.

"I do not want to drink that."

"You will not leave this room until you swallow this potion," said Septi.

Jeryl sat up slowly and accepted the mug. Its contents smelled vile. He swallowed the bitter potion in one gulp, then returned the mug to Septi.

"May I rise now?"

Septi shrugged.

The potion had made Jeryl's stomach queasy. He threw back the furs, reached for a robe, and struggled into it. His thigh no longer hurt; the new skin was a shiny golden-pink color, smooth and soft. He bent to pull on boots, and his head swam.

"Sit still for a few moments," said Septi. "Hanra-bae said that you might feel dizzy."

Jeryl leaned back against the wall and tried to quell the nausea.

"What else did Hanra-bae say?"

"He left this message for you." Septi handed Jeryl a scrap of writing-cloth.

The runes were indecipherable. Jeryl stared at them for a long time before he threw the cloth aside.

He swung his legs over the edge of the platform and stood, bracing his left hand against the wall to keep from swaying. The room shifted in his sight, the floor dropping away before him and then rising up again. He closed his eyes, took two deep breaths, realized that his head felt like someone had been stuffing wool into it.

"You really should remain in bed for the rest of the day," said Septi.

"No, no. I must be ready when Hanra-bae returns. Come down to the kitchen with me."

The corridor seemed longer than usual, the stairs narrower and steeper. Jeryl walked slowly, one arm pressed against the wall. At least the floor had stopped moving. The kitchen was warm, filled with bustling younglings responding to Ortia's familiar commands. Septi poured Jeryl a mug of tea, added several spoonfuls of sweetener, and brought him a plate of warm bread.

"Thank you, friend." Jeryl sipped and tried not to make a face. The tea was far sweeter than he liked.

"Mentor." The harsh, familiar voice of the clan's Healer came from the doorway.

"Yes, Viela."

"I wish to apologize for my behavior in council yesterday. I was overcome by my concern for Poola and House Actaan. I acted rashly." Viela hesitated, then came into the kitchen and approached Jeryl. "I have come to ask you to accompany me to House Actaan. Ertis is endangering his House by postponing this cocooning. He will not listen to my pleas."

Jeryl swallowed the rest of the tea, then poured a second mug and did not add sweetener. "If Hanra-bae returns before sunset, we can brew the potion. I will drink it, and tomorrow I will attempt to cocoon naMieck while Ertis cocoons naOflea."

"You risk the future of House Actaan on this venture." Viela was angry. "It would be better to let Ertis cocoon naOflea now, and wait for the next cocooning to try your experiment. You will have more time then."

Jeryl shrugged. "Ertis asked to be a part of this. He wants House Actaan to have the honor of spawning the first daughter House in memory. Would you take that from him?"

"We dare not risk losing Actaan!"

"We have another day before Ertis must perform the cocooning. Let us use it as best we may."

Viela stepped back. His reddening aura billowed out
around him. "You are no Healer!" he shouted. "You cannot know the limits of Poola's time. Mind your Mentor's
business and leave healing to me. I will not allow this cocooning to be postponed any longer!"

"You have no choice," said Jeryl, pushing back his
bench and rising. The bench's wooden legs scraped angrily
along the stone floor. Jeryl's ruby aura expanded to match
Viela's, pulsing in time to the angry throbbing in Jeryl's
head. This Healer had been allowed too much power in Clan
Alu. It was time he learned the limits of his authority. Jeryl
lifted his hands, palms turned toward Viela, and uttered a
challenge. "Leave be, or feel the extent of a Mentor's
power!"

"I am not powerless," cried Viela, raising his hands to
answer the challenge. Younglings ran to the far corners of
the kitchen.

Energy flowed down Jeryl's arms and into his fingertips.
His palms tingled with power. "Step aside, Healer, or die!"

"No!"

The shout came from Septi. Jeryl turned, saw the young
Master standing before the hearth, arms held rigid at his
sides, palms open and fingers spread parallel to the floor.
"Mentor, do not do something you will later regret. You
cannot afford to deprive Clan Alu of its Healer."

Septi was correct. Jeryl let the power dissipate. "Healer,
the cocooning will take place tomorrow morning, whether
or not Hanra-bae returns with the windwort this evening.
Now leave us."

Viela glared at Jeryl, his aura still showing his anger. He
dropped his hands. "I will be at House Actaan until the
cocooning is completed. Be there at dawn if you intend to
take part in the ceremony." He turned and stalked from the
room.

Jeryl swayed, caught the table's edge with his hands, and
sat heavily on the bench. He was exhausted.

"Can you find it?" asked Secko.

Hanra-bae pushed through the waist-high snik-grass
searching for the trailing stems and leaves of windwort that

sometimes grew among its roots. He spotted one of the gold-green leaves, reached down and grasped the snaky tendril of the stem. "It is here. Bring my pack!" He followed the stem farther into the snik-grass patch, until he found the parent plant.

Secko trudged after him with the pack. "You must finish this quickly. It is nearly midday. It will be dark before we return to Alu Keep."

"I cannot harvest the herb without blessing the plant." Hanra-bae reached into his pack and removed his curved iron knife. He held the carved bone handle, touched the shiny blade first to the center of his chest and then to his forehead. Then he gathered three of the plant's stems into his left hand and cut through them with a single stroke of the blade. He whispered his thanks as he coiled the long stems into a bundle and put them and the knife into his pack. "Finished," he said. "We can go now."

The weather quickly turned colder as the sun moved across the western sky. By mid-afternoon they had returned to the storm-ravaged area of the plain. Their mounts trudged through drifts, backtracking the trail they had made that morning.

Hanra-bae shivered despite the warmth of the sun on his back. He was concerned about the time; it had taken them much too long to traverse the snow-covered trails. If he did not reach Alu Keep before dark, he would not have time to brew the potion and prepare Jeryl for the cocooning. He tried to hurry his alep, but it plodded along on its six legs, carefully picking its way through the ice and snow.

"The stream is just ahead," called Secko. "The water is higher than it was this morning. It has almost reached the bottom of the bridge. The snow in the mountains must be melting."

The Healer could hear the sound of rushing water. He trembled, from fear rather than cold. To a fisher, water was both life and death. To Hanra-bae, who had nearly drowned as a youngling, it was only death. He had never conquered his fear of water. "Can we not find another route back to the keep?"

"Not if we intend to reach it before dark. The bridge is damp from the spray, and it is a little slippery. We should walk our aleps across."

Hanra-bae dismounted and stood at his mount's head. He

stared at the swiftly moving water. The stream was narrow. The rushing water climbed the banks, snatched lumps of snow and chunks of ice, and twirled them away downstream. The bottom of the bridge was only a hand's span above the water. Spray had coated it with a fine layer of ice.

He closed his eyes and remembered sliding from the side of the fishing boat into cold, clear water. His heart thudded in his chest.

"Come," said Secko. He led his mount onto the bridge. "Be careful where you place your feet."

Hanra-bae gripped the rein just under his mount's nose. He led the animal forward to the edge of the stream. He wanted to turn back, to ride away from the rushing water to a place that was safe and dry. Then he thought of Jeryl and Ertis waiting at Alu Keep. He grabbed the railing with his free hand and stepped out onto the bridge.

The keep's wooden gate opened for them. Secko led the way to the stable. There he dismounted and called for a youngling to take their aleps. No one appeared.

Hanra-bae struggled out of his saddle and slid to the ground. His legs and back ached. He pulled his pack from the alep's back and looked down the road toward the clanhall. "It is nearly dark."

"I know," said Secko. He called again for a youngling. There was no response. "Give me your mount's rein. I will care for the animals. You go to the clanhall. Quickly!"

Hanra-bae ran. His foot slipped on a patch of ice and he almost fell. His pack bounced against his back, bruising the already stiff muscles. He crossed the wide circle in front of the clanhall, climbed the steps to the door, and started pounding. A youngling opened the door and stared at him, its eyestalks crossed and its tentacles waving.

"Where is Jeryl?"

"In the kitchen, Healer."

Hanra-bae pushed past the youngling and ran down the hall. He stumbled across the kitchen's threshold and handed his pack to Jeryl. "Windwort," he said, pointing to the gold-green leaves and stems that trailed from beneath the flap. "Get me a pot and I will brew your potion."

Jeryl snapped his fingers, and more younglings came running to heat water and take the Master Healer's cloak.

Hanra-bae ground dry larkenleaf to a powder by rubbing

it against the inside of a stone bowl with the handle of one of Ortia's wooden stirrers. Then he tore the fresh windwort leaves into small pieces and sprinkled them over the powder, and added bits of other herbs from his pack. He pounded the mixture into a dry paste, kept pounding and stirring until it began to flake and powder. Then he called for boiling water.

He sifted the green powder into the bottom of a large wooden bowl and added a few drops of water. He stirred slowly, wetting the powder evenly. Still stirring, he had Jeryl pour in more hot water. He stopped when the bowl was half full, covered it with a plate and set it aside.

"How long?" asked Jeryl. He did not take his eyes off the bowl.

"A few moments, or half the night." Hanra-bae shrugged. "I cannot tell. Let it be for a while. May I have something to eat?"

Jeryl brought tea and bread to the hearth.

"If the potion works . . ." said Jeryl, still watching the bowl.

"It will work." Hanra-bae seemed certain. "I followed the instructions exactly. By morning you will be spinning silk to cocoon naMieck."

"I hope so. If I am not ready at dawn, Ertis and naOflea will perform the ceremony without naMieck and me."

"Then we must make sure that you are ready on time." The fisher lifted the cover and peered at the mixture in the bowl. Most of the solid material had settled to the bottom, leaving a layer of transparent liquid above it. "It is green enough, I think. Give me a mug. . . ."

Jeryl handed Hanra-bae a cup and watched as the Master Healer spooned some of the liquid into it. The potion smelled musty and sour enough to make Jeryl back away. "That smells terrible!"

"It probably tastes worse. Are you certain that you are strong enough to do this?"

"If I do not, who will?" asked Jeryl. He reached for the cup.

"Then we must go upstairs to your chamber. You should drink this just before you sleep."

Jeryl rose and led Hanra-bae up the back stairs to his chamber. The younglings had rekindled the charcoal in the brazier and had closed the shutters. The room was comfortably warm. Jeryl blinked, and shimmer-light appeared in one of the wall sconces. He stripped off his outer robe and boots and sat on the edge of the sleeping platform.

"I will drink it now," said Jeryl, reaching for the potion. He took the cup from Hanra-bae's hands. The liquid smelled even worse than it had in the kitchen. Jeryl took a deep breath and held it, then brought the cup to his lips. He took a sip and grimaced as if the potion tasted vile. Jeryl gulped it quickly and handed the cup back to Hanra-bae. He was asleep almost before the mug left his hand.

The Mother's chamber in House Actaan was beautiful. Clusters of quartz and amethyst crystals projected from the natural matrix of the stone walls. They reflected and re-fracted shimmer-light, casting tiny rainbows on walls and floor. Above the open, vine-covered skylight, leaves rustled in the dawn breeze.

On the floor under the skylight was a low stone platform. It was draped with furs—curly white wool-deer, silvery tol, and brown borra. Poola lay in its center, wearing her finest, sheerest lavender robe and humming softly.

Ertis and naOflea knelt beside her. Ertis stroked Poola's arms and tentacles. He dipped his fingers into the puddled secretions of her reproductive glands and anointed naOflea with the liquid. The youngling swayed for a moment, then tumbled forward into Ertis' arms. The metamorphic process had begun.

Ertis carried naOflea across the room to a small grotto in the rock wall. He propped the youngling against the yield-ing stone and began spinning silk fibers to cover and bind its body. As the threads emerged from his fingers, he an-chored them to the wall. Then he wrapped them back and forth across naOflea's body.

Jeryl watched from the far side of the room. He missed his House and all that he had lost when his mate was killed. He had not felt whole since then.

The silk glands in his arms felt incredibly full, and his fingers itched to begin spinning. He rubbed his palms to-gether, then examined the tiny orifices at the tips of his fingers. How would it feel to spin silk into a cocoon? He waited until Ertis finished cocooning naOflea; then he ap-proached Poola's platform, leading naMieck.

Jeryl bowed to the Mother before kneeling at her side.

He performed the ritual exactly as Ertis had, communing with her for a moment before stroking her arms, then anointing the youngling. The ceremony was a painful reminder of the joyous union he had shared with his own mate, and of all he had lost with her death.

naMieck was light and easy to carry across the room. Jeryl propped its body against the rock, settling it into the shallow indentation in the wall. Then he touched his fingers to the stone to anchor the silk and began spinning. The threads were smooth and taut as they left his fingers, and where they touched, they adhered to each other, making a soft fabric that bound naMieck to the wall. In moments its body was completely hidden by the white silk.

Jeryl turned and bowed to Poola once more. The ritual was over, and it had not changed him, had not brought him the completion he was seeking. He was an interloper, a stranger who did not belong at this most private ceremony. He retreated to the door, slipped out and was relieved when it closed behind him.

He walked past House Ratrou, with its darkened windows and vine-covered walls, and suddenly knew that it was no longer his House. It belonged to Mieck now, and to those Masters who would follow him. By cocooning naMieck, Jeryl had cut the last tie to his old life as Master of House Ratrou. He was truly a FreeMaster now, bound to no single House. He was Mentor of Clan Alu, and it was his destiny to help bring new life to each empty House in Alu Keep.

DAW

NEW DIMENSIONS IN MILITARY SF

C.S. Friedman
☐ **IN CONQUEST BORN**   (UE2198—$3.95)
Braxi and Azea—two super-races fighting an endless war. The
Braxana—created to become the ultimate warriors. The Azeans,
raised to master the powers of the mind, using telepathy to
penetrate where mere weapons cannot. Now the final phase of
their war is approaching, spearheaded by two opposing gener-
als, lifetime enemies—and whole worlds will be set ablaze by
the force of their hatred!

Kris Jensen
☐ **FREEMASTER**   (UE2404—$3.95)
The Terran Union had sent Sarah Anders to Ardel to establish
a trade agreement for materials vital to offworlders, but of little
value to the low-tech Ardellans. But other, far more ruthless humans, were also after these materials—and were about to stake
their claim with the aid of forbidden technology, double-dealing,
and threats of destruction to the clans of Ardel. Yet the Ardellans
had defenses of their own, based on powers of the mind, and
only a human such as Sarah could begin to understand them.
For she, too, had mind talents locked within her—and the Free-
Masters of Ardel just might provide the key to releasing them.

John Steakley
☐ **ARMOR**   (UE2368—$4.50)
Impervious body armor had been devised for the commando
forces who were to be dropped onto the poisonous surface of
A-9, the home world of mankind's most implacable enemy. But
what of the man inside the armor? This tale of cosmic combat
will stand against the best of Gordon Dickson or Poul Anderson.

DAW

BESTSELLERS BY MARION ZIMMER BRADLEY
THE DARKOVER NOVELS

DAW

Exciting Visions of the Future!

W. Michael Gear

☐ **STARSTRIKE** (UE2427—$4.95)
The alien Ahimsa has taken control of all Earth's defenses, and forces humanity to do its bidding. Soon Earth's most skilled strike force, composed of Soviet, American and Israeli experts in the art of war and espionage find themselves aboard an alien vessel, training together for an offensive attack against a distant space station. And as they struggle to overcome their own prejudices and hatreds, none of them realize that the greatest danger to humanity's future is right in their midst. . . .

☐ **THE ARTIFACT** (UE2406—$4.95)
In a galaxy on the brink of civil war, where the Brotherhood seeks to keep the peace, news comes of the discovery of a piece of alien technology—the Artifact. It could be the greatest boon to science, or the instrument that would destroy the entire human race.

THE SPIDER TRILOGY

For centuries, the Directorate had ruled over countless star systems—but now the first stirrings of rebellion were being felt. At this crucial time, the Directorate discovered a planet known only as World, where descendants of humans stranded long ago had survived by becoming a race of warriors, a race led by its Prophets, men with the ability to see the many possible pathways of the future. And as rebellion, fueled by advanced technology and a madman's dream, spread across the galaxy, the warriors of Spider could prove the vital key to survival of human civilization. . . .

☐ **THE WARRIORS OF SPIDER** (UE2287—$3.95)
☐ **THE WAY OF SPIDER** (UE2318—$3.95)
☐ **THE WEB OF SPIDER** (UE2396—$4.95)

Charles Ingrid

THE MARKED MAN SERIES

☐ **THE MARKED MAN** (UE2396—$3.95)
In a devastated America, can the Lord Protector of a mutating human race find a way to preserve the future of the species?

☐ **THE LAST RECALL** (UE2460—$3.95)
Returning to a radically-changed Earth, would the generational ships aid the remnants of a mutated human race—or seek their future among the stars?

THE SAND WARS

☐ **SOLAR KILL: Book 1** (UE2391—$3.95)
He was the last Dominion Knight and he would challenge a star empire to gain his revenge!

☐ **LASERTOWN BLUES: Book 2** (UE2393—$3.95)
He'd won a place in the Emperor's Guard but could he hunt down the traitor who'd betrayed his Knights to an alien foe?

☐ **CELESTIAL HIT LIST: Book 3** (UE2394—$3.95)
Death stalked the Dominion Knight from the Emperor's Palace to a world on the brink of its prophesied age of destruction. . . .

☐ **ALIEN SALUTE: Book 4** (UE2329—$3.95)
As the Dominion and the Thrakian empires mobilize for all-out war, can Jack Storm find the means to defeat the ancient enemies of man?

☐ **RETURN FIRE: Book 5** (UE2363—$3.95)
Was someone again betraying the human worlds to the enemy—and would Jack Storm become pawn or player in these games of death?

☐ **CHALLENGE MET: Book 6** (UE2436—$3.95)
In this concluding volume of *The Sand Wars*, Jack Storm embarks on a dangerous mission which will lead to a final confrontation with the Ash-farel.

PENGUIN USA
P.O. Box 999, Bergenfield, New Jersey 07621

Please send me the books I have checked above. I am enclosing $_____
(please add $1.00 to this order to cover postage and handling). Send check or money order—no cash or C.O.D.'s. Prices and numbers are subject to change without notice. (Prices slightly higher in Canada.)

Name_____

Address_____

City _____ State _____ Zip _____
Please allow 4-6 weeks for delivery.